SAVAGE
NEWS

SAVAGE
NEWS

JESSICA YELLIN

mira

mira

ISBN-13: 978-0-7783-0842-3

Savage News

Copyright © 2019 by Jessica Yellin

For questions and comments about the quality of this book, please contact us at
CustomerService@Harlequin.com.

BookClubbish.com

Printed in U.S.A.

Sam & Aby, Jon & Mary
For sanctuary

SAVAGE
NEWS

THE EARLYBIRD™/ WEDNESDAY / 5:43 A.M.
THE E-NEWSLETTER TRUSTED BY WASHINGTON'S POLITICAL ELITE

Good morning, EarlyBirders™. Here are the morning's need-to-know stories:

¡CUIDADO! It's going to be awkward today when the White House rolls out the red carpet for the presidents of **Venezuela** and **Colombia**. Can the feuding Latin leaders put aside their differences? ***PRO TIP:*** What's slick and floats on troubled waters? The theme of this summit.

EARLYPOLL™: AMERICA LOVES THE FIRST LADY.

FLOTUS is more popular than ever. POTUS, not so much. **BE SMART**: The White House will try to convert her sky-high favorability into support for the president's energy agenda.

Must See TV: All cable nets will be live at 1:30 p.m. from the White House press room. Who'll get under the White House's skin today? Send guesses to earlypoll@theearlybird.com!

Spotted: Socialite **Karima Sahadi** and **Shakira** to plan Dancing with the Enemy gala, healing partisan divides through lyrical contemporary dance.

1

THE GIRL ON THE BUS

Natalie Savage stepped onto the asphalt driveway ringing the North Lawn, looked up, and felt her breath catch. She was hit with the sense that she was on a Tilt-A-Whirl, unsure which side was up. How many years had she imagined this moment? Her first time walking up the curving path to the White House's James S. Brady Press Briefing Room, her first time passing the tents where the network news reporters go live from the White House, her first time looping by the marine at the West Wing entrance, mere yards from the Oval Office.

You've made it. She smiled to herself, wrapped in an almost giddy delight. *You're here.*

What are you doing? her self shot back in a tone Barbara Walters might have used to greet a bright-eyed intern. *There's no time to be awestruck. Get going.*

With little warning, the White House had moved up the briefing by an hour and she was about to be tardy her first day on the job. Hurrying up the driveway, she said a silent prayer that she wouldn't be captured barging into the White House

briefing late, excuse-me'ing into her seat, on every cable channel in America.

She reached the white door to the briefing room, pulled on
the brass handle, and—

Inside reporters were moving at double speed: barking into
cell phones, madly texting or tweeting, bouncing in and out
of their chairs.

Thank god, it hadn't started.

Flooded with relief, Natalie pushed into the scramble of
bodies and felt the intensity of a breaking news event in the
air: a pupil-dilating flush of oxygen, the heart-pounding thrill
of being at the center of an all-eyes-on-this story. She made
her way to the American Television Network's (ATN) seat
in the third row and relaxed enough to look around. At the
back of the room was a warren of cubicles, each assigned to a
network. A row of cameras stood in front of the cubicles like
leggy sentries, and in front of those were the seats for the correspondents. She closed her eyes and inhaled deeply.

It smelled of mold and sweat.

Why does success always smell like a men's locker room? she wondered.

Objectively, it was a crap hole. Despite the administration's
claims to have no money for infrastructure projects, Natalie suspected that the shabbiness of the tiny press room was by choice,
not necessity, like an aging duchess who uses chipped Limoges
not because she can't afford better but because she likes it and
relishes the discomfort of her judgmental guests.

She heard the crackle of static and a young man's voice came
through an overhead speaker. "Sorry for the change folks. The
White House briefing will now be delayed by fifteen minutes."

All around Natalie reporters collapsed back into their chairs,
shaking their heads and murmuring as they began angry-texting
on their phones. Everyone had rushed here and now this delay
would throw live shots and lunch plans into chaos. But for Nat-

alie it was a relief. Fifteen minutes to get used to breathing the air of a White House correspondent.

One of Natalie's phones buzzed and she pulled it out to watch it fill with messages from her mother, Noreen.

MOM: Why haven't you been answering my texts?

MOM: You're being very selfish.

MOM: This is about my special day. My wedding. My chance at happiness. Are you trying to destroy it?

The temptation to write back, Yes! Yes I am! was almost overwhelming but she was saved by a text from her sister.

SARAH: So, you're trying to ruin Mom's wedding.

NATALIE: Either that or it's my first day at the White House.

SARAH: Excuses excuses. Are you excited? Nervous?

Natalie hesitated for a moment and then typed: I miss Dad.

SARAH: Well, you know what he'd say right now?

Natalie smiled as she remembered their dad's favorite advice. *I didn't raise my girls to be shrinking violets. Silence helps no one. Be noisy!*

NATALIE: Be noisy?

SARAH: Or maybe that he's really proud of you. You're going to be great.

NATALIE: Thanks for saying that. But I could easily land on my face.

SARAH: When have you ever failed at anything?

NATALIE: I call your attention to the eighth grade high dive. Hives at prom. The scorched earth that is my dating life.

SARAH: Character building moments. On the topic of scorched earth, will you please pick a bridesmaid dress so our mother will stop looking like a boiled owl and torturing your little sister? Her wedding is in less than two weeks. I'll re-send you the pics right now.

NATALIE: Gotcha. As they say in DC I'll make it priority No. 1.

SARAH: God bless. A grateful nation thanks you. Can't wait to see you live from the North Lawn!

Not if I face-plant first, Natalie thought.

Putting down the phone and looking around the press room, Natalie was struck by how little it had changed since she used to watch the briefings on TV with her dad years ago. How many hours had she and her father spent sitting on the couch in his study watching what happened in this space? The memories came back to her now with a painful clarity, how grown up she'd felt sitting next to him, the smell of books and furniture polish, the sound of ice cubes clinking in his big crystal tumbler of bourbon.

"That's history being made, right in front of our eyes," he'd say, gesturing at the TV with his glass. Sitting on that couch, with their basset hound Murrow between them, her dad had imbued the James S. Brady Press Briefing Room with a kind of enchantment that still held her in its sway despite the coffee-stained institutional blue carpet and balled-up newspapers on the floor.

He'd died sixteen months ago and she thought she'd done her grieving. But being here now brought back an unexpected flood of missing him that had tears pricking at her eyes.

At that moment, one of her phones vibrated again, saving her from an unforgivable lapse that might have risked ruining the fake eyelashes and mask of professional makeup she'd applied that morning. She had gotten used to torturing her hair into silky straightness and wearing one percent of her body weight in foundation and eye shadow, but the lashes were now a compulsory, and already itchy, new addition applied at the insistence of ATN's head of talent. "*Everyone* at the White House has lashes. They are a *must*. Otherwise viewers won't *see* you!"

When Natalie had protested, "But *I* can't see so well when I wear them," the head of talent had given her a pained look and said, "Many people can't see at *all*, dear," as though Natalie had been brazenly taking sight for granted up to that point.

Natalie angled the screen so it was easier to read through the forest of lash and watched it fill with the dress pictures from her sister, providing vivid evidence that their mother was going through an unfortunate hippie phase. The dresses looked like they'd been designed by someone who hated women or eyeballs or both. She tried to come up with a criteria for evaluating them—"Well, at least I can wear a bra with that one" versus "Well, at least that one doesn't look like Janis Joplin's burial shroud"—when a smug male voice over her shoulder said, "The one on the left."

"I beg your pardon?" Natalie twisted toward the guy speaking. Her first impression was one of doughy plumpness. He looked about her age and wore a dark suit and a rumpled blue button-down shirt that she would have bet was chosen by a woman who told him it brought out his eyes. Probably his mother.

"The dress on the left," he repeated, looking not at her but her phone. "Absolutely. A classic of the 'I hate my bridesmaids' genre. You can't go wrong. When's your wedding?"

He unbent and Natalie saw that he was tall, taller than she'd realized. His brown hair was a little too long and his mouth a little too small for his face, giving him the look of a naughty toddler. His lips were pressed together in a tight smile but he looked like he'd be more at ease with a smirk.

"It's not my wedding," she said. "It's my mother's. The dress is for me."

"And therein lies a story," he said, folding himself into the seat next to hers and immediately taking out his phone. "Don't worry, I'm not asking to hear it unless it's scandalous and on the record."

Natalie stared at him.

He glanced up from his screen and held out hand. "Matt Walsh. Beltway dot com. Uh-oh. I see the nickel dropping. Now you're thinking, 'Ah, that explains the smell of sulphur in the air.'"

Natalie laughed but her guard shot up. Beltway. The website was the gossipy mean girl of the political set, bringing the same cannibalistic enthusiasm *Us Weekly* brought to uncovering affairs and baby bumps to its coverage of the Bubble. The Bubble being what Washington Insiders—the types who read Beltway—called themselves, as opposed to everyone else, whom they referred to with subtle condescension as "regular" or "real" Americans. That sorry-not-sorry superiority suffused Beltway. Written in the key of snark with an undertone of kissed-it-fucked-it-over disdain, the posts glorified the most banal aspects of politics, sucking any whiff of substance from a story with the efficiency of a college student taking a bong hit.

She was shocked when her first news boss had told her every

important political reporter reads Beltway and if she cared to be one, she'd better start. The last Beltway story Natalie had read covered a White House meeting about the president's energy goals as "Kiss My Fat Ass? Elizabeth Warren Eats a Cookie for the First Time in Six Weeks While Talking Solar in the Oval Office!"

What kind of reporter would do that, she'd wondered.

Well, now the answer was sitting right next to her. The man who had, in fact, written that very story. She was wary but fascinated, as if she'd found herself dining with someone who'd asked the waiter to remove his steak knife, explaining, "I don't trust myself around weapons."

She aimed for a warm but not too friendly tone and shook his hand. "Natalie Savage, ATN."

Matt appeared impressed. "Any relation to the esteemed First Lady of News?"

"You mean Jessica Savitch?" Natalie asked, trying to keep the sound of her mental eye roll out of her voice. "No, we're not related."

Natalie was baffled by the way news people always asked with unbridled excitement if she was perhaps a niece or cousin of the trailblazing news anchor Jessica Savitch. True, as one of the first women to anchor network news, Savitch had been a talented pioneer. But she'd also led a slightly tragic life that included a string of broken relationships, an on-air meltdown, and an early death by drowning in a car that flipped into a canal. Natalie hoped she would have a slightly different trajectory. She was fairly sure that Savitch, with her clear-eyed view of the world, would have wished that for her successors as well.

"Our names are spelled differently," Natalie explained.

"Too bad. Always good to have a famous relative. Anyway," Matt said, gesturing grandly to the podium at the front of the room, "welcome to the Big Show. First day at the White House?" he went on. "Nervous?"

"No."

"Liar?"

"Yes."

He snickered. "Good, we have something in common." Typing on his phone, he continued, "If you'll take a bit of advice from someone who got here before you, there's no reason to be nervous. You're thinking it's the White House, the big top. Screw up here and it's available for viewing on YouTube for the rest of your life! Worse, YouTube is the only place you'll ever be seen. But the truth is, it doesn't matter what you say at this briefing. Nobody listens or cares."

Natalie gave him a look of wide-eyed admiration. "Are you a doctor? I feel so much better now."

He laughed again but didn't look up. "It's not just you, it's everyone. The Reals think there's news at the White House briefing, but inside the Bubble we know it's just theater. Everyone plays a part. It doesn't matter what you say, only how you say it. Nothing worth reporting gets said here."

Natalie performed a mental eye roll (a physical one was counter-indicated by the fake lashes) at the posture of bland unconcern that he was working so hard to effect. As if not caring about the issues or the state of democracy was proof of his objectivity and superior reporting. She wasn't buying it; if he was as blasé as he pretended, he'd have a different job and not be frantically glued to his phone.

Matt went back to his phone, which was quivering in his hand spasmodically like a heart waiting to be transplanted. Natalie stared at her lifeless device. He had to be getting a dozen messages and updates to every one of hers.

It wasn't just Matt, she realized. Everyone there was crouched self-importantly over their phones. It was a room full of fucking transplant surgeons all waiting for the go signal, ready to jump in and save a life, while her patient was going limp and cold on the slab because she wasn't important to anyone. She found herself half wishing for a text from her mother.

It's only your first day, the sane part of her thought. *And this is not heart surgery.*

You could have married a surgeon, the part of her that did an excellent imitation of her mother's voice said. *Remember that nice boy you dated sophomore year? Joey Arburson? I hear he has a very successful practice in Baltimore, lots of important patients.*

Natalie had received this assignment, unexpectedly, the week before. Nelly Jones, the previous occupant of the ATN seat, had been abruptly removed by network brass after she tweeted that the female secretary of defense had dressed for a White House dinner as though she was auditioning to join the president's fantasy bordello team. This triggered a firestorm of criticism, which ATN fanned into a weeklong cable news food fight, landing Nelly an exclusive with the secretary of defense and an anchor job on ATN's 10 p.m. show *TalkTalk Live*. Since *TalkTalk* taped out of New York, Nelly had abruptly left DC, and Natalie had gotten the call to take her spot at the White House.

Temporarily, the DC bureau chief, Bibb Connaught, had stressed when she'd met Natalie the previous Friday. "I don't want you to be disappointed," Bibb had said. "Management is looking for someone else to take the job long-term."

After twelve years in TV news, five of them at ATN, Natalie spoke fluent Network Politics and did the translation in her head. *I'm a seat warmer until someone younger and more connected comes along.*

But Natalie hadn't spent more than a decade swimming in those shark-infested waters without developing at least a slight taste for blood. Even though Bibb saw her as a fill-in, she knew that she had to treat this gig as an audition. In the parlance of mixed sports metaphors so beloved by network executives, here was an opportunity to take the bull by the horns and knock it out of the ballpark. She was not going to fumble this ball.

Getting here was the reason she'd sacrificed her twenties working local news in Bakersfield, Phoenix, and Orlando, then doing the overnight shift in New York, before making it to *Daybreak* at ATN. It was the reason she'd covered quintuple murders, house-devouring sinkholes, and lung-clogging wildfires; going to sleep—alone—before sunset in parts of the country she'd never known existed so she could be fresh for the morning shows while her old college pals were hooking up, getting married, and having kids in New York, Los Angeles, and Chicago.

On the bright side, having no roots meant it was easy for Natalie to jump when she'd gotten the call two days ago. She'd put her New York life in storage, and found a temporary corporate apartment in DC, all in time to have a meet-and-greet with the management of the DC bureau.

Matt chuckled. Unable to resist her curiosity, Natalie glanced over at his phone. "What's happening?" she asked impatiently.

"BamBam brought his son, the rape-y one," Matt said, grinning as he typed furiously. Then he looked up and declared, "Henceforth we shall call this the Regrettable Sex Summit."

Until this moment, the biggest news of the day had been the start of the PanAmerican Summit, a White House gathering of the leaders from seven Latin American countries. The president had ruffled some official Washington feathers by inviting the undemocratically elected, human-rights abusing president of Colombia, Carlos Lystra, aka BamBam, who derived his nickname both from his preferred method of silencing critics and his adoration of the TV show *The Flintstones*.

Matt's news about BamBam's son, Rigo, was certain to light up *tout l'DC*.

Twenty-one-year-old Rigo Lystra was a gossip column gold mine. He'd cut a name for himself on Page Six and the *Daily Mail* for his frequent visits to New York nightclubs on his G5, his late-night drives through Bogotá brandishing an AK-47 while shouting slogans for his father, and as of last week, a rape accusation lodged against him by the most famous ex-child actress in Latin America, Sonia Barbaro. Sonia was Venezuela's beloved twenty-one-year-old star of stage and screen who had accused Rigo of violently attacking her in a hotel room after some celebrity wedding in Caracas. Venezuelan politicians, already at odds with the Lystra family, were taking this as an assault on their national identity. Rigo had dismissed the encounter as a night of "unfortunate sex" with a girl who was too "flat chested to be memorable," and had spent the last week in Bali swimming with the sharks and a number of scantily clad models. Celebrity gossip sites had been saturated with the Rigo photos, while speculating that Sonia Barbaro was pushing the rape accusation as part of a publicity campaign around her soon-to-be released film *Trafficked*. Now with Rigo in attendance at the president's summit, any fireworks between Venezuela and Colombia were liable to erupt into a four-alarm blaze.

"Can we work some puns into the story?" Matt was barking into his cell phone. "Summit Without Consent." He paused. "Or is that too insensitive?"

"That's not insensitive. That's neuropathy," Natalie mumbled as she looked down at the list of priority questions she'd painstakingly prepared for the briefing.

BamBam Lystra is accused of jailing critics, harassing business leaders who deny him kickbacks and there are even reports he's killing his own people. Why is the US extending him a White House welcome and does the president plan to address these human rights abuses?

As she glanced over the paper, she felt her stomach begin to tie itself into a bowknot. Her questions were, in the parlance of her four-year-old niece, *booooring*.

The sound of Matt's voice broke into her thoughts. "Did you truly print out your questions? I'm afraid that puts you squarely in the nerd clique. Hot Nerd, but still."

Natalie stifled a groan. Over the room's loudspeaker, a man's voice announced, "The White House briefing will begin in two minutes."

The words sent a flash of adrenaline rocketing through Natalie. In an instant, Matt, nerves, second-guessing were all gone. Pure white-hot excitement shimmered through her.

In front of her, the front row reporters stood up and turned, rears to the podium, facing the cameras in the back of the room for their live shots. From her seat, Natalie could hear their half of their conversation with their producers in New York: "You're going small-box, big-box, right?" "So how many of us are in the show of force off the top?" "No, it's not Ferragamo. Made for me by a family outside of Florence. It's a bitch to find pocket squares with hand-stitched edges these days. Dying art."

Adrenaline pulsing, she pushed her own earpiece deep into her ear and turned up the volume on the box at her waist. There was no sound. She jiggled the volume again. Still nothing.

"Hey, guys. It's Natalie," she said. "I'm here and can be live anytime." She held her breath, waiting. "Anyone? Can anyone hear me?" Gaping, eternal quiet.

She turned around to face the ATN camera in the back and gave what's-up eyes to her camerawoman, who shrugged. Apparently no one from ATN was talking to her either.

If she'd been outdoors doing a normal live shot—say at the scene of a murder or a dog mauling or a celebrity balcony suicide attempt—Natalie would have stood up and, after a few moments of silence, started waving her arms to get the control room's attention, first subtly, then moving gradually into c'mon-down-you're-the-next-contestant-on-*The-Price-Is-Right*! territory. But the White House was no place for Showcase Showdown moves, so instead she called the Washington, DC, news desk.

"ATN," a sleepy desk assistant answered.

"Hey, it's Natalie. Does New York know I'm at the White House, wired up and ready to go live?"

"What?" the girl said, making the word sound three syllables long, and dangerous. Despite having only had a handful of interactions with them, Natalie had taken to thinking of the whole cadre of DC desk assistants as the What Girls, in honor of their ability to turn that innocuous word into an implement of obstruction.

"Natalie Savage. At the White House—"

The What Girl sighed. "Hold on, I'll see if I can find her." And hung up.

Natalie called back and got a different What Girl, whom she hoped she'd convinced to track down someone other than herself.

And then a miracle happened. Natalie's earpiece crackled to life. Suddenly she could hear ATN broadcasting its show, the anchor talking about the White House briefing that was about to begin. She perked up and said into the mic, "Hey! New York. I'm here, you coming to me?" When no one answered, she tried to get the control room's attention with a delicate princess wave—hand in front of her chest, just her wrist moving from side to side.

Her cell phone started to vibrate.

"Natalie, you do know you're live on TV, don't you?" the voice barked. Natalie's stomach tightened. It was another What Girl.

"We're live? Are they coming to me?" Natalie asked.

"No. You're live on CNN and Fox and it looks like you have palsy. What are you doing? Bibb says to stop waving like that."

"No problem," Natalie said brightly, dropping her hand. *Never show annoyance, never be less than enthusiastic*, she intoned her mantras to herself, two rules she had learned early on. Calmly she said, "I was just trying to get the control room's attention. No one is talking to me. Do you know when they're coming to me?"

"They're not. They don't need you on camera. They're having Heath cover it from the studio. Bibb says you should concentrate on prepping for the briefing. Maybe you'll get to ask a question."

The What Girl said it as though it were a joke rather than a real suggestion. Natalie's chest went tight as fear welled up inside into her, that echoing, hollow-inside emotion that felt just like a breakup, being found not good enough, not loveable enough—*We don't want you.*

She hung up, sat down, and removed the earpiece as her mind launched into a mess of recriminations. She'd done everything they asked. She'd run toward the Biloxi inferno when everyone else was running away; stayed outside during Hurricane Moe when everyone else evacuated; waded hip deep into snake-infested flood waters because they wanted the shot. And for what? To get here. Where they wouldn't come to her.

The mechanics of the briefing clicked on around her, the wall of famous faces was now ramrod straight in the front row, each of them wearing their own version of The Look of Deep Concern (furrowed brow, nodding head), and yelling to be heard over one another at the cameras in the back of the room.

"We don't know what he'll say."

"Expecting the press secretary at any moment."

"I'd hate to speculate, so I can only guess."

They were all saying the same thing—absolutely nothing.

The blue door on the back wall of the briefing room slid open, sending a flutter along the edge of the flags on either side of the podium with the great Seal of the President on it.

Matt tapped his left eye with his phone to get Natalie's attention. "One of your lashes is falling off."

Of course it was. She was even failing at keeping her eyelashes on. She reached up and ripped it off, flinching. She crunched the lashes in her hand and didn't know if it was the pain or the subtle air of excitement that swept over the room, but in that moment her nervousness transformed into resolve. Maybe she was only temporary, but she wasn't going to give up without a fight. She just had to play their game, and do it better than they did.

She watched as three serious young White House aides carrying clipboards and wearing unfortunate suits marched through the door and sat poker-faced in classroom-style chairs against the wall, looking as though they'd just been told they were going to have to retake driver's ed. About four paces behind them came Adam Majors, the White House communications director. Natalie had seen him on television so many times she felt like she knew him. As usual he appeared to be in a state of pique. He stood behind the podium surveying the room with the pinched look of a bachelor tasked with changing a dirty diaper.

"Welcome to your White House briefing. I'm here to talk about the summit. It's a glorious event organized by our president, meant to strengthen America and our alliances. And to keep gas cheap."

He gazed across the room again like a general studying the horizon for an ambush before looking down at a piece of paper. "I'd like to begin with a statement about this summit. The president of the United States is extremely pleased to be greeting the leaders of seven Latin American nations. Good fences make for good neighbors, and ours are good." He nodded, seemingly satisfied with the goodness of it all. "We face enemies around the world. That's why it's important to be close to our neighbors at home. More so when they have oil. Make friends. Keep gas cheap. America's going the distance." He looked up, and Natalie felt her brain try to make sense of those words, but as usual, Adam Majors was conveying a sentiment without a coherent meaning.

"And now I'll take your questions about the summit. Melissa?" Adam called on the curly-haired woman in the first row.

"Thank you," Melissa said. "There's a report that President Lystra of Colombia has brought his son Rigo with him to the US. Now we at the AP are is reporting that the Venezuelans are seeking to extradite Rigo. They want him to face rape charges in their country."

A shiver of excitement raced through the room as people picked up their iPhones and started tweeting and emailing the latest breaking news from the AP. Melissa continued, "The US has no extradition treaty with Venezuela. If they should attempt to arrest Rigo here on US soil, how will the US respond?"

Adam sighed, flipped his briefing book to a tab and read, "The president welcomes all invited leaders with the traveling parties they choose. We will not sit as judge and jury. We do not conduct foreign policy on a he-said-she-said basis. Next question!"

"That didn't answer my—" Melissa attempted, sounding upset.

A forest of hands flew up.

"Charles?" Adam said, pointing to the front row and silencing Melissa.

Charles's face was a mask of weighty thought. "A *New York Times* report quotes three anonymous White House staffers saying they raised objections with the president and told him not to let Rigo attend the summit, but the president overruled them—"

Adam cut him off. "I don't respond to anonymous, nonspecific leaks. You know that."

"This is pretty specific," Charles said as he lifted his iPhone to read directly from it. "One staffer says, quote, 'The president doesn't understand the potential for an international crisis because he has the attention span of a fruit fly with ADD.'" Charles put down his iPhone and asked, "Now do you care to comment?"

Though Charles's velvety rumble gave his question a bouquet of Depth with hints of Importance and Urgency, it was nothing more than a voice exercise. There was only one possible answer—"No"—which was what Adam said, through tiny puckered lips.

Looking around the room, Natalie saw that most people were

busy on their phones and those who weren't stared into space with a dead gaze like actors waiting for their cue. Then Adam said, "Next question," and everyone sprang back to life, hands shooting up, eyes sparkling intently. Natalie put up her hand with the others even though she wasn't sure what she planned to ask. Adam wouldn't address the news, and her policy questions were too dull.

"In the back," Adam said, looking in her direction.

Matt said, "Thanks, Adam," and Natalie bit her lip. She'd thought—

Adam shook his head. "Not you, Matt." Pointing directly at Natalie, he said, "Brown hair, purple blouse? You had a question?"

In her peripheral vision, Natalie could see every camera now turn in her direction. She could feel them zooming in on her face, live on TV from the White House briefing room. Her heart pounded and her tongue felt huge in her mouth.

"Thank you, Adam," Natalie heard herself say. She glanced down at the paper with her questions on it but her eyes couldn't focus. She was too busy thinking, *Here's your shot. Ask something memorable.* There was something about live TV and instinct. When she was on air under pressure, instinct took over and usually delivered. Trusting that, Natalie swallowed and hoped the right words would come out of her mouth.

"Does the First Lady believe that the US should grant Venezuela's request to extradite Rigo? And, keeping in mind that she is originally from Venezuela, will Mrs. Crusoe speak with the presidents of Venezuela and Colombia about the rape accusation when she attends the summit this evening?"

Out of the corner of her eye, Natalie saw Matt sit up straighter and felt a tinge of pride that she'd surprised him. This was quickly followed by a dose of self-loathing for caring.

At the podium, Adam seemed to sneer slightly before flipping a tab on his briefing book. He began reading. "I am sorry to inform everyone that the First Lady will be missing tonight's dinner for the summit. She sends her regrets and best wishes for a successful meeting. But she is home with a migraine."

Natalie felt the blood rush in to her cheeks and heard her heartbeat in her ears. She'd gotten some news. In the high school cafeteria atmosphere of the briefing room, this was like getting asked out by the hottest guy in school and getting an A all in the same day.

"Honey, I have a headache," a male voice called out from the back of the briefing room in a bad imitation of Ricky Ricardo, shaking Natalie out of her reverie. The room turned to check the source of the outburst and then broke out in laughter.

Natalie was not laughing. She was frozen at the sight of Ryan McGreavy, a correspondent from her own network, who was standing in the back like he'd sneaked in after everyone was seated. *"¡No esta noche, Presidente!"* he singsonged, a big grin on his face, in a shitty falsetto imitation of the First Lady.

What is Ryan doing here?

"Excuse me!" Adam Majors snapped, though Natalie could tell he was swallowing a laugh.

What about this is funny?

If a Nazi-looking quarterback was your platonic ideal, McGreavy was a 26-year-old corn-fed exemplar of human perfection. The progeny of a former Nevada governor and a casino heiress, he'd parlayed his regional celebrity into an on-air job in Los Angeles local news. There, he'd staked his claim to immortality by going undercover as a contestant on the reality show *Eat Me*, where he'd gathered hours of hidden camera video. Ryan's subsequent report, *Reality UnReal*, showed *Eat Me*'s producers staging conflicts between the contestants, and aired the same week as the show's finale, proving a ratings juggernaut for his network.

Natalie had seen only one scene—the only one she needed to see—in which Ryan downed a plate of raw pig scrotum to win the competition. The resulting viral video won him a job at ATN, where his star had been on the rise all the way up to becoming ATN's crime and justice correspondent.

Natalie hadn't noticed Ryan before the briefing, which meant he'd crashed—both the briefing and her moment in the spotlight. The feeling of getting wantonly screwed intensified and not in a controllable way.

When Adam Majors closed his binder and exited the room, Matt turned to her. "You really went off leash there with your question. I'm impressed Bibb Connaught sanctioned that."

Natalie tried to keep her face blank. "I write my own questions."

"Oh please, Hot Nerd, don't get defensive. I'm just saying you've got moxie. For a TV reporter." He turned to the back of the room where the blond man-boy was yukking it up with fellow twentysomething reporters. "What's he called again?"

"Pendejo?" Natalie suggested, then added, "I thought you knew everyone." It must have come out a little meaner than she'd intended because Matt stiffened slightly. "Ryan McGreavy," she added, relenting.

"Ah, the governor's kid." He gave her a knowing smile. "If you ask me, that *pendejo* is going to be stiff competition. Looks like he's destined to become a crowd favorite."

Matt stood and began to move off. "I think I'll go introduce myself."

What is the plural of pendejo? Natalie wondered, watching him leave. Then she moved her gaze to the vibrating phone in her hand and found that Bibb had sent her an email.

To: Natalie Savage
From: Bibb Connaught, DC Bureau Chief, ATN
Subject: Your Future

I was not happy with that performance. And what is wrong with your hair? I expect better at the White House. We need to talk. Come to my office. Now, please.

2

HAIR AND LOATHING
IN THE DC BUREAU

When Natalie walked onto the seventh-floor newsroom at ATN's DC bureau, the only sounds were coming from the dozen TV monitors ringing the assignment desk, flashing local news, cable news, and multiple iterations of article-plus-meaningless-noun shows:

The View, The Chew, The Real, The Buzz. Too bad there wasn't a show called *The Condemned*, she could have been its poster child.

At first she'd been puzzled by what she'd done that warranted being summoned by the bureau chief. Her question wasn't the classiest but it had elicited a new piece of information, which was her job, wasn't it? In the taxi on the way to the meeting, she'd looked to Twitter for clues and found only that #NoEsta-Noche was trending and Ryan McGreavy's followers seemed to be climbing by the minute.

She threaded her way through the mazes of desks where colleagues were staring at massive computer screens, monitoring

incoming digital news like air force controllers on high alert for
a bogie. Eyes unblinking, they were refreshing Twitter, Facebook, Snapchat, Instagram, Drudge, the *Daily Mail* gossip page,
the *New York Times*, the *Washington Post*, *POLITICO*, Axios,
BuzzFeed, TVBuzzster, The EarlyBird, and various social media
mining apps, making sure that no vital item—"Shocking Video
of First Lady's Indigenous Cousins Performing Ancient Voodoo
Ritual"—got overlooked and became The Story We Should
Have Had!

Lucky for her, the news cycle was churning so rapidly that
her colleagues were too busy keeping up with the latest White
House leaks to note her presence. At least none of them scooted
away as she passed them.

"Natalie Savage. Great! You got a question today!" a voice
boomed in front of her.

Natalie stopped, just managing not to run into the large,
fortysomething man who had spoken. Hal Thomas, the deputy
bureau chief, was giving her a broad nicotine-stained smile. As
the number two boss right under Bibb, Hal had a reputation as
a petty tyrant who punished reporters who had the audacity to
question their assignments or the bureau's management. Natalie
had heard him referred to even by women outside the bureau as
Handsy Hal. Now, as he gripped her arm while standing a little too close and squeezing a little too long, she could see why.

Natalie gave him a bright smile and disengaged her arm.
"Thanks, Hal," she said in her friendliest voice and, trying to
project urgency, continued toward the news desk.

Hal walked with her. "You looked really great on camera
today. *Really* great," he said, at her elbow. "But have you considered pulling your hair back? You've got great eyes. We could see
them more if you'd just pull it back like—" Natalie, too stunned
to move, watched as Hal leaned in to pull strands of her hair
up and away from her face. Her stomach was mid-somersault
when, mercifully, they were interrupted.

"Natalie!" It was the voice of an angry mom.

She turned to see a figure rushing toward her in a blur of khaki, diamonds, and white blond hair. Bibb Connaught, her bureau chief.

"We need to talk," Bibb snapped.

Before Natalie could reply, Hal said to Bibb, "They want you—"

"I know, I know." Bibb waved him off, then impatiently looked at Natalie. "I need to handle something. Come with me, then we're going up to my office to have a talk." She hurried past and disappeared down a second hallway, leaving the scent of Chanel No. 5 and fear in her wake.

This is not good. Natalie felt as though her stomach was trying to crawl out of her body.

Jogging to keep up, Natalie had a chance to take in Bibb's outfit. She was dressed like the Georgetown version of Isak Dinesen wearing a yellow linen shirt with a high popped collar, khaki pants, a cloth belt, and knee-high riding boots. There was a hint of jodhpur in the cut of the pants, not enough to make them look like she'd just bounced over from the riding stables but enough to give the impression that at any moment she might throw a machete over her shoulder and lop off some heads.

Bibb didn't lead her to a conference room for a quiet execution. Instead, Natalie found herself pressed against the back wall of the DC control room, where producers were directing the network's live coverage in a state of mayhem unusual even for live news. Three people were simultaneously screaming.

"How about Developing Story? Do we have Developing Story?"

"Can we reboot?"

"Graphics, that name is BRIT not TIT. Fix it now!"

Their voices layering over each other.

In the otherwise pitch-black room, the thirty monitors up front were filled with images of older men in bad suits aimlessly milling around a stage. The sound was muted but Natalie deduced the network was covering the group photo for the PanAmerican Summit now underway at the DC Convention Center. Cleary the sedate scene on air had nothing to do with the panic in the room.

Bibb, who had raced to the front of the room, was red faced. "We lose ten percent of our tune in for every five minutes the Breaking News banner isn't up," she snapped at a haggard producer who was in turn barking into a tiny microphone attached to a headset. Natalie noticed that even in a state of clear agitation, Bibb's forehead maintained the smooth satin glow of Botox. "The earnings call is around the corner. *We can't afford this right now!*" As Bibb barked, the producer twisted around to look up at her, making the headset cord look like a noose around his neck.

"What's going on?" Natalie whispered to a young African American man, probably an associate producer, seated at a desk to her right.

"The Breaking News banner crashed." He shrugged, laconically. "So they're freaking out."

Natalie's eyes got big as she registered the full weight of the situation. "You mean we're live on air without the words Breaking News on the screen?"

The producer met her gaze with a nod of mock horror. In a deadpan, he said, "Indeed. No news can be broken without a Breaking News banner."

She swallowed back a laugh. It would have been funny if the mood among the terrorized producers didn't give the impression that someone's head was likely to roll. Clearly one of these people was going to pay for a computer bug taking out the network's guaranteed ratings generator.

Natalie watched Bibb, the EP, and a tech guy huddled over a master computer trying to get the machine to summon the magic words. A flash of color drew Natalie's attention back to the monitors. She watched the silent show as BamBam made a dramatic late entrance to the summit stage with Rigo by his side. Even with the sound on mute, the duo was entertaining and expressive. BamBam looked like he could have stepped out of *Modern Dictator Catalog* in his signature tight orange Nehru jacket and his purple-black hair fluffed out beneath a beret. The son, Rigo, appeared fresh from a shoot for a hip-hop yachting line, wearing an ascot and a navy double-breasted blazer festooned with gold braid. Looking more closely, Natalie saw that the blazer bore the insignia of the Colombia Navy in which, according to his epaulettes, Rigo held the position of admiral. Not bad for a twenty-one-year-old who had surely never worked a day at sea, or anywhere for that matter. Natalie realized she didn't even know whether Colombia had a navy.

BamBam had a gregarious smile and a jovial bounce that made him seem charming when he refused leaders' outstretched hands and instead leaned in for a full embrace with the presidents or foreign ministers of Mexico, Peru, and Brazil. Natalie glanced over at Bibb who was now on headset berating another poor soul about the Breaking News banner fail.

This is not breaking news, Natalie thought. *A Happening Now banner would be just fine. In fact, if eyeballs are the goal, a* #HeWore-What *tag is probably the better way to go.*

With every uncomfortable embrace, BamBam and Rigo edged closer to the president of Venezuela, Luis Gomez. Natalie could sense the tension rippling across the stage. Only Paraguay stood between the two adversaries when BamBam, already approaching President Gomez, arms outstretched, was blocked by four men in identical dark suits and mirrored glasses as they materialized onstage. Almost instantly, Rigo Lystra was surrounded by the men and then whisked away. Without the sound, it looked like an old-timey magic trick: Rigo there one minute, gone the next.

The camera, trained on the scene, caught it all.

Now BamBam was waving his arms frantically. Security details from every country swarmed onto the stage, hustling Pan-American leaders off to safety this way and that way until only the president of Paraguay remained onstage, alone, dazed, and confused.

It had all taken less than sixty seconds and, best as Natalie could tell, none of the people running the ATN control room had noticed.

"Excuse me, Bibb? Did you see that?" Natalie called out. Even without a banner, this was news worth breaking.

The laconic producer she'd been talking to earlier gazed up at her. "Don't bother. I used to try. They never pay attention to what's happening on air."

"But—"

"If you really want them to notice, tweet it. One of the websites will pick it up and then someone in the newsroom will spot it. Probably off Drudge. If it comes from one of us, they'll just ignore it."

As if on cue, three wild-eyed producers came racing into the control room, shouting.

"Rigo was kidnapped!"

"Drudge says he was shot!"

"Beltway thinks he might be dead!"

"Where?"

"Is there video?"

"Who is reporting this?"

Various mouths screamed at once.

Natalie looked at the producer and then back up at the monitors. She had been in enough control rooms in meltdown to know the wise choice would be to stay silent and make herself invisible. But conveying facts was her *job*.

"No one was shot," Natalie shouted over the din, in her most just-trying-to-help tone.

The room didn't notice that she'd emitted a sound. Producers were yelling, "Beltway says they were Venezuelan security forces."

"Fox is calling it a foreign attack on US soil."

"What do we want to go with?"

Bibb started barking orders like the commanding officer on a sinking submarine. "People, rerack the video! I want a Developing Now banner on air, and a headline. 'Colombian Leader's Son Abducted! Summit Attack!'"

The video started running in slow motion replay live on air with the banners Bibb requested. There was Rigo smiling and extending a hand when he was again surrounded by big men in earpieces and whisked away.

"Unlikely," Natalie murmured to herself.

"What is?" the associate producer asked.

"Kidnapped? I just don't see how Rigo Lystra gets abducted in the middle of a high security White House event in the heart of DC. On live TV," Natalie said in a low voice.

"Eh." The producer shrugged. "These days anything's possible."

"That place must be crawling with Secret Service," Natalie insisted to the producer. "How would kidnappers get around them?"

"Who knows," the producer said, in the tone of a man who witnesses the improbable on a daily basis.

Bibb's voice pierced the room. "As soon as we can, we're switching to New York control! I'm getting New York on the phone."

"Or maybe the Service took him," Natalie said. "Maybe he's in US custody."

"I buy that," the producer said, nodding as he pulled out his phone. "Do you want to tweet it or should I?"

Natalie shook her head. "Bibb," Natalie said, walking up to her boss. "Bibb, do you think maybe the Secret Service took him?"

"What?" Bibb snapped, turning on Natalie with a look of rage in her eyes.

"I'm thinking it doesn't make sense to assume he was abducted? Maybe we want to pull back on the—"

Shaking her head, Bibb gave Natalie a dismissive wave. "Wait for me in my office. I'll be there when this is done."

The producer glanced at Natalie's phone, then back at her.

"You do it," Natalie whispered to him, as she walked out of the room.

Natalie studied the decor in Bibb's office while she waited. It was an eclectic mix of British colonial and deconstructed Serengeti. Many of the pieces had begun life grazing the land on four legs, and those that hadn't were carved in the shape of things that had. For example the elephant feet on Bibb's mahogany desk, and the gnu figures to one side of the uncomfortable wooden chair that Natalie would be expected to sit in.

"That was a gift from the headman of the Maasai tribe," Bibb had told her during their meeting the prior Friday. "And so was my throwing spear." Gesturing to a human-size harpoon hanging within arm's reach of the desk. Airily, Bibb had explained that she'd collected all these artifacts while working "in country" as a young producer, but Natalie would bet her agent's cut that Bibb had picked up most of them antiquing in Virginia.

After what felt like an hour, Bibb rushed into the office wearing the look of an exhausted school principal, albeit a principal who could afford three-carat diamond stud earrings and the expensive balayage required to turn her hair that especially natural-looking shade of blond.

"You have no idea how hard my job is," Bibb sighed. She sank into the chair behind her desk and grabbed one of the six remote controls arrayed on top of it, stabbing the volume to high. Natalie momentarily turned around in her chair to take in the wall of monitors. Every channel was replaying the Rigo "abduction" with pundits doing live play-by-play analysis. The ATN monitor now had the words Breaking News in shouty all-caps in the bottom crawl along with the banner "PanAmerican Summit Mayhem." At least they'd dropped the abduction line.

"Thank god, they got it fixed," Bibb said with relief, punching the volume to low. Then her eyes shifted to Natalie and her voice got stern. "So. You," she said and Natalie felt dread rise in her chest. "Today," Bibb said, tilting her head with either sympathy or contempt, Natalie couldn't tell which. "The briefing."

Natalie swallowed. "In retrospect I realize I should have cleared it with you before asking but at that moment I thought—"

Bibb frowned. "Cleared what? I don't know what you are talking about."

"My question?" Natalie said. "About the First Lady?"

A shadow of a line appeared between Bibb's brows. "Oh that was fine. That's not the issue." She sighed. "Natalie, dear, I want you to succeed. Do you want to succeed?"

"Yes," Natalie said breathlessly. "Yes, I do."

"Well, if that's the case, let's talk about the hard things." She pushed a stack of glossy magazines across the desk toward Natalie.

Reaching for them, Natalie saw they were copies of *Hamptons* magazine, *Greenwich Style*, and the *Washingtonian* open to at-home profiles of women news anchors. The spreads showed perfectly groomed TV ladies posed in their decorator-perfect homes, making breakfast for their three—always three—handsomely scruffy children, hard at work in their immaculate offices filled with a row of designer dresses on hangers and boxes of carefully stacked eight-hundred-dollar shoes, captioned with sentiments like, "I love getting up at 3 a.m. for the morning show because I get off work at noon, and that gives me a full nine hours to be wife and mom." And "On my days off, I like to whip up homemade butter, do triathlons, and make mosaics with the children."

"This is what I need you to shoot for," Bibb said.

Natalie almost choked, trying to swallow back her laughter as she imagined a photo shoot at the shabby breakfast bar of the UnComfort Inn where she was currently staying. "This is where I eat processed turkey out of the package alone for dinner after work," she would say with a comely smile.

"I—I don't have kids," Natalie said when she realized Bibb was waiting for a response. "Or a place."

"What?" Bibb asked tersely, jamming a finger at one woman's head. "Their hair. It's the hair you should be looking at."

Suddenly Natalie felt she was on familiar ground. Of all the things she'd mastered in her years climbing the news ladder, giving herself the perfect straight blowout was at the top of her list. In news, a good blowout was an essential survival skill.

"How would you like me to change my hair?" Natalie asked, thinking, *I got this.*

"To start with, it is about an eighth of an inch longer on one side than on the other. Is that meant as a statement?"

"A statement?" Natalie repeated, flustered.

Bibb nodded. "Do we think it is uneven or do we think we're tilting our head?"

"We're talking about my hair?" Natalie asked, just for clarification.

Bibb sighed. "Please understand, I am on your side. You may think this doesn't matter but it does. It will have a direct bearing on your ratings. You can't be cavalier about it."

"I'm not cavalier about my hair. Not at all," Natalie protested. Bibb looked toward the door and as she motioned, Natalie could feel someone enter behind her.

"Hal, join us. We were just talking about Natalie's hair," Bibb said as Hal took a seat and scooted close to Natalie.

"It's one of your best features," Hal said, looking like he was dangerously close to touching it again. "So full-bodied."

"True, but there's just so much of it," Bibb said. "I'm think-ing The Treatment."

"Great idea." Hal agreed as he inched his chair a smidge closer to Natalie.

"It's a chemical straightener that will do wonders reducing the volume." Bibb smiled warmly-ish. "I'll give you the name of a place. It's six hundred dollars but so worth it. You won't believe the difference it will make."

Natalie became aware of a tingling in her arm and realized she'd pushed herself so deeply into the corner of the chair to get away from Hal that her forearm had gone numb.

"Okay," Natalie said noncommittally, thinking there was no way she was spending six hundred dollars on hair chemicals. "Well, thanks, then," she added and, assuming the meeting was over, made to get up and away from both of them.

"It is not just your hair," Bibb said, sending Natalie back into the chair. "It is, well—" Bibb paused. "It's you. I worry you're a little too outside the lines." Bibb tilted her head. "What are you? What's your thing?"

Natalie frowned, speechless.

"See even you aren't sure. That's a problem," Bibb said.

"What should I be?" Natalie asked, genuinely uncertain.

"We need you to be very authentic," Bibb said.

"Viewers love authenticity," Hal said, nodding enthusiastically.

Were they serious? Authenticity, like relatability, was one of those words news managers loved to throw around without bothering to assign it a meaning. "So you're saying I should be more myself on air? Show more personality?" Natalie asked, trying to sound open-minded.

"No!" Hal shook his head violently with a look that said, *Eeek! Not that! Anything but you!*

"More authentic," Bibb repeated, as if it were a tonal language. "Develop something you're known for, a texture and personality that is uniquely your own. A character. To make viewers want to know you and know about you."

What about the news? Isn't the point that viewers want to know about the news? Natalie wondered but managed not to say.

"Look at the reporters in the front row at the White House," Bibb went on. "One looks handsomely intellectual, someone you'd love to sit next to at a dinner. Another is dapper with well-coordinated pocket squares and ties, like he'd be fun at a cocktail party. Even the curly-haired girl—it's a terrible look, but you recognize her instantly. She's that neighbor you can leave the dog with when you go out of town. Bring her back a dish towel or pot holder, something small."

"So I need to develop a *thing*." Natalie was trying to play along. "What about a pair—?"

"No glasses," Hal cut in, apparently reading her mind.

"No glasses on a woman over twenty-five *ever*," Bibb added with finality.

Hal looked at Bibb, with earnest concern. "Did you mention the, ah, you know?" As Hal spoke, he did a circling motion near one eye.

"Oh yes," Bibb said. Looking pained, she leaned forward. "Natalie, are you aware you have on only one set of eyelashes? Did you forget to do the other eye?"

In all the rush she'd forgotten. "No, the other one fell off," she said, embarrassed, reaching up to peel the remaining lash off her eye.

"I see. Well, we can't have reporters looking like one-eyed raccoons—"

"In the land of the blind, the one-eyed reporter is king," Hal intoned enthusiastically.

"Please, Hal." Bibb shot him a dismissive look and, turning back to Natalie, assumed a patient smile. "All right, I'd like this to be productive. Natalie, the truth is that in this business, hardworking women are a dime a dozen. Especially at your stage of the game." Bibb said this with an intonation that meant only one thing: *your age*. As in, over thirty. She continued, "Frankly, talented men are the rarity. They are prized. So in order to stand out as a woman in the news business, you have to display something special." Bibb paused to smile in sympathetic understanding. "That means you need to consider what is special about you."

Natalie began mentally flipping through her résumé with a creeping awareness of how irrelevant all the actual items—class president, valedictorian, magna cum laude, twelve years in news trenches, eight hurricanes, five celebrity trials, Emmy winner— would sound to her present judge and jury. To win in this court of law, she'd need more Sparkle! Vivacity! Enthusiasm!

"The thing that most sets me apart is that I do all my own reporting," she offered. "And I'm good at developing sources, winning their trust."

"Winning the source's trust?" Bibb repeated. Then tried in a different, more patient tone, "Natalie, you should know that last night our ratings were worse than both CNN and HLN. And the morning show?" Hal shook his head mournfully, and Bibb waved the thought away as if it were secondhand cigar smoke. "The parent company wants the Chief to increase profits ten percent over last year. And he's counting on us to deliver at least those numbers. The better we do, the happier everyone is. So."

"So?" Natalie asked, warily.

"The question you need to ask yourself, the question the Chief will be asking, is do you appeal to our key viewers? Do you have what the Demo wants?"

"The Demo?" Natalie hadn't meant to say it out loud.

"The Demo," Hal repeated reverentially.

"Men ages eighteen to thirty-five." Bibb said it as if "Men, Ages Eighteen to Thirty-five" was a mantra she whispered to herself during quiet moments and every night before bed.

Natalie became aware that she was grinding her teeth. Of

course she knew who made up the Demo. It was the hallowed demographic, so desirable because it was said to be the hardest for advertisers to reach and hold. Earlier in her career she'd asked her first boss, Len, "Why not just focus on the viewers who actually want news instead of chasing after boys who don't?"

In response he'd shrugged and said, "In news that's what we call a Zen koan."

That was eight years ago. Since then, she'd accepted that her career was going to be run on the rules of dysfunctional dating and had stopped being incredulous about anything, even the price of water at the airport.

"Natalie, let's look at this a different way. How did you get here?" Bibb stood up from her desk and walked across the office toward a mirror in a carved-teak frame and got busy adjusting the starched collar of her blouse. "In life there are two kinds of people," she began, and from her tone Natalie half expected her to pull out the human anatomy charts she'd seen in her eighth grade health class. "There are those who rise to the top easily because they have an ineffable quality that makes other people want to work with them, even *do their work* for them. And then there's the second kind of people." Bibb paused for effect. "Those who have to make their own way to the top. They have to do more with less, relentlessly keep their eye on the ball, never let up. They have to work harder than the others to get to the same place and that might not be fair but that is how it is. We call the two groups—"

"Men and women?" Natalie said, unable to stop herself.

A painful silence fell over the room, then Hal barked out a laugh. After a beat Bibb joined him.

"Very cute, Natalie," Bibb said. "But this is serious. I call them elevator people and stairs people."

"I see," Natalie replied, aware that she was supposed to say something.

"You are a stairs person," Bibb said.

"It's because you're such a go-getter. You're so smart," Hal said, smiling cheerily.

"And we need to see those qualities on display," Bibb added.

Natalie had no idea how to respond and was grateful to be saved by Bibb's intercom, which now buzzed with a call.

"We'll keep working on this." Bibb gave her gold stickpin an adjustment, then turned and headed to the other side of her elephant-footed desk. The intercom buzzed again. Bibb took a deep breath and, picking up the phone, said with exaggerated drama, "Andrea, tell me you've got a location. You...what? Oh. Oh my... I am sorry. I knew your father was ill but I had no idea...hospice. I see. You poor thing." She covered the mouthpiece with her hand and hissed at Hal, "It's Andrea, with Ryan. Her father is dying." Bibb's expression was filled with alarm. Hand still covering the mouthpiece, she scowled. "I mean, really. Is she going to leave us hanging now? The timing couldn't be worse."

Hal returned her frown. "Just explain that to her. She'll understand."

"People are so difficult," Bibb sighed, then took her hand from the phone and said, "Of course you need to be with your father, Andrea. You need to do what is right for him. But don't forget, the question is also, what is right for *you*?"

Natalie felt like she was having a flashback, hearing echoes from less than two years earlier, her father fading quickly.

"After all the work you've put in, it would be a shame if your career went off the rails right now," her boss on the *Daybreak* desk had said, all sympathy. "But it's your call. Do what's best for you. Just let us know what you decide by 5 p.m. please."

She'd told herself her dad would wait for her. She was covering a major hurricane and she knew that of all people, he'd get it. After all, he'd missed her sixteenth birthday and her graduation, all the while insisting she had to understand because he was pursuing a whistleblower with cold feet.

"Dad, I just have to be reliable, do what they need," she'd told him over the phone. "But I'll be there as soon as I can."

"I understand, honey," he'd said. "Stay where you are. What would we do if you were here? You'd just be sitting next to an old man, driving your mother crazy." His voice was thin and weak but she could hear it swell with pride. "Watching you on TV is the best medicine. It gives me peace to know you're going to be on the North Lawn soon. Here, talk to Cronkite." And Natalie had laughed as she heard the panting of her father's dog fill the line.

Her mother's voice interrupted, her tone hushed. "He's fading fast, Natalie. You should come home. Your sister is spending a lot of time here with the baby."

"But Dad just said—"

A long pause. Then the formal tone, knife-edged with disapproval. "Well. It's your choice, of course. Let us know what you decide."

There had been so many similar dialogues with other people over the years, so many missed dinner-and-a-movies, missed friend's weddings, Thanksgivings, New Year's Eves. Not as intense, but always played in the same tune. It felt like a form of emotional jujitsu, using the dedication and ambition that had gotten her that far against her.

Andrea was holding out a long time with Bibb, not giving in to the pressure, Natalie noted with admiration and a pang of shame. She had caved every time. Even at the very end.

"I'll see you on Friday," was the last thing she'd told her dad, and it had turned out to be a lie. She hadn't meant it to be. He'd held on, her mother told her, two days longer than anyone thought he could, waiting for her. But not long enough for Hurricane Leon to spell itself out so she could get there.

Don't give in, Natalie wanted to shout to Andrea. *Go be with your dad. Nothing they promise or threaten is as important.*

But she knew it wasn't entirely true. *You gave in*, she chided herself, *and look where you are. Right where you wanted to be.*

Or almost. Temporarily.

"Of course we'll need to know as soon as possible so we can have someone take over for you," Bibb was saying into the phone. "Don't worry, it will be someone wonderful, someone just as good as you." Bibb was playing the we-can-replace-you card. That was the closer; it always worked. "What...!" Bibb chirped, sounding delighted. "You think so? You're a trooper! Absolutely, we can do that." Bibb was now magnanimous. "One or two more days here with Ryan and then off you go to see Dad. I bet they can even wait to start the morphine. What difference can a day here or there really make?"

Bibb hung up, closed her eyes, and sighed. "I bought us a few days anyway. Managing people is so draining." She rubbed her temples and looked back and forth between Hal and Natalie. "Andrea's been working with Ryan all week. Who does she think will write his live shots for him if she leaves?"

"She's probably just emotional, not thinking clearly," Hal said as if the problem was that Andrea's father was dying. Or that Andrea *cared* that her father was dying.

"Can't Ryan handle his own live shots?" Natalie asked, unable to bite back the words. It was one thing to have a producer show him the way, but if the guy couldn't speak without someone dictating every word, maybe he was in the wrong line of work?

"Have you met Ryan McGreavy?" Bibb asked.

"I only know him by reputation. And his, ah, *Eat Me* investigation," Natalie said judiciously.

"If you know him, you'll understand," Bibb told her. "Ryan is a work in progress. He is teeming, bursting with potential. But he needs a little—I was going to say grooming but that's the wrong word in his case." To Natalie's horror, Bibb tittered.

Hal joined her. "Ryan has great hair."

"For someone like Ryan, we're happy to hire producers to

write their scripts and conduct their research. Do all the hustly-bustly stuff," Bibb said. "And it works very well, as long as they stick to their lines as written."

I suppose for a guy who's eaten pig sac, putting other people's words in his mouth must feel like child's play. "So you're saying Ryan is an elevator person," Natalie stated more than asked.

"Exactly," Bibb said with pride, like a teacher whose slowest pupil finally learned to read. "I'm glad you understand, because we feel Ryan could make a wonderful reporter at the White House."

For a moment Natalie stopped breathing, as her mind raced. Ryan. It was true. They were grooming I-Eat-Balls McGreavy for the White House job. *Her* White House job.

"Surely you're not surprised. Ryan has politics in his blood," Bibb went on. "You understand your assignment is only temporary." She smiled. "Of course none of this is set in stone. The Chief is in town tomorrow. He's holding an impromptu town hall, to reassure staff about his plans for the network. You should be ready to wow him. At the very least, I'd suggest getting a blowout."

This time, Natalie understood, she was being dismissed. Absently, she promised to blow out her hair, thanked Bibb, and in a daze she stood and headed for the door, all the while hearing the words *Ryan McGreavy, White House correspondent* echo in her head.

"Wait, take these!" Bibb called out, forcing her to circle back and take the glossy magazines out of Hal's outstretched hands. As she headed down the hall, mind racing, she heard echoes of all the other "helpful advice" she'd gotten over the course of her career from women in news management. From women who were *just* trying to be honest or *just* trying to be helpful or *just* thought you might want to know. She wondered if it was like this in other businesses. Or at other networks. What ever happened to sisterhood?

She stalked past the stairs and punched the down button on the elevator. *Stairs person*, she fumed. Then realizing that she was still clutching the magazines she looked around for a recycling can and, not seeing one, shoved them in the trash.

Bibb was in for a surprise. Natalie Savage was not going away. She'd stayed and covered Hurricane Leon and she would stay and cover the White House, too. Permanently.

Although, seeing her reflection in the elevator door, she decided it wouldn't be a bad idea to get a blowout.

3

A SUITE OF ONE'S OWN

Despite the promise of its name, the Executive Comfort Inn where ATN was putting Natalie up—"Temporarily," the woman in HR had stressed—was anything but. It was adorned with plaid drapes and a painting of a sad cowboy who looked like he was going to shoot himself. All the furniture sloped slightly toward the floor as though it had been designed by a team of sadists to ensure she could never relax. At night, Natalie kept waking up in a twisted position halfway off the bed with her forearms aching from bracing against the slope.

On the bright side, it was spacious enough to include a "living room" with a "breakfast bar," which is where she'd eaten her dinner to-go while watching—no, torturing herself with—online clips of Ryan McGreavy's *Eat Me* investigation. Her reaction careened between hilarity and horror as she watched the weekly ritual of degradation. Witness McGreavy's determination as he polishes off a liter of rat-tailed maggots with a shot of horse semen! Enjoy McGreavy's smoldering gaze as he and his inexplicably wet eight-pack race through the jungle and trip into a slick of rhino dung! Admire McGreavy's craftiness as he sneaks his hidden camera into the producers' tent, capturing proof the competition is staged. Such commitment to the truth! Such bravery in holding power to account! What a tribute to the virtue of a free press.

Natalie wasn't sure what to deduce from the clips about Ryan's style of competition—except that the guy would eat anything—when Ryan wrapped up his report by telling an anchor, "I'll do whatever it takes to win." He was so brazen about championing his own success Natalie felt a flash of envy. If only she could summon that kind of attitude. *I win, therefore I'll win.* She cringed, thinking the words felt hollow. *Bibb wants me to win, therefore I'll win.* She smiled. *Yes, that makes more sense.*

She was wrested away from her efforts to channel Ryan's ego by the sound of her phone buzzing.

HAL: Hey! You busy?

Reflexively she leaned back and away from the phone, as if Hal's creepiness could leap out of her screen onto her breakfast bar and start stroking her hair. She checked the clock. 10:35 p.m. It was kind of late to get an assignment but not unthinkably so. She wanted to ignore Hal, but what if he had a killer story and gave it away because she didn't answer?

NATALIE: Hey, Hal. What's up?

HAL: Checking in on the new girl. Hate to think of you sitting home alone.

She clenched her jaw.

HAL: Actually I sort of like the thought of you home alone! How's the hair?

Was it possible he could reach through the phone, after all, or poltergeist-style appear in the screen to haunt her?

HAL: Hahaha just kidding! Want to grab a drink?

She grimaced. He'd just exited the Land of Creepy and entered the Forest of WTF. She wanted to tell him not a chance but she remembered the advice she'd gotten. *Hal weaponizes assignments. Don't mess with him.*

NATALIE: Sorry I'm wiped and have an early am. Need to read up and get rest. See you at work.

She hit Send and her relief went to war with worry. Had she been too dismissive? Too cold? If she bruised his ego, there was no telling what punishment he'd mete out. Still, she reminded herself, she'd experienced enough closed-door come-ons from news executives to know that you have to draw the line when they bypass the gray and enter the danger zone. Leave no room for confusion. She stared at the phone waiting for the inevitable follow-up—a plea to meet for a "quick drink" or a "don't be a bore" nudge—but mercifully there was none.

Chalk that up as a victory, she thought.

Feeling pleased with herself for dodging that bullet, she looked round the room to decide what challenge she'd conquer next. Already she'd taken Bibb's advice and blown out her hair, sort of, by washing the front half of her head, blowing it dry, and leaving the stuff in the back untouched. It was a time-saving trick she'd learned from a globe-trotting war correspondent. "On TV, they only see the hair in front anyway," the correspondent had explained with an insider's wink and a toss of her half-cleaned brunette tresses.

She tried to imagine what her friends in New York must

be doing right now. *They're probably listening to baby monitors over glasses of wine with their extremely attractive and attentive husbands, debating whether they should have hot married sex or organize photos of their perfect lives,* she thought. They always claimed to covet her glamorous TV life, though she was pretty sure none of them had ever shared a temporary corporate suite with a sad cowboy.

Her laptop flashed with an alert from the *Washington Post*. "BamBam Lystra Ordered $10,000 Bottle of Wine at a Jefferson Hotel Dinner with Top Caruso Administration Officials." She logged into Facebook and found paparazzi photos of the Colombian leader very nearly sticking his head into the G-cup bosom of a D-list reality star while the secretary of energy laughed and illegally smoked a cigar indoors.

Guess he's not too worried about his son, Natalie thought, as she scrolled absentmindedly through her feed. Steadily she found herself sinking into the Facebook blues until she was staring at an image of Derek Bomgard, her most recent crush. After two dates Derek had left for an aid trip in Sri Lanka and had clearly returned with more than good memories. As she studied the woman he was kissing in the image, a familiar feeling of tightness crept into her chest. She called up the meant-to-be-reassuring words a veteran news anchor had shared when she'd found Natalie hyperventilating about a breakup in the ladies room: "There's a bright side to being a news nun. We get to skip the divorce bills."

She gulped in a deep breath. *This isn't healthy,* she thought and, pushing her pity party away, reached for her phone. Her sister, Sarah, answered mid-yell.

"Hi, Ms. White House Correspondent. You were amazing today. So smart! You looked born for the briefing room!" Sarah was like a human chill pill.

"My boss doesn't share your optimism," Natalie sighed, feel-

ing the breath come back into her body. "Anyway, there's competition."

"Of course, there's competition. It's the White House," Sarah
said.

"Is this a good time to talk?"

"Wait, that's Mom on the other line, give me a sec," Sarah
said and disappeared. When she came back, she was sighing.
"Mom suggests that instead of getting dinner tomorrow night,
we should go for colonics."

"I hope you said you'll be too busy steaming your vagina,"
Natalie laughed.

"I don't know how much more of her holistic hippie phase I
can take," Sarah said. "So, what's up?"

Natalie felt a tinge of guilt for bothering Sarah. Sarah was a
single mom dealing with responsibilities that were more conse-
quential than anything Hal or Bibb could think up. She didn't
need to manage Natalie's insecurities. Casually Natalie said, "Oh
it's nothing. The head of the network is coming tomorrow. The
new guy. I have to impress him."

"Great. Pitch him a story you're passionate about. Something
you can really dig into. Find some good injustice or cover-up.
That's when you shine."

"I wish," Natalie said, meaning it. "If it doesn't involve a
White House misstep or a foreign leader in meltdown, I'm not
getting it on air."

"Listen, you always told Dad you wanted to be at the White
House because what you did there mattered. You could shine
a light on injustice. Impact people's lives. So do it!" Just then
Sarah's four-year-old daughter, Lulu, let out a shriek and Sarah
said, "I gotta go, I think Lulu just woke up," then abruptly
hung up.

Natalie was thinking that Lulu had an impressively powerful shriek for a three-foot-tall person when her phone buzzed.

MOM: Hi, dear. I just re-watched you on TV. Please don't get mad at me but your skin is looking a little sallow again. Are you taking the CoQ10 I sent you?

MOM: It's important to look healthy. Good health attracts people. It's probably good for ratings, too.

MOM: Have you seen your ratings? How are they?

Giving in, Natalie typed a reply:

NATALIE: Hi, Mom. How are you?

MOM: Great! Gerald and I just did a hot tub together. He is wonderfully flexible.

Shuddering, Natalie redirected.

NATALIE: Guess what. My boss asked me to shell out $600 for a chemical hair straightening treatment. Can you imagine anything so crazy?

MOM: Why not try? We need to invest in our success.

NATALIE: I Googled. It's made with formaldehyde. It causes scalp cancer in lab animals! Who pays $600 to get scalp cancer?

MOM: No that's terrible for the environment. No. My healer gave me a recipe for a wonderful earth-friendly conditioner: aloe vera cooked with agave nectar, a ripe banana, flat beer, and an egg. If it's too emollient, add a touch of apple cider vinegar or urine. Human is fine.

NATALIE: I think I'd prefer scalp cancer.

MOM: Dear is there a date you can bring to the wedding? It's important that you find a partner—not just for the wedding. For life. I read that people who don't have regular sexual activity die early.

NATALIE: I'll make a note of it. Love you. Going to sleep.

She put down the phone and stared at the wall. She wished her dad was around to commiserate. Mom used to be hard on him, too, she remembered, always complaining that he spent too much time on the raft of Sobby Sauls and Heartbreak Hollys, as she used to call her dad's largely pro bono clients. Even at the age of ten, Natalie understood how important his work was, how he helped people who had no one looking out for them.

Then he'd gotten sick. That first time Natalie had arrived for a visit after the diagnosis, she'd found her mother out and her father watching the news. He'd motioned her into the chair next to his bed. "Just like the old days," he'd said. Cronkite, a black Lab who'd been in the family a few years, was curled by his feet. "That'll be you some day," her dad had said, pointing to the television where a network correspondent was doing a live shot. It was Nelly Jones, the ATN reporter she was now replacing. *Temporarily.*

"Don't worry, Dad. I'll get there for you. You'll be proud," she'd said.

He'd smiled back and said, "Get there for you, not me." His eyes were glistening as he spoke. "I know how hard you work, how much you're giving up. We all have to pay our dues. I couldn't be prouder. You know that, don't you?"

An unfamiliar buzzing noise broke through Natalie's thoughts and she looked around to find her phone. Only the buzz was coming from the wall. She spotted the source of the interruption—an intercom—and frowned. She didn't know anyone who could be visiting her now.

When she hit the speaker, a familiar male voice came crackling over the line. "Hey, it's Hal. I figured you can't move the mountain, so I came to you."

Her body went on alert. *Surely he isn't here at the building.*

"Where are you, Hal?" she asked cautiously.

"I don't like the thought of you going to sleep so early on one of your first weeks in Washington. I think you should come down and grab a drink. We can talk White House stuff."

A flash of anger shot through her calm. He hadn't just crossed a line, he'd obliterated it.

"How do you know where I'm staying?" It came out like an accusation.

"It's in the master file on the assignment desk, silly. We have to know how to find everyone in the bureau." He sounded deeply unapologetic.

Her body tensed in disgust as she imagined Hal looking up her personal details in the manager's file after she'd told him to back off.

"Sorry, Hal, but I can't," she said firmly.

"Oh you're such a goofy bore. Come down. I want to give you advice on the bureau," he replied cheerfully. "Anyway I'm feeling all alone tonight. Keep me company."

Over my dead and lifeless body, she thought. "Maybe we can get lunch near the office later this week, okay? But I'm going to bed now. Good night."

"I'll get you out one of these days," he said, sounding untroubled. "Rain check, then."

The intercom clicked and there was silence.

Shuddering she walked to the door to double-check that it was locked and bolted. She stared at the bolt for a few seconds, half convinced Hal would turn himself into a puddle, ooze under the security door, and reemerge in the living room to pay her another visit.

When she was finally sure that the coast was clear, she turned off the lights and climbed into bed with her cell phone set to speed-dial Sarah, just in case.

4

NOT CAMELOT

Heat. Hot. It was painful but it felt so good.

First Lady Anita Crusoe was wrapped in a too-large terry-cloth robe, perched at the edge of a sunken bathtub, hot water running in a fat stream over her feet. For a moment her mouth fell open in joy and relief. So nice, this heat.

The First Lady was too chilled to remove her bathrobe, so she sat at the edge, examining her toes under the hot water. They were starting to turn red and sting; her body was betraying her. As First Lady of Colorado, she'd learned to be rock steady, braving the elements at endless outdoor events. Now, after less than one term in the White House, just a few hours outdoors felt like roughing it. These days she was used to heated trailers and aides handing her blankets or hustling her into warm cars. She had every luxury in the world. At this very moment she was at an estate with a prosciutto room. Truly, a room dedicated to slicing smoked meat!

Estoy mimada, she told herself. Her nostrils flared with a bleak laugh as she considered how quickly she had accustomed herself to VIP living. And just as quickly learned its costs.

Her mind flashed back to the scene in the Blue Room last week when she, Anita Crusoe, had knelt on her hands and knees vacuuming the drapes live on *The Today Show*, yammering about "the dangers of dust, mites, and mold stuck in your household fabrics." Now, from her perch on the edge of the tub, she chirped, "Cleaning is good medicine!" with the same false excitement she'd oozed that day. Ridiculous. It was absurd that she'd allowed herself to be talked into taking on allergens as a cause. "I am a mechanical engineer," she'd wanted to scream. Used to be, she corrected herself.

Her husband's team had insisted that taking on a health issue would be a good way to "soften her image," make her "more palatable to voters who worry about a South American immigrant as First Lady."

"But I'm an American citizen," she'd protested.

"And Spanish is your first language," her husband's communications director had replied. "Half our supporters would like to deport you."

She'd gone along with it. Stayed quiet, done as they'd asked. As always.

God, what a mess I've made, Anita thought bitterly. ¡*Que desastre!*

She let the bathrobe fall off and she slid into the bathtub. She stretched her legs in the water and let out a long breath.

It was nice here. Here she didn't have to acquiesce. Comply. *Vacuum.* How did other First Ladies do it? she wondered. She couldn't be the only one who thought the job was torture. On the other hand, the idea of being the first First Lady to murder her husband while in office did have some appeal. Just think of the cleaning special she could do after that!

There was a knock at the door.

"Ma'am?" It was Beth, the head of her security detail.

She liked Beth, liked the Texas twang in her accent, and the fact that though she was smaller than the rest of the detail, she clearly commanded their respect. Beth had put her job on the line by agreeing, without her boss's approval or the president's, to the First Lady's insistence that they get out of town—now.

"Yes?"

"It's Anthony. He wanted me to let you know he's arrived. Downstairs."

Anita Crusoe smiled as she felt a calm wash over her, slide deep into her core. Anthony. Thank god for Anthony.

"Please tell him I'll be down in ten."

THE EARLYBIRD™/ THURSDAY / 6:02 A.M.
THE E-NEWSLETTER TRUSTED BY WASHINGTON'S POLITICAL ELITE

Good morning, EarlyBirders™. Here are the morning's need-to-know stories:

DRIVING THE DAY: *Where's Rigo? Colombia's 21-year-old wild child is still MIA. Abductions of international celebs don't just HAPPEN in DC! Who took him and where? Venezuela denies involvement. Should make for an awkward day two at the president's summit. Developing...*

QATAR HEROES: On the heals of Crusoe's recent DISASTROUS SPEECH in the Middle East, the region's oil ministers are meeting in Qatar, threatening to halt oil exports to the US.

MMMMM: On the **MENU** for tonight's official **PanAmerican Summit Dinner:**

Green Delicata Squash Soup
Chili Cheese Grits Soufflé & Roasted Figs with Speck
Thyme-Roasted Rack of Lamb
Pear Torte with Huckleberry Sauce
Hungry yet? We are!

5

THE POWER OF NOW-NESS

There were people three deep waiting for the elevators in the lobby when Natalie arrived at the ATN building the next morning. The stairs beckoned—*look at us! No waiting!*—but she ignored them. Screw Bibb, she was going to ride the elevator.

When she was jostled out of the elevator, for a moment she worried she'd gotten off at the wrong floor. The seventh-floor ATN newsroom was nearly unrecognizable. The desks had been cleared away and in their place was a sea of empty ergonomic chairs arranged like an amphitheater, rippling out from an open space with a small black platform. The scene reminded Natalie of a picture she'd once seen showing the remnants of a suicide cult: all that was left of them were the posture-friendly chairs in which they died. Only in this case, a massive sign was slowly spinning over the black platform. The sign read Town Hall with the Chief and featured a bright orange countdown clock that showed thirteen minutes, twenty-nine seconds until his arrival.

The media coverage about the appointment of Reginald Bounds—aka, the Chief—as the new president of ATN, split between describing him either as a visionary or as the antichrist of news, but both sides agreed on one thing: he was going to shake things up. "I'm not in the business of tending sacred cows," he'd been quoted as saying, "I'm in the business of making hamburgers."

The comment had played well with the stock market, giving ATN's parent company, American Services Industries, a healthy boost, but less well with the livestock on the news floor who were now eyeing one another with an unhinged, predatory vibe. Weaving her way between her colleagues, Natalie felt like the atmosphere was hovering uneasily between a psych ward and *Lord of the Flies*.

Without either friends or a desk—"No need for you to do all the work of getting cozy since who knows how long you'll be here," Bibb had explained—Natalie wasn't sure where to go or who to talk to for the next twelve minutes and twenty-four seconds until the town hall.

Glancing around, Natalie spotted a tall, Asian camerawoman pressed against a wall with Handsy Hal leaning way too close. As Natalie watched, the woman managed to wriggle free and Hal's eyes began moving deliberately over the crowd. Natalie looked away quickly and, head down, began threading her way through the clots of people gathered on the perimeter of the floor toward a row of empty seats at the back. She settled into a chair and glued her eyes to her phone.

After checking her Twitter numbers—a healthy follower bump since appearing at the White House—Natalie made herself look very busy scrolling through news articles: "Lystra Family Has A History of Paying Off Women"; "World Leaders With Migraines"; "Orlando Woman Makes Jewelry from Dehydrated Breast Milk"; "Is Porn A Public Health Crisis?"; "Justin Bieber Sings Duet With Down Syndrome Girl."

So Justin Beiber really is still a thing? Why would—?

"How's your mother, the bride?"

Natalie looked up to see Matt Walsh sliding into the seat next to hers.

"She's fine," Natalie said warily, wondering who invited a Beltway reporter to ATN's town hall. "Why are you here?" she asked, caving to her curiosity.

Matt feigned hurt. "Is that any way to greet your new colleague who's just trying to be friendly?"

She felt panic course through her. "New colleague?"

"Someone is out of the loop," he chided. "ATN acquired Beltway last week. The official announcement is today." He grinned into her frown. "I know, I couldn't be happier either. You and I, together at last, like the besties we were meant to be. Should we share passcodes now or wait until after we've had our nails done in the same color?"

"Maybe we should skip ahead to the part where we both like the same guy and have a falling-out and never speak again," she suggested.

"I just love your sense of humor, Savage," he went on pleasantly, ignoring the Chicago-in-February cold shoulder she was aiming in his direction as well as her question.

"Are you sure you want to sit here? There are so many other nicer seats closer up," Natalie said, trying to figure out whether he was serious about being her new colleague.

"I'm good." He said studying her.

Her iPhone buzzed with a message from her sister, which usually made her feel better. At least it was a perfect excuse to ignore the swamp creature next to her.

SARAH: Are you sitting down?

Usually.

NATALIE: Yes. But I'm going to stand up now because I don't

want to hear anything that's prefaced that way. Nothing good ever comes after those words.

SARAH: I think Gerald and Mom are going to a nudist resort for their honeymoon.

NATALIE: I AM STANDING UP. I AM NOT SITTING DOWN. YOU CAN'T SAY THAT WHEN I AM STANDING UP.

SARAH: And when I say I think, I mean that they are. I wanted you to know so you can get used to the idea.

NATALIE: THERE IS NO IDEA. I CAN'T HEAR YOU BECAUSE I AM STANDING.

SARAH: And not freak out.

Natalie had, in fact, stood up, though obviously it had not done her any good. But it did give her a perfect vantage point to see Bibb walk onto the now nearly full newsroom floor—with Reality Show Ryan right beside her.

Bibb's affectionate description of Ryan as an elevator person shimmered through Natalie's mind like a xylophone playing in the chord of anxiety. She was starting to think that rules of the TV news game trumped things like news standards, and if you landed on the Win Genetic Lottery and Be Unhampered by Modesty (or Shame) spaces, you got a Become the Darling of Your Bosses card and advanced directly to Shot at High-Profile Career.

Matt looked up, saying, "Who's the chummy mummy clinging to Ryan McGreavy?" He craned his neck around Natalie to get a better glimpse.

"What is a chummy mummy?"

"Older woman who would like to be more than 'just friends' with a younger man," Matt recited. "It's the update to 'cougar,' now with less sexism."

Natalie frowned. "How is chummy mummy less sexist? At least cougar is a metonym."

Matt frowned at her and hissed, "Metonym? That's very Hot Nerd. It's also the kind of talk that will get you fired." He shook his head in disbelief at her carelessness, repeating, "Metonym," under his breath.

Natalie wondered if talking to Matt made everyone want to research euthanasia or only her.

"Jesus, this place has the atmosphere of an embalming room," Matt was going on. "I assume it's always like this. Or is this special because of the bloodbath to come?"

Natalie glanced at her phone, praying for an interruption. Breaking news? A text from her mother? *Maybe he'll just stop talking.* "What are you talking about?" Natalie said unwillingly.

Matt lowered his voice. "The words *merger* and *revenue* don't occur in nature without the presence of layoffs," he said. "Especially when the new boss has five mortgages, a hefty alimony payment, a pricey new wife, and three kids in private school."

Now he had her interest. "How do you know all that?" she asked, impressed.

"I pulled his divorce filings," Matt said. "Obviously."

Natalie had read some things about the new boss, too. He had been with American Services Industries for fifteen years, where he'd grown profits at every division he'd run by at least ten percent. Now, according to the *Wall Street Journal,* the ASI honchos were testing to see if he did well with "content," in which case he'd be queued up to replace the current CEO. She'd noticed that all the profiles also described the boss as a "family man."

"I don't know, I read that he's turned over a new leaf. New wife, new life. He doesn't believe in working weekends," Natalie said, groping for the bright side. "Maybe he's a good guy."

"I bet anything you're wrong," Matt said, giving her a knowing look. "C'mon, he's the Candy King."

"Candy King?" Natalie asked, torn between the twin poles of her personality: curiosity and not wanting to engage with jerks.

"You know. Pushing candy on kids?" Matt said, looking so pleased to be holding her interest that she felt herself softening a little. "Remember when ASI had that scandal around organic food?"

"Sort of," she lied.

"Let me take you back to the crux of the matter," he said dramatically. "EatRiteFoods had added refined sugar to their supposedly natural snacks. The public discovered this when several unfortunate diabetics ate the stuff and went blind." Matt gestured to the stage where, according to the circling clock, the Chief would appear in five minutes and thirty-seven seconds. "Our new boss was put at the helm of the food division to make it profitable post-scandal. Everyone expected him to cave to the eco-weenies and turn it sustainable times ten. Instead he scrapped the organics line and doubled down on high-fructose corn syrup and trans fats. Earnings went through the roof!"

"From this you conclude he's here to announce layoffs?" Natalie asked, incredulous.

"He understands the proposition that businesses do well when they give the people what they want. Candy," Matt said grandly, as if Natalie hadn't been following. "Translation, increase profits, by any means necessary. Which means layoffs. Which means no one's safe. Which means odds are, one of us is out of a job—soon."

At that moment Bibb ascended the stage and tapped on the microphone. "Welcome, everyone!" she chirped in a childish high-pitched tone Natalie had never heard her use. "Everybody! Take your seats!" She was wearing a red dress with a white Peter Pan collar, white tights, and black ballet flats. The hem of the dress almost, but not quite, made it to her knees.

Matt nudged Natalie and pointed at her phone.

MATT: The woman obviously mugged Little Orphan Annie for her clothes. My god, hasn't that poor child suffered enough?

NATALIE: How'd you get my number?

MATT: Do not doubt me, grasshopper.

Natalie struggled not to laugh. She didn't want to encourage him.

Bibb continued. "You guys, I'm so happy I have the privilege of introducing the man of the moment who has a unique track record of disruptive success…" Her voice trailed off as if in awe. "Welcome the new man in our lives, the Chief!"

Bibb stepped aside and heads began to turn, hoping to catch sight of the Chief coming toward the stage from one of the side doors. Natalie had imagined that in person the Chief would look like most executives—a baldish, mid-height man with a melancholy bravado.

A bright beam of light projected down from the ceiling like the holodeck on *Star Trek*, recalling Natalie's attention to an empty space at the center of the room. And the Chief appeared, a shimmering image floating just above the ground.

MATT: What the fuck is our new boss doing arriving as a beam of light? Is this normal?

Natalie couldn't refrain from replying.

NATALIE: It's a hologram.

MATT: Sure. Well then it all makes—WHAT THE FUCK IS HAPPENING.

The image of the Chief had gray eyebrows, an ample gut, and a mane of gray hair brushed back from his high forehead. He looked like the love child of a Viking, Sasquatch, and a hair-dresser, an impression that was enhanced by the fact that his white cambric shirt was slashed up the front giving his audience brief glimpses of a hairy chest with a tacky gold medallion.

He flashed a bright movie-star grin and thrust his arms out wide like he'd just finished a magic trick—*ta-daa*.

"ATN! So glad to be here!" he boomed. His voice was the deep baritone of a radio announcer. "Hope you don't mind I'm making a special entrance!"

People began to clap. Soon the whole auditorium was on its feet. Natalie, too, though she wasn't sure why.

MATT: We are applauding a 3D image created by wave diffraction. Are we sure this boss even exists?

"ATN, first, I'd like to say I'm so glad to be joining you!" the Chief declared. "I hope you enjoy this new hologram technology. We're giving it a test run, see if it's up to standards for air." He grinned. "If we like it, soon *you* will be using it, too!" A pocket-size dragon crawled up from the Chief's back to perch on his shoulder. He made no notice of it but there were a few *ooh*s from the audience.

Natalie had to admit the Chief projected a confidence that made him almost attractive. The kind of man Natalie always felt both repelled by and drawn to, the charming manipulators, men who were the opposite of her father. "Men who resemble Mom," Sarah had often pointed out, causing Natalie to give up on dating altogether for a few months.

"All right, let's get down to business," the shimmering image declared. "Perhaps you've noticed that we've made some changes to programming, and already viewers are responding. I'm pleased to say our 10 a.m. hour is number three among cable news channels!" The number three appeared over his shoulder as he spoke and the tiny dragon now stood up, stretched, and blew fire across the word MSNBC, incinerating it. People laughed and applauded. "Also the first half of the bottom half hour of our 9 p.m. show is number two, up twenty-five percent in total viewers year-to-year." The dragon sat on his shoulder and stared out at the room with rainbow eyes. "We are gaining on the digital front as well—with ATN.com up forty percent in the last few days on the strength of the Rigo Lystra story."

MATT: You do know those are not impressive numbers.

NATALIE: All news execs make bad numbers sound good. Did you see his dragon?

"This is a great time to be covering politics!" the Chief continued. "The White House is swimming in scandal and viewers have been loving it." The 3D image lunged to one side of the stage. "But we can't get complacent. Even scandals can get stale. We need to change it up." The dragon jumped. "We have to lead the charge." The dragon did a flip and flew straight up toward the ceiling. "We have to innovate—with new technology, like this hologram." The dragon began to do loop-de-loops in the air, picking up speed as the Chief spoke until it was only a blur. "We need new approaches to take ATN all the way to number one!"

All at once the dragon vanished and the words ATN burned in flame above the Chief's head.

The Chief continued, "To that end, I got my quant guys to break down the numbers. Here's what we've learned—the news is making people sad." The hologram paused and looked around the room, letting that sink in. "That's a worrying trend. Increasingly our customers associate our brand with negative emotions. They're tired of hearing us tell them awful things every day. They're starting to tune us out."

He turned and smiled a shade too enthusiastically. "Now, I'm not here to tell you what to do. You're the journalists. I'm here to study at your feet." He nodded at someone off-camera, then said, "But I want to share with you a secret weapon." A crew of What Girls began to march importantly through the aisles like ring girls at a cage fight, handing out sheaves of paper.

MATT: Who are these angels?

MATT: I can't believe I found my future wife here at work.

MATT: What is taking them so long to get to us? And what is it with handing out paper? I haven't had a piece of paper since 1998.

"Assistants are handing out a document that will change your life and, if you embrace it and use it, will change our collective destiny. A team of top data scientists has developed a simple technique that will empower all of us to make our news more attractive to viewers. I believe this cheat sheet can help us reshape this network, supersize our ratings, and make news hot again."

A What Girl bearing tree-pulp technology reached their row. Matt gazed at her euphorically. Natalie looked at the paper and nearly choked on her tongue.

The Chief said, "I present to you, the game changer. The secret weapon. Our List of Forbidden Words." He turned and looked somewhere off-camera and said, "I thought we decided to call them Traffic Killers. I hate Forbidden Words, Larry, it sounds Chinese or something. I—"

All of a sudden the bottom half of the Chief's body disappeared and his large torso hung in the air, legless, for an impossible series of seconds. There were some strange sounds before his full body reappeared.

"Sorry about that. They're still working out the kinks in the technology." He shot another disgusted look off-camera before he continued, "As I was saying. The short version—when our brainiacs did the math, we learned something extraordinary. By using these guidelines, we changed key words in the headlines for our online stories. With the new headlines, the stories got an exponential increase in traffic! We believe this will work for TV as well. All you have to do is avoid these words in your reporting online or on TV and watch your ratings climb. Boom, pure magic. We are giving you the keys to the kingdom, people, the philosopher's stone of newsmaking, the secret formula to turn any dull report into ratings gold."

Natalie stared at the paper in her lap, fighting down a wave of nausea.

Forbidden Words:
Abortion. Affordable Housing. Africa. Authorization.
Bailout.
Canada. Charity. Climate. Cloture. Compromise. Consensus. Consolidation.
Debt. Devout. Disabled.
Education. Entitlement. Equity.
Feminist. Filibuster.
Gridlock.
In-Depth. Income Gap. Inequality. Infrastructure.
Justice.
Lesbian. Last Night. Last Week. Low Income.
Medicaid. Moderate. Monopoly.
Native American.
Poor. Poverty.
Reauthorization. Reconciliation. Reform. Regulation.
Sanctions. Sequester.
Underclass.
Wages. Working Poor. Welfare. Women's Health. Women's Rights.
Yesterday.

MATT: Goodbye poverty, malnutrition and women's health. Hello, Third World Diet Craze: What Keeps Refugee Women Looking So Thin?

NATALIE: You're heartless.

MATT: I'm NOW!

The Chief, blissfully oblivious to the shock he was inflicting on his troops, grinned. "And now I'm ready to take your questions," he said happily.

To the left of the ergonomic chairs, a line had formed behind a microphone. The first speaker was a frizzy-haired man in mom jeans and a puffy vest who, judging by his look, might have been one of the production technicians, which, Natalie guessed, would soon be one of the newsroom jobs handled by a robot. His voice was thin and plaintive, like he was born to receive bad news. "Thanks. I'm very worried about what's going to happen if it's true that we bought Beltway. What about our jobs? Do you plan to start layoffs? Thank you."

Assuming a decidedly serious look, the Chief nodded. "Thank you for the question, and the answer is yes. We've just purchased Beltway. And I couldn't be more excited about this merger."

MATT: Translation, there will be layoffs.

"I know there are worries about job losses. I understand the anxiety. Losing a job is one of the most stressful experiences a person can have, after the death of a child or receiving a terminal diagnosis."

MATT: Translation, very very painful layoffs.

"We're very excited about this acquisition. It will give us a prominent digital presence in the political world. I also hope ATN learns to take on Beltway's more irreverent approach to news. It's time to make politics entertaining."

MATT: You should make me your producer.

Natalie glanced at him, horrified. Surely he was kidding.

The Chief signaled for the next question, and Natalie was nearly blinded by the flash of yellow hair and clinging red dress standing at the microphone. It was their twenty-seven-year-old morning show anchor, Jazzmyn Maine, who could best be described as energetic. "Thank you, sir. I wanted to ask, do we still get a clothing budget? I mean those of us who are anchors?"

MATT: Why on earth would he pay for her to wear anything else?

The Chief nodded. "Jazzmyn, I'll take that in two parts. First, this is a visual medium and viewers want something to look at. Especially you ladies. Let viewers see more of your beauty and they'll appreciate your brains. I promise." He grinned and Natalie imagined him working a quick fantasy of Jazzmyn stripping down to her brains. "Now as for the clothing budget, that's only a concern for anchors, not for everyone. So, Jazzmyn, why don't you come see me privately? My assistant will reach out," the Chief said and Jazzmyn grinned enthusiastically, while a wave of knowing glances rippled across the room.

NATALIE: Is he flirting with her via hologram?

MATT: Don't be bitter. I bet he likes slightly older uptight reporters, too.

Natalie was grimacing at him when she heard a familiar voice at the microphone.

"Mr. Bounds, thank you for your inspiring talk."

Natalie looked up just in time to see Reality Show Ryan read off a piece of paper, assuming the overdone seriousness of a mediocre actor playing the part of a lawyer. "Looking through the list of forbidden words...and it's incredibly helpful. I see it says we can't say 'yesterday' or 'last night'? Why is that?"

The Chief beamed at him. "Thank you, Ryan. An excellent question."

MATT: He's a plant.

NATALIE: No, I can guarantee he is genetically human. Plants might be more intelligent.

MATT: I meant the question. Someone gave it to him to ask.

NATALIE: Yeah I got it. I was making a joke.

MATT: 80% less funny if you have to explain it.

"The answer is simple. Urgency. We need urgency in everything we do. The data team says viewers respond whenever we declare an event unfolding now, breaking as we speak! If viewers feel our reporting is dated or old, why should they watch? Rigo missing? He's still missing, something terrible could happen any minute! NOW-ness! Stay tuned to get the latest! For the same reason we need to use the Breaking News banner as much as possible. It's shown to increase viewership by up to ten percent every five minutes it's on air. That's why I've asked that all producers should assume everything out of Washington is breaking news unless you're told by management that it's not."

Ryan's smile made it clear he found the answer steeped in

wisdom. "And if something really did happen yesterday? What do we say?"

The Chief nodded patiently. "Another great question, and easy. Some options—'this just in' or 'we've just learned.' Might have happened yesterday, but *we* have just gotten a line on it. Make it feel NOW! And of course, you might consider the idea that if the news happened yesterday, you shouldn't be reporting it now."

MATT: Because if you learn about the Watergate break-in a month after it's happened, it's lost its NOW-ness.

"Great. So is journalism good or bad for ratings?" Natalie said under her breath, unable to keep the thought in. People ahead of her turned around to stare. Apparently she'd said this louder than she'd realized.

"Ask that," Matt elbowed her.

"Shhhh!" Natalie glared.

"Ask it!" Matt pressed again. "I mean you practically already have."

"Stop," she hissed at him.

"Excuse me?" a woman's voice called out from the front of the room.

The world went into slow motion as, heart pounding, Natalie looked from Matt to the space up front where Bibb was standing and staring directly at her.

"Would you like to share something, Natalie?" Bibb asked.

Please, please let this not be happening, Natalie prayed.

"Surely whatever warranted an interruption is worth sharing with the whole room. Mr. Walsh, would you like to share?"

Matt winked at Natalie and bounced out of his chair. "Hey, everyone. Matt Walsh. First day at ATN, this is exciting." He adopted an overly formal tone as he looked to the Chief. "Sir,

Natalie was saying she wonders whether you think that journalism is good or bad for ratings. Isn't that right, Natalie?"

In general Natalie wasn't a person who believed in hexes or wishing harm to befall others, but in that moment she would have traded at least one of her lives to see a bolt of lightning smite Matt right in his seat. She knew she should have gone with her first instinct and ignored him.

"Suck up," she hissed to Matt, then stood up and approached the mic like a convicted person heading to execution. She swallowed and smiled at the shimmering image of her new boss.

"Mr. Bounds, thank you for making yourself available to us. I guess my question arose because the last president of ATN told us it's not our job to worry about ratings. It's our job to do good journalism. So it would be great to know, what's your idea of meaningful journalism? Do you think reporting the news is good or bad for ratings? Thank you."

Natalie could feel the room stare at her with admiration mingled with terror. It was the look you give a dictator's failed assassin or Martha Stewart's tardy assistant: you know the person will be disappeared within the hour.

The Chief's features softened. "Glad you asked. It's Natalie, right?" he said pleasantly. "I want to say—and I mean no disrespect—there's a reason that your former boss is, well, *former*. And a reason we're number four."

The tension in the air made the room feel alive. "I'm going to give it to you straight. Your job, each and every one of you, is to grow viewership. Viewership grows ratings. Ratings grow profits. Profits keep the shareholders happy. Happy shareholders mean we all get to go to work tomorrow." He stared intensely around the newsroom until the silence became uncomfortable. "We are not a star chamber elite, deciding what people *should* know. This is the news *business*. Starting today we give our viewers what they want, not what we say they want." Natalie felt a chill creeping down her back. "Starting today, we win. If anyone has a problem with that, I invite you to leave now."

He paused to see if anyone would go. No one did.

The Chief went on. "Good. Remember, people, news is our brand. But what we *do* is tell stories that viewers want to watch. Got it?" He stared out at his audience expectantly. No one spoke. "I didn't catch that," the Chief said. "Got it?"

"Yes," a few people called back.

The Chief's face got a little flushed. "What did you say?" he demanded.

"GOT IT," people called back.

He smiled and relaxed. "Good. And we're going to be distributing a survey to let us know what you think of this new hologram technology. We'd like to work it into our shows." He glanced off-camera. "As soon as we iron out those kinks." He turned back to face the room. "Thanks to all of you! And see you on TV!" He waved and the hologram vanished.

The lights got brighter. People began to shift and whisper. Natalie felt chilled from the inside out.

"Sorry, Savage," Matt said, sounding not at all sorry. "It was you or me so—" He shrugged. "You okay? You look a little green. Need something to take the edge off? I always carry a few Xanax in my first aid kit." He extended his hand, a tiny blue pill in his palm.

It wasn't the first time Natalie had been offered other people's prescription drugs while working, but it was the first time it had happened on the newsroom floor. She glared at Matt. "Can you just let me out, please," she said, desperate to get away from him.

"Let me know if you change your mind."

She walked down the hall toward the ladies room and checked her email. To her relief, there was nothing fatal. No note from Bibb. No urgent message from Human Resources demanding her immediate presence.

Dodged a bullet.

"Natalie?" She turned to see a miniskirted What Girl walking toward her. "I have a message from the Chief. He'd like to see you. Fifth-floor conference room, one hour."

No, she corrected herself. *You're about to be taken out behind the building and eliminated.*

6

THE AGE OF NIELSEN

Natalie stepped into the fifth-floor conference room for her meeting with the Chief and beheld a sight that looked like Bad Dream Mt. Rushmore: Bibb sitting on one side of the lacquer table, with Handsy Hal capering alongside a What Girl at the coffee urn behind them.

Of course.

Of course, Natalie realized she should have expected Bibb to be here. But during the hour she had spent plumping her personality to make sure to sparkle enthusiastically in front of the Chief, it hadn't crossed her mind that Bibb and her underlings would commandeer front-row seats to her humiliation.

Natalie had been raised since her earliest days in the school of Always See the Glass Half Full. Her mind was ready to switch to "Well, things could be worse…" mode when Reality Show Ryan sauntered in, grinning. Yes, things had definitely gotten worse.

Ryan looked like he'd tanned and whitened his teeth in the time since the town hall. "Am I late?" he asked, in a pleasure's-all-yours way that that made clear he really didn't care. His eyes landed on Natalie and he lit up.

"Natalie Savage!" Ryan was now giving her an Engaging Smile. Somehow every one of his expressions looked preprogrammed, as if he'd copied them from a book called *How To Be a News Reporter or Just Act Like One!* "I am so glad to meet you in the flesh. I'm a huge fan!"

Smile! Natalie ordered herself as Ryan opened his arms in a hug and crushed her into his chest. It was like being smothered by an overzealous yellow Lab. She felt relieved when she was released without being licked.

"I've been watching your work since I was a little kid," Ryan said with his most Endearing Eyes. "I just have so much respect for you and women of your generation. All the struggles you've been through."

My generation, Natalie thought. She was only six years older than him.

At the table, an African American woman with dangling turquoise earrings began to choke, her earrings swaying mightily.

Ryan shifted expressions from Endearing to Perky to say, "I know I'm going to learn a lot from you. Can't wait to steal all your tricks!" He winked and circled around the table to take the empty seat next to Bibb, leaving Natalie to ponder the cruelty of a world in which conference rooms were not built with escape hatches in the floor.

The earrings woman, with short cropped hair and eyes that seemed locked in a look of permanent skepticism, held out her hand toward Natalie and said, "Nice to meet you. Andrea Johnson." As Natalie shook it she realized this was the producer who had been working with Ryan.

"I heard about your dad," Natalie told Andrea quietly. "I'm really sorry."

Andrea's eyes got wide and filled with tears. She turned away abruptly for a moment. Then, regaining her composure, she gave Natalie a watery smile and gestured toward the empty place next to hers. "Here, have a seat."

The day before, Natalie hadn't realized that Ryan's Andrea was Andrea *Johnson*. She was something of a legend in the business. Spoken of by some people at ATN in the same awed tones as war correspondents who'd been kidnapped on assignment and Sunday show regulars who traveled with Clooney in Africa and knew the Dalai Lama personally. Natalie had heard other correspondents say that Andrea was one of the reasons the ATN DC bureau still functioned. She managed to get news out despite ownership changes, management shuffles, and an office culture that produced so many experts at passing the blame it could have replaced curling as an Olympic sport.

"You're the Natalie Savage that handled the obese airlift, aren't you?" Andrea said.

"Yes," Natalie said, her voice sounding less confident than she would have liked. That had been a challenging assignment and Natalie was unnerved to think what intel Andrea might have gathered about it.

"Heard you wrangled the best spot for a live shot and stayed up on air for forty-eight hours through the whole deal."

Natalie nodded.

"And missed a friend's wedding without complaining," Andrea added.

That was true, too. But it had happened two years earlier. "How did you hear about that?" Natalie asked.

"Producers talk. A friend in New York told me to look out for you. Said you've got talent, brains, and tenacity—her words— and that DC is lucky to have you. It'd be good to make sure we keep you."

Natalie felt like she might cry. This from a woman the Pentagon had on speed dial? "Thank you."

Andrea eyed something over Natalie's shoulder. "Oh crap. Brace yourself," she sighed and Natalie turned to see Hal incoming.

"Room for one more?" he asked. Without waiting for the

answer, Hal moved a chair from one end of the table around to be next to Natalie. "I just wanted to say hi," he said, leaning much too close. "We're still due for drinks."

"Good to see you," Natalie said as she slid her chair slightly toward Andrea but somehow didn't avoid the arm that brushed her knee.

"I'm so sorry," Hal said, contrite. "Did I hurt you? I can be so clumsy."

"I'm fine," Natalie insisted, even as she shrank away from him.

"Ah, I found you guys," a familiar voice said. Natalie's nerves shot to attention when she turned to see Matt saunter in.

"What are you doing here?" she asked out loud, before she could think better of it.

"I was invited," he said smugly. He nodded at Hal. "Thank you for including me."

"No problem." Hal smiled in reply.

Hal invited Matt? Natalie wondered, eyes darting from one to the other. Maybe this was Hal's way of doling out punishment because she'd turned him down the night before.

Now, judging by the stares around the room, and the look on the What Girl's face as she pulled out her phone and started texting, Natalie deduced the rest of the group knew something about Matt that they weren't sharing. She narrowed her eyes at him and opened her text messages under the table.

NATALIE: Why are you here?

She watched Matt read the text and ignore it. *Jerk.*

He dropped into a seat opposite Bibb, smiled brightly, and added, with pep squad vigor, "Did you guys see the Dow? I caught CNBC on my way in. Our stock is up!"

"Awesome!" Ryan said enthusiastically.

"Looks like the Chief is great for the share price," Matt continued.

"From your lips to god's ears," Bibb replied with zeal, before returning to her conversation with Ryan. Now Natalie's eyes narrowed as her mind raced to horror scenarios—was the Chief going to fire her and make Matt the new White House correspondent? Were cameras hidden in the ceiling, set to capture her humiliation?—when a voice seemingly from heaven boomed, "Goddammit! I said a—never mind."

Everyone was immediately on alert. Natalie looked up at the ceiling expecting the Chief to arrive in another stream of yellow light. Instead the big plasma screen at the front of the room flickered to life and filled with the image of the Chief minus the flowing hair and karate outfit.

"Hello, group," he boomed. "Sorry to be late. Somehow our tech wizards can produce a hologram but can't figure out how to get the video conference up and running." A look of anger flickered across his face before he rearranged it into a smile. "Well, good to be here with you all! My A Team."

A Team! That had a positive ring to it, Natalie thought.

Seen close up, the Chief's face was like a carnival caricature, a collection of rough-hewn features whose only unifying principal was that they had been ordered in size extra-large. The one exception was his teeth, which Natalie could now see were small and slightly pointed. They lent his smile a subtly sinister aspect, giving the impression that this was a creature to whom other creatures submitted.

His eyes moved abruptly around the room, pinning each person with his gaze as he spoke. "I'd like talk about what's next for ATN. We special few in this room will be the vanguard as we revamp news and give the viewers some relief."

He searched the faces around the table until he located Natalie and smiled. "Natalie, I'd like to thank you for asking the question that was on so many people's minds. A frank conversation about priorities is the perfect way to set the stage."

She froze. *Set the stage for what, my beheading?*

"I've brought you here today because we have one job, for White House correspondent, and two of you who are suitable for it."

From the corner of her eye, she caught Bibb and Ryan sharing a meaningful look.

"I'd like to take the next few weeks to see what each of you can do. Who can bring the stories with the most novelty and surprise? Who can give our customers the relief and diversion they crave?"

The Chief turned to face Ryan, who angled forward in his chair like a Labrador eagerly awaiting a pat on his head. "Ryan, your appeal to the Demo is a thing of beauty. Women, men— they love you. Hell, why wouldn't they? Just look at you!"

Ryan flashed his best Bashful Look.

"And you, Natalie." She felt her stomach go watery, panicked at what the Chief might say. "Natalie, you have credibility. We live in serious times and I have a hunch that some of our customers crave reporters with credibility."

Natalie couldn't hold back a smile. *I'm still in the game!* she thought, relief coursing through her.

"A couple notes for you, Natalie," he said in a stern voice. "I want to see you smile more on air. People like people who smile. It's attractive. Everyone has assets, so find yours!" Natalie felt herself blush crimson as the room turned to assess her assets. "And we need you to step up your hair and makeup a few notches." He shifted his eyes to Bibb. "Agreed?"

Across the table, Bibb and the What Girl looked at Natalie with the pained, pinched expressions of popular girls forced to eat carbs. "Absolutely," Bibb said, her eyes giving Natalie an I-told-you-so look. "We're working on it."

"Ryan, Natalie, this is your chance. I've got an algorithm we'll use to measure your performance every day. We'll call it the VOP—Voice of the People. It's your Q score, plus your overnight rating in the Demo, your social media following, and online presence. We'll track your VOP every day, and whoever has highest cumulative score wins the job."

Natalie felt like she had rapid onset vertigo. The room was spinning so fast she had to grip the table to keep from leaning into Hal. "I'm sorry, sir, but are you saying you want us to compete against one another for the White House job?" she asked, hoping she'd managed to keep the panic out of her voice.

"Yes!" The Chief laughed as if Natalie had asked a hilarious question.

"Jeah!" Ryan punched his fist into the air. "I love games."

Natalie swallowed hard. Ryan leaned across the table toward her. "I know you're more experienced with news than me, Nat," he said, saving her most loathed nickname for this prime moment, "but I got to warn you, I'm a quick learner."

The Chief nodded. "The fact that the two of you are so different will make it that much more fun."

Natalie heard the Chief's words but none of them made any sense, like the way the word *fun* now seemed to rhyme with *hell*.

Under the table her phone buzzed. She glanced down.

MATT: And that's just surprise number one.

Natalie was trying to remember if auto-da-fé was a method of suicide involving throwing herself out a window or setting herself on fire when the doors to the conference room flew open, delivering three What Girls into the room, all wearing their karate-shirt minidresses and carrying red jars.

"Now I have a fun surprise," the Chief continued, still abusing that word, as the women placed the jars in the middle of the conference table. "We want to bring the people some relief. And you know what people like?"

Natalie studied the jars and saw that they were glass containers filled with red candies in various shapes.

"Candy," the Chief said as Ryan exclaimed, "Red Hots!"

"Yes." The Chief beamed. "And red sours and red taffy. People, this is what we need more of on ATN."

Andrea looked like she might be sick. "Red dye number forty?"

"Titillation. Delight. Relief," the Chief said, pronouncing each word with the excitement of a child on a sugar high. "Natalie, dig in. Have some fun. Tell me, why do people like candy?"

"Um, it tastes good?" she asked tentatively.

The Chief seemed to like her answer. "Yes. It stimulates the senses. It awakens an excited response. It satisfies a craving for distraction."

"Candy makes people happy," Ryan added, helpfully.

"Yes, my boy. And that's what we need. We need to make our customers feel joy. They're burned out from all the negativity we've been giving them. We must find new ways to generate an excited response."

"I bet he thinks the Fourth Estate is a vacation house," Andrea said under her breath.

The Chief looked around the room. "Take this week's Pan-American Summit for example. We've dedicated too much airtime talking to serious PhDs about melting ice, a depressing future environmental crisis none of us can fix."

Natalie's eyes flicked to the wall of TVs where ATN was featuring a panel of twelve pundits over a banner that read, "Friends With Gas: Colombia's Oil Appeal." Whatever dull climate change coverage bothered the boss, Natalie had missed it.

"There's another way to get at that same story. One filled with the kind of excitement and diversion the people crave. Through characters. Through the rich, beautiful people who occupy the White House and the exotic, devious foreigners they work with."

Andrea was staring a hole in the conference table.

"Let's begin with Rigo Lystra," the Chief said. "The rape charges against him are very exciting. They involve celebrity, sex, scandal. And an important question of prejudice. A young man's future is at stake. So many men can relate to this. How can we know what's true? If unprovable out-of-nowhere accusations can take him down, no one is safe!"

Natalie and Andrea looked at one another, straining to hold back an eyeroll. Had the Chief missed the fact that Rigo's accuser had reported a rape immediately? That Rigo had left the country to jet-set off to Bali? Who exactly was stealing his freedom?

Bibb, who had been busy on her iPhone, now placed it on the table in front of Ryan and pointed at a message on the screen.

Ryan glanced down to read and yelped, "This is huge!"

"What's huge?" the Chief asked.

Ryan pulled out his own iPhone and started typing away feverishly.

Placing her elbows on the table, Bibb rested her chin on her hands girlishly as she said, "Chief, I think we have an exciting development in the Colombia rape story. Ryan, care to explain?"

"I have one of our star reporters from the New York bureau on that," the Chief said dismissively. "He's close to learning where this kid is."

"Sir! I have an exclusive!" Ryan blurted. Then he looked to Bibb and, after she nodded her approval, continued, "According to my source, Venezuela wants to kidnap Rigo and make him stand trial in Caracas. The US Secret Service took him away for safekeeping. He's at the Colombian embassy on Massachusetts Avenue."

Natalie felt a pit open in her stomach, remembering the conversation she'd had with the associate producer. She'd been right. Of course it was Secret Service. And now Bibb was feeding Ryan the story! *No, this isn't Bibb's fault. You could have pursued your instinct but you didn't. This is on you*, she scolded herself.

The Chief looked concerned. "How good is your source, my boy?"

"Solid. White House," Hal said firmly, looking from the Chief to Ryan, then smiling smugly at Bibb.

Wait. Hal did this?

"And," Ryan continued excitedly, "I was just invited to play hoops with the White House communications director this week," Ryan said, winking at the boss. "He used to work for my dad's last chief of staff. It's a good connect."

"This is fantastic, wonderful," the Chief said, sitting forward. "Ryan, I want you outside that embassy. And keep working those relationships. Bibb, let's keep Ryan there live till that kid leaves the embassy."

"Awesome!" Ryan said.

Andrea let out a long sigh. Matt was shaking his head. Natalie felt like she might asphyxiate on frustration. The Chief seemed to be enjoying the tension in the room. Natalie imagined him envisioning *Last Reporter Standing: Editorial Meeting* as a new, behind-the-scenes show about the newsroom.

"And now, how about Natalie?" Bibb purred. There was a cat-who-has-just-committed-canary-genocide look on her face that confirmed what Natalie had suspected: Bibb had a plan, and Natalie knew it did not involve her own success.

The Chief looked delighted by what he was about to say. "I'd like Natalie on the First Lady's migraine."

"Sorry?" She was certain she'd heard that wrong.

The Chief was serious. "I'd like you to dig into the migraine angle. How long has the First Lady had these headaches? Are they real? If so, do they stop her from performing other wifely duties?"

Natalie tensed, hoping that didn't mean what she thought it meant. She realized she must have been visibly gritting her teeth because Matt gave her big eyes that either said Don't Fuck This Up or I Need to Pee Real Bad.

"I recognize that headaches are a serious issue and impact many people," Natalie said, doing all she could to keep from screaming. "But I'm wondering if maybe the medical unit might be better suited to tackle that angle? I bet one of our doctors would have great insight. And I could do something a little more squarely focused on White House policy. Like—"

"Excuse me," Matt piped up. "Matt Walsh, hi. I'll be producing Headache At 1600. America's Royal Pain. Chief, I want to let you know both of us are excited about this assignment and can't wait to get started."

Producing me? Natalie heard the words but couldn't process them.

"You're a funny one, my boy," The Chief's eyes weren't smiling. "But let's not make light of headaches. Twenty-eight million American women experience migraines. Headache meds are huge advertisers. This is a story that brings it home."

"The parent company has a big pharma division," Hal whispered to Natalie, as she leaned away.

Driven to the far corner of her chair and desperation simultaneously, Natalie said, "Why not do boys against girls? Andrea and me versus Ryan and Matt?"

The Chief shook his head. "Out of the question."

Bibb's eyes flashed with disapproval. "That kind of talk is inappropriate, Natalie. Gender is not a factor in assignments." She shook her head. "Besides, as you know, Andrea and Ryan are already accustomed to working together. They are a well-oiled team. I'm sure you and Mike—"

"It's Matt," Matt put in.

"—will do very well," Bibb finished, ignoring him. Something in Bibb's tone suggested she thought exactly the opposite. Something that kindled Natalie's competitive spirit. She looked at the Chief, weighing her options. She could say no and get sent back down to general news purgatory. Or she could play the game, get the White House job, and do the work she believed in. Eventually. Candy now, protein later.

"I'm in," Natalie told the room, with fake enthusiasm. She felt something in her soul contract and burrow into a ball. *Might that be your professional integrity?* She silenced the voice in her head. "When do we start?"

The Chief was beaming. "Wonderful. It looks like we have our plan. Each night I'll circulate the VOP. This is only for our internal use. So Ryan and Natalie know where they stand and what they have to do to improve. Sound good?"

Natalie glanced around the table. Bibb was scowling, which seemed like a good sign. Ryan gave her a thumbs-up, which could mean anything. Matt was nodding, engaged. Andrea was looking jaundiced. Hal was staring at Natalie's legs.

"Arrange it!" the Chief boomed happily. "This is going to be great! Two stories full of intrigue. Two stories that will make you believe rich people's lives are worse than yours! I'll see both of you on TV!"

The screen went black.

Bibb turned to Andrea, all business now. "Andrea, you're going to have to postpone your trip home, I'm afraid."

"Of course," Andrea said quietly.

Natalie felt like a knife had been plunged through her own chest. She looked at Andrea from the corner of her eye, holding back the impulse to scream *no*!

Bibb was gazing adoringly at Ryan who leaned forward to grab a handful of Red Hots. "We'll get you the best crew we have."

As Andrea leaned over to gather her things, Natalie heard her whisper, "My money's on you to kick Ryan's ass. No one who thinks a filibuster is a sex act should be allowed to cover the White House."

For a moment Natalie froze, then her heart filled with affection as she realized what Andrea had said. "Thank you."

"If you can push through their bullshit, you can still do some really spectacular reporting at ATN. It's hard but it happens."

Andrea paused before adding, "You'll just have to live up to your name."

Natalie's breath caught. "Oh I'm not related to Jessica Savitch. I—"

"Savage," Andrea interrupted and smiled. "I'm saying, be savage. You got it in you. I can tell."

She turned and walked toward the door. As Ryan caught up with Andrea, Natalie heard him say something about "making sure the camera crew uses the Caucasian Blur filter on me because it really makes my skin pop."

Bibb was right behind him. "Good luck, Natalie," she said with a smile that shared almost no genetic markers with genuine. "Watch your hair."

As soon as they were gone, Natalie walked over to Matt. "How long did you know this was happening?" she demanded, aware that Hal and the What Girl were staring.

Matt stood and shrugged. "Long enough."

"Why didn't you tell me? Whose side are you on?"

"Mine," he said.

"Natalie, you're going to do great," Hal interrupted, crowding into her personal space as the What Girl let out a low snort of laughter.

"Thanks, Hal, but can you give us some privacy," she snapped, then seeing Hal's stricken face, regretted it.

The What Girl pulled out her phone and walked out of the room tittering and typing with Hal walking too close behind her.

When they were gone, Matt shook his head. "You're too wound up. You need to calm down or you're never going to win this thing."

"Thanks for the moral support," Natalie said. "I cannot believe that just happened."

"It'll keep happening until you get tips like Ryan's," he grumbled as he tapped something out on his phone.

"Oh thanks. And what do you recommend?" She scowled.

"Unless you take up golf or hoops, I suggest you start sleeping with someone in the White House. Adam Majors is single."

Her mind flashed to an image of Adam Majors in bed, referencing his briefing binder for answers to questions like "Does this feel good?" The next moment she felt a wave of self-loathing for entertaining the thought.

This was Matt's fault. He was like some kind of gremlin, bent on torturing her.

"Why are you doing this?" Natalie asked.

"I need you to succeed so I can ride your coattails," Matt said, his tone of voice shifting from ready-for-combat to let's-try-mediation. "With this merger, my future at Beltway is up in the air. I need to make myself a burrow at ATN. And you need me, so it's win-win. You can show me how to work the dysfunctional network and I will give you wisdom about how to make DC buzzworthy."

"Maybe you should be the one sleeping with Adam Majors."

"You're focused on all the wrong things," he went on, ignoring the comment. "There's a network full of reporters who would kill or die to be in your position. Why don't you try to make it work?"

"Isn't that what I'm doing? By agreeing to this charade?" she demanded.

"That's not enough. You've got to step up your game. You can't afford to continue like this." He did a sweeping motion up and down her body. "You need new hair. Maybe a spray tan. And get some fitted clothes that show off your body. You do have a body, don't you?"

Natalie stood agape. Was she really going to take style advice from a man who looked like the Pillsbury Doughboy's cousin? "You are one to talk. Are you aware pleated pants went out of style in 1992?"

Matt flinched. Was it possible she'd hurt his feelings? Was it possible he *had* feelings?

He shook his head. "I'm not criticizing you. I'm just trying to help," he said and walked out the door.

Just trying to help. Everyone was just so helpful. She stared after him, considering her next move.

7

ON TAKING LIBERTIES

It was 8:45 p.m. and Natalie was at her sad temporary desk, sandwiched uncomfortably between a retaining wall and a garbage can on the outskirts of the newsroom floor. Whoever had replaced the furniture after the Chief's town hall meeting earlier that day had wedged the tiny aluminum desk into the mix, positioning it so Natalie could barely see the TVs, but offering her an unobstructed view of the What Girls up at the news desk. The vibe up there was like cheerlead squad auditions: No Outsiders Welcome.

Having discovered, too late, that after 7 p.m., ATN was in a veritable food desert—no restaurants nearby, no delivery in under ninety minutes—Natalie had gone through four bags of vending machine pretzels. The growl in her stomach was made worse by the sounds of the What Girls sharing freshly delivered organic salads just feet away.

"Oh my god, I'm so sorry we didn't think to ask if you wanted anything!" one of them had called out when she'd caught Natalie eye-drooling at the food. "Whoops!" they'd tittered, then gone back to looking incredibly busy on their iPhones, meaning they

were probably YikYaking or BackStabbing or some other app
she'd never heard of that had nothing to do with news.

That was an hour ago. Now, Natalie watched them giggle as
Hal, perched opposite a What Girl with big blue eyes, beseeched
her for help with a birthday gift for his sister. "Please try it on,"
he said as he held out a piece of lime green fabric that looked
alarmingly like a sports bra. "She'll be so angry if I get it wrong
and I swear you're her size. Just please put it on real quick?"

The Whats seemed unfazed. "Hal, why are you buying your
sister a bra?" one teased.

"Wait, do you also want us to try on some lingerie for your
mom?" another asked, prompting tittering all around. The scene
was troubling in more ways than Natalie wanted to count.

She moved her chair around to block out the Hal Show and
get a better view of ATN's prime-time news show, *TalkTalk
Live*. Nelly Jones, her predecessor at the White House, was on
set looking arrestingly beautiful in a dare-to-bare spaghetti strap
dress, her golden gams flashing from behind a see-through desk,
her once straight amber hair now undulating tresses of champagne blond.

Where is it written, Natalie wondered, *that the higher you climb
the blonder you get? Or does it work the other way around?*

Nelly finished teasing her first hour-long special—*Who Hates
the Bunny: America's Assault on Easter*—and the show cut to boxes
of pundits shouting at one another over live pictures that alter-
nated between the summit dinner now underway at the White
House and Ryan McGreavy stationed outside the Colombian
embassy. Every time Ryan popped up in his superhero stance—
hands on hips, legs just beyond shoulder distance apart, chest
jutted forward—Natalie felt a tiny little stab in her heart. He
looked born for the part of news hero. All he lacked was the
cape flying behind him.

During the six hours since Ryan had broken the story of Rigo's
embassy sanctuary, the other networks had descended on the site at

Seventeenth Street, drawing an impressive crowd of protesters—
mostly women—now chanting, "Hey hey, ho ho, Crusoe's rap-
ist has got to go."

The chair that had come with the sad desk periodically emitted a deep sigh and Natalie had started to think of it as a sort
of mood chair. For hours she'd been dialing doctors, searching
videos, scrounging for anything that might help fill in details
about the First Lady's history of migraines—and kept coming
up empty. *Sigh*, said the chair. *Sigh*, Natalie agreed.

When she'd called the White House press office, she'd been
told, condescendingly, that any questions about FLOTUS's health
should be directed to FLOTUS's press office. When she reached
FLOTUS's press office, she was told, equally condescendingly,
"The First Lady's health is a private matter. We can't discuss it."

"But Adam Majors discussed her migraines in the briefing,"
Natalie had replied. "It's public information. I'm just looking
for a little background."

"We can't help you here. I suggest you reach out to the president's press office."

"I just spoke with them and they referred me to you."

"Tell them I referred you back to them." The line went dead.
Sigh, said the chair. *Sigh*, Natalie echoed.

The rest of her research was equally frustrating. Considering that Anita Ramirez Crusoe was constantly in the public
eye, there was a surprising lack of detailed information about
her—and not just about her health. Descriptions of the First
Lady's early life in Venezuela were so banal they read like tourism brochures.

FLOTUS had grown up in Maracaibo, a coastal city near
Venezuela's northern border with Colombia. As everyone knew,
she'd been Miss Venezuela in her late teens and come to America on an engineering scholarship in her midtwenties. Her father was a judge. Her mother, once a bookkeeper, had become
some kind of activist. Both her parents had opposed Venezu-

elan President Hugo Chavez and served a brief stint in prison for speaking out against him. American campaign reporters had descended on her hometown during the primary and though they'd unearthed kindergarten teachers and the owners of local *panaderías* searching for any whiff of scandal about young Anita Ramirez, they'd found none.

FLOTUS herself had never mentioned headaches in any interview, or any ailments at all. The only instance Natalie could find of FLOTUS discussing her own health was in a two-year-old video from a small summertime campaign event in Eau Claire, Wisconsin. In front of a group of fifty or so women at a rec center, she'd made a joke about wearing a turtleneck in summer, explaining she'd just had a worrisome mole removed from her neck. There was nothing in any way relevant to migraines, apart from the fact that researching them was giving Natalie the beginnings of a migraine herself.

Now she stared at the script, what little she'd written.

IT'S A HEADACHE FOR THE WHITE HOUSE... FIRST LADY ANITA CRUSOE—REPORTEDLY DOWN WITH A MIGRAINE... AND SKIPPING TO-NIGHT'S SUMMIT SOIREE... WILL LATIN AMERI-CAN LEADERS TAKE HER ABSENCE AS A SNUB?

At the end of the line, the cursor was blinking angrily, waiting for Natalie to come up with something—anything—Urgent and Now to wow the bosses and get her home for the night.

The chair sighed. Natalie moved her eyes back to the television monitors just in time to see Nelly Jones lean in intently and ask the camera, "Is there trouble in the First Marriage? What's the real reason the First Lady's a no-show to tonight's state dinner?"

Before Nelly could toss to one of the boxes of pundits, music blared and a JUST IN graphic rolled across the screen. Ryan popped up, announcing that he had a statement from White

House Communications Director Adam Majors, and Natalie's stomach coiled into a tight knot. Ryan had snared the White House's most senior press wrangler as a top source.

On TV, Ryan began reading. "President Crusoe will not take sides in a he–said–she–said. No doubt both sides have reason to be upset. No doubt both parties bear some blame. The Crusoe administration will not put its finger on the scales of justice." Ryan looked up at the camera and explained that Rigo Lystra has every right to stay at the Colombian embassy until Venezuela drops these "unproven charges." Embellishing, he added, "The White House is taking a stand for letting the truth come out. We are at ground zero of a fight for freedom."

Natalie's hands tightened into fists. Ryan's self-importance was bad but his unquestioning embrace of the White House's line of absurdity was infuriating. Was he really going to pretend that Crusoe's team was keeping its hands to itself when clearly it had its fingers up justice's skirt? It sounded like they'd gotten to at least third base.

In a way this is Andrea's fault, she thought angrily. *She has to know better if Ryan doesn't. And speaking of producers, where the hell is Matt? Shouldn't he be landing some ONLY ON ATN tips for me?*

Her phone buzzed.

MOM: Do you know this new reporter, Ryan? He's very good.

MOM: He seems to be very well informed. I hear he's from an important family. And so handsome!

MOM: Maybe he's single? You could bring him to the wedding. Women go with younger men all the time these days.

"I'm going to kill someone," Natalie muttered.

Natalie jumped when a female voice at her shoulder said, "This is a joke? About killing. You do not mean to do a killing?"

Natalie turned to find the Asian camerawoman who'd narrowly escaped a mauling by Handsy Hal before the town hall standing behind her desk.

"It is a joke. I'm not planning on doing any killing," Natalie said, hoping whoever this was would leave her alone.

"I see," the woman said, extending her hand. "I am Dasha, camerawoman."

In black jeans, a black long-sleeved T-shirt, black ankle boots, and a navy-and-white check scarf wrapped several times around her neck, she looked more like a guerilla fighter styled by Benetton than a camerawoman. She had unusually high cheekbones, a broad face, flaxen-toned skin, dark hair pulled severely back into a pony tail, and slate-gray phoenix eyes that were now scanning the room as if by instinct. She held out her hand.

"Great. You two met," Matt said, appearing out of nowhere like the ghost of Christmas Unwanted. Looking at Natalie, he explained, "She's our new camerawoman, most recently posted in Kabul where she shot for BBC and Sky News for the last decade and a half." Then he added in a whisper, "She's from Kazakhstan."

Dasha gave a curt shake of her head. "Not Afghanistan since '09. Yemen, then Damascus. Tripoli for nine months. I was embedded with Alawite forces fighting ISIS in Raqqa the last five months. I have gotten every crew out safely, not many people can say this." She paused to let that sink in.

Natalie was searching for an impressive sounding reply—"I once helped an obese man get airlifted out of his house without him missing a turn on Xbox" was the best she had to offer—when Matt pointed insistently at the TV behind them. "Check out McGreasy."

Natalie spun around to see Ryan McGreavy live outside the Colombian embassy with a First On ATN banner running above the Breaking News banner.

"Thank you, Nelly, I'm about to bring you an exclusive, only-

see-it-here interview that no other network has. Just us. Exclusively." A graphic reading ONLY ON ATN rolled across the
screen and then shattered into a million little pieces over *Star
Wars*-sounding music.

"Huh, do you think it's an exclusive?" Matt said. None of
them looked away from the screen.

"I'm here to bring you the first interview with Rigo Lystra
from inside the embassy."

Holy shit, Natalie thought. *How the hell did he land this?*

A still photo of Rigo Lystra appeared at the corner of the
screen next to a symbol for a phone.

Into the camera Ryan said, "Folks, we're on the phone now
with Rigo Lystra, who is holed up inside the embassy behind
me. *¡Rigo! ¿Estás bien, amigo?*" Ryan winked into the camera.
"For everyone at home, I'm asking, are you okay, my friend."

A young man's voice came over the line. "I'm okay! Let's
speak English, my friend. I'm so grateful to the United States
of America for letting me keep my freedom. This is all baloney.
I did nothing wrong and you will know it. Justice will win."

"We believe you," Ryan said. "And we're sorry you are going
through this."

We do? We are?

"I think this McGreavy does not use your word 'we' cor-
rectly," Dasha said and Natalie wanted to hug her.

"Man, we want to know," Ryan continued on behalf of all
of them. "What's it like up there? How you doing?"

Rigo began describing the hospitality of the wonderful embassy staff.

Natalie turned to Matt. "How did he get this interview?"

"Oh, grasshopper, you must understand, for a man who is
willing to do anything, there are always many doors open,"
Matt said.

"Or for a correspondent with an ace producer," Natalie shot back.

Matt was unmoved. "Don't look to me. Look at you," he

said, gesturing to her body. "I want to get my news from a girl who looks like she takes her style cues from the *Shapeless and Rumpled Catalog*, said no one ever." Matt's eyes got hard. "You have to look like someone worth listening to in order to get the attention of people worth talking to. No one is going to spill high-quality dirt to someone who won't be able to get it in front of an audience."

Dasha made a clicking noise with her tongue and frowned at Matt. "Do not listen to him." The camerawoman's eyes focused on the television with an expression Natalie would not have wanted turned on herself. "You will do better. I hate the fake bozos. Matthew, what do we know of Greasy?"

"Not Greasy, Mc—" Matt cut himself off. "Anyway, that's mine. I want credit if you use it. And I prefer Matt to Matthew, Matthew is the name..." His voice trailed off under Dasha's stare.

On screen now, McGreasy was telling a story about Rigo's love of basketball and how successful he'd been with his brackets three years running.

Around the room, computers began emitting a high-pitched beep. Soon the whole newsroom was chirping with the sound of an urgent AP news bulletin:

URGENT
Washington, DC—First Lady photographed with Colombian strongman Carlos Lystra. A photograph appearing on gossip site TMZ shows First Lady Anita Crusoe, laughing with Colombia's president before the summit dinner.

Natalie's chair sighed as her mind began to race down Worst Case Scenario lane.

What about her migraine? Had there even been one? The story she'd spent all day chasing was gone—*poof*—just like that.

Taking with it her VOP.

And her career.

At least you didn't spend six hundred dollars on your hair, her mind offered up as a consolation prize.

Her chair gave a sigh bordering on a moan as she leaned forward, pulling up the photograph to study it. There was Bam-Bam standing with his arms stretched out wide, as though the photo was snapped right in the middle of a funny story, with the First Lady seated on an upholstered chair smiling up at him. She had her hair pulled up, was wearing a long-sleeved navy sheath, and her head was thrown back as if she was delighted by his wonderful joke.

"Flirty FLOTUS Digs the Dictator," Matt said, studying the photo on Natalie's monitor. "Or better! Dick-Tator. It's a Dicki-leaks dump!" He launched into a smug laugh.

"This is not funny," Dasha said to Matt, then turned to Natalie. "Often people joke to cover up with laughter the sadness inside of them."

"This is bullshit," Matt said, reaching for his phone. "I'll call the White House and see what Adam Majors has to say about this."

"It's weird," Natalie mused mostly to herself. The setup, the photo. None of it made sense. Was the migraine a lie?

In the back of her mind, Natalie felt a familiar prick, the prick of instinct that told her there was something more here. *Try harder,* her first boss used to say. He'd also insisted she had an antenna for The Story and over the years she'd learned to trust it.

She zoomed in to study the picture more closely, as though it were one of those images in a kids' magazine where you have to circle the incongruities—a book hanging in midair, a clock with the numbers backward, a tiger in a baby carriage, a mole on the First Lady's neck.

A mole on the First Lady's neck!

Quickly she opened her internet browser and pulled up photos of the First Lady and felt her heart beat faster. "Dasha, can you look at this picture? Do you see something on the First Lady's neck?" Natalie asked, trying to keep her voice level, not let her excitement get out of hand. Because the First Lady was in profile, her neck—and the mole—were easy to see.

Matt crowded in uninvited. "It's a mole. A beauty mark," he said. "Why?"

Dasha nodded. "Matthew is not wrong," she agreed.

Natalie beamed at them. "She had that mole removed two years ago," she told them. "During the campaign."

Matt looked at her skeptically. "How you know that?"

Natalie's chair sighed, but she was ebullient. She pulled up the video from the Wisconsin women's event she'd been watching earlier and hit Play. There was FLOTUS apologizing for wearing a turtleneck in August, explaining she'd just had a mole removed from her neck.

"There!" she said. "You see?"

Matt was staring at the screen. "It could be a different mole."

Natalie wanted to scream. Instead she opened a new window and Googled videos of the First Lady from the campaign. The first thing that came up was a *People* magazine cover shoot. She was in a red blouse, with a mole clearly visible on the right side of her neck.

"See right there?" Natalie said, pointing at the First Lady's neck. "A mole."

Then she found the most recent video of the First Lady, a *Today Show* appearance about allergies. "There!" Natalie said, freezing the video when FLOTUS was in profile. No mole. It was gone.

Now she pointed at the photo TMZ had just released. "She had that mole removed two years ago." She turned to grin at Matt and Dasha. "That means this photo is either old or doctored."

"Shit, that's amazing." Matt said as Natalie eyed him to make sure there wasn't a *but* coming.

"What did the White House say?" she asked.

"No response. Which means something's up," he said, pulling his phone out. "And now I am going to produce the hell out of this piece. Let's get you on air."

Natalie glanced at the television where Ryan, looking a little flustered, was wrapping his interview with Rigo. Already other stations had gone wall-to-wall FLOTUS.

My turn, Natalie thought. *My chance.*

8

THE RIGHTS OF MANAGEMENT

Despite the breaking news on air—a panel of pundits in boxes engaged in a shoutfest over FLOTUS's photograph with BamBam—the wattle of What Girls didn't seem to be doing anything more than ignoring Matt and researching the calories in toothpaste. "I had no idea it could make you fat but GMA did a whole segment on it," one of them announced.

Fifteen minutes earlier Matt had marched over to the desk, declaring he was going to personally track down an executive producer and get Natalie on the air pronto. That had been long enough for her to fix her hair and freshen up her makeup. Now she was getting restless.

After checking her eyelashes one last time, Natalie put down the mirror and walked over to the desk. "I still don't get it." One of the What Girls who had been squinting at Matt shifted the squint to her. "A mole? Who else is reporting that? Does, like, the *New York Times* or, um, Beltway have it?"

Natalie frowned and looked at Matt who looked back at her with an expression of humility she wouldn't have guessed he possessed. "You try," he said. "I am completely defeated," and walked off, leaving Natalie on her own.

With a deep breath, she steeled herself and explained, no. No one else was reporting the mole. "We have it first," she said, flooding her voice with enthusiasm.

The What Girl frowned, unmoved. "I don't understand. If no one else is reporting it, how do you know it's true?"

Patience, must exercise patience, she told herself.

"Because I've confirmed it myself. With my own eyes." Natalie inhaled again and tried for an approach with less logic. "Can you help me get it on air before the other networks do?"

The What Girl stared at Natalie like she'd just asked to open the airplane exit door at thirty-thousand feet. "I'm sorry but no," the What Girl said, clearly not sorry at all. "I'm under orders not to bother the show with anything unless I'm one hundred percent sure we have something reportable. I can't confirm what you say unless a trusted news organization is reporting it. Otherwise, how would I know it's right?"

Natalie felt like she'd tripped into an alternate universe. In What World, following the crowd, playing catch-up, was the winner's move; new information was Bad and something to be scorned if not outright avoided.

Not What World, she thought. *WhatTheFuck World would be more apt.*

Was she going to be reduced to tweeting Drudge about the mole?

There had to be a better way. There had to be someone she could appeal to.

Like a fairy godmother, a man's voice rang out from her left. "Hey, lady! You're here late."

A fairy godmother she'd been anxious to avoid—until now. Even without looking in his direction, Natalie could feel Hal smiling at her admiringly. "I don't think I ever noticed how fit you are!" he went on. "Seeing you from a distance just now I realized you must go to the gym a lot?"

He really just said that. Surely Bibb, somebody, has told him it is not okay to talk to—

Focus, she told herself. *Bibb. Hal talks to Bibb all the time.*

She turned and grinned at him "Hey, Hal. Am I glad to see you," she said with all the warmth she could muster. "I have a big story. Think you could help me get it on air?"

To Hal's credit, he instantly appreciated the newsworthiness of her mole discovery. "That's killer! What does the White House have to say?" he asked, looking concerned.

"Nothing. Matt tried Adam Majors twice, and by email," she said, wondering whether he was going to hold up her live shot pending White House comment on a mole.

"Well then, way to start off on the right foot," he replied, beaming. "I'm calling Bibb now and getting you up." He walked away, punching numbers into his iPhone, prompting Natalie to think that maybe Hal wasn't so bad after all.

As Natalie walked back to her desk, Dasha materialized by her side. "I do not like this, asking help from Hal," she said.

"Oh he's harmless. At least he can be useful."

Dasha narrowed her eyes. "Lie down with fleas, swim with fishes."

Natalie squinted at her for a moment and decided it was probably best not to correct her.

When they got back to her desk, Matt was standing there, shaking his head. "Bad idea, very bad idea."

Natalie waved him off. Why was everyone second-guessing her? "You're just mad I got this scoop without you, producer," She pulled the mirror out of her makeup bag to do the once-over—hair, eyelashes, smile—and felt uneasy about what she saw.

"Earth to Natalie," Matt said, perched at the edge of her desk. "I'm saying, you're not going to get it on air. Not if Bibb's involved. She is not, repeat *not*, your friend. She is one hundred percent Team Ryan."

Why was he so opposed to everything she did?

"Bibb may not be the best bet for my future success, or humanity's, but she won't want another network to report this first," Natalie said, determined to cling to something. "Besides," she added, pointing at the TV where Nelly was doing rapid-fire questioning of all twelve pundits in boxes. "It would be impossible for me to get on air without her."

"You should have told her you have big news, without saying what it is," Matt said. "Whet her appetite without showing all your cards."

"Should I also beware of putting the cart before the horse but hold off on counting my chickens? I'm not entirely clear on the rules of mixed-metaphor cage fighting, but I'm pretty sure the fact that mine at least are somewhat consistent makes me the winner."

If his dourpuss expression was anything to go by, Matt did not agree. "Make fun if you want, but I'm trying to help you. She's a Machiavellian monster and she's going to screw you if she gets the chance."

Natalie put up a hand. "Abuse metaphors if you must but please leave screwing out of it."

"Ho ho, sounds like I came in at just the right time," Hal said, bustling between them. He looked flushed, and Natalie hoped it was because of his errand, not what he'd overheard. "Great news! Bibb is dying for the story. We just spoke to New York, they want Natalie on air ASAP. Live from the third-floor flash studio now!"

"Thank you, Hal!" Natalie smiled at him, hating herself for feeling gratitude. For a moment she almost understood why management kept Hal around. He got things done.

She turned her beam on Matt. "Aren't we lucky to have Hal and Bibb in our corner?"

"You're going to regret this," Matt said in a low voice.

"**Want to** bet?" she yelled back over her shoulder as she walked toward the elevator. At the last moment she swerved and turned to take the stairs instead.

She practically skied the four flights down to the studio in her excitement. Her hand trembled a little as she ran a pass over the digital lock from the stairwell. She had a scoop about the First Lady of the United States! This was nearly the pinnacle of the scoop pyramid and by far the highest level story she'd ever broken. *Stairs one, elevator zero*, she thought. *Let's hear it for being smart and not dropping the ball. And having big hair.*

The door to the flash studio clicked open and she stepped into inky darkness. It was dead silent and cold enough to freeze meat. The room had the quality of a morgue.

The only light came from a picture of the White House projected on a plasma screen behind a large news desk. In front of it stood a robotic camera with lights hung overhead, still dark, which was odd because the control room in New York should have known she was coming by now. Shivering, she made her way to the news desk, fished around for a microphone which she ran up her shirt, and plugged in the earpiece. She could hear the anchor in New York talking about the photos. A TV monitor in front of her was flashing Breaking News!

"Hey, guys, I'm here!" Natalie said to anyone who might be listening. "Can you turn on the lights?"

As she waited, Natalie started rehearsing what she would say. "Heath, these photos are many things. Unexpected, controversial, and ATN can exclusively report—fake. What we can definitively say is they raise questions about the First Lady's migraine and her whereabouts." She stopped herself. The build had taken too long. "Heath," she tried again, "ATN can exclusively report that this stunning photo…is a fake. This image of the First Lady was taken months if not years ago. And we know because of the tiny telltale mole on her neck."

The room was still pitch-black, and she hadn't heard anything from the control room. Her fingers felt like icicles.

Impatient, she was reaching for her phone to dial the news desk when a voice spoke in her ear. "This is Mitch in New York with *TalkTalk Live!* What do you have for us?"

Classic. The control room, in charge of everything that went on air, was always the last to know the news. "Hi, Mitch. I've got a scoop about the photo. It's about the mole on FLOTUS' neck."

"Cool. I heard something about that. Stand by."

The lights came on, the room began slowly to brighten, and Natalie waited, counting seconds as she practiced the words she would say. "If you look closely at the photo, you'll see a mole on the First Lady's neck that was removed six months ago. No—" She stopped, took a breath and restarted. "If these photos had been taken today, even this week, that mole would be missing."

Another voice spoke in her ear. "Hi, this is *TalkTalk* in New York. We have a lot to get in, a lot to juggle. What do you have?"

Quelling her rising frustration, she went through it again. The mole. The photos. FLOTUS. "No one else has it," she finished, hoping to instill a sense of urgency.

"Yeah. I think I heard something about that," the new voice said. "Not sure we'll need you, but stand by."

How would they not need the mole? It proved the pictures were fake, that the White House was covering something up, that the First Lady was—

The show's theme music came on. "Lets all talk, talk, talk, talk! Let's keep up the talk, talk!"—and they dipped to commercial break.

Natalie was incredulous. Instead of coming to her they had gone to an ad for prescription pain medication, giving someone else and some other network the chance to scoop her.

I could tweet it, she thought. On the monitor an older man in a doctor's coat was asking if she or anyone she loved suffered from back pain, neck pain, shoulder pain, or any other kind of discomfort.

But if I tweet it and no one else has it, then other networks might pick it up from me before ATN runs it.

Now an oil company was explaining its plans for sustainably powering America, which had something to do with family picnics in racially diverse parks and the migration of monarch butterflies.

On the upside, it could lead to a huge bump in my Twitter followers—

At a chain restaurant that had recently suffered an E. coli outbreak, a family who had been fighting was brought back together by free breadsticks and one large pitcher of either soda or iced tea.

—on the downside, it could incite the wrath of Bibb and ATN and bump me out of the running for the White House, cuing of plagues and locusts, etc.

And then the commercial break was over. The screen went dark, Breaking News music soared, the photo popped up in the video monitor along with a now countless number of pundits shaking their heads in boxes. Nelly, looking especially excited, announced an "exclusive development."

Someone in Natalie's ear said, "Stand by to go live on *Talk-Talk*. We have two photos. The doctored one with the mole and one without."

"Great, I'm ready," Natalie answered, putting her phone aside.

The rush of excitement surged again. On camera, Nelly said, "These photographs are as new to us as they are to you. We have our experts poring over them and one of our experts has made a discovery. Ryan, tell us, what you've found."

Natalie stared. Had he just said—? Did she hear—?

On screen, Ryan, once again in his superhero of news stance outside the Colombian embassy, began to speak. "Nelly, it's a stunner but your own eyes will tell you the truth on this. If you look at the leaked picture, you'll see a mole on the First Lady's neck. Look carefully. You see it? Now, look at this video from the First Lady's appearance on a morning show last week." The screen cut to the First Lady dust-busting on *The Today Show* wearing the red blouse.

"No mole," Ryan intoned. "That's because she had it removed a while back, and that means this image is fake, certainly not from tonight's dinner. Which leads us to wonder." He leaned forward and shot a molten look into the camera. "Who faked this photo? What do they hope to achieve? And where is First Lady Anita Crusoe now?"

Not just Natalie's fingers but her entire body felt frozen. They had given her scoop, her research, the photos she herself had found, to Ryan. Ryan, who knew nothing about the First Lady.

Her mind got loose and jumpy. Was this Bibb's doing? Or the What Girls'? Hal? What if Bibb didn't know? But Hal had said she did, that she was excited.

He could have lied.

Surely he wasn't still punishing her for refusing to get a drink with him?

Was it a mistake? Was it a cabal?

She forced herself to inhale deeply, working to keep her voice even as she spoke into the microphone to whoever was listening in New York control room. Establish facts. Don't accuse or protest. Avoid sounding like a crazy person. Casually she said, "Hi, control room. Um, why didn't you guys come to me?"

"Really sorry," a deep male voice spoke into her ear. It wasn't one of the people she'd talked to earlier but another one. "That was a terrific tidbit," it enthused. "We've had Ryan on the show all night so he's part of our narrative. Just wanted to stick with him and get that great piece of information on as soon as we could. No one else has the mole yet. Glad we got it on air in time. Thanks for the reporting. You're clear."

"But I still—"

The lights went off in the studio. She felt suddenly exhausted, as if someone had turned off her power, too. Unable to move, she sat alone in the dark watching the TV monitor. "ATN's Exclusive: First Lady Molegate." They already had a name for it.

Ryan was on camera again. She couldn't bear to listen to him. Natalie closed her eyes and removed her earpiece.

She wanted to cry and scream "it's not fair" like a five-year-old having a meltdown. It was an inviolate rule of reporting that if you got a scoop, you got the credit. That was how you made your name as a reporter. If they were going to give your reporting away, what was the motivation to skip Thanksgiving or Christmas or your father's fucking last month alive? And what reporter would take someone else's scoop?

Someone who would put anything in his mouth, Natalie told herself.

When the phone rang, she realized she was in tears. She composed herself and heard Bibb's voice in her ear.

"I heard you are upset," Bibb launched right in. Apparently she hadn't done as good a job of sounding composed and casual when talking to New York as she'd thought. "This is not a beauty pageant, it's a team sport. What matters here is that we— our team—got the information on air before anyone else. That is a home run for us. And I'll be sure the right people know your contribution. ATN owns the mole. Thanks to you."

She wanted to scream at Bibb and Hal and all the What Girls and especially Ryan. But, exhausted, she'd just hung up.

The door opened and Matt sauntered in. "That went well. Still happy to have Hal and Bibb in your corner?"

For a moment she looked at him silhouetted in the light from the hallway and let the basics of the situation really sink in. Characters. Narrative. It was all so ludicrous.

She unplugged the microphone and stood up from the desk. "You must be happy," she said.

He shook his head. "No. That went the way I predicted, not

the way I wanted. There's a difference." He held the door for her and then followed her out of the studio.

Dasha was waiting in the hallway, arms crossed. "I do not like this Greasy. He is cheating."

"It is what it is," Matt said. "It's up to us to be better."

"Oh this is my fault? What's my problem now, I was too thorough? I shouldn't try to be a good reporter?" Natalie knew she sounded bitter but she couldn't help it.

"You're missing the point, again," Matt said, irritation replacing smugness in his voice. "I know you're not stupid so you must be in denial. Let me spell it out. It's not about the reporting. It's about TV." He fixed her with a steady gaze. "It's about looking and sounding the part."

She started walking down the hallway, Matt and Dasha scurrying behind. Things had to change, but how could she compete with Ryan? He wasn't even a reporter. He was like a news actor playing…a part.

And like a sea wall giving way under the thrashing of a storm, awareness came crashing into her exhausted mind: Matt was right.

They're news actors, Natalie told herself. *Everyone's acting a part in the drama. Play the part. Play the game. Win the game.* Natalie exhaled. *Rate now to report later.*

"I see it on your face," Matt said, now at her side.

"See what?" she asked, reluctant to give in to him.

"That you know I am right." He looked smug. "That you know I know how to win this."

"Really, Newstradamus?" she said as they walked past the elevators toward the stairwell.

He moved to stand directly in front of Natalie, stopping her in her tracks, until she relented. "Okay, okay!" she said. "What do you think I need to do?"

"Step one. Hair. Makeup. Tan."

"I knew you'd say that," she moaned. But she understood.

Matt knew how to play the game. Why not take some advice from an expert? Turning, she walked to the elevator and hit the down button. As they rode to the lobby, she made a decision.

Deep breath. She'd do it.

9

SOME OF THE
PRESIDENT'S MEN

"Absolutely not." The First Lady was on the phone, her dormant incredulity flickering to life. "I will not play along with your reckless games. Don't ask again."

She stabbed End and handed the cell phone back to her agent Beth.

"They've lost their minds," she said and started pacing the room, replaying the conversation in her head. It was her chief of staff calling to say the president's team wanted to issue a statement in the First Lady's name, blaming Venezuela for the doctored photo and demanding an apology from President Gomez. Of course such an accusation by the First Lady against her country of origin would be convincing. It would garner international attention.

There was no evidence the photo came from the Venezuelans. It could just as easily been produced by BamBam's people, or any *huevón* with access to Photoshop. Hell, the White House could have made it up to serve some interest she hadn't considered.

They want me to attack my own people. For this? No.

The president's staff consistently treated the East Wing, where the First Lady's staff worked, as an inferior rival faction of the White House, undeserving of real information which had to be kept and protected by the big boys in the West Wing.

As she worked it over in her mind, the First Lady's incredulity grew into anger.

It was Majors who had come to her team last week announcing that Mrs. Crusoe would be seated next to that criminal BamBam Lystra at the summit dinner. Majors planned to announce this to the press to "demonstrate our absolute neutrality on the question of the purported rape," and make clear that "personal disputes won't get in the way of the summit and our mission to secure a stable energy future." She'd nearly exploded with fury, instructing her staff to send back a message: if the president wants his wife next to BamBam Lystra, he'll have to get himself a new wife.

That had seemed to put the issue to rest. Until her husband had extended an invitation to BamBam's monstrous child, Rigo.

She stared at the Persian rug, unseeing and now nearly shaking with restrained fury. The manipulation was never ending. It was as though she was meant to stand for nothing, no values, no loyalties. Just play along.

Truth was, she'd been compliant, for years. Well before they took office. Before the campaign. From the beginning. She'd so rarely spoken up, so rarely made demands. She closed her eyes. She couldn't fight them, but she could create trouble. She could make her husband's life difficult. She would make sure of it.

THE EARLYBIRD™/ FRIDAY / 5:32 A.M.
THE E-NEWSLETTER TRUSTED BY WASHINGTON'S POLITICAL ELITE

Good morning, EarlyBirders™. Here are the morning's need-to-know stories.

SIREN: MORNING MYSTERY! WHO FAKED THE FLOTUS PHOTO!? WHO LEAKED IT!? Send your tips to earlytipster@theearlybird.com**.**

Outrage at 1600: *White House Comms Director Adam Majors in a rare overnight statement: "The press's reckless decision to broadcast a doctored photo of First Lady Anita Crusoe is exactly why America hates the media. As I previewed, the First Lady was home with a migraine and not with Mr. Lystra at the summit dinner. The president is disappointed in this coverage but continues to do the important work of ensuring America's energy security."*

KUDOS: To ATN newcomer, eagle-eyed *Ryan McGreavy.* **The first to** spot the fake!

The Look: If FLOTUS *had* gone to dinner, two designer gowns were ready to go. A pink Alexander Wang cold-shoulder in silk-georgette or an ombré Kate Spade sequined strapless illusion gown. See them here: www.TheEarlyBird.com/theLook. Tweet our link!

10

WHATEVER IT TAKES

Three hours. That was how long the receptionist at Salon Badem had told Natalie The Treatment would take.

"We process candidates for The Treatment a month in advance," the receptionist had added, making the salon procedure sound like the CIA's extraordinary rendition program, only less enjoyable and harder to get into. When Natalie had mentioned she was calling at the suggestion of Bibb Connaught, the woman's tone changed. "Why didn't you say? With this referral, we can place you immediately."

The receptionist had requested a two-hundred-dollar nonrefundable deposit and for a moment Natalie had hesitated. What kind of person would pay six hundred dollars to get scalp cancer at 6:30 a.m. on a Wednesday? Then her mind had flashed to the studio, to Ryan on air, and she'd mentally raised her hand and shouted, *Me! I'm that kind of person! Sign me up!*

Badem was the It salon of Washington, DC, located, like its clientele, as close as possible to the White House. Made of enough white marble to qualify as another monument, it was as famous for its blowouts—the first one at 5:45 a.m. to accommodate those in early news slots—as it was for the ugly rumors about its flamboyant owner, Osman Badem.

Based on the profiles she'd read to steel herself for the experience, Natalie wasn't sure if it was despite or because of Osman Badem's reputation for abuse that the A list flocked to the place. Magda, the hairdresser Bibb had insisted she see, laughed when Natalie had asked about this. "You are a smart report, *habibi*," she said with a friendly wink and a vaguely Moroccan accent. Magda wore elbow-length black rubber gloves, clear safety goggles, white pants, and a white lab coat cinched at the waist with a belt that managed to showcase her ample cleavage. With her shoulder-length auburn hair brushed back off her forehead and her full mouth carefully made up in plum, she looked like a biological scientist from a future styled by John Galliano.

Natalie had been sent off with an assistant "to blank the slate," as Magda said, which meant having her hair washed and blown dry. "We will speak when you come back."

With her head in the sink, Natalie felt a rising tide of anxiety. She should have been at the office, or at least on her way there making calls and looking into the fallout from Molegate. The White House had put out a statement reaffirming that FLOTUS had indeed been home with a migraine, meaning that the photo had been a fake. Now she worried about White House reaction. What if the First Lady showed up to speak to reporters while she was at the salon and unavailable?

"No point in stressing," Matt had scoffed. "You won't get on air if you don't get that hair. Do you want me to go with you and hold your hand?"

The only thing worse than missing out on a mega-story while paying to possibly get scalp cancer, she thought, would be listening to Matt the whole time.

Her phone buzzed.

MOM: Gerald's son Trace says if you don't have a date he thinks one of his friends would be willing to sit with you.

MOM: There is no reason to be embarrassed about needing a setup. According to New York Magazine, 32% of educated women in their thirties are single. Your group has a name: The 32%.

MOM: Also I was watching your clip on YouTube and I wonder, have you run out of the placenta-based moisturizer I got you? Don't be mad but I think your skin could use a little buff up before the wedding. For the sake of the photos!

MOM: And before you accuse me of being critical, remember, I only tell you this for your own good.

MOM: Would it hurt you to respond now and then?

Natalie dropped her phone in her purse, closed her eyes, and tried to practice one of the deep breathing exercises Sarah was always trying to get her to do. "Imagine you are somewhere safe, you feel comfortable and totally yourself," Sarah had recommended and Natalie pictured sitting at her desk, in front of her computer. She wondered if everyone would agree that there's a thin line between relaxation and hyperventilation.

Forty-five minutes later, Magda was carefully measuring chemicals into a mixing bowl, talking as she worked. "You ask about Osman. The clients, they love his attitude. He is rude, he is risqué yes? This must mean he is the best! Only the best dare to be rude!" She smiled. "The people who love power, they love the challenge from the rude people. They must work to prove they are important, you see?"

Natalie laughed. "It sounds like you've spent a lot of time around politics."

Magda clucked her tongue. "Too much and also too little. Yes and also with the report like you. Your type is not so different."

Questions started popping like corn kernels in Natalie's head, but before she could start asking, Magda's easy, playful manner vanished. She'd suddenly become withdrawn and stiff and Natalie was wondering what she'd done to offend the woman when she realized that the atmosphere in the whole salon had become tense, with a hushed expectancy that made the six flat-screen TVs hanging on the far wall seem loud.

Osman Badem came striding into the room trailed by three assistants, his thin, shoulder-length hair flying out behind him. He sent ripples of confusion across the calm surface of the salon, barking an insult here, a compliment there, growling, ordering coffee, tea, juice, goddamn not that green juice, and get rid of that fucking cushion, can't you cunts get anything right? As he passed Natalie's chair, Magda bent down to receive a kiss on each cheek and Natalie was surprised at just how short he was.

The next moment he was gone and a moment after that the normal sounds of the salon reemerged, like a jungle after a tiger stalked through. It struck Natalie that the salon embodied something she'd begun to notice about DC in general: there was a collective agreement to conform, to bend toward a sameness—the blowout, The Treatment—while celebrating and feeding off of the outrageousness of a few.

And here she was, paying extravagantly to have a woman in a push-up bra apply a compound that smelled like rotten eggs and car exhaust, a compound which had been shown to cause tumors in lab rats just so she could pass as one of them—someone with Sparkle! Authenticity! A permanent beat!

You'll make a fine conformity model, the voice in her head taunted her.

Did everyone have a subconscious always set on Mock? she wondered. She would have preferred a subconscious set on Sympathize or Encourage or I Got Your Back.

"Plenty of people make sacrifices for their jobs," Natalie said, speaking to her reflection.

She was surprised when Magda answered, leaning close and speaking in a low tone. "It is true. But sometimes it is dangerous to notice this. As we were saying, people like the rudeness over the kindness. And the pity."

Natalie realized that Madga had thought Natalie was talking about her. That Natalie had noticed her discomfort with Osman.

"I wasn't— I didn't—" Natalie stammered.

Magda's smile was warm and her voice jocular again as she stood. "Of course not. You are correct, *habibi.* We all do things for survival. Do I want to be sniffing chemicals all day? No. But I have a child and responsibilities. I must take care of myself. Also, I have the fans," she said, gesturing at the circle of three large fans ringing them. 'They protect me. It is important, as a woman, to protect yourself."

Natalie nodded. "You're right."

In that light, Natalie saw that her hair was kind of an armor. One more thing to strengthen her defenses and make her less vulnerable to danger. And it wasn't as though she hadn't been to other salons for equally byzantine treatments involving chemicals and procedures that sounded more like weapons—lasers for her legs, boiling wax for her bikini, electrical shocks for her eyebrows—than beauty regimes. Those incursions had been waged in the name of some abstract notion of beauty; maybe she should just be grateful that this current foray had professional backing.

Her eyes wandered to the mirror and she stared at the salon

behind her, taking in the other women in identical robes sitting on carefully placed poufs and chaises, also investing in the defense of their realms. She wasn't looking in judgment, it was just—there was something about the people, or maybe the atmosphere, in this salon that was different from other parts of the beauty industrial complex she'd known.

"Washington, DC, is not like other places, yes?" Magda said and gave her shoulder a supportive squeeze. "I tell you what it is. Other places there is something that stands for power. Money or beauty or youth or sex appeal, yes? Here, power is power."

Natalie nodded, and as the thought sank in, she realized what was unusual about the salon—she kept meeting people's eyes as she looked around. "Everyone is looking at everyone else in the mirror," she breathed.

Magda clapped her hands delightedly. "That is it! Exactly right! The people here, they are not always looking at their phones like New York or themselves like California. Here they look at each other. Because Washington, DC, is a city of who you know. Also, unfortunately a city of very ugly clothes." Magda shook her head. "But that cannot be helped."

Natalie laughed. She liked Magda a lot. "What is your secret of survival?"

"My life story is for appointment number three," Magda teased. "You have already gotten me talking more than I should because you pay attention." Magda's eyes moved beyond Natalie and a slow smile spread across her face. "Ah, this is good."

In the mirror Natalie followed Magda's gaze to the front desk where a beautiful, cartoonishly thin woman with ink-black hair to her waist was checking in. "Karima," Magda said in a hushed whisper. "Karima Sahadi. You know who she is?"

Natalie nodded. "Yes." Everyone knew who Karima Sahadi was. Even people who were not (slightly) obsessed political reporters would have caught the profiles of the DC hostess of record in the *New Yorker, Wired,* or *Vogue.* Wife of the ambassador to the Arab League, a coalition of Arab nations, she was the vortex of the social whirlwind around which boldface DC swirled. According to the *Vogue* piece, Karima's living room was "the capitol of the Capitol" because it was one of the few places Democrat and Republican, junior staffer and chief of staff could comfortably mingle with one another. According to *Wired,* you could always find the most important figures on the frontier of tech and policy in Karima's living room. According to the *New Yorker,* she occupied a top tier in the hierarchy of access in the city.

"She loves to know all the reports. I will introduce you." Magda winked. "This will be a very good thing."

Natalie's excitement at the opportunity dimmed slightly as she caught sight of her own reflection in the mirror. An introduction to Karima could be invaluable, but with her red-rimmed eyes and toxin-slathered hair, she did not look the part of the smart young reporter on the rise.

"Hello, darling." Karima leaned in to air-kiss Magda. She had just the slightest British accent. "You look like you just stepped out of a Luc Besson dream, as usual. I wish I had time to chat but I've got to be at the Portrait Gallery in an hour and I must have Osman give me a fluff." She leaned close. "I hear he is in a mood."

Magda nodded as she put her hand on Natalie's shoulder. "Karima, before you go, I would like very much to present to you my new *amie,* Natalie Savage. She has come to do the White House for ATN. She is a smart one." The warmth of Magda's introduction was beyond anything Natalie could have hoped.

Karima's face lit up with a magical smile that made Natalie feel at once important and awed. She offered Natalie her hand. "How lovely. You have already started at the White House?"

Natalie stammered, not wanting to miss her opening or get

caught in a lie. "So happy to meet you. I did my first press briefing this week." *See, not a lie.*

"Ah!" Karima's eyes lit up in recognition. "I have heard of
you. You asked after Anita, the First Lady, yes? They said it was
a new girl. That was you?"

Natalie felt herself blush, deeply. Was it possible someone was
talking about her—to Karima Sahadi?

Karima was regarding her with interest. "You are very smart.
Thinking of Anita, looking where others aren't." She leaned toward Natalie as if she was going to impart a secret and Natalie
caught the scent of her perfume, burnt wood and roses, marvelous even through the haze of chemicals. "Anita is a good
woman. This is all too terrible." Then she seemed to alight on
an idea. "We will have lunch, you and me. Yes?"

"Oh that'd be so nice," Natalie murmured to the lovely
woman who called the First Lady by her first name and was
undoubtedly just being polite. There was no way Karima Sahadi
had time for lunch with temporary White House correspondents.

"Wonderful," Karima said, pulling out her phone. "Bombay
Club on Monday? 12:30 p.m."

Stunned, Natalie just stared at her.

"She'll be there!" Magda said, giving Natalie's shoulder another squeeze. "This is wonderful, *habibi*—"

They were interrupted by the sound of a man yelling, straining like an unbroken stallion. Karima straightened. "Oh dear,
there's Osman. I must hurry before he tramples someone." She
turned toward Osman who was brandishing a hair dryer at his
three assistants with increasing violence. "I'm coming, darling."

As Natalie watched the delicate woman cross the floor, she
breathed deeply and caught another whiff of Karima's perfume.

"A custom blend of pure oils," Magda explained. "The ini-
tial work costs tens of thousands. She goes through two bottles
a month and every refill is—" She waved a hand as if numbers

that size were incalculable. She gave Natalie a confidential smile. "She liked you."

"I'm sure she was just being polite," Natalie said.

"Trust Magda, *habibi*. When I do The Treatment to Karima's hair, it takes five hours. In five hours one can learn many things. You go to lunch. Karima can make things happen in this town."

For some reason it made Natalie feel better to know that a woman like Karima dealt with the same chemicals—and pressure to pass—that she was enduring. Like they were part of a sisterhood.

"Now you sit," Magda said and disappeared. Magda's assistant rolled a massive heat lamp over to Natalie's chair, saying, "It will open the cuticle," as if that explained anything. Then she handed Natalie a dry hand towel and gestured to cover her mouth. "If you do not like to breathe with the chemicals."

Even with the towel, her nose began to sting after a minute. Soon she was more than uncomfortable. On the scale of sad to happy faces they show you at the doctor, she'd have assessed her level of misery at "the one who looks ready to impale himself on a sickle."

Don't panic. Don't overreact. Still breathing through a towel, she slowly texted her sister, Sarah, using one finger.

NATALIE: Can you die of a hair treatment? If it's made with formaldehyde?

Sarah was a naturopath, and while she could be a little *too* naturo for Natalie's taste—Natalie had an abiding faith in the power of prescription medication—she knew her stuff.

After what seemed like six eternities, Sarah replied.

SARAH: I feel like I want more details before I answer that question.

NATALIE: If something gave monkeys scalp cancer, would it also give a human scalp cancer?

SARAH: There is no such thing as scalp cancer.

NATALIE: Tell that to the internet. It thinks scalp cancer is totally a thing.

SARAH: On the other hand, if you are starting to talk about the internet like it's your boyfriend, you do have a serious problem.

NATALIE: The internet would make an excellent boyfriend. Always available and fully versed on Top Ten Sex Tips.

SARAH: Although kind of into conspiracy theories and porn. And prone to spreading viruses.

NATALIE: Happiness crusher.

SARAH: Speaking of which, Mom asked me to tell you about the bridesmaids activity Saturday morning before the wedding.

NATALIE: Oh god. Don't tell me. Is it organic douching? Group sensual massage?

SARAH: No. We're having an apothecary blending party. Making custom scents to "amplify the energy of love," I'm told.

NATALIE: As long as it doesn't involve any bodily fluids.

SARAH: I can't guarantee that. Anyway, the Gerald-in-Laws will be there and she wants to make a good impression.

NATALIE: Got it. Attendance mandatory. I'll be there!

Natalie felt the dryer lift off her head and looked up to see Magda scrutinizing strands of her hair like a computer programmer scanning software for signs of malicious code.

"Are you tweeting?" Magda asked as she rubbed the hair through her fingers. "This is very good for you to do. It is like vitamins for the reports. Makes them strong. This is what everyone says."

Natalie laughed, guilty that she had been texting her sister, not building her brand. "It makes me crazy."

"This is also what everyone says." Magda smiled, then replaced the dryer over her head. "Ten more minu—" Magda broke off and lowered her voice to an urgent whisper. "Look as if you are very busy. Maybe an important fact has come for you? Keep your eyes down." Natalie did and heard Magda say, "Ah, Karima, you look wonderful of course. What? Oh yes."

The drier came off of Natalie's head. "*Habibi*, Karima would like to say goodbye."

"It was a pleasure to meet you, Natalie Savage." Karima's smile glowed and her hair shone like a cascade of blue-black silk. "We will have a lovely chat on Monday." She offered Natalie a cheek to air-kiss, gave Magda a hug, and floated off.

Magda beamed. "I told you she liked you."

Natalie felt starstruck. "It was so nice of her to say goodbye."

"Nice?" Magda snorted. "You are smart and stupid all together, *habibi*." Magda reverted to the urgent whisper. "Keep your face down but look in the mirror at the manicure section. Do you see a girl in a very unfortunate blue sweater? Yes? That is the assistant to the editor of The EarlyBird. Karima made sure she saw you. She has done you a big favor." Magda purred, self-satisfied. "You will appear in the newsletter tomorrow. Spotted at Salon Badem."

Natalie felt a flash of panic. "Magda, no! I don't want people knowing I'm getting my hair done when I should be at work."

Magda smiled magnanimously. "*Habibi*, spotted talking to Karima? This is better than work. It will be very good for you, you will see. And now you owe Karima a favor in return."

Natalie was wondering what she could possibly offer Karima in return—her grandmother's apple crumble recipe? Wardrobe advice if she wanted to go to a costume party as one of the 32 percent?—when she felt Magda's hands on her shoulders. "At last we come to the happily-ever-after," she said. Looking up, Natalie was astonished by her reflection in the mirror. Her hair was not simply straight, it was Drowned Rat straight. Lifeless, dead, cooked. Tortured, sucked dry as if by hair-vampires, eviscerated—

Magda spun the chair around and explained, "For the full effect, The Treatment must stay on for twenty-four hours. You wash it out tomorrow. Today if you have a party, no dancing and no you-know-what-ing. Sweat, wet, touch too soon and is all a waste." Magda winked at her. "You will have to be hard to get for one night."

Natalie appreciated Magda's notion of what her life must be like, the parties, the dancing, the men throwing themselves at her and her catching them.

Slightly shell-shocked, she thanked Magda and went to pay. On her way across the salon, she caught the woman in the ugly blue sweater, the assistant to the editor of The Early Bird, looking in her direction. The woman smiled. Natalie smiled back.

Natalie considered her cynicism about conformity in DC, about how Badem was like some kind of female indoctrination facility where individuality was leeched out from the roots of your hair on down. Now she was aware of what she'd missed, the undeniable current of power in the salon. As if here, tucked unobtrusively in the White House's backyard, was a potent nexus of influence. One that decidedly did not smell like a men's locker room. The Treatment *was* almost like a badge of solidarity.

Albeit one that was going to take out its practitioners young through early onset scalp cancer. Which meant she'd better get going.

11

SOLITARY COLORS

It was still early in Colorado. Anita Crusoe didn't want to reach for the phone to check the time but she assumed it had to be close to 6 a.m. She was lying in bed, her mind racing, imagining what that poor girl, Sonia Barbaro, a compatriot, must be thinking. Was she up, too, trying to make sense of the world, grasping for steady ground? She was desperate to reach out to her, just reassure her. To say, *I know. I know what it is to be disbelieved or worse, muzzled. Your truth brings us trouble so you'll have to swallow it.* No seas difícil. *Don't be difficult.*

But that was impossible. A call could be taped or tapped or simply leak. It would trigger international headlines, then an international incident, and then what?

Her mind turned to her husband. This was his fault. He was putting her in an impossible situation. He had to appreciate what it would stir in her. What it would unleash. She felt a welt of anger rise. She knew he could be cold, calculating, but she'd had no idea he had the capacity for this depth of cruelty.

The memories she'd worked so hard to push down, lock away, were now rushing to the surface, clamoring for her acknowledgment. She rolled onto her stomach, pressing her face into the pillow, trying to hold it all back. But it was no use. They came tumbling in. The acrid smell of his sweat. The ravenous look in his eyes. The stillness of everything in the world except his body. But what haunted her most from that night were the sounds. The hungry, defiant groans. They say it's about power not pleasure but like everything they tell you, it's not the whole truth. There was pleasure for him. She'd heard it.

Ese cerdo.

When she'd gathered the force to kick, she'd been as surprised as he. The crunch of bone giving way under her foot. He'd started screaming, cursing them with threats and warnings. But he'd stopped. He'd dressed and left through the front door. It never happened again.

Less than a week later, she'd passed him in the street and again for so many days after that. He'd looked away, *que cobarde.* She'd had to see him in the papers. Watch him on television. Pretend it hadn't happened. Didn't matter. Pretend they'd all moved on.

Was this what Sonia was living through? Was this what her own silence was now abetting?

Her husband had to know what this meant to her. He was giving sanctuary to Rigo, a man who had his freedom because he was powerful. Patrick was putting so much on the line for these monsters. Why? It made no sense. As she felt her frustration grow into rage, she told herself she had to know the answer.

12

THE TOTAL WOMAN, UPDATED

On the street Natalie felt a little woozy, which she assumed was either due to her impending scalp cancer or her anxiety about being out of the office in the middle of Molegate, a veritable breaking news tsunami.

Or maybe this is how your soul feels when you start selling off parts of it.

She checked her watch: 10:15 a.m. That was late for work but early for doing battle with herself, which meant she needed coffee, and not the thin and watery blend they sold at the kiosk outside ATN's offices.

Turning, she walked two blocks to BrewHouse, known as the unofficial coffee spot of the DC media-political set. With exposed brick, Marshall McLuhan quotes on the blackboard, and bearded baristas ready to tell you the birth-origin of each bean in your coffee, it was the most hipster place in the District.

Still, this being DC, it failed to attract a crowd that bore any genetic resemblance to hip. She entered to find it crowded with men uniformed in loose-fitting khaki pants and women sporting unkempt hair with not a fake lash in sight.

That could be you if you didn't work in TV, she thought. *If only you could go back to your twenty-one-year-old self and tell her to pick print instead.*

Checking the time (10:21 a.m.) and the line (at least a dozen people ahead of her), she started feeling flush. Could these chemicals really be poisoning her? Maybe this was Bibb's intention all along. Or Matt's. He's the one who'd insisted she listen to—what had he called her? The Machiavellian monster. Yes, this was Matt's fault.

Her phone rang.

She put in her earpiece and answered, "I was just thinking about you."

"I'm flattered. How is the hair?" Matt said, oblivious to the menace in her voice.

"Terrific," she replied with a mirthless laugh. "I look like a malnourished meth head in summer."

"I was hoping more for a Connie Chung, Lucy Liu look."

"I'll be sure to add Asian fetishism to your list of attributes," she said. "What's happening at the office? I saw the *Washington Post* has a story about Crusoe's plan to increase oil imports from Latin America. We should try to get on that."

"No go. Ryan is on the substance angle," Matt said without a hint of irony, adding, "The Chief wants us to follow up on the mole."

Natalie repeated his words in her head, trying to make sense of them. "How do you follow up on a mole? Especially one that's been removed?"

"Great question," Matt said. "But we've got to make a mountain out of it."

She stifled a groan. She had important things to worry about, like how to make an impression with her journalism when the network wouldn't let her cover actual news? Scanning the coffee shop, she searched for anyone here who could give her a hot breaking news tip—maybe a White House official, a First Lady confidante, someone with expertise in Latin American dictators or international oil politics, when she turned and spotted the man in line behind her. His liquid-green eyes met hers and she felt like she'd been tased.

She had seldom seen other men like this in DC. He was tall, African American, broad shouldered, with close-cut hair and a kind of hipster confidence that just emanated hot.

She smiled, and watched as he leaned toward her infinitesimally and—sniff, had he just sniffed?

"You smell like my aunt Mina," he said with a one-dimple smile, as if it this was the most charming thing in the world to tell a stranger.

Feeling herself blush furiously, Natalie stared at him, torn between It Wasn't My Idea and How Dare You.

"Excuse me?" she stammered out of sheer mortification. Yes, he smelled like soap and sweat and pure masculinity while she smelled like a morgue and looked like she'd been skinny-dipping in an oil spill. But, still, it was not cool to point that out.

"Sorry, I said that out loud, didn't I? Bad habit." His lopsided smile made her stomach tingle. "It's to make your hair straight, right? You know they make it with lye."

"Formaldehyde," Natalie corrected him, hoping she sounded confident and affronted.

"Ah, you got the organic blend?" he said jovially.

She appraised him with his single dimple and eyes that seemed permanently set to mirth. His slim-cut pants hit him in all the right places and his white broadcloth oxford managed to appear sharp and casual at once. It was all definitely working for him.

"Lucy Liu? Connie Chung?" It was Matt's voice in her ear. "You there?"

"I'm here!" she said, turning her back on Mr. Hot Dimple.

"On Molegate, I'm thinking we should make some kind of interactive graphic. We can put it up on social media. The Chief will love it. It'll drive up your followers."

"Graphic of what?"

"FLOTUS's distinctive markings. We can map all of her moles and freckles."

"Are you kidding me? We can't map that. We don't know about other markings. And anyway even if we did, that's just rude. And wrong."

"Is not."

"Is too."

His tone of voice changed. "Hold on. Something is happening."

She heard him put the phone down, without hanging up. Rude. So rude, she fumed, wanting to hang up but also dying to know what was happening in the newsroom.

She was staring into the sea of khaki in front of her when a sound broke through her thoughts.

"I couldn't help overhearing. You're looking to do some map-making? I'm happy to recommend an app."

She turned and confirmed Hot Dimple was, again, speaking to her.

"Don't tell me, Aunt Mina is an app developer?" she asked, weighing whether he was mocking her or flirting, then reminding herself that, in her current state, the latter wasn't an option.

"Nah. But I am a cartographer." He tilted his head to one side. "And happy to help."

Oh really?

"You're the neighborhood mapmaker? What do you map?" she asked, certain he was pulling her leg.

He got an excited look as he spoke. "Well, everything. Business networks. Market patterns. Topography. Maps are really just a picture of how different things relate to one another. My primary interest is boundaries, spaces between different states or states of being. Doorways. Weather systems. Neighborhoods."

"Who is this guy?" It was Matt's voice in her earpiece. She'd forgotten she was still on the phone with Matt. "What a total nerd. Get rid of him."

"Don't be an ass," she snapped.

"Sorry." Hot Dimple had his hands up in feigned surrender.

"No, no, I didn't mean you," she said, shaking her head so forcefully she hit herself in the cheek with a cancer tendril. "I'm talking to someone on the phone." She indicated the headset.

Hot Dimple nodded, looking uncertain. She noticed that his green eyes were flecked with gold and she shivered, feeling a deep attraction.

This is what happens when you don't have sex for five months, said a voice in her head that sounded like her sister, Sarah.

Only four-and-a-half, Natalie's brain corrected.

She had to drag her eyes from him to keep from making a fool of herself.

"What's this guy want?" Matt asked.

Ignoring that, she asked, "So what's going on in the news-room? You said something's up?"

"I don't know. Bibb rushed to the assignment desk and now she's in a closed door with Hal. I'm trying to find out," he grumbled. "Meantime, let's pick up the mapmaker. Ask him if he went to school for that."

"I thought you wanted me to make him go away," she chided.

"I did. But I changed my mind. Because if you get laid, you're going to be more relaxed on air."

"Jerk."

"I'm just trying to help you hook up with a guy who sounds like he might be nearly as nerdy as you."

"Call me when you know what's going on."

"You are terrible at flirting."

"Hanging up now!"

When she'd finally reached the front of the line and paid her $5.75 for a four-ounce pick-me-up, she walked to the other side of the bar and pretended to be busy on her phone as she watched Hot Dimple say something to the cute female barista who laughed and blushed up at him. Clearly every woman's reaction to him, she thought.

She made herself busy on her iPhone until she felt Hot Dimple walk her way and stand next to her.

"Hi, again. Sorry about that introduction." He held out his hand. "I'm James."

"Hi, James," she said, looking up from her phone. "If you're not put off by the formaldehyde, I guess I shouldn't be put off by the association with Aunt Mina."

He laughed, and as they smiled at one another, Natalie groped for something to say, ending up with, "What do you have against straight hair?"

"Nothing really." He shrugged. "Just that it's controlled. Predictable. Careful." He looked at her mischievously. "I'm always telling the women in my family that curly is way more attractive. If God gave you the curls, let them run free." He smiled and she felt like a sparkler was crackling in her chest.

"It's not my choice. It's for work," she managed.

"Really? Aren't there laws against that?" he asked. "I thought the rules say the boss can stare at your chest and underpay you, but he can't tell you to change your 'do."

Her phone buzzed and she hit Ignore without even looking at it. Matt would have to wait.

"Unfortunately that's not the case in TV," she explained. "In TV, they can tell you how to look. Also how much to weigh, what to wear, how to do your hair."

"You're on TV?" He sounded surprised. "You must be a reporter. What do you cover?"

"I cover—" She didn't want to lie but wasn't about to tell him about the mole. "Politics, DC, whatever the echo chamber is buzzing about."

Her phone rang again. She hit Ignore.

"And what is it they're buzzing about today?" he asked.

"The First Lady's headaches. A creepy twenty-one-year-old. An incompetent White House. The usual."

Her phone rang again and this time phones all around the café started ringing at the same time. Glancing at hers, she saw that it wasn't Matt but Bibb.

James gave her that lopsided smile again. "Sounds like the echo chamber is calling."

Flashing him a look of apology, she answered it.

"Natalie, there is video of FLOTUS having an affair," Bibb said, skipping the hello. "We need you on set, top of the hour."

Natalie's heart soared. An affair! Breaking news! *And they want me in the middle of it.*

Immediately, the only thing on her mind was the fastest way to get in front of a camera. This was, apparently, the single thought of more than half the customers in BrewHouse because people were now popping up from tables like pieces in Hungry Hungry Hippos, forming into inefficiently rushing crowds, reporters and politicos stabbing at their phones, ordering Lyfts while rushing the door. She checked her watch. 10:33 a.m., it was going to be tight.

Catching her eye, James indicated the mass of people. "Want to avoid the Great Wall of Chinos?"

"Yes!"

He waved at her to follow and started walking behind the coffee bar, through a doorway marked RESTROOMS, and into a narrow pathway.

"I'm here way too often," he said, "and doorways are kind of my thing."

He pointed to an emergency exit door in the back.

"Amazing!" she gushed.

"Wait." He stopped her before she could go. "How do I find you? In case you need any help mapping something."

He wants to find me! For a moment she was at a loss for words before saying, "I'm Natalie. Natalie Savage. But I don't have cards on me." It was true.

"Okay, I do," he said, handing one to her.

"Got it! I really gotta go," she said, apologetically as she stuffed the card into a pocket.

"Say it back!"

"James, I'm not going to forget," she said, pushing open the door and calling back. "The formaldehyde hasn't triggered brain damage yet."

As the door closed behind her, she could have sworn she heard laughing.

13

THE BEST IF NOT THE BRIGHTEST

Matt met her by the ground floor elevators, looking like a nervous stage mom waiting for her toddler beauty queen.

"You've seen the tape?" he demanded.

Natalie walked past him into the elevator. "Can you be helpful and tell me which studio I'm in?"

"Studio A," he said, scurrying in next to her. "We've got to make sure you own this story. It's huge. Tell me you've seen the tape?"

Yes, she had on the cab ride over. And though she would avoid saying the words to his face, Matt was right. It was going to be huge. Incontrovertible evidence of the First Lady getting intimate with a very handsome—and unidentified—man. It was black-and-white surveillance footage in three parts. The first part showed the First Lady and Mystery Hunk sitting on a couch eating popcorn together. The second was the two of them in a bedroom, FLOTUS wearing only a bathrobe receiving a kiss on the forehead from Mystery Hunk before allowing him to hug her, tenderly. The last part of the tape showed two figures throwing handfuls of leaves at one another in a garden. Notably there was no mole on the First Lady's neck in any of the shots. This video was new.

"They are so clearly doing it," Matt said enthusiastically as the elevator reached their floor. "Days like this I fucking love the job."

"I don't know," she said, leaving the elevator and walking fast down the hallway so he had to jog to keep up. "The video is surprising. Provocative. Train-wreck-un-look-away-able. But it's not proof that the First Lady is doing it with someone else. There's nothing explicitly sexual in it at all."

"Great, go with that," Matt said. "That should be your on-air posture. While everyone else is hyperventilating about FLOTUS the floozy and shouting sex, sex, sex, you can play Miss Goody Two-shoes, the voice of reason. No sex to see here," he said, imitating her voice. They reached the big door marked Studio A. "It's the one position I'm confident you can sell."

"What is that supposed to mean?"

"I'm simply suggesting you play to your strengths. The world's last thirty-two-year-old virgin."

"I am not—"

"*Shhh*, save it for the show," he said, pushing her through the door.

Inside the studio, the air-conditioning hit her like a polar blast. A stagehand wearing an orange parka, ski hat, and gloves greeted her, his breath forming a fog cloud as he spoke. He ushered her toward a half-moon set surrounded by seven robotic cameras on wheels. There were two other production assistants, one wrapped in a Snuggie, the other wearing camouflage survival gear and snow boots.

Natalie found Heath Heatherton sitting behind his desk, bob-

bing his head to his Bose headphones like a prizefighter, studying a stack of blue notecards.

She stilled for a moment. This was the first time she'd seen
ATN's top anchor in the flesh.

"Natalie Savage! Welcome to Heath's show," he boomed,
not bothering to remove his headphones. "Great job out there!"

She wasn't sure to which "great job" he was referring but she
smiled and said, "Thank you so much. A pleasure to be on with
you," as she allowed herself to be led to a stool behind the desk.

In his seven years of national fame, Heath Heatherton had
adopted and shed a number of identities. Just forty-one years
old, he'd already written three best-selling autobiographies. The
first, *From Nothing*, was his up-by-the-bootstraps story of growing up "Greenwich poor," the son of two midlevel corporate
lawyers coming of age in a world of hedge fund families. Next
came *Man-o-Rexic*, a revealing look at his fight to maintain 3
percent body fat through a lean protein and vegetable diet which
triggered a years-long struggle with body dysmorphia. In his
latest, *All of the Above*, Heath claimed either a genetic or emotional identification with every racial and religious group and
sexual orientation recognized by the US Census Bureau. "I'm
an intersex, Judeo-Christian, Islamo-Buddhist, descended from
every race on earth," he'd enthused, insisting his multifaceted
identity enabled him to empathize with a wide array of guests
and news stories. "When I'm with an interview subject, I sometimes *become* that subject."

Critics eviscerated his anchor involvement style of report-
ing as "an extreme distillation of the narcissism of the TV age."
One *New York Times* columnist summarized his show this way:
"Coming up next, more about me." But he made for great TV.
And thanks to his ratings, Heath had almost unchecked power
to do what he wanted on his show.

Seated in such proximity to the great anchor, Natalie did her
best to stare at her hands and not at the star while a stagehand

untucked her shirt and ran his cold fingers and a microphone up it. The cold fingers stopped at her breasts and clipped the microphone onto the shirt fabric then reached around to repeat the procedure with her earpiece up her back. When the stage-hand finished, Natalie retucked her shirt and, glancing down, did up an extra button on top just to be sure there was no cleavage showing. She smiled at Heath but he seemed to be studying his notecards too intently to notice.

"Five minutes to air!" someone shouted.

"We have the video, right, guys? Any ID on the man?" Heath said, talking to the people in the control room. Natalie could not hear their reply.

"Great. And how do you want to play this?" Heath paused. "Mmm-hmm. Natalie. Right. Great. Great." He looked up and smiled at her again.

On TV, Heath was heart-meltingly alluring, handsome with big eyes, a round childlike face, and the honey-colored skin of a Brazilian model. But Natalie observed that seeing him in person was like standing in front of one of these heat-free TV lights—sunny glow but eerily lacking in warmth.

The door slammed open and Ryan McGreavy bounded into the studio and vaulted onto a stool between Natalie and Heath like a pro gymnast.

"Not late after all!" Ryan declared to the room, then turning to Heath, enthused, "Killer video."

"Totally!" Heath replied. "We're gonna crush it!"

Natalie watched as the two men high-fived one another.

She fidgeted in her chair and wondered if she should make some kind of sporty noise, too.

"Whoop, whoop," she mumbled, trying to mimic their enthusiasm.

"Three minutes to air!" a voice shouted.

Ryan pointed at a monitor where Jazzmyn Maine, the morning anchor, was live on air, sparkling like a brilliant-cut diamond. As always, Natalie was struck by Jazzmyn's allure. With her big blue eyes, bright blond hair, and chest-baring blouse, Jazzmyn was mesmerizing, even on mute—scratch that, especially on mute.

"She really pops on camera," Ryan said worshipfully. Natalie looked up to see both Ryan and the stage manager staring at Jazzmyn's image on the TV, as though they'd become the subject of a secret Illuminati mind control exercise.

"Mmm-hmm," one of the guys on set murmured.

Jazzmyn's show went to break and, mind control shattered, Ryan proclaimed, "I hear she's into threesomes." Abruptly he swiveled to face Heath. "Did two guys on the Judiciary Committee staff. It's all over Capitol Hill."

"Really?" Heath mumbled without looking up from his notecards while Natalie started fidgeting in her seat, suddenly intensely aware that she was alone with five men.

Ryan pressed on confidently. "I know a guy from her last station. And they say she's into group sex." He paused for a reaction but Heath, still studying his notecards, merely frowned whether in disbelief or disapproval Natalie couldn't tell.

"Ryan," Natalie began, feeling duty bound to speak up on behalf of another woman, "that's uncool of you to say."

"I don't know. I think it's cool," said the stagehand who'd no doubt had his cold hands up Jazzmyn's shirt, too.

"That mental image will keep me warm at night," a voice from the control room added in Natalie's ear.

"Hey," Ryan said, putting up his hands. "Just repeating what I heard." It took all Natalie's willpower to stay quiet. This was not the time to pick a fight, especially not about the Hefner-at-home vibe in the room. She had to be focused and ready for air.

The seconds stretched on in silence until someone on the floor yelled, "One minute to air!"

Natalie inhaled sharply then exhaled, giving a fluff to her

drowned-rat hair with one hand and smoothing out her blouse with the other.

Heath had started making big movements with his mouth, like he was warming up his lip muscles. Ryan, watching him, started doing the same. When Heath moved from making big OOs to EEs, Ryan stopped to wipe away drool that was pooling at the corners of his mouth.

"We're live in 15…10…5, 4, 3, 2…"

The stage manager pointed at Heath, whose face transformed into a stunning smile. "Hello, world. It's 11 a.m. on the East Coast, 8 a.m. on the West Coast. Welcome to a special edition of *Big Politics* with Heath Heatherton."

Heath was live on monitors on every surface in the studio. He turned to look at a second camera, which afforded viewers an extreme close-up of his pretty honey-toned face.

"The hidden camera video you're about to see gives us rare insight into the private lives of our leaders. It's about lust. Betrayal. Duty. Freedom. A story older than time."

Natalie checked the teleprompter. It did, in fact, say "older than time."

Was it possible for a thing to be older than time? she wondered, then realized that in a world where the boss could arrive in a ray of light, questions like that were just childish. Who was to say that time didn't have an older sister or maybe a cousin?

The teleprompter read "pause for graphic," which Heath did. The screen exploded into the tiny red and green shards from which the words ONLY ON ATN came bursting forth, followed by the video. Heath provided voice-over narration, which included the phrases "treasonous love" and "way hotter than the president."

The video rolled and as Natalie watched it for the second time, she tried to discern if the two people in the video seemed to be sleeping together. FLOTUS looked more relaxed than Natalie had previously seen her. Hair down loose, she seemed soft and vulnerable. Which suggested an affair, but didn't prove it.

When the show came back from tape, Natalie saw the shot of herself on set next to Heath and Ryan, in a monitor out of the corner of her eye. A thrill of excitement shimmered through her. For the first time it felt real. She was "live, in studio" for *Big Politics* with Heath Heatherton. Her heart started to pound so fast she was sure the microphones could pick it up. *This is making it.*

She couldn't wait to tell Sarah.

Heath turned to his right. "Ryan McGreavy, fresh from the Colombian embassy where you broke the news about Rigo Lystra. Tell us—the First Lady of the United States and another man. What do we have here?"

"What we have here is a shameful, un-American betrayal." Ryan was somber. "There is nothing acceptable about committing adultery against the White House. Mrs. Crusoe has a solemn duty to be faithful. She's violated her vows to her husband and to America. And there will be consequences."

Natalie was staring at Ryan, dumbfounded. *What kind of consequences? Does he think it's unconstitutional to cheat on the president?*

She was sure Heath would make Ryan clarify himself. Instead, the anchor nodded gravely and tossed the ball her way. "Natalie?"

"I think we need to be cautious," Natalie said, trying to sound energetic and *NOW!* while also not sounding too alarmed. "The video is provocative. It raises many questions. But we can't tell the nature of the relationship between the First Lady and that man. Surely we can reach a consens—"

She stopped herself before uttering the word *consensus*, recalling in the nick of time that it was one of the Chief's Forbidden Words.

She started again. "Surely we can agree that this is hardly a sex tape—"

"Disagree," Ryan declared, interrupting her.

"Sorry?" She frowned at Ryan, startled.

"It's a sex tape. That's clear as day," Ryan said.

Natalie looked from Ryan to Heath and back. Was he really denying the sexlessness of the tape?

"Don't you need sex for it to be a sex tape?" she asked.

Heath clapped his hands, enthusiastically. "Love it. This is a he-said, she-said live in studio!" He beamed. "How's this? What if we call it a caught-red-handed tape? Or a smoking-gun tape?"

"I like that, a smoking-gun tape," Ryan said, swiveling to face Heath. "I'm not saying that cheating on the president is necessarily treason. But it makes you wonder why we can't impeach a First Lady."

It does? "Because the First Lady is not an elected office," Natalie said with more edge in her voice than she'd intended. The two men raised their eyebrows and looked at one another sharing some kind of silent language. Natalie felt her stomach knot.

Down, girl, she berated herself. *No one likes a scold.*

Just then a voice crackled in Natalie's ear. "Hey, can you unbutton your shirt?"

Natalie froze, trying to figure out if someone had accidentally keyed into the person's wrong earpiece.

No way that's meant for me.

The voice continued, "Don't say anything, you're on camera. But the Chief called and thinks you're too buttoned-up." There was a pause and Natalie remained still. "We'll switch to a solo shot of the boys, if you can just unbutton your blouse one button?"

Wrong again.

Natalie flicked her eyes over to the live-to-air monitor, which showed that she was indeed out of the shot.

"Of course I meant that symbolically, not literally," Ryan was saying. "When my dad was governor, my mom understood that she had to play hostess. It's part of the deal." With a sinking feeling in her stomach and a rising blush, she undid one button and looked down to confirm nothing was showing. Close, but still PG.

"That's great. Great," the voice said in her ear as Natalie imagined the entire control room staring at her chest in the wall of monitors.

No biggie, she told herself. *Not like you're doing a live shot in a bikini.*

"You know what this brings to mind, Heath? It reminds me of what's going on with my friend Rigo Lystra, over at the Colombian Embassy," Ryan was saying emphatically. He was facing Heath, his back turned to Natalie. "I've been on the phone with him again today and he says what bothers him most is the betrayal. The deliberate attempt to humiliate him and ruin his reputation for no reason. And how willing the public is to go along with it. I imagine the president has similar feelings."

Now he's comparing the president to a child playboy accused of rape? Surely Heath will point out that Ryan's case is packed with nuts.

"Interesting point," Heath said, nodding meaningfully, not doing any pointing out at all. "Natalie, let's do a hypothetical. If you were First Lady and unhappy in your marriage, would you consider it acceptable to step out on the president with another man?"

Natalie looked around with some desperation. Seriously, was no one going to stop this? It was like being inside one of those dreams where the stairs turn into a lake and then you have no teeth, and when you try to fly, all your friends start cackling and then you wake up relieved to be in your own bed in a world that made sense. Only she was already awake.

"I'm not entirely comfortable with that hypothetical," Natalie said, summoning all her will to make sure her voice sounded demure. "Just a few days ago a doctored photo of the First Lady became big news."

Wait, am I allowed to say a few days ago? She panicked. *Or, like yesterday, is that phrase forbidden?*

"Again I'm talking about brand-new, just-in-now video of the First Lady," Natalie said, forgoing clarity in the name of pleasing the Chief. "For all we know, it's doctored, too, and—"

"That's a reach." Ryan was frowning. "Why are you working so hard to protect the First Lady?"

Flummoxed, she replied, "I'm not. I'm just—"

Ryan interrupted again. "Heath, I think the press tries to protect the First Family. No offense, Natalie." Turning his back to her, he swiveled to face Heath. "What you're hearing from Natalie now is typical Washington speak. She wants you to doubt what you see with your own two eyes. I say we trust the people to know."

Natalie looked at Ryan, or rather his back, wishing brains could maim. "No, I'm saying we should verify—"

"Oh like we're the information police? Why should we decide what people see?" Ryan interrupted, craning his neck to glance at her.

Natalie's fingers curled into fists. "No, like journalists. Otherwise we're just the internet. It's our job—"

"Down, guys, down," Heath cut her off, making let's-get-calm gestures with his hands. "You both make important points." He looked to Ryan. "We have a responsibility to speak truth to power, even when it will upset people in power." He turned to Natalie. "And we have a responsibility to verify what we report." Finally he turned to one of the robotic cameras. "As a journalist, I won't back down. I'm going to do my job. And no one in power will stop me." He continued looking into the camera, with a smoldering intensity.

In her ear Natalie could hear, "Hard out in five!"

Ryan broke the silence. "Heath, fearless journalism is the best journalism."

"Four, three, two," the voice in her ear said.

"Amen," Heath said with a satisfied smile.

The show cut to commercial.

★ ★ ★

When the lights went off, Heath high-fived Ryan and made a shooting gun gesture to Natalie.

"Great job, guys! Loved the conflict. You're like the Bicker-sons!" he said, putting on the Bose headphones and picking up another stack of blue cards for his next segment.

Natalie was shaking. That had felt like a setup. Had they agreed ahead of time to make her their foil? Or had she been too passive, too polite, about getting her points across?

She thought of her dad's words, *be noisy*.

If he'd seen that segment he probably would have said *be absent*.

She made her way to the door with her head down, wanting to get out of there fast.

"We've got chemistry, girl." Ryan said, giving her a hip bump as he caught up with her. "Total TV chemistry. Was it as good for you as it was for me?"

She said nothing, caught off guard.

He flashed her a big smile and said, "Let's definitely do it again," and hurried away.

Matt was waiting in the hall outside the studio.

"What was that? You didn't get yourself in the conversation enough," he said, hands on hips, in the voice of an angry stage mother.

Natalie shook her head. "Are you kidding? They didn't—"

Matt put up a palm. "No excuses," he said and from the tone he might as well have followed it with *young lady*. "You let Ryan take over!"

"Let him? What was I supposed to—"

"Ignore him!"

"—do when he kept interrupting—"

"Talk over him! LIKE YOU DO WITH ME!" Matt yelled.

She stared at him. He nodded at her smugly. "You're fully capable of it."

"On the bright side," he said, "it's going to be great for your VOP. On the less bright side, it'll help Ryan's, too, so we need to find a way to differentiate ourselves."

"Oh sure," was all Natalie could manage. She felt the phone in her bag vibrate. Summoning up the last of her will, she reached for it.

"Natalie, that was gold, pure gold." It was the Chief. "I loved the back-and-forth with Ryan. I loved your just-the-facts-ma'am attitude. And I love how you defended the First Lady."

Her heart revved like a race car. She had defended the First Lady! And it was good! "Thank you," she stammered.

"This is a huge story. FLOTUS is out on a sexcapade, the president is being de-manned before our eyes. It's pure candy and viewers are going to eat it up. You've just shown me what I needed to see. I want you to be our First Lady correspondent." He paused. "Remember, cable is all about attitude. So keep up the attitude."

"Okay, Chief, will do," she said, though she had no idea what attitude he wanted her to keep.

For a moment, she enjoyed the warm glow of approval spreading through her body. "That was the Chief," she told Matt at last. "He wants me as the First Lady correspondent!"

Matt smiled. "I told you, Savage. That was great TV. And if you just listen to me and do what I say, you'll—"

"Stop talking," she said, not willing to let him ruin her moment of triumph.

He grinned. "Good practice. Keep that up and we'll have McGreasy by his McBalls in no time."

Natalie was back on the newsroom floor, at her desk, rewatching the FLOTUS video, hoping to find some clue about when or where it was shot, when she realized she'd just watched the same clip three times and not seen it once.

She was distracted, and not by the video. The Chief's excitement had awakened a sense of optimism, which had her thinking about James, the hot cartographer from the coffee place. She reached into her pocket and thumbed his card.

Seriously, who was a cartographer these days? It sounded like something made up for a period drama, a globe-trotting cartographer who traveled the world studying boundaries and seducing ladies.

She had his info. She should email him.

Absolutely. Right after you get an apartment. And clean hair.

She went back to the video, still not seeing it. What was the big deal about writing a random hot guy you barely knew? She was an adult. More, she was the First Lady correspondent. The First Lady correspondent couldn't be shy about making contact.

Before she could lose her nerve she pulled out his card and started a text.

Natalie: Thank you for your navigation expertise today. It was invaluable.

She hit Send before realizing she hadn't said who this was.

Natalie: This is Natalie, I forgot to say that.

How would he remember which Natalie? Had she even introduced herself earlier? She couldn't remember.

Natalie: From BrewHouse. The one with brown hair, in front of you in line?

Keep going! Her brain urged. *Boys like crazy people! Maybe next you can suggest moving in together and favorite baby names!*

Her email dinged.

James: Formaldehyde? Of course I remember you, Natalie Savage. I just watched you on TV. Nice work. But I was disappointed there was no mention of mapping.

Natalie felt her stomach do a backflip. Cute James had been watching.

Natalie: Moles are so two hours ago. We're onto impeaching the First Lady.

JAMES: So I heard. Maybe we can have her beheaded?

NATALIE: Send her to the Tower! Lock her up!

JAMES: I would offer you my cartography skills but since the news cycle has moved onto witchcraft and martyrdom, I don't have any applicable talent. Guess I should just straight up ask you out. Dinner?

Natalie blushed deep into the roots of her hair. May as well have some fun before the scalp cancer set in.

NATALIE: That'd be great. You're on.

JAMES: Fantastic. I'm a little busy with family obligations this weekend. How is Tuesday night?

Cute. He took family seriously.

NATALIE: Yes, I'm game.

JAMES: Great. I'll text you a place closer to the date. Looking forward!

He'd just said date. *It's a date!* She sat at her desk, grinning. So far today she'd been on set with Heath, impressed the Chief, and now had a date with a hot guy who spent time with his family.

"Whoop whoop," she said under her breath.

14

THE SELLING OF
THE PRESIDENT'S WIFE

"My talent? Freestyle roller-skating, choreographed to the national anthem," Anita Crusoe said with feigned pride as Anthony doubled over in laughter. They were sitting in the TV room, having tea before dinner where he'd been pressing her for details about her days competing for Miss Venezuela.

"And in a bikini, no doubt?" he asked.

"Of course! You can't roller-skate to the national anthem with pants on," she said straight-faced. She'd forgotten how ridiculous it all was and how good it felt to laugh. Spending time with Anthony was so different from being with Patrick. He was always tied to an agenda and the clock, no space for quiet moments. As she watched Anthony now, she couldn't help but wonder how her life might have been different if she'd found a man like him. A man who wanted to soak in life rather than mold it.

"That's a high stakes situation for a sixteen-year-old," Anthony said.

"You have no idea! I was up against a ventriloquist and a dog act," she said, noticing how the corner of Anthony's eyes wrinkled upward as he laughed, as though his eyes laughed with him.

"Mrs. Crusoe, sorry to interrupt." It was Beth, her lead secret service agent, looking tense. "Ma'am, have you seen the news? I'm afraid we're going to have sweep the house."

A look of irritation crossed Anita Crusoe's features. How many times had she been forced into a security hold because some harmless crackpot had threatened to bring hell and fury to the Crusoe family, or some Secret Service agent had discovered a stray paper bag in her vicinity and called in a bomb-sniffing robot to disarm what turned out to be a tuna fish sandwich?

"Beth, is that necessary? I can't imagine anyone knows we are here," she said more plaintively than she'd intended.

Beth had reached for the TV remote. "You should see this, ma'am. Do you mind?" she said, turning on the television without waiting for a reply.

When Anita saw the story, her blood went cold.

On TV, a bright red banner screamed, "Breaking News: Anita Crusoe Hidden Video," which rotated with another that read "New Video: FLOTUS with Mystery Lover." She couldn't believe what she was seeing. Surveillance footage taken from this house—including the bedroom—blasted out for the world to see. Suddenly she felt chilled, exposed. She reached for a blanket as she turned on Beth.

"Who did this? It's one of your people!" She could hear her own voice rising in panic. "No one knows we're here!"

Beth remained calm. "Not entirely true. My director knows we're here, Mrs. Crusoe. If he didn't, you'd be a missing person. There'd be a manhunt for you. He's known since we arrived. Which means some at the White House know, too," Beth said steadily. "Headquarters would have access to the camera feeds—"

"Camera feeds?" the First Lady asked, confused, enraged.

"Ma'am, you know we're under full surveillance here. For your safety, we need eyes, but it's a highly secure feed."

"Apparently not," Anita Crusoe spat back. She noticed Anthony shift uncomfortably in his seat.

Anthony! Poor Anthony. He was in the video, too. They had exposed him.

"Oh my god," she turned to him. "I'm so sorry. I never imagined I'd get you caught up like this!"

He held up a reassuring hand. "Don't worry about me. It comes with the territory, I'll be fine. I'm only worried about you." He turned to Beth. "What would you like us to do?"

"We'd like you to hold in this room until we've swept the house to ensure there's no physical breach. My guess is someone took this from the feed. The director will have the cyber guys on that back at home. But we have to check."

"Thank you, Beth," Anthony said.

The First Lady was lost in thought.

Of course, someone took it from the feed. Patrick's people did this. It was a warning shot. They wanted her to know how displeased they were that she stymied their plans. And they didn't mind exposing her and her secrets to keep this under control.

How far would they go? she wondered.

"What are you thinking?" Anthony asked warily.

"Patrick hates it when things don't go as planned," she said. "I think he's underestimated me."

THE EARLYBIRD™/ MONDAY / 5:43 A.M.
THE E-NEWSLETTER TRUSTED BY WASHINGTON'S POLITICAL ELITE

Good morning, EarlyBirders™. Here are the morning's need-to-know stories.

SIREN: ILLICIT VIDEO OF THE FIRST LADY WITH ANOTHER MAN—WHITE HOUSE DOESN'T DENY AFFAIR—FIRST LADY'S OFFICE SILENT—DEVELOPING.

WHITE HOUSE BLASTS VIDEO: *Adam Majors:* "*It's a sad day when leading news organizations air illegally obtained surveillance footage of Mrs. Crusoe. This endangers the First Family. We will find and prosecute the leaker to the fullest extent of the law.*"

RATINGS BONANZA: The video boosted cablers. Look for **OVERNIGHT NUMBERS** soon!

EarlyReaders™ Want to Know: Who's the man in the video? What's his relationship to the First Lady? What does the president know? Where is the First Lady now?

Paging All Lobbyists: The *Washington Post* reports on a secret White House plan to freeze oil imports from the Persian Gulf and boost our oil exports from Latin America.

Spotted: ATN newcomer Natalie Savage and Karima Sahadi confabbing at Salon Badem.

15

BAND OF SISTERS

The website for the Bombay Club boasted of an environment that "emulates the characteristics of the old clubs of India." An apt description, Natalie thought, of both its Raj-era decor and its clientele.

Sitting there, she felt as though she was radiating excitement. Today her hair surpassed her fantasies of smooth silky manageability. And the timing couldn't have been better. She and Karima were seated at a prime corner table that commanded a view of the entire room—and allowed the entire room to see them. At the table on their left, Karima had explained, a lobbyist for the private prison industry was meeting with a lobbyist for the frozen foods industry. To their right, a deputy treasury secretary was meeting with a representative from the payday lending industry. Sprinkled among them were media celebrities who carried the regal bearing of representatives of the Crown, mingling with their subjects.

It didn't escape Natalie's notice that, even in the pinnacle of Empire ambiance, Karima seemed to occupy a place of honor. During the fifteen minutes since they'd been seated, a steady

stream of well-wishers had been eddying past to thank the socialite for hosting a fantastic luncheon/cocktail/fund-raiser/ball
which, each of them in turn insisted, was either "magical" or
"pure perfection."

The conversations followed a set pattern. First, Karima would
say, "Not at all, my darling," and then offer a thoughtful comment on a well-observed detail of their last conversation or
something wonderful they'd worn. After a moment the visitor would lean in close and ask how Karima was handling the
Terrible News in today's *Washington Post* (which said that the
administration was looking at a total shutdown of oil imports
from the Middle East). The question was always delivered in
the tone of a concerned friend but there was something almost
gleefully predatory lurking behind it.

Karima seemed not to notice. In the same warm, generous
tone, she would offer one of three replies: "Ah, this is the world
we live in," with the slightest arch of her delicate eyebrows; "It's
all a negotiation," with a subtle shake of the head; or "Friends
must remain friends. All will be well," capped with a reassuring smile.

Finally, she'd turn and introduce them to Natalie, as ATN's
newest rising star. "You must get to know one another," Karima
would insist, with a wink. "I will connect you by email."

Natalie understood that these introductions were worth
Karima's weight in career gold, catapulting her almost instan-
taneously into a new stratosphere of DC status and access. With
Karima's stamp of approval, she could officially become a person to know, and court. The only thing that marred the otherwise triumphant feel of this moment: her gratitude for Karima's
generosity was tempered, at the back of her mind, by a fear. It
was the antsy concern of a guest who isn't quite sure how much
the hotel bill will be, or if she'll be able to pay it. Because there
was no question that an operator with the experience and con-

nections of Karima Sahadi, wife of the ambassador to the Arab League, would want something in return.

Natalie's best guess was that Karima would want her help with the Terrible News, which could mean a loss of trillions in oil wealth for the countries her husband represents, and Natalie was growing increasingly uneasy about the approaching moment when she would have to tell Karima that she did not cover energy or oil and probably couldn't offer her anything even remotely useful.

When the stream of ill-wishers dissipated, Karima squeezed Natalie's hand. "Thank you for your patience. Everyone is so hungry for bad news. It is why they all come. Also they know what they read in the papers is nothing. It is—" She made a gesture like she was pushing away dirty air. "It is the amuse-bouche. Everyone wants the main course."

She lifted a single well-manicured finger to the maître d', and silver dishes of food materialized out of nowhere, though Natalie was sure they hadn't shown Karima a menu.

"The food here is quite good," Karima said. "It is a pity so few of us eat."

Natalie was uncertain whether that meant she should or shouldn't eat the food, but asked instead, "How did you learn to handle all the prying questions and people?"

"Ah, they just want to know if I will continue to be useful to them. And of course I will be. It is what it is." She winked. "But we are not here to talk about my troubles. We are here to talk about you and your career." Karima placed saffron rice and mango curry chicken on Natalie's plate, while leaving her own plate glaringly bare. "Since we met I have seen you on air. You are very good. Precise. Smart. Well informed. Why aren't you standing outside the Colombian embassy right now? Why did you let this boy take the big story?"

Unsure how to explain—or justify—her predicament and increasingly ashamed, Natalie stammered, "The short answer is, because Ryan got the scoop. His dad had a connection and now he's tight with Adam Majors."

Natalie did not expect Karima's big, genuine laugh. "I doubt it," she said. "His father was not particularly well liked as governor. Surely you know how this works. Bibb Connaught speaks to the White House all day long." She shook her head. "Adam Majors was an intern for Bibb's husband many years ago. I would assume she got the information and passed it to her protégé. It is useful to know the history of people," she said, tapping her forehead with a perfectly manicured nail.

Of course. She should have guessed Bibb was behind Ryan's perfect placement. Matt had been right. She was fully Team Ryan.

"Do not look so concerned, my love. There are ways around this. You have one thing going for you that the boy does not."

Natalie had to struggle to imagine what that might be. "A catchy last name?"

Karima chuckled. "No. You are a woman. In this town, women have a special kind of power."

Natalie felt a crushing disappointment. Of course, that's what Karima expected. She was an older generation.

"I don't think I'm cut out for that," Natalie said, aware how prudish she sounded. "Morality aside, I just can't manage to fake interest in a guy if I'm not actually interested. It doesn't go well." She didn't want Karima to start setting her up with married senators and lobbyists.

A line appeared between Karima's brows as she frowned with confusion. After a beat she gave another trill of laughter. "Oh. No, I did not mean—" She laughed a little more, then wiped her eyes. "Pardon me. No, I was not suggesting you use your female charms in the bedroom. Although, there are, of course, the network executives." Karima sighed. "The men in New York, they like to date the female staff in Washington and Chicago. Bureaus they can visit away from their wives. Do you golf? They like to take the girls to 'corporate golf tournaments.' This way they can expense it." She winked. "And Bibb would be powerless to stop it." For a moment Karima studied Natalie. "But no. I do not think you have what it takes to make it that way."

Where Natalie should have felt indignation and pride, she was instead overcome by a gaping vacuum of insecurity. She forced a laugh and said, "I guess I don't really have the looks for that. Or the lingerie."

Karima smiled. "I was thinking more you don't have the stomach for it. I wouldn't worry about the looks. Several of the men in the restaurant got cricks in their neck watching you when you walked in." She shook her head. "No, it is better the other way. You rely on our network."

"Your network?" Karima made it sound like a spy organization.

"Of women. In this town, the women help one another," Karima confided with a smile.

Bibb must not have gotten that memo, Natalie thought.

"Of course, not all of them," Karima added, as if reading Natalie's mind. "Your Bibb for example. She doesn't play well with other women. She only helps herself. But others..." Karima pointed across the room to a woman with a neck like a goose and short salt-and-pepper bobbed hair. "You see over there? That is Helen Cay."

Helen Cay needed no introduction to Natalie. She was one of the most respected political reporters in town.

"Seven years ago, she was hired from radio to cover Congress for network TV, but the executives in New York refused to put her on air. They said she was too ugly. Of course they knew what she looked like when they'd hired her." Karima made a gesture to convey the absurdity of this world. "The female senators she'd been covering for years saw what was happening and started feeding her stories, turning down interviews with anyone else. Left with no choice, the network eventually put Helen on air. Now they say she will get the Sunday show as soon as the anchor chair opens up."

Karima shifted, turning her gaze to an Indian woman in a bright blue silk blouse. "That's Carla Jacobs, one of the top lobbyists for the tech industry. Three female clients put her back in business when her husband ran off with the masseuse. Apparently he's since contracted an STD." She gave a mischievous wink. "Chasing youngsters comes with its risks."

Natalie flashed back to the moment she'd met Karima, and the feeling of secret sisterhood she'd felt at Salon Badem. She loved the idea that there might be an alternate hidden power structure in DC, one that let women like Helen Cay and Carla Jacobs wend their way around the obstacles that faced them. One to which Karima was offering her access.

"I would like very much if you could join me at my home for a cocktail party next Friday night," Karima said as she reached for her phone and started typing. "You will receive an invitation from my office. I've just asked them to email you." She placed her phone on the table and smiled warmly. "There will be many wonderful people for you to meet there. I will introduce you."

"Why are you helping me?" Natalie blurted, the question finally too loud in her head to hold in. "I know there are reporters who can give you more for a lunch than I can."

Karima didn't hesitate before answering. "I am helping you because you will owe me." She looked Natalie full in the eye and unapologetic. "And I am helping you because you are young and new and smart. You will figure this town out and I want to be among the first on your team. I require friends in the press and you will remember the people who helped you at the beginning."

"But I don't cover the energy sector. Or foreign policy. I really won't be able to report on oil," Natalie explained, wishing it were otherwise.

"You needn't report on my world to be helpful!" Karima said, looking amused. "I have many friends from the White House,

Congress, the business world, always looking for a way to place information. I help them reach you, they help me reach my goals." She smiled warmly. "Everyone wins."

"And what are your goals?" Natalie asked.

Karima smiled in a genuine way that made creases at the corners of her eyes.

"I like that you ask this. Many wouldn't. You are a good reporter."

Karima's cell phone, sitting on the table, began to buzz. When Natalie glanced at the screen, it read Jimmy's. Apologizing, Karima answered the call impatiently.

"Goodness, no!" she cried. "All of it must be out until I say so. No deliveries, not even wine. I thought we explained. Nothing at all." She paused. "Yes, the whole wine cellar. Dry." She hung up the phone, shaking her head. "I am trying to rid my house of alcohol. It's impossible to leave anything to others. Is it so difficult to understand what 'all of it' means?"

Until now, it hadn't occurred to Natalie how strange it must be for Karima Sahadi, a Muslim, to play the part of American hostess while following Islamic law. Did she have to have a dry house always, she wondered, or just when she entertained Muslim guests. That had to be complicated.

Karima's eyes went to Natalie's plate. "You have not touched the food. You do not like it?"

Embarrassed, Natalie glanced at Karima's plate and saw that it was still bare. She hadn't even taken any food. Apparently she wasn't one of those women who pretended they could eat anything they wanted and still keep a waiflike figure. She just avoided food altogether. In a twisted way, it endeared her to Natalie. Maybe this meant Karima made her moves in the open, Natalic thought, and didn't engage in elaborate pretend.

"It looks delicious, I'm just—I feel a bit overwhelmed," Natalie answered candidly.

Karima smiled at her with understanding. "Washington, DC,

can feel unnerving at first. It appears to be a place of much guile, but really it is very simple." She gestured to the room. "Here's what you should know. Everyone here wants more power. Mostly power comes through access. Of course, with money, too. You ask my job? My job is to be a fulcrum, the delicate point that maintains balance. Between the US and the Arab world, between my friends who are sometimes enemies with one another. If the balance is overturned, hurt feelings can become a tantrum. From spark to fire in no time."

"All relationships here are transactional," Natalie said, more as an observation than a question.

For a moment Karima seemed distracted, lost in thought. "You remind me of Anita when she and Patrick first got to DC. He had been preparing for it for years. But she—she was still surprised at how things worked." She shook her head, withdrawn. "Poor Anita."

At the mention of the First Lady, Natalie perked up. She understood that Karima was name-dropping, her relationship with the First Lady was likely no less transactional than all other DC relationships. Still any insight was valuable.

"You know, I urged her to stay with him. I told her they are good together," Karima said.

"So, she did leave him?" Natalie asked, on alert. "Are they separating?"

Karima tensed. "I meant early on, when they were still dating. We've known them for years. Raheem worked with Patrick in his mineral and gas days, before he made his money." She sighed and her eyes became slightly unfocused. "They were perfectly matched. Her beauty, his drive. And Patrick was a good friend." She shook her head and her gaze became direct again. "His speech in Dubai was a deep disappointment. You know about it, of course? Dismissing years of alliance between the US and the Middle East. It's put a real strain on the relationship, as you might imagine." She frowned. "And now he sits by as

Anita's good name and reputation are slandered. It's astonishing he's doing nothing about it!"

"In fairness, the First Lady hasn't pushed back either," Natalie said, seeing an opportunity to get information. "Why do you think she isn't appearing in public and answering reporters' questions? She could just tell us who this guy is. It'd be really easy for her to put this to bed." She stopped when she realized that might not sound good. "I mean, put this whole thing behind her."

She was relieved to see Karima chuckle. "Why should she come out and show herself? If she were to state the truth, she would be disbelieved, attacked—by the press, by the public. Surely by Washington. Too much truth makes you a threat. No, they would ruin her reputation beyond what we've seen." She paused, as if she was trying to convince herself. "No. The White House should be expressing outrage. Her husband should defend her. That would, as you say, put it to bed."

Natalie leaned forward. "You're convinced she's not having an affair?"

"This is silliness." Karima waved her hand.

"But the video," Natalie said. "It might not prove an affair, but it certainly suggests it. Do you have any idea who leaked it?"

Karima shifted in her seat. "These are good questions. But as you know, the public story is so rarely the real one. Like with your little Ryan getting his scoop. Ask yourself who stands to benefit from that tape? From making it? From leaking it?"

"I don't know," Natalie said, feeling frustrated with herself.

"Not yet," Karima said. "But you are smart. And if you keep your ears open, you will."

After a moment of consideration, Karima added, "Here's a bit of a head start. Perhaps you will do me a favor? Look into a company called Sallee LLC. You can remember that name? Let me know what you find."

"Do you have a—?" Natalie was interrupted when her cell phone started to jump. *Bibb.*

Glancing apologetically at Karima, she answered it.

Bibb was speaking before Natalie finished saying hello. "An aide from the First Lady's office was overheard on his cell phone at a Starbucks. He said the First Lady is in St. Tropez. You're on a 3 p.m. flight out of National Airport. Get there ASAP."

Natalie's heart soared. Breaking news—and a trip to the French Riviera. *Score!*

Karima took it well. She stood and kissed Natalie on both cheeks. Right before they parted, she whispered. "Sallee LLC. Don't forget."

THE EARLYBIRD™/ TUESDAY / 6:34 A.M.
THE E-NEWSLETTER TRUSTED BY WASHINGTON'S POLITICAL ELITE

Good morning, EarlyBirders™. Here are the morning's need-to-know stories.

BREAKING NEWS: *STAFFER OVERHEARD—FLOTUS FLEES TO FRENCH RIVIERA—WHITE HOUSE PANICKED—IS THIS A RUNAWAY WIFE?*

Situational Awareness: An EarlyBird™ Timeline of FLOTUS Developments

*8 Days Ago: First Lady a No-Show at Summit Dinner
*4 Days Ago: Video Surfaces of FLOTUS with Mystery Man
*1 Day Ago: Late Word Leaks FLOTUS on Escapade in St. Tropez
*This Morning: No White House Comment, No First Lady Sightings
  Networks will be live from St. Tropez's white sand beaches all day.

¡ATENCIÓN! With 21-year-old Colombian party boy Rigo Lystra still in hiding, Venezuela's president tells the *Washington Post* the situation is "ridículo."

HOLLYWOOD LOVES SONIA: Lystra's accuser, Venezuelan actress **Sonia Barbaro**, set to arrive in US this week. Her prize winning film *Trafficked* premieres in Los Angeles, Friday.

EarlySponsor™: GlobalCom™** Is Proud to Support the **Union of Latin American Nations**. In Times of Crisis, **ULAN** Boosts Regional Cooperation for Peace and Stability.

16

THE CAMERAMAN AND THE SEA

Natalie sat motionless in a desk chair in front of the muted TV in a room at the Miami Beach Hampton Inn, longing for at least twenty minutes of uninterrupted silence. She was tired of all the voices, including her own. The last time she'd been by herself was in a stall at the Miami airport bathroom seventeen hours earlier. Now she found herself fondly recalling the comparative quiet of flushing toilets and Dyson hand driers.

Her reverie was interrupted by the sound of Nelly Jones's voice, suddenly at full volume, asking, "How would a White House divorce work? We'll tell you, tonight. 10 p.m. Eastern on *TalkTalk Live*."

Opening her eyes, Natalie looked at Matt, seated next to her. He was gripping a remote control which was wrapped in a plastic bag.

Eyeing the baggie, she tried not to giggle.

"What?" Matt asked, spinning toward her. "Why are you smiling?"

"I'm glad to see you're taking precautions with the remote control. Are you practicing safe TV set?"

"The hotel remote control is a biological petri dish. Touching it would expose me and everyone around me to near-certain contagion." He said holding the plastic-covered device up for her to see. "The front desk was kind enough to provide this remote control sanitation option and I feel it is prudent to use it."

"Is bag from ice bucket," Dasha said from her chair by the camera. "Maybe used. For sure not clean."

Matt squinted at her and went back to the TV.

"I smoke," Dasha said, exiting the room.

Natalie, Matt, and Dasha had been holed up in the ground floor suite at the Miami Beach Hampton Inn, "Where Breakfast Is On Us! And The Fun Is On YOU!" for seventeen of the longest hours of her life.

This was not what Natalie had expected when she'd boarded the flight out of DC the prior afternoon. At the airport they'd received a call from a What Girl: "You're ticketed to go to Miami on the 3 p.m. flight."

Foolishly leaning on logic, Natalie had attempted to clarify, "You mean St. Tropez, right?"

This prompted the What Girl to scoff, "No. Bibb says you'll be out of position if we send you to St. Tropez. Plus it's too expensive. We got you a hotel not far from South Beach."

The words hit Natalie like a noxious cloud. All her journalistic instincts told her to run. Flee. Get on a flight to St. Tropez where she'd find the real story about FLOTUS and career oxygen. But Dasha was on the phone lining up a rental car and Matt, maneuvering his roll-y bag with one hand and a Starbucks and his cell phone with the other, announced that the control room needed them live on air from Miami ASAP. She took a deep breath—*better get used to this*—and followed Matt's roll-y bag through the terminal.

They'd arrived at the Hampton Inn just before 6 p.m. and made their way to suite 155 which was decorated with matching comforter, drapes, and upholstery in a motif that could best be described as monkeys having sex.

Instantly Dasha had swung into gear. In a feat bordering on genius, she'd removed a pane of glass from the window, instructed the satellite truck to back up right outside, then she'd run cables from the truck through the empty window frame, hooking them up to the lights and camera inside. By 6:45 p.m., Dasha had positioned Natalie on top of a stepladder, which meant that on camera all you could see was Natalie's torso against a dusk backdrop of the sand and darkening sea beyond.

"Is how we do in Irbil," Dasha had explained as she was setting up the camera. Gesturing to the windowless indoor set, she'd said, "Is safer from shrapnel."

Natalie understood that reporting from the Miami Beach Hampton Inn was a bad idea, a news disaster waiting to happen. It might lead viewers to believe she was reporting from St. Tropez, which would be a lie. It also might cause her to tumble three feet off a stepladder onto the floor of a Hampton Inn while live on TV. One of these fears was confirmed when, during her first live shot, the anchor tossed to her, saying, "We go to our Natalie Savage, live from St. Tropez."

As soon as the camera was off, she'd called the news desk. "We'll get crucified when people figure out we're in Miami. Can you imagine the item they'll write in TVBuzzster?" she'd moaned to Hal on the phone. "Would you please get me reassigned to St. Tropez where the story is actually happening?"

"You're right. We can't mislead viewers," Hal replied, followed by, "So I will personally make sure the anchors never again say where you are. Everyone is good with it," he assured her. Implying she should be, too.

A tingle of apprehension shot down her spine. Before getting off the phone, he advised her to disable the location settings on her Facebook and Twitter apps.

"In fairness, we're not misleading anyone," Matt said. "As

long as they don't say you're in St. Tropez, we're in the clear. It's on viewers if they assume you're in Europe."

"Great. I'll remind my credibility of that when it's taking a beating in a dark Twitter alley," Natalie said, wondering whether it was a coincidence that the very characteristic for which the Chief had praised her—her credibility—was being tested by Bibb.

The more she thought about it, the more it seemed deliberate. Now her mind was stuck in a loop, playing out the dual admonitions she seemed to get from everyone in the business. "Be a team player" and "beat them at their own game." Did no one notice that the two things were at odds?

Her stomach grumbled and she realized she hadn't eaten in forever. She glanced at the clock. 11:35 a.m. Well past breakfast time, for normal people. In her current world, nice distinctions like breakfast and lunch had simply become a question of Doritos or Cheez-Its.

Natalie's phone buzzed and she welcomed the distraction, until she saw who it was.

MOM: Hi, dear. I was away from the TV for the last 20 minutes. Were you on again?

MOM: Judging by the bags under your eyes, I think you might have blocked sinuses. Am I right? Maybe you want to do a steam in the shower, it will loosen your mucus.

MOM: When you're home for the wedding, I'll give you a saline rinse for your sinuses.

MOM: I say this to help you!!! Love you.

Natalie shut her eyes, jammed her palms into her sockets and did silent screaming in her head. Did everyone's mother notice these things? Was thirty-two too old to care when your mother noticed these things?

"What has happened? Greasy have news?" It was Dasha, back from her smoking break and mistaking Natalie's fetal position for a Ryan-reaction.

"Don't mention McGreasy," Matt said in a loud fake whisper. "*Someone's* in a mood."

"Greasy always has news!" Natalie said in a voice that sounded a little borderline hysterical even to herself. She glared at the TV. As if by magic, Ryan appeared on screen. He was live! From the Colombian embassy! (The real one.) Looking Earnest and Sincere! The headline blared: "When Girls Make Good Boys Go Bad."

"Turn it up," Natalie and Dasha said at once.

"I know the pain Rigo is suffering because I have lived through it myself," Ryan was saying, with Heartfelt Intensity.

Natalie and Matt exchanged horrified looks. Was Ryan about to confess to something?

"In college, one my closest friends, we'll call him Jeff, was on the wrong side of a false accusation." Ryan paused for a Deep Breath. "Jeff had it all going for him. Six-three, thick hair, arm like a rocket launcher, headed to a big-time career with a hedge fund that had more than five billion in assets." Ryan hesitated, looking like he might cry. "Then, his senior year, a sophomore accused him of raping her—on a night when he was too drunk to do anything like that!" Ryan's face was a mask of horror and disbelief. "It ruined his life."

On TV, Heath asked, "What happened to your friend?"

"He graduated a year late. Lost the hedge fund job. He's working at a mutual fund in Boston now." Ryan shook his head, looking dejected. "Compared to where he was headed, it's real bad."

"This is tragedy?" Dasha said, her body nearly vibrating with anger. "Why does he say these stupid things?"

Heath looked like he was working hard to appear moved by the story. "And what happened to the woman?"

For a moment Ryan looked truly surprised, as though the thought hadn't occurred to him. "Great question," he said, reporter speak for I-have-no-fucking-idea. But Ryan bounced back fast, or Andrea, in his ear, did. "Maybe she's somewhere in that crowd." He gestured toward the protesters behind him. "My point is, these things ruin lives. And Rigo's story is putting an important spotlight on this crisis of false accusations."

"There's no way we're going to beat Ryan," Natalie sighed, falling back in her chair. "There is no way I can match him for drama and absurdity."

"We must crush him," Dasha said.

"Yes, and I know how we can start." Matt fixed Natalie with a meaningful look.

"I'm not wearing a bikini top, we've been over this," she replied to his unspoken demand.

"I wasn't going to say that. Yet. But you could show more skin," he said, "Maybe a tank top?"

"No."

"What's wrong? Are you malformed? Do you have an embarrassing tattoo? That's it, isn't it. What does it say?"

"You wouldn't ask Ryan to wear a tank top," she countered.

Matt looked offended. "If Ryan could come up with a reason, he'd be on air in a muscle shirt in no time. In fact if I were Andrea, I'd be racking my brain trying to figure out a way to make that happen." He gestured to the beach out the window. "Meanwhile we're in the land of fun and sun, and you won't even wear something sleeveless."

"Let's play a game," Natalie said. "Whoever is quiet the longest wins."

He turned away. She closed her eyes and noticed that it was starting to get hot in the room. With the glass missing from the window, she knew the air-conditioning wouldn't stand a chance against Miami humidity. *Let's hope The Treatment holds.*

Standing up, she walked to the bathroom, closed the door, and looked in the mirror. In thick TV makeup, she looked like the wax museum version of herself. Or a corpse ready for an open casket funeral. She would have killed for a shower but with the mask of makeup, she couldn't even splash her face with water.

Leaning toward the mirror, she studied her reflection. Her mom was right: there *were* bags under her eyes. At least her hair was straight. Remarkably straight, given the humidity. Victory! she thought and managed a smile.

She dampened a washcloth, unbuttoned her shirt, and wiped down her neck, upper chest, and armpits. *Relief.* She closed her eyes and was feeling some calm when there was a banging on the door.

"Go time." It was Matt. "The chopper is up. They want you live."

"What's happening?" she asked, opening her eyes and buttoning up her shirt.

"The photographer found a yacht. FLOTUS is on it," Matt told her. "They think it's Leonardo DiCaprio's boat."

Heart racing, she flung open the door. "FLOTUS is doing Leonardo DiCaprio?" Hell, if that were true, she might even consider a bikini top.

Natalie was standing on the stepladder three feet off the ground staring straight ahead. There were two diva lights shining in her eyes, one with diffused color to soften her features and make her glow, another under her chin to fill shadows under her eyes cast from the bright sun. Two high-intensity HMI lights were flooding the space around her to create a sunlit look to counter the brighter sun outside. She knew that if they were in St. Tropez they'd be outside and none of this would have been necessary. Not for the first time, Natalie was struck by how much more work faking it took than the real thing.

"Stand by to go live. Your anchor is Heath," a voice said in her ear. "You ready?"

"Ready!" Natalie chirped as a flash of excitement raced to her stomach.

Bibb had hired a helicopter and a paparazzi to troll the coastline searching for signs of FLOTUS. According to Hal, the helicopter pilot had located a VVIP yacht in international waters; the pilot was now hovering overhead with a cameraman ready to go live.

A new voice said in Natalie's ear, "Coming to you in 30. In 15. In 10."

Silence. Followed by a clash of symbols and thunderous music—the ATN breaking news intro. A tingle ran up her spine.

The next voice was Heath's. "Welcome back to ATN and our fast-developing breaking news. All eyes are on the glamorous beaches of St. Tropez, a playground for the rich and famous. It's known for its ten-thousand-dollar-a-night hotel rooms and all-night party scene. And now, perhaps, as the hideaway for the First Lady." He turned to another camera. "We go now to our own Natalie Savage, who has been tracking Anita Crusoe to the sandy beaches of the French Riviera. Natalie, we have news?"

Natalie smiled, admiring the smooth way Heath handled her intro. Tracking the First Lady to the French Riviera. It was close to the wind but not flying right into it, she thought, wondering if that was actually a valid nautical metaphor.

"Hello, Heath," she said cheerily. "It's nearly 4 p.m. St. Tropez time, where the party kids are just starting to wake up from their disco naps. In an exciting development, a member of our team has located a mysterious luxury yacht. There is reason to believe the First Lady could be on board. Luques Frier, a local photographer, is joining us now from a helicopter above the Mediterranean Sea. Luques, tell us what you're seeing."

An image of an exceedingly long white yacht floating on teal blue water filled the screen. Its name, the *Xury*, was stenciled on the transom. The scratchy sounds of a Frenchman talking into a headset came into Natalie's ear.

"Natalie, we believe this is the yacht of Leonardo DiCaprio." It came out *zuh YAAT of Le-O-NAR-doh Dee-CAP-rio.* Luques went on to explain that when the yacht docked the night before, there were reports that the captain had requested extra security to escort his guests to a restaurant on the coast. Paparazzi had materialized, the yacht had pulled away without disgorging any of its elusive guests, and for these reasons, Luques believed the First Lady was on board.

"Interesting. So you believe the First Lady is on board because the guests required security? Do we have any other information validating that?" Natalie asked, troubled he'd jumped to such a conclusion.

"Hey! Go along with it!" a voice in her ear said. In her peripheral vision, she could see Matt putting his head in his hands.

Be a team player. Increase your VOP, she told herself. *Rate now, report later.*

Working to sound coolheaded and in command, Natalie did as the voices in her ear advised. "Luques, is there any indication who is on board the yacht now?" she asked. "Any signs of DiCaprio, the First Lady, or the Secret Service?"

"We'll get a closer look," Luques declared, and to Natalie's surprise the helicopter dropped twenty feet closer to the water as the camera zoomed into the ship's tinted windows.

"I cannot see zee persons, but we know they are there!"

Someone in the control room yelped into Natalie's ear, "We've got a photo of the First Lady receiving an award with DiCaprio. We have it ready to go whenever you want to toss to it."

Natalie took a breath. "Luques," she said, "I want to show our viewers this photograph. It was taken—"

"—two years ago," the voice from the control room said in her ear.

"—at a charity function two years ago. Leonardo DiCaprio and the First Lady receiving an award together," Natalie said.

The voice in her ear added, "For the environment!"

"In recognition of their work protecting the environment."

"Natalie, have him get closer—zoom in," the voice said.

"Luques, do you think you can get a closer look? Those windows are awfully dark."

The camera zoomed closer until she could see the silhouettes of several people inside. It was impossible to make out their faces. Still, Natalie's heartbeat started racing, like she'd just run a red light.

"Luques," she said, "think we could try zooming in on the other side of the yacht?"

"Great, great direction," someone said in Natalie's ear. "Just keep it moving. More angles. More questions."

As Luques started to answer, a figure in a crew uniform raced out from behind the smoky sliding glass doors onto the deck of the yacht. He was just below the chopper shaking his fist directly at the camera, screaming, his face nearly purple with rage. It was impossible to hear him over the roar of the propellers.

"What's he saying?" the control room yelled.

"Luques, can you make out what he's saying?"

The uniformed crew member stalked back into the boat and Luques launched into a disquisition about the maritime rights of photographers. He was in the middle of insisting "zee photographers have zee right to film zee boats" when another man, presumably the captain, emerged on the deck, brandishing a long black gun. It looked just like the ones Natalie had seen in the hands of the Big Horn survivalists when she'd covered their standoff with the Wyoming National Guard. That had ended badly for everyone involved, except ATN, which blessedly had time to black out the gory parts before the video made air.

Now, Natalie stared into the camera, feeling one part worried she was about to watch a live shooting on television, one part thrilled that it would be hers, *exclusively.*

"Is Remington 700," Dasha said from behind the camera. "Good gun. Has laser sight."

Natalie didn't wait for direction this time. "Luques, he's got a rifle," she said urgently.

Suddenly there were multiple voices shouting in her ear. "Stay! Hold the shot!"

Natalie's heart started racing in a new way. Like she was watching someone get targeted by a massive-rifle-with-laser-sight kind of way.

"Stay on the shot, Luques," she heard herself say.

The helicopter circled the boat while the captain screamed and, gripping the rifle, ran to the other side of the deck. For a split second Natalie was outside the moment, watching it. The two high-intensity lights in her eyes, TV makeup spackled on her skin, a piece of plastic wedged in her ear, Matt five feet away, laughing, while she stood perched above the ground on their make-believe set in their midlevel motel room. *Is this really happening? Any of it?* In that moment the scene on the monitor seemed as fake—or surreal—as her beachside backdrop.

"Luques, you're doing a great job, just hold that shot," Natalie said, fighting to ignore the awful feeling of dread flooding in with her adrenaline. Without warning the captain raised the gun to his shoulder and fired. In her ear Natalie heard a scream and then the shot went black.

Behind the camera Dasha nodded. "Is very good gun."

The next five minutes were chaos. With no video, Natalie was forced to sift through the voices screaming in her earpiece. She tried to deliver salient information about what had just happened. Relief flooded her when she learned that she had not, in fact, participated in broadcasting the death of two people.

The captain had aimed not for the chopper but for the camera, shooting it out of Luques' hands. By shooting him in the wrist. The helicopter pilot reported that there was a lot of blood, so he was flying Luques to the hospital.

Since New York wasn't interested in that part of the story, Natalie signed off and unplugged her earpiece. Her body felt clammy and her mouth felt dry.

Matt helped her down off the step stool, his face split by a huge grin. "How do you feel?"

"Like I've just taken part in something unclean," she said. *I pressured a man to risk his life, for nothing.*

She was headed to the bathroom to splash cold water on her face when her phone rang.

"Natalie, my girl, that was phenomenal. High stakes. Real tension. Totally diverting. Felt fresh. Well done!" It was the Chief. "You are surprising me, Natalie. I'm very happy with your work."

"I'm so glad, Chief," she said, feeling not so much glad as opportunistic. She decided to seize the moment. "Sir, do you think it's possible we could report the rest of the story from St. Tropez? I think—"

"Oh no need," the Chief interrupted with a chuckle. "We spoke with the Mayor of St. Tropez. The First Lady isn't there." He paused. "I stuck with the story because I had a feeling it'd be great TV. Good thing I did. I suspect your VOP is going to be in the stratosphere today."

Natalie looked at the hotel TV where ATN was rerunning video of the yacht with the Breaking News banner "FLOTUS on DiCaprio Boat?"

She felt her surprise shift to anger. The boss knew FLOTUS wasn't on the boat, and he made her play along with the cameraman anyway? This was a whole new class of pushing the limits. Not only ethically, but personally. They'd put her credibility on the line and Luques's safety. They'd set her up, used her, let a man get shot—

"Sir, are you saying—?"

"My dear, I have to jump," the Chief said. "You've got to watch what our boy Ryan is about to do!" And he was gone.

Natalie's mind was spinning.

"Holy shit!" Matt yelped and Natalie watched him stab the remote control through his antibacterial plastic baggie. He and Dasha began staring like zombies at the TV. Natalie shifted her gaze to see what they were looking at.

On air, Ryan was standing in front of the protesters outside the embassy and—

Natalie blinked to make sure her eyes weren't lying.

"Is he—undressing?" Natalie asked slowly.

Matt and Dasha were too mesmerized to respond.

Ryan's hand had moved from his top button to the second, and third, and was now unbuttoning his shirt to reveal his chest.

"They say only women are sexualized in our culture. Well, are we sure?" Ryan said as he continued the slow tease, now down to his navel. He looked somewhere outside the shot, presumably at his producer, Andrea, and winked. "To challenge that theory, I am removing my shirt on camera." He shrugged out of it and let it drop giving the camera a stunning view of his eight-pack. "If this video of my naked chest goes viral online, if it shows up in chat rooms," Ryan said, sounding Defiant and Full of Intent, "if it is discussed on entertainment shows, if I'm booked on talk shows or the subject of other reports simply for showing my chest on air, I say we rethink this whole idea that women are the only ones being objectified."

He was standing, somehow glistening and shirtless, in front of a sea of female protesters, delivering a polemic about the plight of hot twentysomething dudes with TV gigs.

This should be a soda ad, Natalie thought.

That was drowned out by another thought. Matt was right.

The mind control shattered. Matt was now looking at Natalie. "Do I get to say I told you so now or should I—?"

"Shut up."

An hour later, the breakfast Doritos weren't aging well nor was Ryan's stunt striptease. A What Girl had called and ordered the team to "shelter in place" until the Chief decided their next assignment. Natalie had found a French florist to deliver flowers to Luques's hospital room—the least she could do—and was now in the hotel gym, in exercise gear and crouched over the handlebars of a rusty Nautilus bicycle, her mind running in circles with her legs. She was cycling through a mess of self-recrimination and doubt. Turning up the music, she tried to focus on Beyoncé, but the image of Ryan unbuttoning his shirt had taken up permanent residence in her mind. *How did I not see this coming?* she thought as Bey belted it out. *What can I do to compete? Surely there's an obvious way to up my game or lower my standards and beat Ryan.*

She was moving double time nearly at the end of the song when she noticed her phone ringing. "Hello," she answered without looking at the caller ID.

"Natalie, my girl, it sounds like you're in a wind tunnel. Where are you?" It was the Chief.

"Sorry, I'm at the gym," she said trying to slow down her legs.

"Fantastic. Important to get in those workouts and stay trim. Speaking of which, can we get your cameraman to frame you a little looser? Don't sue me for saying this but you have a nice chest and we're a visual medium. I'd like to see more of you on camera, if you know what I mean."

"Of course," she said, telling her dignity to stand down. This was an opening to speak up and ask for an assignment that would play to her strengths. One that involved actual reporting.

"I was very impressed with your work today," the Chief was saying. "I like bringing your gravitas and smarts to more entertaining stories. Powerful combination."

There's nothing wrong with entertaining viewers, she told her conscience before it could protest.

"How would you like to get together and discuss new ways to pursue this?" the Chief asked.

Okay, this is going in the right direction. "I'd love that, Chief," she said hurriedly. "I can be on a plane to New York tonight. Do you want to meet tomorrow?"

He chuckled. "No need, my dear, I'm in Miami Beach. Flew down with Jazzmyn this morning for a golf tournament."

She felt a chill, suddenly sensitive to the air-conditioning and her clothes, damp with sweat. Karima's words echoed in her head—*The New York executives like to take the girls to corporate golf tournaments. This way they can expense it*—and she was hit with a reflexive wave of judging Jazzmyn.

"Oh. I hope it was a successful," Natalie said, aiming for a neutral tone.

"Yes, great game. Jazzmyn had to head home with a family emergency. Maybe you want to join me for dinner?"

Shivering, she got off the bike, found a gym towel, and wrapped it around her shoulders. She'd heard the Chief's words and knew she should be excited—dinner in Jazzmyn's place. In Miami. That's an offer any reporter would kill for—but instead felt rolling anxiety. *What if he wants more than dinner?* Pulling the towel in tight she thought *no, there's no way. With all the MeToo stuff, there's no way he'd risk it. Would he?*

"I really want to see you do well, Natalie," the Chief was saying. "And I think if we put our heads together, we can make it happen."

An offer you can't refuse.

"That'd be great," she heard herself agree.

"Wonderful! I'll have my assistant contact you with details. See you this evening," the Chief exclaimed, as if he was surprised by her reply. As if he thought she had a choice.

17

SEXUALPOLITIK

The Nuit Noir Lounge had a certain brothel feel to it, with indigo velvet curtains you didn't want to brush up against and the kind of seedy splendor that only sticky seats and the scent of Pine-Sol-over-dried-beer confers. It was still early afternoon so the dim interior was cool and relatively quiet. There were plenty of booths but Natalie, Matt, and Dasha had slid into seats at the bar, drawn by the warm glow of several television sets. It was a professional hazard, particularly when the screens were all tuned to local news.

They'd agreed to meet for a midafternoon council of war which they now put on hold to watch a wide-awake-looking anchor nod emphatically at her coanchor and say, "That was a really fascinating story, Rob."

Matt pointed at the TV. "That means, I wasn't listening to anything you said, in Reportuguese."

"In what?" Natalie asked.

"The language of television reporters," he said. "It's probably more like a dialect, actually, but it's totally different than print. I'm studying it."

Perched on her stool, Natalie leaned slightly away from Matt. "Really? Give me another example."

Matt pointed at the screen where a reporter had just said, "Time will tell. Back to you, Rob." Matt continued, "Time will tell. Translation, I have no fucking idea how to end this live shot."

"Yes!" Natalie laughed, getting into it. "Sometimes that also means 'Olive Garden closes in twenty minutes so let's wrap this up pronto.'"

"Or Yarmouk Martyrs Brigade has laid siege to the town," broke in Dasha. "Turn off all lights and take cover before RPGs strike."

"Wow, duly noted," Matt said as he stared straight ahead, eyes wide.

After a moment of consideration Natalie added, "You know which is my favorite? Stay tuned."

"What does stay tuned mean?" Matt asked.

"It means, I have a lead on a story and I'm not letting you in on it till I've got it solid. So get ready." For a moment she remembered that feeling, the satisfaction of being on a killer story.

"Stay tuned," Dasha said and nodded. "Is good."

When the TV cut to commercial, the group got silent and Natalie suspected they were all having the same thought: how nice it'd be to chase down a real lead on a real story. For example, they could be investigating where the First Lady *really* went. Her mind flashed to an image of herself walking in slow motion, coat flapping behind her, hair perfectly silky, through the streets of the First Lady's hometown of Maraicabo, hunting down clues to her disappearance. Watch out, people, reporter on the case.

"All right, cell phones out, everyone," Matt ordered, interrupting the reverie as he spun around on his barstool. "Time to research the opposition. We need to know just how strong the opponent is. We'll devise a strategy for attack."

Acquiescing, Natalie pulled up her social media accounts but she already knew what she'd find: a total ass-whooping by Team Ryan.

On Twitter #McChesty was trending; a Facebook page called Ryan Raw had 13,200 followers; and he'd already inspired a BuzzFeed listicle of the top topless photos of the decade.

"It hasn't even been a full five hours," Matt marveled, looking at a POPSUGAR slideshow of screenshots of his bare chest which they'd edited into a montage over the song "I Don't Know How to Love Him."

"He's a genius," Natalie murmured. "He's made himself a victim, a sex symbol, and an advocate all at once." She shook her head. "An absolute genius."

Dasha, who had been staring at the pictures of Ryan, grunted. "Too many muscles. Why chest so shiny? Why hair so greasy?" she sneered. "This is boy, not man."

The waiter came by to take their orders.

"Who's ready for shots? Tequila?" Matt asked.

"I'm not drinking," Natalie said.

"Come on, Savage. Don't be a bore. We all need a drink. It's the only move."

"We bond," Dasha said, knocking on the bar. "We drink."

"Nah, I don't drink," Natalie said firmly.

"What do you mean you don't drink?" Matt looked bewildered. "All reporters drink. It's mandatory."

"Where I am from, many people *maskünem*. Is okay," Dasha said and mimed taking a shot in an imitation of a drunk.

"I'm not an alcoholic," Natalie shot back, more sharply than she'd intended. Then, feeling she'd been rude to Dasha, added, quietly, "My dad was."

Stop this at once, young lady, she heard her mother's voice in her head. *There is no need to air the family's dirty laundry in front of everyone.*

"I am sorry," Dasha said, with a softness that surprised Natalie.

"Oh it's fine," Natalie waved the sympathy away. "He quit when I was a kid."

As she explained, she flashed to a memory of her dad at his desk littered with empty green bottles of Canada Dry ginger ale, his go-to addiction after he'd gone sober.

"Beats taking up smoking," he'd tell Noreen whenever she'd harangue him about the link between sugary beverages and heart disease.

"Wow, a crack in the armor," Matt said, eyeing Natalie with surprise and something that approached compassion. "She admits a vulnerability."

"I hardly see how *not* drinking is a vulnerability," she countered.

Matt ordered two tequilas and picked up a menu. "How about food?" he asked, checking his watch. "It's only four o'clock but we may as well eat. Who knows where in the world we'll be by dinner."

"I think we'll be here in Miami tonight," she said vaguely. "Pretty sure."

"Why do you say that?" Matt asked, looking surprised.

Natalie stared at the bar top, simultaneously wanting to come clean about her dinner plans and dreading Matt's response.

"The Chief's in town," she said quickly. "He came with Jazzmyn for a golf tournament but she had to leave, so he asked me to have dinner."

"What? That's fantastic!" Matt lit up. "Best news all day! This means he's leaning Team Natalie. It could increase our VOP."

She smiled, telling herself Matt's right. *This is a good thing*, she intoned silently, trying to beat her intuition into submission. She looked over at Dasha, who let out a slow whistle, then made a clicking sound with her tongue.

"What?" Natalie asked defensively.

"You meet at restaurant or hotel?" Dasha asked.

Natalie shook her head slowly. "I don't know."

"Avoid hotel," Dasha said ominously.

"What are you guys talking about?" Matt asked, incredulous. "The head of the network wants a one-on-one with you. This is great!"

Ignoring Matt, Natalie shifted to face Dasha. "But what do you think he'd do?"

Dasha considered this a moment and then offered, "Maybe is like Abu Fazl, from Saddam's army. Always asking girls for dinner in hotel room. He put pills in wine, then put wang in girl." Her eyes got a faraway gleam in them. "Abu Fazl had very bad death."

A shocked laugh burst from Natalie. "Of course he did."

"You guys are being crazy," Matt insisted. "There is no way the Chief wants you to be his sloppy seconds."

Dasha shot him a dose of Watch Yourself eye and he amended, "I just mean that he'd get fired if he tried anything. Too many guys have been taken out for MeToo stuff. No way he's risking his career to play hide the sausage with you."

Natalie shot Matt a quizzical look and let out a hollow laugh. "Who are you kidding? He wouldn't lose his job because I'd never complain."

"*Govno!*" Dasha agreed. "Never. Not after what happen with Raheema in Baghdad."

Natalie spun around to face Dasha. "What happened with Raheema in Baghdad?"

Shaking her head Dasha said. "For sure you have heard this. Raheema had problem with you-know-who whacking off in car on assignment. She report whacking and now she doing weather in Youngstown."

"Oh right," Natalie said with a knowing look.

"What? Who? Who did that?" Matt demanded, nearly hysterical.

Dasha scowled at him and, narrowing her eyes, said to Natalie, "Is also bad with Hal."

"Hal is such a creep," she agreed. "He stopped by my building the other night and asked to come up at, like, 11 p.m. He's been punishing me ever since."

Dasha's eyes darkened and she looked around the room as if to assure herself that Assad's forces weren't lurking in the shadows. "I hear rumor. With the young girls, he presses the wang into the back."

Matt rocketed forward in his chair. "What did you just say?"

"The assignment girls. When she sit at computer, Hal make the wang hard, stand behind, then push wang into her." She made a disapproving face. "Wang attack."

"That's disgusting." Natalie wrinkled her nose, remembering how Hal had grazed her body in the editorial meeting. And Bibb had been sitting right there in front of them. Come to think of it. "I bet Bibb knows. She's an A and A."

"What's this? A and A?" asked Dasha.

"Aider and abettor," Natalie explained. "Enabler. I think there's one at every place. The senior woman in management who scares the female employees under her into silence and submission."

"Yes, they make the system working." Dasha got a faraway look in her eyes. "They punish the women who make the complaint. Too much complaint and they say this girl is crazy. This girl get Abu Fazl killed. This girl is rough."

"Tough," Natalie corrected. "They call us tough."

"Okay, tough," Dasha agreed. "They like better we say nothing."

"I don't understand," said Matt, exasperated. "If Hal's so bad and you guys all know, why don't you turn him in to HR?"

"Haven't you heard anything we've just said?" asked Natalie, indignant. "HR doesn't care. Why don't *you* turn him in? Now you know as much about his creepiness as we do."

Matt threw his hands up. "Okay, okay! I'm not the enemy."

"HR worst," Dasha elaborated. "Like KGB, secret police."

"Yep, if you complain, they paper your file to show that you're the problem." Natalie sighed. "HR exists to protect management from the employees."

"Yah. Nelly Jones, too," Dasha said, shaking her head.

Natalie straightened to attention. "What about Nelly?"

"She taping special on harassment. Big show. Six cameras," Dasha said and gave a hollow laugh. "For sure will not mention problem at ATN."

"Oh my god, could you even imagine?" Natalie agreed, laughing.

Matt held up a shot of tequila and said, "Well, cheers to us. Reporters obliged by management *to expose everyone else's dirty secrets*, while hiding our own."

"Cheers," said Natalie, raising her glass of water. "To the total double standard we live with. Like how Chesty can take off his shirt and he becomes stronger and more untouchable for it. But if I tried—"

"If you did that, our VOP would be through the roof," Matt said, bitterly.

Laughing, Natalie felt herself relax. Strange, but it felt good to say all this out loud. No one ever discussed these things at the office, as if group silence was the price of participation.

"Enough." Dasha banged her hands on the bar. "We make happy conversation. Not work." Dasha crossed her arms, clearly determined to make small talk. "You, Matthew. What sport do you play?"

Matt blinked, confused.

Dasha waved her hands in the air. "You understand what I am saying? Sport. The games. You play?"

"Well, I'm a grown man so I don't *play* games. But if you mean what do I do for exercise, I lift weights and swim." Natalie found this unlikely. "And I played lacrosse in college," he said, warming up to it. "I was the varsity captain."

Dasha frowned. "I do not know this game. Is it like bowling? You look to me like you would do bowling."

Matt turned an interesting color and said, "It is nothing like bowling. Lacrosse is very athletic and exciting. And I was captain of the softball team at the *Post*."

That caught Natalie's attention. "You were at the *New York Post*?"

"No, the *Washington Post*."

Natalie couldn't believe what she'd heard. "You worked at the *Washington Post*?"

"Yes," Matt said slowly.

"You once had journalistic integrity?"

"There's a lot you don't know about me," Matt said, with a challenging gaze.

"Was married," Dasha said matter-of-factly while Matt looked at her, mouth agape.

"How did you know that?" he demanded.

"You were married? You were not married," Natalie said, floored.

"My friend is friends of the ex-wife of Matthew," Dasha confirmed. "She say is nice woman. Move to Iowa."

"You have a nice ex-wife who lives in Iowa?" Natalie asked, still floored. Matt blushed furiously.

"It's old news," Matt said and picked up his phone.

Natalie was searching for an appropriate response when her phone buzzed.

"VOP is here," Dasha called out, scrolling on her own screen.

Holding her breath, Natalie opened the email.

From: The Chief
Subject: VOPS

Ryan 54. Natalie 42. Great work by all today. Keep it up!!!

Twelve points. He was beating them by twelve points. Looking at the numbers, Natalie was overcome with exhaustion. "I
give up."

"Wait, I've got just the thing," Matt said, and Natalie, in a
daze, watched him reach into his satchel and pull out a handful
of little blue pills. "Xanax," he announced.

She looked at them, feeling unmoved.

"It's not addictive. It'll just turn down the volume in your
head," Matt said, sounding a lot like the high school campus
drug dealer.

Lacking the life force to fight Matt, she stuck out her hand,
watched as he placed two pills on her palm, and stuffed them
into a pocket. "Okay, I'm going to my room," she said and with
some effort, hopped down off the barstool. "Then I'm going to
dinner with the Chief. Wish me luck."

18

NATALIE IN WONDERLAND

Natalie was under the monkey fever comforter in her own room at the Hampton Inn trying to breathe through the nauseated feeling rolling through her. Her body was cold and her head felt compacted, like she'd just drunk an entire Slurpee in one go. Shivering, she pulled up the cover and reread the email that was open on her iPhone.

It was from the Chief's assistant, letting her know that the network was sending a black car to pick her up at 8 p.m. No word on her destination. No mention of a return car at the end of the night. She reminded herself of all the articles she'd read calling the Chief a family man, dedicated to his new wife and kids. It was borderline egotistical to think he'd try anything tonight.

Pressing her eyes shut, she tried to make her mind go blank but it was a losing battle. *Twelve points*, her mind screamed. That was the real problem. She was trailing Ryan by twelve points. Yesterday, after the on-set debate about the sexless sex tape, she'd been only four points behind. Now, after a killer story that involved an actual shooting live on air, Ryan had more than doubled his lead. Cancelling dinner with the Chief wasn't an option.

Her phone rang and she glanced at the screen which may as well have been screaming the word MOM. She willed the phone to stop but it turned a deaf ear and hummed right along. As she watched the voice mail arrive, Natalie waited for the flood of texts.

MOM: I heard you were involved in a shooting. Are you alive?

MOM: I'm very worried. Don't ignore me.

With a slow exhale, she started typing.

NATALIE: Hi, Mom. I've passed away and I'm texting from the great beyond. It's okay, though, I'm happy here.

MOM: Don't be glib about this. I don't know what I would do if you died a week before the wedding.

Pulse flaring, Natalie imagined her mother's outrage if she were forced to postpone her honeymoon for something as inconvenient as her child's funeral.

Don't take your mother's bait, said her dad's voice in her head.

She glanced over to the bedside table where she'd put the two little blue pills Matt had handed her. The Xanax seemed to beckon. She was starting to think that if she had many more days like today she could seriously crack up, possibly on air. Considering that prospect, maybe taking a pill would be the responsible choice. Maybe Xanax—like fake eyelashes and The Treatment—was just another necessary compromise for the job.

The phone vibrated and Natalie ignored it. Her mother would have to find someone else to bother for now. The phone vibrated again. And again. She let out an angry exhale and glared at the screen.

JAMES: Hi there.

JAMES: I've been watching your network.

Her heart leaped. James. Sweet James!

JAMES: Hope you don't mind my saying this. On behalf of all men, I apologize for the naked guy.

Natalie's gloom instantly lifted. She'd forgotten there was something to look forward to. She pushed herself up on her elbows, beaming at her phone.

NATALIE: At ATN we're dedicated to exposing the naked truth.

JAMES: Stripping the story bare?

NATALIE: Yes, bringing our viewers true transparency.

JAMES: Does that mean you're going to reveal all?

NATALIE: Not without dinner first.

JAMES: Then it's a good thing I got us a reservation at a great place downtown. 7:30 p.m. Work for you?

Natalie's breath caught. The date. It was tonight? She stared at the phone, frozen. *You've screwed this up, too. The one nice thing and you botched it.* She started typing, wishing she could give a different response.

NATALIE: I'm so sorry. I completely messed up. I'm stuck in

Miami waiting to get our next assignment and not sure if we're flying back to DC tonight. Would you be willing to reschedule?

She stared at the flashing cursor on her phone, damning a world in which she had to cancel dinner with a hot, age-appropriate cartographer to (possibly) dodge advances from her married fiftysomething boss. As she waited for James's reply, her mind did a monologue of his thoughts. *How rude. She's a flake. She's too self-obsessed to remember a date. She's not worth the trouble. Her hair smells funny.*

The Xanax caught her eye.

One Xanax can't hurt.

She palmed one of the little blue pills and, before she could have second thoughts, downed it with water from a bottle by her bed. Feeling very grown up, she lay back on the pillow and waited for it to kick in.

It still hadn't taken effect when the phone vibrated. Reaching for it, Natalie realized she'd been holding her breath.

JAMES: You really have a crazy job. How about Friday?

He's not giving up! Natalie felt a dark cloud lift and was about to type Yes! when she remembered that Karima's cocktail party was Friday night. She couldn't miss it.

NATALIE: I'd love to see you Friday. I have to go to a cocktail party that night. It might be an interesting scene. Want to come to the party and get dinner after?

His reply arrived fast.

JAMES: I'd be honored to be your plus one.

JAMES: Does the ATN dress code require men to be shirt-less? Not to brag but I think I can give this McChesty a run for his money.

Natalie broke out in a grin.

NATALIE: I'd like to be the judge of that.

JAMES: Deal. See you Friday.

Staring at the text, Natalie felt a calm wash over her. Maybe it was James or maybe the Xanax was doing its trick, but suddenly her body felt suffused with a cottony lightness. *Let's get some sleep,* she thought.

She woke up to the sight of Matt and Dasha staring down at her from the end of her bed.

"How many Xanax you give her?" Dasha asked, studying Natalie with concern.

"Not that much," said Matt. "She's a total lightweight."

Natalie was staring up at them, bleary-eyed, wondering if they were apparitions. "What's happening?" Natalie mumbled.

"We've been trying your cell. You've been dead asleep. Management gave us the key," Matt said dismissively.

"Why'd they give you the key?" Natalie murmured, still foggy.

"The Chief is sending us to North Carolina," Matt announced. "Guess your dinner's off. Flight's in two hours."

It was like a thunderclap. Natalie jerked upright and reached for her iPhone. Scrolling, she found an officious email from the Chief's assistant explaining that the boss's wife and children had surprised him in Miami so they'd have to organize a meal for another time. Thank you for understanding.

Hallelujah! Dodged that bullet! She wanted to leap across

the room and hug Matt for delivering the news. Only his back
was to her and he was leaning over the hotel room refrigerator
jimmying open the door. "You didn't get it unlocked? You're
such an amateur!"

"What are you doing?" asked Natalie, gratitude replaced by
Xanax-moderated irritation. "Leave the minibar alone. They'll
charge us and then ATN will charge me."

"You don't have any Funyuns."

"What kind of minibar has Funyuns?"

"*Ax!*" Dasha nearly barked. "No time for this. Chief have assignment. You will be in story more. More action adventure."
She added forbiddingly, "He wants you in field."

In her Xanax haze, Natalie thought Dasha's words sounded
ominous and she suddenly saw herself standing alone in a field—
an actual field, like something out of *Children of the Corn.*

"What does that mean?" she asked warily.

"In *the* field," corrected Matt. "He's sending us to OpSec
Solutions."

"What's—?" she started.

"OpSec is private security, ex-special forces. Experts in hostage and ransom."

"I know these men," Dasha elaborated. "Helmand Province
massacre was very bad. But mostly they are okay."

Concerned, Natalie looked to Matt for reassurance.

"The boss wants to play up the mystery of the disappearance
of FLOTUS." Matt started imitating the Chief's voice. "What
if FLOTUS has been kidnapped? Let's look at what happens if
she's held hostage and needs a rescue."

"Has she been kidnapped?" Natalie asked, certain she'd missed
a key development.

"No!" Matt said, exasperated. "No one knows where she is.
But the boss thinks it's a good narrative. Great characters. Real
drama. Yada yada."

She squinted at him. "Shouldn't we be trying to figure out

where FLOTUS really is, at least why she's left?" Freed of her dinner trap, she felt invigorated. "Isn't that the story we should be on? Or figuring out why Rigo and the Lystras are creating all this trouble?"

Matt flashed her a look of utter impatience.

"Okay. Okay." Natalie relented. "So he wants us to dramatize a fake kidnapping?"

"Yes," Matt said. "And you are doing it in a tank top."

19

ANITA SHRUGGED

Anita Crusoe stopped her hike and cast her eyes up the hill. It was a day of glittering sunshine and she marveled at the sight: blue sky, no clouds, a mountain alive with the sounds of spring coming to life.

She should be enjoying this, she knew. Holed up in the mountains with no commitments and all the time in the world to think. If only she could have calmed her mind. It was so noisy— replaying it all. Their history. Her blindness. Patrick's empty promises.

How had she not seen it from the start?

Her early adulthood had been messy and uncertain and required constant vigilance, so it made sense, she reasoned, that she'd seek out the opposite in a husband. He was cool and contained and as rational and predictable as the laws of classical physics. She appreciated his logical approach to the world. He gathered data, analyzed circumstances before forming an opinion. Once formed, his confidence in his own correctness was almost awe-inspiring. He was the only politician she'd ever known who was free of bombast or hyperbole.

She'd met her husband at one of the excruciating dinners she was expected to attend with university donors. It wasn't lost on her that she was included in these meals far more often than the others in her PhD program. She had no illusions it was because of her fine engineering skills. Inevitably she would be seated next to a wealthy older donor who'd bang on about his philanthropy or his tennis game, then confess that he'd heard she was once Miss Venezuela. How delightful! She'd sleepwalk through the dinners smiling, prompting, and pretending not to notice the way their gaze kept falling on her chest, or how they'd confide that their marriages were loveless, their bodies in need of attention. "How long will you be in the country?" they'd want to know.

She became expert at the delicate art of dodging the advances without scaring away the donor. After all, she was at the university on a grant, in the US on a visa. Both could be revoked. Enduring mawkish, dirty old men for a few hours over dinner each month seemed a tolerable price to pay to continue her work.

Patrick had been different. Substantive, intense. Looking back, she now saw that she'd mistaken his lack of humor for sincerity, maybe even integrity. She'd met plenty of wealthy men, men who could have provided her the security and stability she craved, but she could never imagine giving herself to the others. In Patrick, she saw a sense of purpose. He'd reaped billions extracting oil, gas, and minerals from Latin America; he succeeded where many others had failed. "I won't pretend it was charity work. I was there to make a profit, and many people profited," he'd said with unexpected candor. But he maintained that he always wanted to give something back.

"I create value and promote values," he'd explained that night, as he told her about the schools and hospitals he'd built across Latin America.

Later it would become his campaign message. "Building Value, Strengthening Our Values. The American Way."

Now it seemed so empty. So dishonest.

"If you think you can rebuild without private investment, you've got your head up your ass," he'd said after the salad was served.

"I beg your pardon?" she'd replied, amused.

"I looked into your research. No matter how low cost you make the infrastructure rebuild you're proposing, no matter how promising Venezuela's push to 'democracy'—" he used air quotes around the word "—there is no way you can turn your country around without private corporate buy in."

She'd disagreed vehemently, but was dazzled by his knowledge, taken by his brisk questioning.

By dessert he'd made an offer. If she'd join him for dinner the following night, he'd consider funding her research. To her surprise, she'd said yes. On their third date, he'd flown her to rural Colombia to give her a tour of the hospital he'd built there, his commitment to giving back to the communities where he made his fortune. "I do as I say. Building value, and values," he said.

That day trip had slipped into a weekend and within three months they were engaged. They married quickly; it was the logical way to speed her application for citizenship. Then he'd entered the race for governor and she'd put her research on hold. She was needed on the campaign trail. Later she delayed her return to school because as Colorado's First Lady, there were ribbon cuttings and working groups and endless interviews. She finally withdrew from the PhD program altogether when Patrick's presidential campaign began. Life on the road was too demanding.

"I need you," he'd said early on. And from him, it was better than I love you. "We are great together," he'd insisted with a fervor she believed was reserved only for her. It meant he would reach for her hand under the table at campaign rallies where no one could see. It meant that he would show up three or even five minutes late to meetings just so he could kiss her one more time. It meant that she alone could make him laugh when he didn't mean to, she alone could coax from him the sudden explosions of heat and passion that had surprised him and dazzled her. It meant she was his weakness and he was her strength. Being needed by a man who was so fiercely independent felt like power and a guarantee of stability.

That was before the White House.

She and Patrick had made a deal. If he won the presidency, he'd make life better for her people. There was a new democracy in Venezuela, a president committed to human rights. She told herself that as First Lady of the United States, she could do far more to help Venezuelans than she could as a PhD student in engineering. Patrick had promised her that if he won, he'd ease sanctions on her country, make it possible for the economy to strengthen and democracy to grow.

She laughed at the memory. His self-righteousness, her naïveté.

And the world thinks I'm the one betraying this marriage? What a joke.

Anita took a deep breath, savoring the taste of the wet spring air with its earthy, cleansing scent. She'd been walking for a good thirty minutes and was starting to feel her blood flow. The terrain here was untouched except for a single line of footprints ahead. Usually her detail didn't bother her. They had a job to do, she was used to it.

Today for some reason their presence was enraging. Was it really necessary to have snipers ahead and armed agents behind while they were in the middle of nowhere? Wasn't it possible for her to have the illusion of privacy here? The sense of being a lone explorer? The whole point of getting away from the White House was getting *away*—leaving the trappings of the presidency behind. She might as well go surrender herself at a prison.

Childish. I'm being childish, she scolded herself. The team was giving her as much space as they could, more than they were supposed to. She knew that. What if some lone wolf lunatic was hiding in the woods waiting to assassinate her?

"Ma'am?" It was Beth, the head of her security detail, from behind her. "If you wouldn't mind, ma'am, I'd suggest we return to the house. It is beginning to get dark. Makes the team nervous."

Anita nodded. "Ten more minutes," she said.

She closed her eyes and tipped her head back and slowly breathed in three more lungfuls of the crisp, tingling air. Silently she dared any snipers to take a shot. *Go on, hit me*, she challenged.

Not a one. Too bad. Would have saved everyone a lot of trouble.

THE EARLYBIRD™/ WEDNESDAY / 6:46 A.M.
THE E-NEWSLETTER TRUSTED BY WASHINGTON'S POLITICAL ELITE

Good morning, EarlyBirders™. Here are the morning's need-to-know stories.

WHITE HOUSE MYSTERY: *One story will dominate the day. WHERE IS THE FIRST LADY?*

CRUSOE SHOCK: *FLOTUS hasn't been seen with POTUS since the Fashion Fights Fascism gala honoring Tory Burch ten days ago. Time to ask the obvious: IS FLOTUS LEAVING POTUS?*

VENEZUELA PRAYS: Makeshift shrines are popping up across Venezuela. In FLOTUS's hometown of Maracaibo, hundreds hold vigil praying for her safety.

EarlyTipsters SHARE THEIR THEORIES ABOUT FLOTUS: She could be sick with cancer. Recovering from plastic surgery. On a sensitive diplomatic mission. Helping a loved one through a tragedy. **EarlyFact:** No president has ever gotten divorced while in office!

Spotted: *Pentagon officials seen entering Colombian embassy. If they're negotiating safe passage for Rigo, why isn't State Department present? No comment from Foggy Bottom.*

20

MANUFACTURING CONTENT

Wedged in a middle seat on board a flight back to DC, Natalie was sitting with her eyes closed trying to deep breathe. Her piece with the OpSec guys was scheduled to air at the top of the hour and she was expecting the worst.

As soon as they'd finished the shoot, Matt had hustled them into the rental car insisting it was time to get to the airport. "But what about the script?" she'd asked naively. She wanted to write the script and oversee the edit.

You know at heart I'm a stairs person, part of her protested.

Her input wasn't needed, said Matt. The script and edit had been left "in the trusted hands of the network," a phrase that had caused her to start hyperventilating. "This is good news," he continued. "You don't have to bother with the work part, like Ryan."

You're an elevator person now, she thought, and hated herself for it.

Eyes still closed, she felt something knocking on her skull.

"Hello? I know you're in there." It was Matt, from the seat behind her.

She opened her eyes and checked her watch. Two more minutes till the piece aired. "I feel sick," Natalie said.

"At least get to the bathroom first," Matt said, prompting the woman next to Natalie to scoot slightly away.

"It was a figure of speech," she assured the woman, who still looked suspicious.

"Do you want the good news or the bad news first?" Matt asked her from between the seats.

"Bad," Natalie said.

Matt ignored her. "The good news is that after previewing the piece, Bibb called Hal into her office to rant about it."

Natalie pulled up onto her knees to look over the back of the seat at Matt. "Bibb and Hal got to see the piece already? Why do they get to see it before us?"

"You're focusing on the wrong thing," Matt told her. "You've made Bibb very unhappy. You should be proud."

Natalie felt herself brighten a little. "Good point."

"The Chief is over the moon," Matt went on. "He told Bibb to increase your budget. He said to reimburse you for hair and makeup."

"What, I'm getting my own hair and makeup?" This was unprecedented in Natalie's career. "That's amazing. How do you know?"

Matt put on an expression she felt was supposed to make him seem wily but really just made him look constipated. "I have my sources."

She squinted her eyes at him. "What's the bad news?"

He pointed at the monitor on the back of Natalie's seat. She turned in time to see Ryan standing outside the embassy, this time wearing a shirt. She checked the clock—it was the top of the hour. Which meant—

"They're leading with Ryan instead of me?" Her hands curled into angry fists, and it started getting hard to breathe.

"Do you need to get out?" the woman next to her asked, looking concerned.

"No, thank you," Natalie said, trying to sound normal as she jammed in a single earbud.

She was just in time to hear Ryan say, "—the first time they will be in the same country since the night in question." The monitor cut to video of Sonia Barbaro, her long black hair shining, wearing a white T-shirt and blazer walking through a crowd. It was followed by more video of Sonia, now in an emerald green sheath on a red carpet.

"Barbaro lands in the US tomorrow night ahead of the American premiere of her new film, *Trafficked*," Ryan went on. "She hasn't spoken publicly since accusing Rigo Lystra two weeks ago. This weekend, she'll be angling for publicity, and we can only imagine what she'll say next. The world will be watching."

"Everyone knows Barbaro arrives tomorrow," Natalie snapped. "Why is this the lead story?"

Her phone buzzed and she glanced down to find a text from Hal complimenting her on her beyond awesome work today, adding, you were smoking hot in every sense of the word!

Wincing, she flicked her eyes back to Ryan on the monitor. *This was probably Hal's doing.* It made perfect sense.

"Hal must have done this," she said out loud. "When he heard the Chief liked our story, he probably lobbied for Ryan to be the lead. He's a human barricade to the White House."

"Table for one at Conspiracy Café?" Matt replied. "Someone's paranoid."

Before Natalie could respond, the woman next to her started pointing at the monitor. "Excuse me. What channel is that?" She gave Natalie a conspiratorial smile. "I want to see if he takes off his shirt again."

From behind her, Natalie heard Matt start to sing. "And I guess that's how you get the lead on the news," to the tune of "I Guess That's Why They Call It the Blues."

"Bet that you wish now, you'd worn that bikini…"

"You are lucky they don't allow weapons on planes," Natalie muttered.

"What was that?" the woman next to her asked.

Natalie tried for a reassuring smile. "Nothing."

On the screen, Ryan was still talking, "You can be sure she'll be swarmed with press attention on her arrival and ATN will be there." He paused and smiled at the camera. "Also," he said and dramatically moved his hand to the top button on his shirt.

Natalie and the woman to her left leaned forward together in anticipation, but for different reasons.

"Hah! Just kidding," Ryan said, then winked. "That's for the folks at home."

Watching Ryan now made Natalie want to research ritual forms of suicide. She was considering different options when Matt interrupted her reverie.

"Hey, look." Matt pointed at the television where, with soaring music, the First Lady's face had appeared with Natalie's face next to it.

"Someone is getting an elaborate setup," Matt said, in the kind of voice you'd use to appease a toddler.

Natalie glared at the screen, hoping her dagger eyes would somehow project behind her to reach Matt.

Now Heath Heatherton's angelic face filled the screen and the knot in Natalie's stomach coiled more tightly. Heath was reading the top headlines of the day, but she couldn't make out his words over the sheer panic that had seized her.

Peering at her between the seats, Matt said, "Why do you look like you're going to throw up?"

"There's a high likelihood this piece will humiliate me for the world to see."

"The world? I don't want to throw water on your pity party but ATN's cable audience only averages 850,000."

She could barely breathe as the monitor cut to a shot of a

sparsely furnished room. At the center was a figure seated at a table, head covered in a burlap bag, hands tied down to a chair, and surrounded by tattooed he-men in ski masks. It was the makeshift interrogation room at OpSec Solutions, the private military camp in North Carolina where they'd just spent the day. She'd been careful to wear her shirt buttoned extra-low with a push-up bra, and noticed with some satisfaction that—with a bag on her head—her cleavage commanded attention.

One of the "hostage takers" was reading from a notebook: "President Crusoe, we have your wife. If you want her back, you will do what we say. If you want her back *alive*, you will do it quickly."

In the room, in real time, Natalie had thought that the ransom statement felt completely clichéd, overly dramatic, and stagey, but on camera it was tense, powerful. From a purely entertainment perspective, she had to admit, it was good TV.

Amazing what good lighting and the right cameraperson could do.

On screen, one of the he-men snatched the bag off Natalie's head and now her face was on camera looking like a #BadMorningAfter. She had the hair of an unkempt child and eyeliner smudged under her eyes.

Real Natalie shot an angry glance at Matt, who gave an exaggerated shrug, miming powerlessness. "What could I do? It looked authentic. They love authenticity! Anyway it's good."

Natalie looked around and saw that people all over the plane were watching the piece. Including the woman to her left. Part of her had to admit the setup was pretty captivating.

On screen, a voice barked, "We've got company! Breach! Move the package now!" The camera wavered crazily as the *pling pling pling* sound of gunshots erupted. Then came a bright flash of light and smoke filled the room. The smoke parted and suddenly a huge bronze-colored forearm with a tattoo of an eagle wrapped itself around Natalie's waist.

"This is X Team 1. I've got the package," Eagle Tattoo barked into a wrist radio.

It seemed to Natalie as though the passengers were holding their collective breath as the monitor cut to a great tracking shot of Natalie and Eagle Tattoo bolting down a corridor running hard—did they have a Steadicam on this shoot?—weaving back and forth, then out a door. They were running across a vast lawn when Eagle Tattoo pushed her into a waiting Jeep, climbed in after her, and took off, spraying gravel everywhere. Natalie remembered that two cameras had been locked down on the dashboard. She now saw that as the car rocketed forward through a flurry of gunfire, smashed through a chain-link fence and went careening down a steep rocky slope, they captured her doing an excellent imitation of Edward Munch's *The Scream*.

Natalie's heart sped up as she watched Eagle Tattoo deftly maneuver the Jeep over a small stream, then stop beneath a leafy tree. Then Tattoo pulled off the mask and unfolded a slow, simmering smile. "Hey. I'm Julia."

Tattoo, it'd turned out, was a massive woman. She'd looked like an action hero: at least six-two, ripped, with a chiseled face, cropped brown hair, gray hooded eyes, and a jaw so square it could chip ice. It was as if The Rock and Joan of Arc had a love child who grew up to do private security.

In her airplane seat, Natalie leaned forward in anticipation of what she knew was coming next. She watched as Julia expertly ran her hands over Natalie's arms, stomach, chest, and then grazed her nether regions, while looking into Natalie's eyes. "Just checking for any breaks or serious injuries," she'd said, leaning in close, "I'm sorry if we hurt you." On the monitor, it looked as though they were about to kiss.

"I'm, *um,* okay," Natalie had replied nervously, thinking the TSA would disapprove of this pat down.

In real life, they'd had to wait twenty minutes for the cam-

eras to reset and Natalie flashed back to the conversation they'd
had during the break.

"Sorry about the pat down. I hope they warned you?" Julia
had said with a self-deprecating laugh. "Reg said he wanted it
slow and personal. Better TV."

"Reg?" asked Natalie, searching her mind.

"Reginald," Julia said, then added, "Oh wait. You guys call
him the Chief, right? You're lucky you get to work for him."
She looked almost wistful as she said the words.

Natalie let that sink in before asking, "How do you know
the Chief?"

"I've done a lot of work for your parent company and their
high-value targets," explained Julia, shading her eyes from the
sun. "When he was overseas, I handled personal protection for
him, Katie, and the kids." She got a gleam in her eyes. "Such a
great dad. Heart of gold. He really helped me out."

"The Chief. Helped you out," Natalie repeated, trying to
square Julia's picture of a sensitive, openhearted "Reg" with
the boss she knew.

"Yeah, my line of work isn't great for women. Especially,
you know, dykes like me." She shrugged. "Reg was kind of
my champion."

Before Natalie could ask a follow-up question, a twenty-
foot-long drone—a fucking military-grade drone—had come
streaking through the sky, giving them "cover" for their escape.

That's when Natalie had realized ATN was spending a small
fortune on this shoot. It was more elaborate than anything she'd
ever been part of—in fact, more elaborate than almost any news
story she'd seen outside an election, a tsunami, or maybe a wedding on a morning show. At her first local station, she'd been
asked to limit her use of lights because the bulbs were so expensive.

Leaning over her chair, Matt poked Natalie on the shoulder.
"This is great. You're—"

"Stop talking." Her eyes were fixed on the screen and, privately, she had to admit he wasn't wrong. This wasn't anything she would ever have put together, but it was kind of thrilling TV. If reporting actual information weren't a consideration.

The piece ended with a flourish, Natalie escorted away by a cordon of sixteen motorcycles. At the end of the spot, Natalie had appeared on camera explaining that all of what had been shown had been made up, hypothetical—ATN had no reason to believe the First Lady had been kidnapped. She'd tried to make that point as forcefully as possible.

Still, as soon as the piece ended, the woman in the seat next to Natalie said, "So, who do you think kidnapped the First Lady?"

Didn't she hear me say it was hypothetical? Natalie thought, feeling something that approached panic but stopped short.

"We made it all up," Natalie said, trying to impress on her the meaning of hypothetical. "We don't have any reason to believe that she's been kidnapped."

Shooting Natalie a disapproving look, the woman said, "Please. You wouldn't do a kidnapping story if you didn't know something we don't. Was it the Arabs? Or the Colombians?"

Seeing the pointlessness of any counter argument, Natalie offered her a stiff sort of smile and said, "I sure wish we knew."

"Mmm-hmm," the woman continued, as she glanced down to Natalie's lap and back up. "Word of advice? You should button up that shirt. No one's going to take you seriously if you don't dress like a lady."

"Thanks for the feedback," Natalie said, hoping she sounded cheery rather than homicidal.

Matt's hand appeared from around the back of her seat with a handful of Xanax. He mimed taking one. She didn't even have to debate this. Natalie accepted the blue pills and swallowed one without water.

She sat back in her chair and closed her eyes, embarrassment warring with gratification. Natalie knew the proper reaction

was to shake her head at the incredible waste of resources for
the pretend news story that had just aired. *Imagine if we'd poured
all that time and money into investigating where FLOTUS really is, or
figuring out what the Lystras are up to.* But a part of her felt almost
giddy at the network's support for her story.

"Excuse me."

Natalie opened her eyes to find the same woman pointing at
the arm rest and glaring.

"We're supposed to share armrests."

Sitting up, Natalie silently fumed. *You don't approve of me and
my sleep style? I don't approve of the tuna fish sandwich you're eating,
so we're even.*

Now too annoyed to sleep, Natalie grabbed her phone and
opened her Twitter feed to see how the world was reacting to
the piece. She read messages from strangers that ranged from
You RULE to Stupid cunt, racy dating profiles, and a DM from
a personal trainer offering to share his patented interval training workout guaranteed to thin your thighs. But the vast majority said some version of ATN reports FLOTUS was kidnapped.
Who has her? There were at least five hundred tweets guessing
where she'd been taken.

Her phone buzzed with a text.

MOM: Great story, dear! You looked more flirty than usual.
Much improved.

MOM: When do you get the ratings? Think they'll be on
TVBuzzster soon?

Natalie searched her mind, trying to remember when she'd
told her mother about TVBuzzster.

She was about to check Ryan's feed when she saw a text from
the Chief's personal cell. It was all emojis. Positive emojis.

Excited in a hazy, buzzy kind of way, Natalie held the phone between the seats to show Matt. "That's good, right? I mean they are all positive emojis."

Matt nodded. "I guess. I'd say the Chief is giving us two thumbs-up. Although that's the only emoji he did not actually give you."

"I think he's post-language," she giggled.

"I think you've had too many Xanax."

Ho ho, Matt was hilarious. But she had to admit he'd been right. Not about the Xanax but about how to fight Ryan. The straight hair, the push-up bra, letting someone else edit the piece, doing what the Chief wanted had paid off. Their segment had been terrible by the standards of journalism, but amazing TV by any other measure. And in her relaxed state, she was starting to see that maybe this wasn't selling out. The truth is, she had to get people to like her, to care about her personally before they'd care about what she said on air. Once they were invested in her, Natalie, as a reporter, a character on TV, then they'd pay attention to her reports. Ryan had a platform. And if she kept playing by the Chief's rules, she could, too. For the first time since the competition started, she felt like she was getting traction. She was on solid ground again and well on her way to...

To what? she demanded of herself.

Time will tell, her self responded as she closed her eyes and dozed off.

THE EARLYBIRD™/ FRIDAY / 5:53 A.M.
THE E-NEWSLETTER TRUSTED BY WASHINGTON'S POLITICAL ELITE

Good morning, EarlyBirders™. Here are the morning's need-to-know stories.

EARLY EXCLUSIVE: *A TOP WHITE HOUSE SOURCE, tells EARLYBIRD™ that the FIRST LADY is recovering from exhaustion at a SILENT RETREAT in New England. No ETA on her return. Anyone have a second source? A sighting? Email: earlytipster@theearlybird.com.*

Say, What? According to *Condé Nast Traveler,* **Silence Tourism** is "the latest in detox vacations." Popular with Hollywood celebs, silent spas offer everything from "naptime" to "forest bathing." We hope it's working for you, Mrs. C!

SONIA'S SUCCESS. *Entertainment Weekly* is calling *Trafficked,* Sonia Barbaro's new film about a survivor of sex trafficking, a **"mesmerizing study of a woman facing human depravity,"** and lauds Barbaro for a **"tour de force performance."** Do we smell an Oscar on the horizon? **Film premieres this Friday.**

Spotted: Defrocked celebrity chef **Mario Batali** on hand at the Colombian embassy last night to serve his signature nacho meatballs to **Rigo Lystra's** guests.

21

INTO THE MADDING CROWD

Natalie was in the collapsed back seat of a Lyft that, like a disturbing number of DC cars, smelled of food and sweat. But between the prospect of seeing James again and the text she'd gotten from Karima that afternoon—Darling, can't wait to see you tonight. You'll be the toast of the town!—she felt like a debutante riding to her coming-out ball.

Did you really just think that? Debu—no. Just no.

She felt like she'd been body snatched by a debutante.

Better.

Thanks to the kidnapping shoot, her FaceTwitSnapGram followers were through the roof: Instagram had doubled to 150,000 and Facebook was up to 850,000. The VOP hadn't come out yet but the Chief seemed so pleased he'd sent her an email promising "more exciting surprises," which augured well for her career if not her professional integrity.

The car snaked up Massachusetts Avenue, a broad tree-lined street bordered by massive stone mansions, the Vatican embassy, the vice president's residence, and the Cosmos Club where, she'd heard, they had a wall of photos dedicated to members who were on the postage stamp. The car started to slow.

"Traffic," the driver said. "It's that guy at the embassy. Everyone stopping to see the protests."

Natalie knew it was a Washington cliché that political reporters resorted to polling drivers and doormen for "public opinion" because it was their only contact with blue-collar Americans, so she was working to resist the urge to ask the driver what he thought of Rigo, when he volunteered.

"I had a guy in the car the other day, from the State Department. He said the Colombians got something on the president. Maybe drugs? Sex with kids? Maybe video of sex with an animal? Something."

Natalie nodded to be polite. She'd heard versions of this before. The car made a right turn onto a leafy residential street and crawled into a line of brake lights. Lincoln Town Cars and black SUVs with satellite antennae stretched in a line as far as the eye could see in front of them. No one else was in a silver Honda.

Note to self, she thought. Next time order the black car.

At the front of the line, one of a phalanx of valet attendants leaped forward to open her door. She looked up to see a sprawling brown Tudor Revival home that was either brand-new or very recently and aggressively renovated, complete with a perfectly trimmed faux English garden.

As she stepped onto the cobblestone walkway, she felt a sizzle race through her veins. She was about to parade into the epicenter of DC power. She was missing her mom's rehearsal dinner, but any guilt she'd been feeling vanished.

Throwing her shoulders back, she envisioned herself cutting a path, unimpeded, into the house. In reality the cobblestones were so crowded with partygoers she found herself inching, rather than marching, into her future.

Making her way forward. Natalie caught a snippet of the conversation in front of her—

"I just started on an anti-obesity campaign for Nestlé. If that's not a contradiction wrapped in a Hot Pocket."

"At least when Nestlé buys your soul, they make it worth your while. I'm trying to get LipoGone FDA approval, and they don't want to pay more than thirty a month. I mean, who does FDA approval for less than fifty?"

Natalie marveled at how precisely these people conformed to a certain Washington stereotype. Political insiders measuring their worth by the company they keep and the companies that, basically, keep them.

She turned and came face-to-face with Justice Ruth Bader Ginsberg.

"Oh excuse me," the justice said, stepping aside to make way for Natalie.

"No, you first. I insist," Natalie said, wide-eyed, as she gestured for the judge to pass.

She was gaping in her wake when Matt materialized at her side. "Jesus, don't eye fuck Ruth Bader Ginsberg," he said.

She hadn't considered the possibility Matt would be here, but she was too starstruck to care. "This is amazing," she gushed, nearly giggling with delight as she watched Justice Ginsberg walk away from her. She could still smell her perfume.

"What is wrong with you?"

"Nothing. I'm great," Natalie enthused, spying her personal reporting heroine, Dana Bash, getting out of a car. "Anyway, what are you doing here?"

"Oh sad, you thought you'd be the only reporter invited?" He looked at her, feigning pity. "I was White House correspondent for Beltway before I became your Svengali, remember?" His tone shifted to worried older brother. "Can we be serious for a moment? You know you are about to physically enter the belly of the beast. You're walking into the actual echo chamber. You have to be chill. You can't embarrass yourself in there."

"Got it," she said and, shivering, nudged Matt forward.

They reached the entrance and Matt pushed open the door. Natalie stood at the edge of the vestibule, gaping.

The wall of sound hit her first, then a smell that reminded her of something from the past, the scent of—

"Is that teriyaki?" she asked aloud as they stepped into the foyer.

The scene confronting her was not at all what she'd expected. This was no sedate gathering of aging elected officials and policy analysts trading favors over canapés and champagne with chamber music in the background. It was more like a frat party for homely drunk accountants. Meatloaf was belting out, "I'll do anything for love," while men in rumpled suits and women with frizzy hair were screaming to be heard over the music. And of course there was the teriyaki smell.

"Intense, right?" Matt hollered over the din, once they were inside. "The political establishment, legacy media, influence peddlers, and Professional-Know-It-Alls-R-Us!" He extended his arms wide. "Welcome."

It was a lot to take in. Every other person was vaguely familiar: a member of Congress, a spokesperson, a pundit. Then Natalie started to pick out faces deeply familiar: Wolf Blitzer, John Dickerson, Katy Tur. DC's most famous reporters were everywhere.

Matt led the way into a living room wallpapered in deep red, watermarked silk fabric. Tucker Carlson—and she felt slightly overwhelmed—Chris Matthews—like she was getting smacked in the face with the heat and noise of hundreds of people's ambition on the move. Gloria Borger, Bret Baier, Andrea Mitchell, Nicolle Wallace, Dana Perino, Judy Woodruff, Kasie Hunt, Hallie Jackson, Jeff Zeleny.

This was the DC version of the champagne room—Newt Gingrich—the VVIP section inside the VIP section—*eeew*, Newt Gingrich?—the secret lounge inside the first-class lounge, the place where DC power players went to let their hair down. It was like being upgraded from American Airlines to Emirates, only with bad food.

Never, never think of Newt Gingrich and the champagne room at the same time again, she admonished herself.

Matt broke away, giving her the universal pantomime for *I'm finding the bar*, leaving her on the threshold of the next room. Clearly this party was not dry.

She began to catch snippets of the conversations around her for the first time. Everyone, it seemed, was talking about Rigo.

"The neighbors are freaking out. The music goes all night."

"He had the chef from Nobu in to cook for the whole embassy!"

"I was there!"

"Oh shit, check this out," a woman in a Tory Burch dress shouted, holding up her iPhone for the group around her to see. Like dancers in a ballet, they all lifted their iPhones in unison and began nodding as they read the latest alert.

Following suit, Natalie found an AP alert that read, Sonia Barbaro gives statement on arrival at Los Angeles premiere.

According to the Associated Press, Barbaro had just arrived at the LA premiere of *Trafficked* and given a statement expressing support for other victims of sexual violence. She said, in part, "We do not need to hide any longer."

"My Humps" began blasting from the sound system. The group started yelling over the strains of Fergie singing about her lady humps.

"Strong statement!"

"Anyone know if they have this on camera?"

While tapping on their screens.

Natalie was awestruck. After reporting for four networks in six cities over twelve years, working the overnights, the early mornings, the all-nighters, she was, at last, covering breaking news with the nation's elite political reporters. Fergie extolling the powers of the junk in her trunk only slightly diminished the profundity of the moment.

There was no telling how long Natalie would have stayed riveted in place if Matt hadn't materialized and broken the spell. "You need to do something about your face."

"What specific thing is wrong with it now?"

"The expression. It's like you've dropped twenty points off your IQ since we walked in the door. You really need—"

She knew Matt was still speaking but she had no idea what he was saying because at that exact moment, James appeared. He was heading toward her but still hadn't spotted her. She watched as the crowd parted effortlessly around him, his eyes scanning the room. She was supposed to meet him here at eight. Was it already eight? He clocked her and broke out into a broad smile.

"Hello, Natalie Savage." When he stood in front of her, she felt like the school nerd meeting the varsity football star in a teen romance. *How is it possible he is here for me?*

"Hi," she answered, aware that she was grinning in the way that her mother said made her cheeks look fat.

"Are you listening to me?" Matt demanded.

"No," she said, without looking at him. "James, this is my producer, Matt."

Matt shot Natalie a disgusted look. "You invited a date, seriously? This isn't a sorority mixer. You can't have dead weight here." He gave James a once-over. "No offense."

"None taken," James smiled, seemingly amused.

"If you want my advice, make this a catch and release," Matt said to James, still assessing him. "She doesn't have time for a relationship."

Natalie's mouth opened but no sounds came out.

"You undersold him," James laughed. "Hard-bitten doesn't do him justice."

Folding her arms, Natalie scowled at Matt. "I think you're wanted in the other room, urgently."

He tilted his head. "Yeah? What are you going to give me to go away?"

"What do you want? A bone, a tennis ball, a dried pig ear?"

"Keys to the minibar next time," he said, crossing his arms.

"Done," she agreed.

"Ha-ha, I was going anyway!" Matt snickered. To James, he said, "Nice knowing you. Good luck."

As he disappeared into the crowd, Natalie looked up at James. "I'm sorry, he's—"

"Protective of his talent. I get it." James smiled, looking down at her.

Natalie felt her breath catch and got lost for a moment in his green eyes.

Before she could think of something witty to say, the scent of wood chips burnt with rose wafted over, bringing her back to the moment. She knew only one person who could afford that custom blend and she turned now to see Karima's thin body slip easily through the crowd. Her hostess's cheeks were even more sunken, her cheekbones even sharper than when they'd met.

Karima sashayed toward them and reached for Natalie, pantomiming a double cheek kiss. "Natalie, I'm delighted to see you looking so well!" She seemed truly happy.

Then she spotted James and her eyes lit up. "James! Darling! I'm so glad to see you here."

"Aasā' al-khayr," James said, leaning in for an air-kiss with Karima. *"Tabdeena alyawma jmeelatan jeddan."*

Natalie did a double take. *James knows Karima? And he speaks Arabic?* Suddenly she was gripped by the fear that she was on a date with a spy.

Karima turned to Natalie, explaining, "James's mother, Anne, is one of my absolute closest friends in the world." She faced James. "How is she? I owe her a call, I've just been so..." Karima made a big sweeping gesture to indicate the maelstrom that was her social life.

"She's doing well, feeling strong," James said. To Natalie, he explained, "My mom has MS. But she's got it under control."

"Ah, you're together!" Karima breathed out a feminine little giggle. "Nicely done, my boy," she said, putting her two hands around James's biceps. Then she leaned in toward Natalie, swallowing her in a cloud of smoky roses. "Very good work. This one is a dreamer. And from an important family. Everyone loves the Hardings."

It was no secret to Natalie that DC was a town filled with VIPs, which meant that if you met a guy in a coffee shop mere blocks from the White House, it stood to reason he might be from an Important Family. But it hadn't occurred to her that James was some kind of DC elite.

Realizing Karima was smiling at her, expectantly, Natalie recognized an opening and leaned in to whisper, "I followed up on your tip. The company you suggested I research, Sallee LLC? I'm afraid I hit a dead end. Is there anything else you can tell me about it?" She kept her eyes on Karima's, measuring her reaction.

"Shh shh." She held a single finger up to her lips. "We will discuss it another time. For now, remember this." Leaning in just a touch closer, she murmured, "It is never too late to be wise." As she pulled back from Natalie, she winked.

What does that mean? Natalie just barely avoided blurting the question out loud.

One of Karima's staff appeared and put a large arm across her back. "Mrs. Sahadi, Senator Jacobs is asking for you. He's by the bar—" And the arm pulled Karima into the crush of people.

Natalie stared at the space where Karima had been with a sinking feeling. *It's never too late to be wise. Is that the polite version of try harder?* She was pretty sure Karima had just told her to step up her game.

The truth is, she hadn't dedicated very much energy to researching Sallee LLC.

A simple search had revealed that Sallee LLC was incorporated in Belize, using a secretive structure familiar to her from her days assisting her dad on some of his more complex cases. Online she'd found a data search company that, for fifty bucks, pulled and scanned the company's incorporation documents. That paperwork had arrived by email and showed that Sallee LLC had been formed in 2003 by someone named Jon Torres. In 2005, Torres had transferred Sallee LLC to another firm that was now out of business. There was no working contact information for anyone.

When she'd Googled Jon Torres, it'd returned more than twelve million results in half a second and, worse, it seemed as though he was the board director for more than five thousand other companies in Belize. Even if she could speak to him directly, the chances he'd remember this one company were minimal. She had no idea what Sallee LLC did or who owned it.

Now she felt guilty she hadn't dug further. *You're definitely becoming an elevator person*, she thought. *It's never too late to be wise*, she repeated in her head as she stared at the space where Karima had just been.

"So, what was that all about?" James was watching her with a kind of benign interest. As she met his green eyes, she forgot all about Karima and her obscure tips.

Natalie put her hands on her hips. "More important, Mr. Harding, you speak Arabic! Are you CIA, undercover Rangers, Mensa?"

"Definitely not the last one," James laughed. "I only know how to say about ten phrases in Arabic. Mostly 'you look beautiful' and 'more red, please.' My dad was stationed in UAE for a few years when I was in high school, so I learned some phrases."

Ah, military. That explained his good manners, too. "What branch is your dad in?"

"Navy. Was," James shifted and looked slightly apologetic.

"But now, he's a player in what your friends in the media would call the military profiteering complex."

"He's a defense contractor?" Natalie translated.

"Close, he's a consultant," James corrected.

"And your mom?"

"She sits on some boards. Her MS is getting advanced." For the first time the playful look in his eyes was gone. "That's why I live in DC. So I can help out."

Cute, smart, loves his family and interested in you? One hundred percent chance that he is a serial killer.

"How long has your mom been sick?"

"It was diagnosed about fifteen years ago. But she can still do a lot of activities. She's in a walking group with Karima." A flutter of discomfort passed over James's features and he added, "I think theirs is a pretty transactional friendship."

"Like all DC relationships," Natalie laughed.

"Not all," James said, looking her in the eyes. "I hope."

As the words penetrated, the room seemed to shrink around Natalie and her face felt hot. "I hope so, too," she said quietly, surprised by her own bravery.

She looked up into James's eyes and the party went quiet around her. Closing the distance between them, he said, "Do you want—?"

But his eyes moved and he broke off when Natalie felt a tug on her arm.

Glancing in the direction of the tug, she saw a very tall, very blond young woman in a sleeveless hot pink dress, her bra straps showing on the sides. It was the morning show anchor, Jazzmyn Maine, looking like the star of a Mommy-and-Daddy-screw-the-babysitter porno.

Don't judge, Natalie's mind scolded as she struggled not to give the woman's nearly naked body a visible once-over.

"Jazzmyn," Natalie said. And remembering Karima's words—

women here stick together—she tried to sound warm. "How are you?"

"I'm great," the girl said excitedly. "I wanted to ask your advice." Her eyes flicked from Natalie to James and back. "Can I have a minute alone?"

"No problem, I'm parched," James said. "I'll go to the bar. What can I bring you?"

"Water, and thanks," Natalie said with a look that she hoped conveyed don't-take-too-long.

Facing Jazzmyn, Natalie couldn't help but glance at her bra straps, which were basically screaming *look at me!*

You should be thrilled she's body positive, her empowered inner voice reminded her. *Ryan wears less to work.*

Please, this isn't progress, it's pandering, her inner Noreen snapped back. *Doesn't she have a mother?*

"I haven't had a chance to tell you how much I admire you," the high-wattage morning show host was saying. "I think you do such good work and have such a good reputation and people respect you and—"

Natalie zoned out while Jazzmyn continued with what she assumed, from experience, was the gratuitous flattery that comes before a totally inappropriate request. She could only imagine what Jazzmyn wanted from her. The secret email address for the White House chief of staff? Help booking an exclusive with the president? Elevator people had a habit of asking for the easy route and getting it.

"So I was wondering how you think I should approach this," Jazzmyn said. "I mean, if you were in my position."

Confused, Natalie frowned. Clearly this conversation wasn't headed in the direction she'd expected. "Sorry, I didn't catch that. Approach what?"

"The Chief. I think he's serious about giving me the 6 p.m. show. Not by myself, but, like with Ryan or something. He said I'll—"

Suddenly the sounds around Natalie turned to a dull hum and all she could focus on was the feeling of her rising blood pressure and the stinging pain of injustice. Jazzmyn, who had likely never read a political piece longer than an Instagram caption, was poised to land a prime anchor slot, a post from which she'd shape coverage of pressing policy issues and conduct interviews with world leaders.

"So the Chief and I are getting dinner at his hotel after the party and I want to be ready to negotiate. Lean in, right?" She beamed proudly. "I'd love your advice on what I should get in the contract. I was thinking maybe they should guarantee one overseas reporting assignment and a sit-down with a world leader every six months? What do you think?"

Natalie flashed to an image of Chinese President Xi Jinping seated for an interview opposite Jazzmyn straddling a bench, back arched with her bra straps showing. Shaking away the image, Natalie reminded herself that Jazzmyn was coming to her for advice as the Older Wiser colleague. *Be nice, help her.*

She was about to offer some mild encouragement when the weight of Jazzmyn's words hit her. "Wait, the Chief wants you to have dinner tonight, in his hotel?" she asked, getting a bad feeling.

"Yes," replied Jazzmyn brightly. "So we can really hash it out."

Just like he wanted to do with me in Miami.

"Jazzmyn. Are you sure you want to do that?" Natalie asked, recalling Dasha's warnings of hotel room treachery. "Have you considered rescheduling for lunch tomorrow, just so you're not alone with him at a hotel. You know?"

"Oh he's not like that!" Jazzmyn said cheerfully. "I was with him for a whole day in Miami and he was a perfect gentleman. We spent tons of time alone and he talked about his wife and kids the whole time. He's a family man."

Natalie blinked, choosing her words carefully. "That might

be true, but still, isn't it smart to play it safe? Even just to avoid gossip. What if someone sees you with him at the hotel? You don't want people to think—" She stopped before the words came out of her mouth.

Jazzmyn's face flushed. "That I slept my way to the top?" Her cheerful tone had vanished and was replaced by an accusatory edge. "You think that's how I do things? Because how could someone who looks like me get ahead any other way?"

Natalie, blanching, wanted to protest, but she stood there too startled to speak.

"Believe it or not, there's no water at the bar." James reappeared and touched Natalie's arm. "They said we have to get it in the kitchen."

Natalie smiled at him and then looked back at Jazzmyn. "That's not what I meant," she began.

"Never mind." Jazzmyn shook her head and looked away. "Stupid of me to think you'd be different from everyone else." With a forced smile, she added, "Have a good evening."

"What was that about?" James asked as they watched her walk away.

Before she could answer, James was accosted by a sixtysomething woman sporting a burgundy coif hair-sprayed into the shape of a large acorn. "James? Darling, how is your mother?"

James gave the same polite answer he'd given Karima, then turned toward the kitchen. They managed maybe five steps before the scene repeated.

"You seem to have found your demographic," Natalie whispered.

James sighed and pointed her in the direction of a white swinging door. "Make a break for it and I'll come find you."

The kitchen was quieter than the outer rooms but filled with clusters of people talking and smoking in groups. Natalie spotted bottles of Evian on the white marble kitchen counter and started making her way toward them when there was a crash as a wine bottle hit the floor. This was followed by a handful of nervous giggles as a gaggle of guests relocated a few feet in the other direction, leaving the mess.

Natalie was appalled. She found a broom by the wall and started to clean up the glass.

"Natalie? Is that *my* Natalie?"

She spun around in the direction of a very familiar voice and was confronted by a large gut and a frighteningly familiar set of eyes all leaning in to hug her.

Is this happening?

"Chief? Hi!" she stammered scanning his little pointy teeth and bullet eyes. In person, he was smaller and more menacing than he appeared on screen, like the chatty customer who seemed friendly until you got a glimpse of his white van.

As the Chief swept, her into his tight and slightly sweaty embrace, she gestured at the wine on the floor.

"Leave that," he said, pulling her away from the spill. "Karima and Raheem are old friends and I can assure you, they have plenty of staff to do the cleaning."

With his hand gripping her elbow, the Chief guided her to an alcove far from the other guests. Natalie felt a chill of discomfort as he let his gaze quickly extend down her body and back up. He nodded in admiration.

"You are looking great, polished. Who knew you had such a nice figure!"

Just take it as a professional compliment, she told herself. She forced a smile. "Thank you, sir."

"You're doing very well, Natalie, you know. Substantive and credible." He nodded in the direction of the party sounds. "Karima clearly likes you and my wife is a real fan of yours. Thinks you do great work."

She swallowed down the sour taste in her mouth. *He brought up his wife. He's a family man. Stop being paranoid,* she reprimanded herself.

"And—" he leaned in a little closer and lowered his voice "—I have some great news for you. I just got the VOPs and you are at sixty-two, five points ahead of Ryan!" He was grinning ear to ear. "How do you like that? Your abduction scored through the roof!"

"That's great!" she exclaimed, flooding her voice with enthusiasm. *It is great,* she told herself. *Be excited.* But she couldn't ignore the fact that he was standing so close, she could smell the liquor on his breath. "You know, I see potential in you and if we can smooth out the rough edges, I think we can get you to the next level," the Chief said, still smiling.

Rough edges? "I'm sorry, sir?" she asked.

"Well, we both know that you have a reputation for being difficult," the Chief said, as he leaned in so close his gut brushed her abdomen.

"You weren't happy we sent you to Miami instead of St. Tropez. You were angry Ryan reported the story about the First Lady's mole. I understand you wanted to edit your own piece for OpSec. It's a lot of complaining."

She opened her mouth but no words came out. Her mind was a jumble of outrage, shame, and confusion.

"I think it's because you're a fighter. Intense. I was a bit like that, too, when I was your age. I was hungry." His gaze took on a sick intensity and he lowered his voice as he said, "It's important to relax. To let loose, get free. Do you know how to relax? I'd love to watch you really let yourself get wild." He winked.

Natalie felt herself go ice-cold. Inside, her mind screamed, *Run! Scream! Escape!* But she did nothing. She stood there with a frozen smile plastered on her face and told herself to make no sudden movements, do nothing to embarrass the boss.

"Savage? Chief?" said a familiar voice.

Natalie spun around, turning her back to the Chief, to see

Matt enter through the kitchen door. Relief coursed through her. She'd never been so happy to see Matt in her life.

"Hey! Come say hi!" she chirped, sounding slightly manic. She took a step toward to him when something stopped her. It was the feeling of a finger running slowly down her spine, stopping at the top of her tailbone, thumbing the top of her panties. Natalie felt a flash of danger as every muscle in her body tightened and her face got hot. She was conscious of seconds passing and she twisted around to make eye contact with the boss to be sure. He casually pulled his hand away and winked.

She heard him say something about "continuing this later," and she mumbled the words "bathroom," "find my date," and "see you at work," as she bolted for the door. Matt looked confused but he let her pass and she could hear him ask the Chief about their VOP as she plunged into the crowd. Once she was surrounded by strangers, safe in the crush of the party, she started shaking.

Fighting against waves of revulsion, Natalie made for the nearest bathroom. Her feet were throbbing, her skull ached, and she wished she could find fresh air that didn't smell of teriyaki. Pulling the door shut behind her, she replayed the scene in the kitchen. Did that just happen? She must have misunderstood. He wouldn't do that, not in public. *He's a family man.* Heart of gold. With shaking fingers, she opened her clutch to find the extra blue pills Matt had given her earlier. "Plenty more where they came from," he'd said.

She put a pill in her mouth and, feeling her heart race, decided it wouldn't hurt to take two. She swallowed and slid down onto the floor, leaning back against the wall and closing her eyes, trying to slow her breathing and her frenzied thoughts.

When she jerked awake, there was a pounding at the door.

Shit. She'd dozed off. How long had she been in here? The buzz had definitely kicked in.

Standing up, she cupped water from the sink to help wake her up and checked her reflection in the mirror.

You look tidy. You look professional. You're good, she repeated like a mantra in her head. Feeling like she was in a fugue state, she did a quick reset of her makeup and headed back out, apologizing to the people in line outside the door.

She had just stepped into the foyer when she ran into James. She resisted the temptation to press her face into his chest and start to cry.

She must have seemed slightly wild-eyed because he gazed at her, concerned. "I've been looking for you everywhere. Are you okay?" he said.

"I don't know," she said quietly.

He tilted his head and, without a word, pulled her in for a hug.

With her head pressed against James, Natalie felt an explosion of warmth. He was nothing like the Chief. James was kind and good—and tall. *I could get lost in you*, she thought.

His voice was a low caress as he asked, "Want to get out of here?"

She pulled back, looked up at him, and nodded. "Yes. I really do."

THE EARLYBIRD™/ SATURDAY / 7:33 A.M.
THE E-NEWSLETTER TRUSTED BY WASHINGTON'S POLITICAL ELITE

Good morning, EarlyBirders™. Here are the morning's need-to-know stories.

BARBARO BREAKS HER SILENCE. Sonia Barbaro at the LA Premiere of her film Trafficked: *"Too often the survivors of sexual assault are disbelieved. I've spoken my truth. Like my character in this film, Loretta, I won't back down. We do not need to hide any longer."* Developing...

World Poetry Day: It's today. And the official @FLOTUS Twitter account posted an audio clip of FLOTUS READING *Diving into the Wreck* by poet Adrienne Rich. *Isn't FLOTUS at a SILENT RETREAT?* What gives, **Adam Majors**?! Please return our call.

Spotted: *At the Sahadi cocktail. MSNBC's* **Chris Matthews** *talking to FOX News's* **Chris Wallace**, *CNN's* **Dana Bash**, **Gloria Borger**, *WashPo's* **Ruth Marcus**, *ATN's* **Reginald Bounds** *leaving with* **Jazzmyn Maine**, *and ATN's* **Natalie Savage** *leaving with* **James Harding**, *son of former DEPSECDEF* **Fred Harding**. *An eagle-eyed tip:* **Jazzmyn Maine** *was seen looking "disheveled and upset" hours later as she left the Jefferson Hotel in a cab.*

22

ONE SECOND FOR SEX

Too hot. Natalie pushed the comforter down trying to get some cool air onto her body, but it wouldn't move. The half-asleep part of her brain told her to ignore it and keep her eyes closed. That seemed right since her body felt heavy and the bed was so soft and warm. Unusually warm. Warm like there was another body there with her.

James!

Her eyes flew open and she found herself in a room that, to the best of her knowledge, she'd never seen. The night before came flooding back. The talk with the Jazzmyn. The Chief. Two Xanax. Leaving the party with James and then…nothing. She couldn't remember getting to his place.

Careful to avoid any sudden movements, she lifted her head slightly. Turning to assess the situation, she came eyeball to eyeball with a golden retriever.

The dog pressed his wet nose against her cheek, trying to push her back to sleep, and she had to swallow back a giggle. When she reached out to pet him, she noticed her blouse was still on.

A quick inventory revealed that except for her coat and shoes she was fully dressed. Had nothing happened?

Flustered, she pushed herself into a sitting position, patted the dog, and scanned the room. There it was, at her four o'clock: one seriously handsome man asleep in a massive easy chair, shirtless. James. He could, indeed, give Ryan a run for his money in the Pectoral Olympics. He was lean and muscular with a smattering of hair at the center of his chest. She felt flushed and knew she shouldn't stare but she couldn't help it. Shirtless, James was sort of breathtaking. Also very far away.

What is he doing over there?

Her mind started racing with possibilities. What if he hadn't wanted to fool around with her? What if he'd just taken her home out of pity or duty or guilt?

While she was assessing the situation, James's eyes opened and her breath caught as their eyes locked.

"Good morning, Sleeping Beauty," he said with a scratchy voice and a smile.

"Good morning," she replied, and, in panic, turned away to wipe under her eyes and remove any stray makeup.

"Sorry to surprise you with an unexpected overnight," he said, still reclined and breathtaking in his shirtless splendor.

Trying to sound composed, she pushed herself up. "How come you slept over there, in the chair?" It came out like a squeak.

One corner of his mouth lifted into the slightest smile. "Well, you kind of fell asleep in the car without giving me your address. And you were pretty hard to wake up. Since you really weren't in shape to consent to a slumber party..." He shrugged and indicated the chair. "You must be really exhausted from all the traveling you've been doing?"

She blushed furiously.

Really smooth, she commended herself. *Step one, go home with the cute guy you like. Step two, kick him out of his bed. You have a great future as a How Not to Have a Life coach.*

"Can I ask a question?" she whispered, anticipating a horrible answer. "Did I do anything really embarrassing?"

"No," he said, shaking his head with a grin. He arched a single eyebrow and she felt her blush deepen. "You did get a little chatty. You said something about a patchouli nudist party. Is that what the cool reporters are doing these days?"

She covered her face with a hand. "I said that? Oh god." She took a deep breath and forced herself to look up and meet his eyes. "It's a nudist resort, and I'm not the one going. I hope that doesn't disappoint you?"

"Not at all. I'm a little relieved actually." He smiled. "Friends?"

"No. It's my mom's wedding," she went on, feeling suddenly exhausted, as if just talking about her mother could suck the life force from her. "She's going through this earth mama phase. At first I thought it was just to get attention, but she seems pretty committed." She sighed. "She's marrying a nudist."

"She's marrying a nudist," James repeated, carefully. "Will the ceremony be—?"

"God, no. No. At least I hope not. No, that's the honeymoon."

A cough of laughter escaped from James before he could clap a hand over his mouth. "I'm sorry, this probably isn't funny for you but—"

"It should be funny," Natalie said, smiling. "If I were in my right mind about my mother it would be but I just—"

Suddenly she froze.

"What day is it?" she asked, feeling a rising sense of panic.

"Saturday."

The wedding. *No, this can't be happening,* her mind screamed.

"What time is it?" she asked. Her body was already in motion, scrambling off the bed, scanning the apartment for her shoes and iPhone and any sign that this wasn't happening.

She spotted the alarm clock. 7:10 a.m. A rush of relief flooded her body. Hallelujah, thank god! The apothecary party didn't start till until ten, the ceremony was at noon. That gave her plenty of time to get ready and hit the road.

"What's going on?" James's eyes were appraising her.

"Sorry," she said. "My mom's wedding is today. It's okay, it's not until later, but I thought—"

She looked around the room and spotted her iPhone plugged in to charge overnight. *James did that?* How thoughtful. Grabbing it, she walked over to the chair where James was now sitting up, shirtless. Just to show him that she wasn't lying or making an excuse for a quick escape, she let him glimpse the screen and the note that read: MOM'S WEDDING!!!!!! DON'T BE LATE!!!!!!

The pulse in Natalie's throat fluttered as she felt James's proximity. He seemed totally relaxed with his chest on full display, as if this was pretty much his normal Saturday routine.

He squinted at the phone. "How much time do you need? If you stay a little longer, I'll make you breakfast."

She could feel his warmth. He smelled so good.

"And what would we do after breakfast?" she asked coyly.

He did that half smile thing again. The smile was warm and inviting and without thinking about it, she bent and kissed him.

Her kiss was cautious and light. When he kissed back, it was hungry and hot. She felt something let go inside her. Now she was against him, moving with him, sending shivers through her body. He shifted and laid her back on the chair, unbuttoning her blouse and exposing her bra. She met his eyes and felt heat diffuse to the very edges of her body. She reached up to trace her finger over his bare chest. He made a sound deep in his throat and pulled her toward him. As she felt his skin hot against hers, he asked what she wanted and she didn't need to think.

"You."

Just then her phone rang.

"Do you need to get it?" he whispered.

She shook her head no and reached for him. His lips were on

hers, moving soft but firm, when the phone rang again. And the dog started to bark. Loudly.

"CP, quiet," James commanded, then went back to what he'd been doing with his mouth.

The barking continued. James stopped and smiled.

"I'm sorry. Would you give me a minute?" he asked, looking apologetic while still on top of her. "I better deal with Colin Powell."

She frowned. "What about Colin Powell?"

Pushing himself up and off the bed, James shook his head. "He needs to pee."

She stared at him. "Colin Powell needs to pee."

He reached for a leash by the side of the bed. "Colin Powell is my godfather. He gave me the dog. So I named him Colin Powell."

She stared at the dog and back at James. She was at a loss for words. James was hot and he was a gentleman and Colin Powell was his godfather?

After he left the room, she stretched out and luxuriated in the feeling of being in James's place. *I could be here all day*, she thought. If it weren't for the wedding from hell.

Her phone rang again and she sighed. She was sure it was her sister, Sarah, reminding her to bring an extra set of stockings and a pair of low heels in case she needed them later that night. Taking her time, Natalie reached for the phone. The screen didn't say Sarah, it said News Desk, and they were calling for the third time.

"Natalie, we need you here ASAP." It was a What Girl.

Calmly, she explained that this was her mom's wedding day. That she'd requested it off even before she'd agreed to move down to DC, temporarily. That even Bibb understood she had the day off.

"Hang on," the What Girl said.

The line went silent and she knew the next voice would be Hal's. This had to be his doing.

"Natalie, I know it's your mother's wedding." To Natalie's surprise, it was Bibb. "But we're doing a special at the top of the hour and Jazzmyn can't make it in. We need a female voice."

Jazzmyn! They wanted her to miss her mother's wedding to accommodate Jazzmyn's morning schedule. *Does that involve breakfast with the boss*, Natalie wondered. *She's leaning all the way in*, she thought, then instantly felt guilty.

"I'm sorry, I have to be at my mother's wedding," Natalie said firmly.

Bibb continued, "I need you at work. Sonia Barbaro is in the US and is saying things that could precipitate an international crisis. We're in major breaking news and need a woman's voice. What time does the wedding start?"

In a low voice, Natalie said, "There's a gathering at 10 a.m. The wedding's at noon."

"I can let you out in time for the wedding. You can skip the pre-wedding activities. You'll be anchoring with Ryan. I'll personally ensure you'll make it in time for the ceremony."

When she hung up, James was standing over her, looking apprehensive.

"What is it?"

"There's breaking news, they want me in," Natalie said, feeling defeated and embarrassed in front of him. "Saying no isn't an option. It's hard to explain—"

He held up a hand. "You don't have to explain. My dad was a deputy secretary at the Pentagon. Forty years in the service. I understand when saying no to work isn't an option."

She stared at him. Who was this guy? A saint?

He reached past her to hang up the leash and she saw his biceps flex. No. Saints definitely did not have arms like those. She thought of the way he'd just kissed her and she wanted to make sure he understood she really didn't want to go. "James, I—" She began.

The phone rang again, like an incantation. *This is your chance. You're on the elevator now.*

She closed her eyes, took a deep breath, and opened them again.

She had to get to work.

23

THE SURRENDERED REPORTER

"I know it tickles, honey, but sit still or the lash won't go on right," the nice woman painting wet glue onto the rim of Natalie's eyelids told her.

"Sorry. It feels like my eyeball is on fire."

"Try to think of something else. Think about how you're becoming a star. You're getting PFE," the makeup lady said.

"PFE?" That was a new one.

"Pure effing exposure. Getting your face on TV as much as possible."

The makeup lady blew on Natalie's lid as she used tweezers to press the lashes into place, making Natalie's lid start to go numb.

Numb is good, she thought. *Numb means your eyeball doesn't burn anymore.*

At 8:46 a.m., even small victories were important.

"Savage in the house! Anchor chair, here we come," Matt's voice said, seeming even louder than usual.

She hadn't expected him to be there. "What are you doing up so early?" Natalie asked, sneaking a glance out of one eye.

"Keep them closed," the makeup lady barked. She went on,

apparently addressing Matt, "Don't you interrupt. She has to be on set in ten minutes."

"I just want to congratulate my reporter on getting an anchor spot with McChesty," Matt said, sounding unusually cheery. "And make sure she understands her role."

"Meaning?" Natalie asked. Even with her eyes closed she could feel him standing too close.

"Meaning DO NOT let Ryan interrupt you. You need to get in there. Equal time. Think of this as a WWE matchup. You're going for the smackdown. Bury him. Have no fear, show no mercy."

"I left my Lycra unitard at home so I don't think WWE is happe—"

Natalie felt a tap on her chin, an indication it was okay to open her eyes. She did and the mirror showed her lashes the size of small tarantulas. Natalie forced a smile at the makeup lady who beamed back and started looking through her kit of lip glosses.

Natalie turned to Matt. "More important, where is Jazzmyn? Any gossip?" She paused while Dusky Rose lip gloss was painted onto her lips. "I'm dying to know why she can't be here."

Matt shook his head. "Other than the thing in EarlyBird, no clue."

"What was in EarlyBird?" Natalie asked, studying the lip color in the mirror.

"She was spotted doing a bad walk of shame out of the Jefferson Hotel last night. Tears 'n' all," he said. "Some Mr. Right must have turned out to be Very Wrong."

Natalie turned to face Matt, realization dawning. "Matt, she was there with the Chief."

"Definitely Mr. Wrong," Matt said, gloating.

"Shit. What if something terrible happened?" Natalie whispered, staring at the floor.

Pulse flaring, Natalie felt her chest pool with dread. Except it wasn't dread, it was guilt. After what happened with the Chief in the kitchen, she should have found Jazzmyn. She should have stepped in. She'd let Jazzmyn march into that. Why? Was she jealous? Trying to hurt her? Honestly, she hadn't even thought about the younger woman. She'd just taken the pills and checked out.

"Listen, lie down with dogs," Matt said.

"Jazzmyn can take care of herself," the makeup artist declared, squeezing Natalie lightly on the shoulder. Turning, the woman faced Matt, brandishing a flatiron like a weapon. "Now back up. We need to get her ready."

"Okay, okay, don't brand me please," Matt said, putting up his hands in surrender.

Natalie's eyes were wet when she turned to Matt. "Matt, can you please find out where Jazzmyn is today and how I can reach her?" Her throat was starting to go sore.

"Just focus on nailing this gig," Matt said. "I like the idea of producing for an anchor."

"Please," Natalie implored.

"Fine. If you're going to be a downer, I'll go raid the office supply cabinet. Did you know they still stock office supplies? Welcome to the modern office of the new millennium, have a number 2 pencil. See you in the studio, Hot Nerd," he said as he ambled out of the room.

When Matt was gone, Natalie wiped away her tears and inhaled deeply. She would check in on Jazzmyn later. There was nothing she could do right now. She had to focus. She apologized to the makeup artist who leaned in for a quick touch-up.

"You didn't get this from me," the makeup artist said. "Better to lie low with the Chief. He can be vindictive. Whatever you think you know, let it go. Jazzmyn will be okay. She's spent a lot of this time in this chair and I can tell you she's tougher than you think. So don't play the hero, just get on that set and do your thing."

When it was complete, Natalie gave herself a once-over and

saw the makeup woman had outdone herself. She'd walked in looking like Humpty Dumpty after the eggpocalypse, but now you could hardly tell she was just off of a week of epic travel, word of a possible assault, and a one-night stand with a golden retriever.

Also a make-out session. She allowed herself one moment to think about James, then, feeling guilty, forced her mind from the past to the future. She needed all the confidence five pounds of makeup, three inches of heel, and a little cleavage could give her to get Savage with McChesty.

The blast of air-conditioning that hit her when she opened the studio door sent a shiver down her spine. She wished she was wearing something more than a thin skirt and silk chiffon blouse. She wished she'd eaten breakfast. She wished she was still in bed with James or at least his dog.

"On this set, they see your whole body. Legs 'n' all, so don't do anything dirty below the waist," the stage manager said as he led her to a high stool with no back. Even with Natalie's heels, the chair was way too high for her, so the stage manager had to heave her up onto the seat.

"These things aren't made for smaller women," he said.

Yeah, she'd gotten that. Between the temperature and the fact that any guest wearing a skirt could accidentally "do something dirty" by shifting in her seat, it was clear the whole set wasn't designed for any women, small or large.

He thrust an earpiece at her and efficiently strung the chord down her back, plugging it into a box affixed to her chair, indicating the volume knob for her to adjust, then repeated the procedure with the microphone and her chest before he headed off backstage.

Natalie was thinking about Sonia Barbaro's comments on the red carpet when she became aware that the studio was rotating around her. Or rather that her seat was turning in a slow circle toward the back of the room. She shifted her weight, trying to make the seat stop rotating and felt around for a footrest for leverage—no luck. When the chair stopped moving, she was facing the back of the room.

And stuck.

She evaluated her options: unhook her earpiece, mic, and the cords going up her back, jump off the stool, and then attempt a remount on her own. Or wait helplessly like a baby in a high chair for someone to push her back into place.

She heard the studio door open.

Please let that be a tech guy, she prayed.

"Nat, is that you?" Ryan's voice asked her.

Not the tech guy.

He stepped into view. "Why are you facing the corner? Have you been naughty?" he said with a smirk.

"Morning!" she said with exaggerated cheer. "Actually, if you could turn me around and push me a little closer to the desk, that would be great." She smiled at him with as much dignity as she could muster.

Ryan did as she asked. "Probably want to hold on for safety," he advised, tapping his knuckles on the gray Formica surface of the desk.

"Thanks," Natalie said, mortified and annoyed at once.

As Ryan perched on the stool next to her effortlessly, Natalie felt a sudden craving for the comfort of warm pants, low shoes, and a workplace designed for her ease.

"We've got to repeat the Bickersons routine from the other day," Ryan said brightly. "That was TV gold."

"I think—"

"Even you can't possibly want to defend Sonia Barbaro. She is shameless," he interrupted as he started stringing the microphone up his shirt. "What a piece of work."

"Excuse me?" Natalie asked, biting back a snarl.

"Save it for air, you two," a voice said into Natalie's earpiece.

As she held onto the Formica and stared into the silent studio, listening to the producers on her earpiece talk about nut allergies, she felt a rising worry. Like she was strapped in to a roller coaster that was missing its safety bar.

Come on, this is exactly where you want to be.

Intense yellow lights came on, flooding the studio like a heavenly intervention. A voice came alive in her ear.

"All right, you guys. We've got the top of the show scripted in prompter. After that, it's all you. Ryan, you're on cameras one and three. Natalie, you're on two and four. We have two-shots on cameras five and six. And we'll be ready with video of Rigo, the protesters, Sonia. You say it, just assume we'll play it. With some surprises to boot. Ready, guys?"

"One minute to air!" someone shouted.

Natalie fluffed her hair and smoothed out her blouse, then realized her stool was rotating away from the cameras again. She pawed desperately at the desk, catching the edge just in time to right herself, looking around to see if anyone had noticed.

"Thirty seconds!" someone shouted.

Ryan was making big movements with his mouth, like he'd done when Heath was on set, only now he was showier and added in big shoulder circles and a tongue flutter.

"We're live in 15...10...5, 4, 3, 2..."

The stage manager pointed at Ryan, who emanated Good Cheer and Down-home Machismo. "Good morning. It's 9 a.m. on the East Coast, 6 a.m. on the West Coast. Welcome to a special edition of *Big Politics This Weekend*, I'm Ryan McGreavy."

The stagehand pointed to Natalie and she began reading off the teleprompter into camera 2.

"And I'm Natalie Savage. Today we lead with the Sonia Barbaro bombshell that is sending shock waves from Hollywood to the nation's capital," she said dutifully.

Ryan took over. "The Venezuelan vixen was strutting the red carpet for the Los Angeles premiere of her controversial new film, *Trafficked*. It's about a young women kidnapped into sex slavery. What a coincidence!"

Following along in prompter, Natalie noted that Ryan had ad libbed generously.

Two can play that game, she thought as she took the baton.

"Her alleged attacker, the Colombian party boy Rigo Lystra, remains holed up in the Colombian embassy in Washington, DC. Lystra says he fears the Venezuelans will kidnap him if he leaves the embassy and force him to stand trial," said Natalie before adding her own commentary. "However, it's important to note that the US State Department has assured Rigo Lystra safe passage home." She turned to Ryan. "Many critics are asking, if he's innocent, why is he so afraid to leave the building?"

A voice in her ear directed, "Guys, this is great stuff but save it for later. Stick to the script for the intro."

Ignoring the prompter, Ryan replied, "Because the Venezuelans will set him up for a trial as fake as these accusations."

"Throw to graphic!" the voice said from the control room.

They did and the screen exploded into the tiny red and green shards from which the words BREAKING ON ATN came bursting forth, followed by video of Sonia Barbaro on the red carpet. Natalie hadn't yet seen the footage. Barbaro looked gorgeous, in a strapless burgundy mermaid gown, cut to show her long caramel legs, black hair shimmering down her back. The woman was flawless.

"Look at that." Ryan said as the video of Barbaro squeezed back to take up half the screen, the other half filled with a shot of Natalie and Ryan on set together. "Does she look like a victim living in fear? I don't think so."

"She looks like a professional actress doing her job," Natalie replied, wondering whether Ryan believed what he was saying or was just posturing for TV. "We're all savvy enough to understand actresses are expected to dress provocatively when they promote their films."

In Natalie's ear, someone said, "Good comeback, Natalie. Keep it going, guys." The monitors switched now to show three boxes. Ryan in one, Natalie in another, video of Sonia in the middle.

"Have to or want to?" Ryan asked. "And I think 'promote' is the key word there. As in self-promotion."

"Love that!" the voice said.

Natalie smiled to soften what she was about to say. "Wait, you're calling her a self-promoter because she's showing some flesh? Isn't that a little close to home?" She batted her false eyelashes and to the camera said, "Hey, control room, can we put up video of Ryan disrobing outside the embassy?"

"Love it!" the control room said as, on cue, one half of the screen filled with video of Ryan removing his shirt earlier that week, on the other half was a live picture of Ryan, looking pissed, on set.

In her peripheral vision, Natalie noticed Matt on side of the studio, making pummeling gestures like he was knocking out a WWE competitor.

"Thank you for making my point for me," Ryan said, recovering.

"Which is?"

"Showing flesh gets attention. So do fake accusations. Do you think it's just a coincidence Barbaro is promoting a film about sexual assault while claiming to be a victim of one? Listen, I grew up in politics and I know how these games go. Claiming assault is a great way to get free media and lots of sympathy, which is exactly what we're giving her right now." He sounded sanctimonious. "If you want to talk about victims, let's talk about the victim holed up in the Colombian embassy."

"Rigo Lystra? He is among the richest people in the world with his own army and a fleet of private jets at his disposal. How on earth is he a victim?" Natalie asked.

"Rich men can't be innocent?"

"Famous women can't be assaulted?" Natalie did her best to summon her version of Ryan's Earnest and Sincere look. "I'm curious, Ryan, what would you like Sonia Barbaro to do? Give up her career, go into hiding? And if you would silence Sonia Barbaro, an international celebrity, what kind of message are you sending far less powerful women who are worried about being shamed for speaking out about assault?" Natalie asked.

"*Alleged* assault," Ryan corrected. "No one has been found guilty here." His eyes shone as he took the high road. He was right. "And let's talk about who's really in hiding. Rigo Lystra is holed up in a building on Massachusetts Avenue that he can't leave. He can't have a life. While Sonia Barbaro is globe-trotting and going to Hollywood parties dressed like a stripper."

"Guys, this is great stuff!" the control room enthused. "We have a surprise caller. Stand by. We're letting him join you now."

The next voice came over the crackling sounds of a cell phone line.

"*Hola, mis amigos. ¡Buenos días!*" said a familiar voice.

"*¡Rigo, mi amigo!*" Ryan broke out in a warm grin. "How are you?"

"To be honest, my friend, it is very hard. Living here in solitude. For me, freedom is a memory."

It took all Natalie's willpower to hold back a groan. According to the *Washington Post*, he'd had the cast of Cirque du Soleil flown in for a show the night before.

"Admiral Lystra, hello, this is Natalie Savage," she said, using his official title. "I understand you're a big fan of acrobatics. You had a Vegas-style show at the embassy last night, with a sushi dinner, yes? Help us understand how that's a life of solitude," she challenged.

"Some of my friends have been kind enough to keep me company, this is true," he said plaintively. "But I am still a prisoner."

"Our own State Department says you can leave any time and they will guarantee you safe passage out of the country."

"No, this is not true. The Venezuelans would take me."

"What evidence do you have to support this claim?" Natalie pressed. "And, respectfully, why should we believe you over our own State Department?"

"Because the Venezuelans cannot be trusted," Rigo said, raising his voice. "In America, you do not understand. Venezuela is very bad country run by very dangerous people. Very dangerous! It is a cancer in our hemisphere! The threat from Venezuela is greater than you and the American people know. Today they threaten me. Tomorrow they will threaten my country. Soon they will be a threat to us all. They must be stopped."

Natalie, surprised he'd veered into a foreign policy argument instead of the he-said-she-said, was formulating a reply when a voice from the control room yelled in her ear.

"Guys, we have breaking news. We're going to bye-bye Rigo. Savage, you're handling the news. Someone should be out with a sheet by now."

Out of nowhere, a hand emerged from under the anchor desk. Looking down, Natalie was startled to see the laconic associate producer she'd spoken to in the control room the day Rigo was kidnapped, crouched under her legs, using one arm to pass her a piece of paper. Accepting it, she resisted the urge to wave hello at him.

Suddenly music was playing in her ear and she looked up to see the monitors fill with bright red graphics and the words Breaking Development, which shattered into a thousand tiny pieces. Natalie faced the camera as a voice in her ear said:

"We are interrupting our coverage for breaking news—"

"We are interrupting our coverage for breaking news," she said.

"From TMZ," the voice said.

"In from the celebrity news organization, TMZ." *Oh god*, her mind screamed, *please let this be legit.*

"FLOTUS lover," the voice said in her ear.

"TMZ has new details about the Mystery Man in those videos with the First Lady," Natalie said. Just then, the monitors went full with the surveillance video of FLOTUS with her unnamed lover, which allowed Natalie the freedom to look down and read from the piece of paper she'd just been handed.

"According to TMZ, the man in the video is named Anthony Cantrell," she read. "He's led quite the jet-set life. He was a model in his twenties, but no known career since then. In recent years, Cantrell has been in residence in Palm Beach, Chicago's Gold Coast, Paris, and Hollywood." Natalie could hear the sound of her own heart pounding in her ears.

"Ryan, we've got photos," someone said in Natalie's ear.

She paused to let Ryan take over. "Let's get a look at Mr. Cantrell," said Ryan. On the monitor, photos of the Mystery Man popped up. He was photographed with one wealthy woman after another. Ryan narrated, "Here he is with an heiress of an automotive fortune. This woman here is married to Brazil's Sugar King. And this woman—a child really—is the daughter of one of France's biggest pop stars."

Ryan paused and shook his head. "Well, Nat, there's one thing all these women have in common. They're loaded."

"If the reporting is right," she said, feeling both defensive of the First Lady and wary of anything that came out of Ryan's mouth, "at the very least it raises a lot of questions."

"Like just how big a gold digger is this guy? And why is the president allowing the First Lady to humiliate him like this?" Ryan asked.

When they went to break, the voice came booming into Natalie's ear. "Guys, this is great stuff! Home run. We were planning to go to taped programming at the top of the hour but New York wants us to stick with the live coverage."

No! Natalie's mind screamed as she flicked her eyes to a clock. 10 a.m. "I can't. I have to go." She powered on her phone and saw it start filling up with texts.

SARAH: Morning!

SARAH: I tried calling and got voice mail. You didn't oversleep, did you?

SARAH: Earth to Natalie?

SARAH: Um, you remember what today is?

SARAH: Holy shit! You're on TV. What are you thinking? It's Mom's wedding. I don't care how important you are or what's happening at work, you need to figure out your priorities and get here. Now.

Natalie jumped out of her seat.

"Today is my mom's wedding," she said, ripping off her microphone and throwing off her earpiece. "You guys can handle this without me. I gotta go."

As she was running out the door, she heard Ryan pick back up.

"Sonia Barbaro has been famous ever since she was a little girl. When she was just ten, she told the Venezuelan press she wanted to get an Oscar before her twenty-fifth birthday. Now she's a seductive, ambitious, grown woman. Some say her claim against Rigo Lystra could earn her that award…"

It is what it is, Natalie thought as she headed out of the building.

24

BURY MY HEART WITH NOREEN'S APOTHECARY

Natalie knew that if she went over eighty miles per hour on the George Washington Memorial Parkway, she risked getting slapped with a misdemeanor reckless driving charge. On the other hand, arriving late for Noreen's wedding guaranteed her a lifetime of weaponized guilt, so she floored it. She'd have to make the remaining fifty-minute drive in forty if she was going to get to her mom's in time to change before the ceremony started. It could be done. Just barely.

"I'm so happy for you," Natalie said aloud as she cruised down the parkway. "I'm so happy for you," she repeated, trying out different intonations. She'd found having a line ready to use on her mother made their conversations easier because she didn't have to think about what to say, which meant she didn't have to think about what her mother had said. Their communication went much more smoothly when neither of them paid close attention.

Natalie pushed her speed to ninety miles an hour when her phone buzzed.

"Siri, please read me my texts," she said to her phone.

"Looking up hexes," the polite British male voice she'd assigned to Siri answered. "There are two million two hundred sixty thousand entries for—"

"No. Read me my texts," she tried again, more slowly.

"I'm sorry, I didn't get that. Do you want a history of vests?"

Third time was the charm.

British male Siri started reciting. "Sarah writes—are you en route? I told Mom you're almost here. I currently reek of something called Wild Woman Luna Drops and am not washing it off till you arrive.

"Sarah writes—I mean it. You better be on your way. I think I'm losing my sense of smell.

"Sarah writes—this is for your sake more than mine. If you are late, you'd better plan to make a new life for yourself somewhere far from Bridezilla."

Natalie laughed. She liked the way British Man Siri said Bridezilla.

"Siri, please reply, tell Mom I'm there but I've gotten so thin she can't see me without her glasses. Mom will be thrilled."

"Sarah writes—pro. Bowly. Mom keeps asking if I've gained weight since my fitting. Apparently my ankles are particularly offensive."

"Siri, please reply, I'm on my way. Be there by eleven forty-five. How is the new McMansion? Is it McDecorated in a McTheme?"

"Sarah writes—are you dictating your texts? I am not sure what a macman sin is but I think I want one. Sounds both tasty and naughty. But if you were talking about the decoration, I promise you will be astonished."

"Siri, reply, say more about that please."

"Sarah writes—let's just say I'm calling it Aztec Barbie Dream House."

"Siri, reply, I am trying to picture that but sort of in the way that you watch horror movies through your fingers."

"Sarah writes—hurry up and get here! Mom's coming at me with a diffuser full of patchouli."

"I'm so happy for you, I'm so happy for you," Natalie intoned as she sped through the suburbs of Virginia. She did some fancy in-and-out-driving, causing two people to honk and one man to give her the finger. "I'm so happy for you," she yelled at him as she sped off and she meant it, especially when she managed to arrive in front of her mom's new house at exactly 11:45. A few hours late for the bridesmaids events, but plenty of time to change for the wedding. It was like not being late at all. She'd run in and change—surely her mother would still be primping.

She jumped out of the car, grabbed her suitcase, and wheeled it to the front door. From inside she heard barking and through the window she could see Cronkite, her dad's black Lab, running in circles of excitement. Her dad used to say Cronkite always knew when she was headed home.

"Hello?" she said, pushing open the front door, getting a face full of furry dog. Paws on her chest, Cronkite stood licking her face in huge long slaps. She laughed, but felt her throat get a little tight and had to close her eyes against an unexpected welling of tears. *Fuck*, she thought. She heard glasses clinking and the sound of people talking in the distance and knew she should go and join the party. She was too old for this. For how much longer would the sight of Cronkite make her feel like her dad was still alive?

"How kind of you to join us. Or did you only come for the dog?"

Natalie felt a jolt of primal fear, like a kid caught wearing muddy shoes on a white carpet. She spun around, pushing Cronkite to the floor. "Mom! Hi! I'm so sorry I'm late." Ignoring the survival instinct telling her to duck and cover, she leaned in and gave her mom a hug. Her mother was wearing a long lace and fringe dress, with feathers in her hair. If she were a doll, she would have been called Original American Stevie Nicks.

Natalie stepped back in a pantomime of admiration. "Mom, you look amazing!"

"I know. I've been using the most wonderful yam and pumpkin enzyme peel. It's just delicious. If it weren't for the hyaluronic acid, I swear I might eat it!" Noreen threw her head back to give Natalie a better view of her throat. "Is the contrast with my neck too extreme?"

"You look great, Mom." If her mother's neck had been covered in irradiated scales, Natalie would have given the same answer. "You look gorgeous and happy like a beautiful bride."

"Actually, I think it's all the orgasms," Noreen said in a whisper. "Your father liked sex well enough, but wasn't very good at stimulating me. Gerald is just so much more gifted in that department. I know he isn't much to look at, but his skills bring out the most erotic response. He's a true sexual dynamo."

Natalie stared at her mother, wondering how normal daughters would react to this information. "I'm so happy for you," she said.

Clearly displeased to not have provoked a more heated reaction, Natalie's mother switched gears. "You are late and we're holding the wedding for you. Just you. I asked you to come yesterday, and you couldn't be bothered, and now we're all waiting on Miss Important TV Star." She surveyed Natalie. "I see the studio did your makeup. The eyelashes are a bit much, don't you think?"

There was no way to win—in this battle, every victory was a defeat. Plus, Natalie really wanted to check her phone and knew her mother would freak out if she did it right there. So she raised the white flag. "I'm really sorry, Mom. I'm sorry I'm late. I'll go upstairs and change and tone down the makeup, okay? I can be ready really fast."

"Natty! Natty!" The squeal was accompanied by the sound of tiny pounding feet and Natalie looked up to see Sarah's four-year-old daughter, Lulu, running straight at her.

"Hi, sweet Lulu! I've missed you," she said, catching the little girl in her arms and spinning her around with a squeeze. She buried her face in her niece's neck and inhaled the feeling of warmth and love. God, she'd missed this. It had been so long since she'd last seen her. "I'm so happy to be with you," Natalie said, lifting Lulu high in the air to get a better look at her. "Don't you look like a big girl in your flower girl dress!"

"Gramma doesn't like my dress. Gramma says Mommy should have got me a more 'ganic dress. But I like this one!"

Lulu twisted her head around to look at Noreen, who said with exaggerated pronunciation, "Organic," then with a sigh explained, "With what we know these days, it's unwise to dress little people in anything other than organics. I read that polyester can contribute to autism, learning disabilities, and several unfortunate skin conditions."

"I'm not little," Lulu declared and, turning back to Natalie, said, "I'm five. Well, almost five. Really four and ten months, but soon I'll be five. I go to kindergarten."

"I know," Natalie said with a laugh. She was filled with wonder and a bit of jealousy of Lulu's calm handling of her grandmother. "I think your dress is beautiful. And I agree you're definitely old enough for it. Four and ten months is super grown up."

Natalie put Lulu down as a group of Noreen's friends came crowding in, followed by Sarah. The sight of Sarah was like a balm for Natalie, giving her palpable, physical relief. More than anything she wanted to run over and hug her but was intercepted by two of Noreen's new friends.

"You must be the *famous* Natalie! I watch you on TV all the time."

"Such a treat to meet you. Your mother is constantly bragging about how successful you are and posting all your pieces on Facebook. She is so proud of you."

Natalie watched her mom transform her gaze into a beatific, maternal glow. "Yes. And her father would be so proud, too. Makes me tear up just thinking about it." Natalie did her best to stop herself from letting her disbelief show. Was it possible her mother, who had nothing but criticism to her face, boasted about her to her new friends?

Sarah shot Natalie a look that said Do Not Make a Scene, and Natalie did as ordered.

The real Noreen returned as soon as the women left. "You know I'd already met your father by the time I was your age," she said to Natalie. "I had your sister when I was two years older than you. Aren't you dating anyone, Natalie?"

You can dress her in all naturals, marry her to a nudist, but you can't take the nosy out of Noreen.

"I'm so happy for you," Natalie said.

Noreen frowned. "What is that supposed to mean? Is that some kind of insult?"

Natalie's thoughts suddenly went to her phone. Had she left it in the car or was it in her bag? She really needed to check it.

"I think it means she's happy for you, Mom," Sarah translated, lunging forward and grabbing Natalie's hand. "I think she needs to change. And I want a few minutes to catch up with her."

Noreen looked unsure then said with a wave. "Fine, but hurry up. Natalie has already done her best to try to ruin my day. I will not accept any more of her chaos."

"Curses, foiled again," Natalie said under her breath and got an elbow in the ribs from Sarah.

With Lulu leading the way, they trooped upstairs and down a hall painted deep red and turquoise with a massive feather serving as wall art. "Is this just for the wedding, or is Mom really this into Native Americana?" Natalie said.

"Unclear. You should see what she did downstairs. It's Southern gentry shabby chic," Sarah said, then pushed open a door and immediately stepped aside, letting Natalie get the first huge whiff of extra sweet cotton candy smell.

Natalie recoiled with a yelp and felt an instant headache bloom. "Seriously?"

Sarah shook her head. "Mom's aesthetic may have changed, but her love affair with department store diffusers is alive and well."

The room was filled with massive pillows upholstered in Native American chevron patterns, not a piece of furniture in the place. As soon as the door of the room was closed, Natalie pulled out her iPhone. Unchecked for a terrifying ten minutes, it was alive with notifications; twenty-four new notifications on Twitter, thirty new followers on Snapchat, twenty-two new friend requests on Facebook. Each notification made her feel more invigorated, just the shot in the arm she needed.

"Natalie? What are you doing?" Sarah asked.

Natalie answered without looking up from her phone. "Checking my messages on social. I have almost five hundred new followers and a ton of messages in the last hour because I got to anchor this morning. It's crazy." She toggled over to Instagram. She'd forgotten to check her Insta account.

"You have a follower right here, who would love your attention," Sarah said and there was an unfamiliar edge in her sister's voice. "Not to mention a wedding that's waiting on you."

Natalie looked up and saw that Lulu was staring adoringly at her. Overcome with a wave of shame, she dropped onto her knees and held out her arms, gesturing for Lulu to come give her a hug. Cronkite rushed in at the same time as Lulu and three of them fell over and started rolling around on the ground, clutched in a big furry ball.

"I'm sorry," Natalie said, looking up at Sarah from the floor. "I'm being a jerk. I'm just distracted and stressed and tired and the traffic was awful."

"Gramma says you're selfish," Lulu offered. "And she says you always put work first just like Grandpa did."

Even in the safe warmth of the hug, the words stung. Since meeting Gerald, her mother had become increasingly critical of her dad. He'd been selfish to work so hard. He was more interested in reading than in spending time with his family. He had punished her by dying. Since her mother enjoyed pointing out how much Natalie was like her father, the insults began to feel transferable.

"I can't remember. Did Mom put Dad down this much when he was alive?" Natalie asked.

Sarah's face wrinkled. "What are you talking about?"

Natalie did her best Noreen imitation. "I used to be miserable, but now with my new life I have art and orgasms."

"What is an orgasm?" Lulu asked.

"Something grown-ups get," Natalie told her.

"Like divorces?"

Natalie shook her head. "Not really like divorces. Nicer."

"Orgasm," Lulu repeated.

Sarah mouthed, "I am going to kill you."

Natalie gave her a wide-eyed look and mouthed back, "I'm sorry."

"Do you like Gramma's new house?" Lulu asked Natalie.

"It's a lot different than the house we grew up in," she answered vaguely. To Sarah she said, "I just don't understand why every time Mom talks about how happy she is, she has to put Dad down. It's like she has to make him awful in order to prove she's better off now."

"Um, I don't think Mom is trying to be happy to get back at Dad. She is just trying to go on with her life." Sarah gave her a concerned-sister look. "Are you okay?"

"I'm great. Why are you asking like that?"

"You aren't using your happy voice," Lulu said.

"No, you're not," Sarah agreed.

Natalie knew that it was Sarah's nature to worry. And as much as she loved and respected her sister, they lived in different worlds. Sarah was a naturopath in Charlottesville and a mom. There was no way she could understand what Natalie was up against.

"I'm fine." Natalie's fingers itched to get back to her phone. "I just need to do a quick change before the hellebration starts."

Her father would have understood. She looked at Cronkite and could swear he understood.

"What's a hellebration?" Lulu asked.

"Something that starts in ten minutes sharp." Sarah was speaking to her daughter, but Natalie got the message.

"Nearest bathroom?" Natalie asked as she pulled her bridesmaid dress out of the closet, then paused a moment to appreciate it. On the hanger, the look was macramé on top, tea cozy on the bottom.

"Whoa," Natalie said.

"Not bad when you consider it's made of soy, spandex, and bamboo," said Sarah, adding, "Use the bathroom to the left. It has only three dream catchers."

"Only three dr—?" Natalie broke off as Sarah nodded solemnly. "Oh. Oh my."

"Yes. You don't want to know about the bathroom down the hall."

Natalie set the timer on her phone for five minutes as she headed to the bathroom on the left to fix her makeup. As she caught sight of herself in the mirror, she gasped and thought her mother had a point. She looked like a drag queen after a long night out. Getting to work, she peeled off her fake eyelashes, pulled out her makeup brushes, and started toning down her fuck-me-now eye shadow.

With one eye still on her makeup, she started thumbing through the messages on her phone. It was mostly more friends and followers, but there was a text from Matt begging her to send a photo of herself in the bridesmaid dress, and another from Andrea, Ryan's producer, that read, I might have something for you. Where can I find you this afternoon?

Natalie frowned, surprised. What could Ryan's producer want to share? Maybe it had something to do with the Mr. and Mrs. Bickerson performance from the anchor set this morning.

Warily, she typed back, I'm at a family wedding but reachable after the ceremony. Call you in a few hours? She paused and, after a moment's hesitation, added, Is it about this morning?

She hit Send and the reply popped up quickly. Great. I'll reach out in about an hour.

Standing in a mango–scented bathroom with three dream catchers and her makeup half on, Natalie's heartbeat picked up a little. What could Andrea want? Why didn't she give a hint?

"Natalie?" It was Sarah on the other side of the door. "Are you on the phone?" It was a judgment, not a question. "It is time for you to get off the phone and join the wedding like everyone else. Lulu and I are going downstairs where we are all waiting for you."

Shit.

"I'll be right out," Natalie called out, shame washing over her. From her toiletries case she grabbed another brush to smooth down her hair and spotted the pills from Matt she'd brought along. Yes, that was just what she needed. She popped a Xanax and cupped her hands to wash it down with water from the sink. Then she checked her watch.

The ceremony was supposed to start in two minutes, perfect timing. Feeling calmed down at the knowledge that the cottony Xanax buzz was coming, she sprayed her hair, added a layer of mascara, slipped on her high heels, and headed downstairs to join the wedding party.

★ ★ ★

The wedding march was already playing when Natalie met Sarah at the back of the lawn. Her sister barely made eye contact which meant she was furious, but she knew Sarah never stayed mad at her for long. Looking around at the attending guests, Natalie saw almost no familiar faces. Blessedly, the pill kicked in when they were halfway down the petal strewn aisle of grass.

As Natalie stood to the side of the minister, opposite her new step-family-in-laws, she found herself wondering how Gerald's long gray ponytail managed to sprout from his otherwise bald head and why he'd decided maroon and orange were the colors he wanted to get married in. She was in such a daze, she didn't register the vows or any part of the ceremony until the minister loudly declared them man and wife. Gerald went in for a full-on French kiss.

As soon as it was appropriate, Natalie told her mother and Gerald she was happy for them and ducked into the downstairs bathroom to check her phone. No voice mails. Not a text or email from Andrea. Pushing away her disappointment, she tucked the phone in a drawer filled with hand towels for easy access and rejoined the wedding party.

The photos went by in a blur. Natalie smiled, sucked in her gut, turned this way, faced that way, and rearranged as ordered. There were shots with Gerald's sons and without, with Gerald and without. This was absolutely the way to attend a wedding, Natalie thought, happy in her buzzy haze. When the Savage women finished posing for a mother-daughter-granddaughter series, the photographer said, "That's all. Great job, ladies."

Natalie excused herself to use the ladies' room again.

Feeling relaxed and like the world was a bit soft around the edges, she sat on the closed toilet and checked her phone. Where before there was nothing, now there were two missed calls, a voice mail from Andrea, and a bunch of emails. While she was sitting there, her phone rang.

"Natalie, it's Andrea. I've been trying to reach you."

Natalie felt her heart race pick up with anticipation.

"I want you to know, I think you're really good at what you do. This is your beat and you deserve this story," Andrea said.

At once, Natalie was no longer feeling relaxed or fuzzy but bursting with curiosity. "I appreciate that, Andrea," she said cautiously.

"Check your inbox. I've sent you a few emails. Obviously you'll need to report it out, but it all fits." Natalie put the call on speakerphone and, heart racing, opened the first email from Andrea. It read, Huntington Recovery Center, Arizona.

Andrea continued, "You'll find the name and address for an addiction rehab center in Arizona. I'm told that's where the First Lady has been hunkered down."

Heart now pounding so loudly she could hardly hear, Natalie opened the second email. There were three photos. She tapped them and they started downloading—slowly.

"There are also a bunch of surveillance pictures of that mystery man, Anthony, arriving at the facility," Andrea was saying. "It's the same guy from the videos of FLOTUS."

Natalie's blood was sizzling with excitement. FLOTUS. In rehab. *And we have the exclusive? Correction, I have the exclusive.*

"How did you get these?" Natalie heard herself whisper.

"I can't say. But you can check my work. You should." Andrea cleared her throat.

There was an angry knock at the door, and her mother's voice saying, "Natalie! Natalie, are you in there?"

Natalie sucked in her breath and covered the phone. "Sorry, Mom. I'll be right there!"

"We need you. You're keeping everyone waiting," her mother hissed.

Turning back to the phone, Natalie asked Andrea the question she had to know the answer to. "Why are you giving these to me? Shouldn't you share them with Ryan?"

Andrea sounded defeated. "I hate how sensationalist and shallow our coverage has been. This isn't why I became a journalist. You know I told you it's still possible to do great reporting at ATN. I want that to be true. It's just—" She stopped herself. "Doesn't matter. Point is, Ryan deserves some real competition and you're a good reporter," Andrea said. "Good luck."

When she hung up, Natalie felt her body start to tingle. The story was going to be huge, and it was her scoop. Hers. She wanted to hug Andrea and shower her with something… Xanax happiness. She checked her watch. There would be plenty of time to get through the rest of the wedding and still get into the story tonight. She'd fly to Arizona as soon as possible and confirm FLOTUS was in residence before anyone else figured it out.

There was more knocking, slightly less angry. On the other side of the door Sarah said, "Seriously, Natalie you need to get out here. The photographer is ready for you and you're holding everything up."

Natalie dropped her phone into the drawer and threw open the door. Her mother was there, visibly seething, with Sarah beside her. "I don't know who you think you are, but you are not acting like the daughter your father knew." Her mother's lips were narrow, her eyes slits. Natalie looked over at Sarah, who again avoided her eyes.

"I thought the photos were over," Natalie said simply. "I didn't know I was inconveniencing anyone."

"I am doing a series with each of my children, alone," Noreen explained. "You are still my child, aren't you?"

"Of course, Mom." Natalie sighed. "I'm sorry. I was wrong to rush off."

"Fine," her mother said. Natalie's frankness seemed to have Noreen on the ropes, but it lasted just a moment. "Please fluff your hair first."

Wearing her best for-the-camera smile, Natalie allowed herself to be led into the backyard where the photographer was staging the photos. She let herself be posed in front of her mother, Noreen's arms wrapped around her waist. It felt more threatening than maternal and Natalie tensed at the proximity.

"You know, Natalie, I'm starting a new life with Gerald. That means I can't mother you anymore," Noreen said as they smiled at the camera. "You're going to have to start taking care of yourself. Be an adult."

Natalie frowned. She earned her own money, paid her bills, lived on her own. How was she not taking care of herself?

"And can we see a smile, please?" The photographer was looking at Natalie, who hadn't realized she was frowning. "Good. Now if the two of you will face each other but bring your eyes here. Lovely."

"I'm telling you this for your own good," Noreen went on through her teeth. They were standing front to front and Natalie could see the small lines around her mother's eyes and lips. They made her seem almost human.

"You know they are now growing organs in laboratories?" Noreen said, still smiling. "Soon people will be able to have a second liver or new lungs on hold. Your generation could live well past a hundred. And if you're going to be here that long and single, you have to start building a future with security."

Almost.

"You ladies are doing great," the photographer said. "I can feel the love there. Let's see some teeth with those smiles."

"Have I told you about my marvelous new guru?" Noreen said, flashing a wide grin. "So wise. Really just full of wisdom."

Natalie doubted it. *Tilt head, breathe, smile*, she began to recite, to tune her mother out.

"He's advised us to simplify our lives," Noreen went on.

Tilt head, nice calm eyes, smile, Natalie recited.

"So I've decided to simplify the dog."

Tilt head, relax—"What?" Natalie asked, bewildered.

"One more pose," the photographer said. "Let's have you turn back to back with your heads touching. Beautiful. Now let your joy beam out through your smiles."

Natalie thought it was amazing no one had murdered this photographer. "What does that mean, simplify Cronkite?" she repeated while beaming her joy.

"Put him to sleep," Noreen answered.

Natalie felt her beam dim. "You're kidding, right? You can't put Cronkite to sleep."

"He's too old to rehome," Noreen warned in a happy sing-song voice. "Even the pound won't take him. He's had a good long life. Why not end it while he's still happy? With the new cocktails, they say it's a very peaceful passing. Really, it's doing him a favor. No need to make a scene."

The photographer said, "And now let's try a saucy hand on the hip. Perfect. Noreen, you're a natural. Natalie, dear, if you could get a little closer to your mother."

A scene? Natalie thought. She wanted to make a whole opera. "There's nothing wrong with Cronkite. You can't kill an animal just because it is inconvenient."

"Well, I don't recall seeing you this concerned about my well-being," Noreen said, smiling over Natalie's shoulder. "When was the last time you inconvenienced yourself for me?"

Natalie's jaw was starting to cramp from all the smiling. "I'm here, aren't I? You have no idea how hard I worked to get here."

"Yes, you are so very important. You and your career," Noreen said, her tone as forced as her smile. "You sound exactly like your father. And if you keep up this way, you'll end up just like him."

"Dead?" Natalie squeezed out from between her teeth.

Noreen shifted to give the camera a different angle on her jaw line. "Dissatisfied and trying to make sure everyone else is, too." She tipped her chin up. "The dog goes with you or it goes to the vet. That's all there is to it. This is the humane thing to do."

Smile, smile, smile. "I don't have my own apartment, and I travel nearly seven days a week. I can't have a dog."

Noreen put her hand on Natalie's arm and smiled up into her face. "No man, no home. No wonder you've been trying all day to ruin my wedding."

Natalie pulled away. "That is not true. I have not been trying to ruin anything."

"Smiles," the photographer said pointedly. "Let's remember to smile."

"Sarah thinks you're unaware of your behavior, but I think you know exactly what you're doing," Noreen told her in a musing sort of voice.

Sarah? She was lined up against her, too? The sharp pain of betrayal she'd experienced earlier came back now, even more keenly. It had always been her and Sarah against the world.

Or so she'd thought. A knot began to form in Natalie's stomach.

"One more and we're done," the photographer said. "Let's make it a candid. Anything you want. Ladies' choice."

Natalie wondered if vomiting on your shoes was an option, but before she could suggest it Noreen pulled her close and tilted to rest her forehead on her daughter's. Smiling into her eyes, Noreen said, "Your father is dead, Natalie. It's time to accept that. There is nothing in the world less attractive than a daddy's girl without a daddy."

The words affected Natalie like a physical slap, jolting her, waking her up from the complacent stupor she'd been in and making it clear what she needed to do next.

"Marvelous. Just beautiful," the photographer said. "I think you're going to be thrilled with those. Real mementos of a very special day."

The inside of Natalie's head was so noisy she probably would not have heard it if someone had tried to stop her from leaving, but no one did. *You're not wanted here, but you're needed at work,* her brain kept saying. Then fury replaced confusion and she was filled with a sense of purpose that quickly silenced any doubts, any misgivings. She'd go where she was welcome.

It took her less than ten minutes to shed the bridesmaid's dress, put on her jeans, and pack her bag, leaving the discarded gown hanging in the closet. She'd have enough baggage courtesy of her mother without that.

She looked down at Cronkite, staring expectantly up at her. "Yes, boy, you, too." She didn't know what she was going to do with him, but she was definitely not going to leave Cronkite here to be downsized to make more room for sex swings.

It was a warm, clear afternoon. The sky was filled with the fluffy clouds that made Virginia feel a world apart from DC. As they pulled away from the Aztec Barbie Dream House and headed toward the District, Natalie started to feel an emptiness in her chest. She was on her own. She'd pissed off her family. There was no one she could really confide in at work. She'd just have to get used to being a one-person operation.

She reminded herself that she was a rising reporter at a huge network with a major scoop. She told herself that she had Cronkite and her smarts. She caught her own eye in the rearview and said, "I'm so happy for you."

She managed to make it nearly a mile before she had to pull off to the side of the road because she was crying too hard to see.

25

LADY OF THE FLIES

As Natalie merged onto the highway, she breathed out a sigh of relief. She felt like a complete fool for having broken down like that, but it seemed to have acted like a rain shower on a hot summer day, clearing the haze from her mind, making everything appear sharp and clean and even a little bit hopeful. She knew that once Sarah saw the story she was about to break, she'd understand and forgive her disappearance today. In fact, once she broke the story, everything would make sense. She'd be a top Washington reporter, and all her sacrifices would be justified.

"Siri, call Matt Walsh," she said into the speakerphone.

"There are one million four hundred eighty thousand results for fat waltz," British male Siri declared. "The chicken fat waltz was performed by the band Monkey Swallows the Universe at the Queens social club in—"

When Siri finally got the right number, Matt answered after just one ring. "What happened? Any wedding cat fights? Any naked selfies?"

"Better," Natalie said. "I think I know where FLOTUS is."

"Oh." Matt sounded like he was watching TV. "How many Xanax have you taken?"

She needed him to focus. "Matt, listen. Put on your serious producer hat, if you even own one. We need to get on a flight to Arizona, tonight. I need you to work on that and get Bibb's approval."

"Bossy today, aren't we?" Matt said distractedly.

"You may refer to me as Ms. Bossy, if that helps."

"Okay, Ms. Bossy, just so I understand, I should casually inform Bibb that we're skipping town on the company's dime. Care to explain why or for how long? Or when she asks for details should I just say this is on Natalie's orders?"

He had a point.

"Okay, you're right. Can you be ready with flight options for Phoenix, and I'll fill you in on the rest when I have more information? I have to make a call and confirm some things," Natalie said and hung up before he could ask more questions. She wasn't ready to trust Matt with the scoop.

Her second call was to Huntington Recovery Center in Phoenix, which Siri blessedly found after just two attempts. The receptionist said she'd have to take a message for the executive director who could only be reached for emergencies, "due to this being Saturday." Summoning her most authoritative slash threatening tone, Natalie explained that she was a reporter for ATN, the national television network, and on deadline with important information about your center so a call back in the next hour would be great.

She hung up, confident that would get a quick reply.

As she rounded a corner on the leafy parkway, Natalie saw the silver water of the Potomac and the Washington Monument piercing the blue sky in the distance, and a sizzle raced through her body. This was the image they showed in every Washington spy thriller—right before the agent nabbed the bad guy and broke the mystery wide open. She grinned to herself, feeling it was a sign, confirmation she was finally on a real story.

Watch out, Ryan.

Turning on the car's satellite radio, she flipped to a simulcast of ATN's live broadcast. "A brand-new poll from ATN and SurveyMonkey shows the nation is divided." It was Nelly Jones's voice, promoting her Monday show. "Half of Americans believe Sonia Barbaro is telling the truth. The other half believe it's all made up," Nelly said. "Does that mean it's impossible to know? Tune in Monday."

Glancing at Cronkite, Natalie pointed to the radio. "Do you hear that? We're not reporting actual information. We're reporting what viewers *think* the facts might be. You get how that's crazy, don't you, Cronkite?"

Cronkite farted, which she took for agreement.

Her phone rang.

"Hi, Ms. Savage," a thin male voice said. "My name is Curtis Norton. I'm the manager on duty here at Huntington Recovery Center." Natalie, heart racing, worked to stay focused on the road. "As today is Saturday, I'm afraid our executive director is unavailable, but I wanted to return your call. How may I help you?"

Natalie's excitement was dulled by a tinge of disappointment. She wanted to speak to the boss, but the manager on duty would have to do.

"Thanks so much, Mr. Norton," she said, slipping into her polite reporter mode. She'd learned that gave her the most flexibility. Start sweet and they had a tendency to underestimate you. "I'm calling from ATN in Washington, DC. Multiple sources tell me that First Lady Anita Crusoe is currently a patient at your center." She waited a beat to let that sink in. The sourcing was a slight exaggeration—it was only one source and she didn't exactly hear it firsthand. "I wanted to give you a chance to comment before we go to air."

There was a pause. "I appreciate the call." Then silence.

Natalie almost felt bad about giving him a panic like this. He had to know that the First Lady's stay would eventually leak, but the poor guy couldn't be excited to field this call. "Ms. Savage, was it? At Huntington, we assure all our patients anonymity. It's part of the ethos of recovery."

Patient! He's just referred to FLOTUS as a patient! In her mind Natalie started doing a jig.

"I hope you understand." Mr. Norton sounded apologetic.

"Of course I understand, Mr. Norton. My own family has struggled with addiction and I respect your commitment to privacy." She felt a tinge of guilt for trading on her father's personal history, but it was a good way to win the source's trust. "This is a great opportunity for you to educate the public about recovery and your good work."

"Well, I do appreciate the offer, it's very kind of you," he said without a hint of appreciation. "I'm sure that you understand we have many high-profile patients. Were I to speak in response to this inquiry, it might lead the press to call about other clients."

Natalie was flush with excitement. The way he said "*many* high-profile patients" was the agreement she needed. He was essentially saying that FLOTUS was one of their high-profile patients but there were many others. Of course he wasn't allowed to confirm FLOTUS was there, but twice declining the opportunity to deny it was almost the same.

When she thanked him and hung up, she smiled at Cronkite, "We have a big scoop." Catching his eye, she felt a flash of regret. Her dad wouldn't like this story, not at all.

When she was a teenager, he'd get mad whenever she'd needle him to reveal whether anyone she knew was in AA. Anyone famous? Any of her friends' parents?

"If I were to divulge that, I would be part of the problem," he'd say.

Guess I'm about to be part of the problem, she thought and dialed Matt.

"Okay, ready?" She smiled absently as the reality of this moment started to sink in. "FLOTUS is in an addiction rehab center in Phoenix."

"What? Are you sure?"

"Pretty sure. I just spoke with the manager. Got as much confirmation as I can without being on the ground. How quickly can we get there?"

"What did he say?"

"That he can't discuss it because of privacy. Then he got silent. Twice."

"He didn't deny it?"

"Nope."

"Holy shit. This is fucking huge."

"I know. I need to do an errand but I can be at the airport in two hours."

"On it," he said and hung up.

For once, Matt's appetite for scandal was a blessing.

With no friends in town and the UnComfort Inn being a decidedly un-dog-friendly environment (more proof that their commitment to comfort was illusory at best), she really had no choice. At least that's what she told herself as she arrived at James's place just before 3 p.m. and prayed that he was home. She should have called, but it wasn't the kind of thing you ask over the phone, and she figured she'd have better luck pleading her case in person.

Buttoning up her pride, she pushed the doorbell and waited. She thought she heard a sound upstairs but when no one emerged, she buzzed again.

Now she heard footsteps on the stairs and felt a sharp pang of worry. What if he slammed the door in her face? He'd have every right to. She'd agreed to go home with him, passed out, bailed abruptly without hooking up or getting breakfast, and was now showing up asking for a favor. *I'd make the worst girl-friend ever,* she thought.

Looking down at Cronkite, she said, "Act cool. And look cute. We really need him to like us."

Cronkite looked at her and she could have sworn he was telling her to take her own advice.

The door opened and standing in front of her was a trim African American man in khaki pants and a blue button-down shirt who looked sort of like James but with graying hair.

"Hello, I'm sorry. I'm here for James. I hope I'm not interrupting something. Is he home?"

The man's eyebrows shot up. "You're a friend of James?"

She nodded, wondering if there was a problem. Maybe James had another girl upstairs? *Maybe? Probably! He probably has to feign illness and fight women off when he wants to spend a Saturday alone.* She should have called first.

"Is this a bad time?" she asked nervously.

The man pushed his lips together and shook his head as if to say not a bad time at all. Then, without looking away from Natalie, he called over his shoulder, "James! Female visitor here for you! Age appropriate. I think you should come quickly."

She heard footsteps on the stairs and then James appeared wearing a crisp blue T-shirt and looking surprised to see her.

"Thanks, Dad," he said. "Can you excuse us?"

Dad? Handsome dad.

When his father went upstairs, James looked at Natalie, confused. "This is a surprise," he said. Natalie noted that he didn't call it a "pleasant" surprise. "What happened to the wedding?"

She tried to achieve a state of inner calm. She needed as much dignity as she could muster. "I had to leave early because there's news and I have to get to Phoenix."

He raised an eyebrow. "You walked out on your mom's wedding?"

"Well, my mom wants to kill the dog so I felt justified," she blurted. Then, registering James's startled look, blushed. *That's the look you give someone you don't want to date*, she thought. "Sorry, it's a long story, but short version, I was at the wedding. I had to leave and take my family dog with me so my mom doesn't put him to sleep. But I also have to fly to Phoenix tonight. So I know this is a huge imposition, but I'm wondering if maybe I could leave him here with you and Colin Powell?"

It sounded insane. Hearing it out loud, she realized just how insane. And rude. She tried for a casual laugh but it came out like she was choking.

"Are you okay?" he asked. "Do you want a glass of water?"

"I'm fine. I was just trying to laugh insouciantly."

"Not for the faint of heart," he said. "That's graduate level. Probably better to start with a jovial chortle."

Ugh. He was smart and cute and funny and she was screwing this up. She should turn and go. Take Cronkite and run. If she dressed him in a sweater and glasses, no one would be able to tell her dog apart from any of the beaten down travelers at the airport right?

But her feet didn't move. She said, "I'm sorry about leaving so abruptly this morning. I was nervous and I needed to get to work, and I was afraid I was going to screw up my mom's wedding." She stopped herself with a laugh. "Actually I did screw it up. Badly." She waved that away. "Doesn't matter. What I'm trying to say is—is that your dad? He looks really young. Super handsome." She stopped herself and shook her head. "I don't know why I said that. I get a little nervous around you. If you can't tell, I'm not always very good at boy-girl interactions."

James squinted at her with a smile. "Oh I don't know. I think you're doing okay."

Her mouth opened and closed twice before words came out. "Please don't say things like that. It makes this embarrassing situation even worse." She looked at him beseechingly.

"James, dear!" It was a woman's voice. "What are you doing downstairs? Why don't you invite your friend up?"

He laughed and stepped back from the door. "Got it, Mom," he yelled up the stairs. And then to Natalie, "Would you like to come in?"

She said, "Yes," and meant it. "But I can't. I have to be at the airport and I need to run to my apartment and get clothes first."

He shook his head, smiling. "Is that your standard don't call me, take my dog, and I'll call you line?"

"No, it's true!" God, it would be easier to concentrate if he wasn't so cute.

Cronkite, who had been doing a jig on the hot sidewalk, now inched up to James and began to nuzzle his leg.

"What's his name?" James asked.

"It's Cronkite." She took a deep inhale.

James shook his head again, laughing. "Okay. Well, we'd be honored to have Cronkite as a guest."

"Thank you," she said. "Really thank you so much."

"One more thing."

He pulled her to his chest and kissed her.

Not hard. Not long. Just perfectly hot.

"Let me know when you're back," he said.

She nodded and got back into her car swooning.

She drove two blocks in a haze, the empty feeling in her chest replaced by rising excitement. It was all coming together at once. The guy. The story. Her future. She started to consider where James might take her on their next date. And maybe they'd go to Miami for New Year's vacation together. He'd look amazing in a tux when she took him to the White House Correspondents' Dinner—or the White House Christmas party—once she was ATN's senior White House correspondent. Good things come to those who persist!

Her phone rang.

"Natalie, Matthew says you confirmed the First Lady is in rehab? Is this true?"

Bibb.

"Hi. He did?" Natalie said, trying to play it cool. "Yes, I've possibly confirmed that. I need to do more reporting."

"We need get this on air ASAP. They'll be ready as soon as you arrive."

Her heart started racing.

"Fantastic. Thanks, Bibb. I asked Matt to put us on the next flight to Phoenix. I will let you know as soon as I have this solid, hopefully in time for the morning shows," she said, offering the best case scenario.

Bibb was firm. "Don't worry about getting to Phoenix. We have an Arizona freelancer on call. Tell me the name of the center, and I'll head our Arizona crew in that direction."

Natalie felt her blood go cold. She'd been here before. If she gave Bibb the name of the rehab center, she'd hand the story to Ryan. Did Bibb really think she'd fall for this twice?

"Natalie?" Bibb said. Natalie imagined Bibb pulling out a whetstone and slowly sharpening her nails as she spoke. *All the better to claw you with, my pretty.* "How quickly can you get to the White House? I need you on the North Lawn ASAP and I need the name of the center so we can get a reporter over there."

"Wait...you want me to go to the White House?" Natalie stammered, thrown.

"Yes. I want you live from the North Lawn, ASAP. I'll have our freelancer in Phoenix chase down any leads on the ground in Arizona. I can't afford to waste time flying you out there. Let's get you out front on this now."

Everything went quiet except those words. Live from the North Lawn. For Natalie, that was the TV news equivalent of getting the Oscar, landing a CEO job, and hitting fifty million likes on your YouTube video simultaneously. Bibb was giving her a break!

Sure, you could insist on going to Phoenix to report this yourself,
but Ryan wouldn't, she chided. Maybe this was the Chief's way
of making up for the situation in the kitchen Saturday night.
Maybe it was the universe's way of ensuring things worked out
in the end.

"I can be there in fifteen," she told Bibb and turned right,
heading in the direction of the White House.

26

COMMON NONSENSE

Natalie pushed open the door of the security guard shack at the White House Northwest gate, stepped onto the asphalt driveway ringing the North Lawn, looked up at the White House North Portico with the expanse of grass and trees stretching out around it, and smiled.

She remembered the way her dad used to go silent whenever this image came on the screen. The way he'd nod at the reporters doing their live shots. How his voice filled with admiration when he'd rhapsodize, "Holding our elected leaders to account is a public service. It's a big part of what makes our country exceptional."

She wondered if her dad would forgive her for what she was about to do. She shook the thought away. This was news. And it was her job to report it.

Sorry, Dad, she thought as she started down the driveway.

She made a right turn onto a stone pathway that ran along Pebble Beach, the area reserved for White House live shots for each national network. (So named, she knew, because the area used to be a patch of mud covered with pebbles. The Bushes had the pebbles covered with more forgiving pavement, but like so much at the White House, it was known for The Way It Used to Be).

Hurrying past the positions for all the major networks—NBC, CBS, ABC—she noted that none of the other networks were lit up and ready for live shots. A few reporters were milling around the pavement talking on their cell phones, but all seemed quiet. She smiled, warmed by the knowledge that the others didn't have a jump on her story.

She arrived at the ATN position to find Dasha behind a camera setting the shot and Matt pacing in front of it on the phone.

"I'm on with the desk," Matt said, covering the mouthpiece. "They have a Phoenix reporter headed to Huntington, but it's going to take another forty-five minutes to get a truck up and live from there. They don't want to wait. Control room wants you now."

Ignoring Matt, Natalie smiled at Dasha and gestured to the White House. "Pretty cool, huh?"

"Yah." Dasha nodded briskly. "Watch out, Greasy."

Smiling, Natalie shooed Matt out of the way and took a seat on a black metal utility box, then grabbed her makeup bag to give herself a touch-up.

"Hello, did you not hear me?" Matt was looking down at her. "They want us ASAP."

While applying translucent powder to her T-zone, Natalie shook her head at Matt. "Don't be crazy. We can't go live until the Phoenix reporter confirms this on site."

"Wrong. They expect us up after the next break."

"We can't go live yet. All I have is a guy not denying she's there." She shook her head. "That's not confirmation. We need a second source."

"We do have a second source," Matt said in a controlled tone. "Photos of Anthony going into the center. What else do we need, God spelling it out in skywriting?"

She made her eyes big, "That would help."

Matt pushed her mirror out of her face. "Do you think Ryan waits for a second source? Do you think he stops the breaking news train to cross every T and dot every I?"

"No, but I also wouldn't swallow horse semen for a sweeps stunt," she said, wrenching the mirror back into her control.

Matt narrowed his eyes. "Is that really what this is about, journalistic integrity? Or are you maybe letting your feelings about your dad's alcoholism cloud your judgment? Maybe you're hesitant to out FLOTUS as an alky because it hits close to home?"

How did he always read her like that? Natalie shot him angry eyes. "That's nasty."

"But true?" he asked. "Someone is going to report this. If it's not you, I guarantee you it'll be Ryan. Do you think he'll even hesitate? And once he's on the story, do you think he'll be at all kind about the First Lady being a drunk?"

Natalie looked over at the monitor playing ATN. There was Ryan, still at the anchor desk, beaming Hearty American Manhood across the airwaves. No, he wouldn't hesitate, and, no, he would not be kind.

Ignoring Matt, she looked up at Dasha. "What do you think?"

Dasha nodded like a loyal comrade. "If you do not want to make the report, I make excuse," Dasha said, shrugging. "Camera trouble. We do this often in Kandahar."

"Stop it, both of you," Matt snapped, then turned to Natalie. "Do you want the White House job or not?"

"Of course I want the job."

"Then stop acting like a baby and do it."

Dasha's phone rang and, after answering it, she covered the mouthpiece.

"They call for us now," she directed this to Natalie. "Want I should say connection is bad?"

Natalie looked from Matt to Dasha and turned to take in the

sight behind her. The majesty of the White House, the wide expanse of the North Lawn.

This is your shot.

"Yes or no?" Dasha asked from behind the camera.

Why are you looking for problems? she asked herself. *You've earned this.*

She looked from the lights to the camera and made a decision. She'd do it. She had the bureau chief and the network behind her. What were the chances this would go wrong?

Natalie stepped up onto a tiny platform under the ATN tent and faced Dasha's camera, three HMI lights on her face, a large diva light casting a warm glow across her features.

Combined with the sun, the lights made it hard to see, and she could feel her eyes start to water, on the verge of tears. She held a hand in front of her face.

"Is bright?" Dasha said. "I adjust. But is very good shot. Very pretty. Very young."

"Does your mom the bride know you're about to break this story wide open?" Matt asked from the sidelines.

Natalie shook her head no. Mom and Sarah would find out afterward. And then they'd understand.

"Savage, we got you live from the White House. Coming to you in thirty. Ryan McGreavy is your anchor," a voice said in her ear. "We have some photos and video of the FLOTUS. We'll follow your lead."

"Is my hair okay?" she whispered to Dasha. Both Matt and Dasha nodded yes, emphatically. God bless Magda.

She took a deep breath and looked into the camera, switching to reporter mode. She put on her formal smile. The Breaking News music filled her ear and she could hear Ryan in studio promising viewers a "major breaking development you'll only see here on ATN." Then he tossed to Natalie, "Live from the White House."

She felt a flutter of anticipation.

She was going to nail this.

"Thank you, Ryan. I have just gotten off the phone with sources who shared with me some very personal, very private information about the First Lady that's never before been public." In her ears, her voice sounded strong, authoritative. "According to these sources, First Lady Anita Crusoe is recovering from addiction. She's currently at a rehab facility in Phoenix, Arizona." She paused to let that sink in. "We have photographs of the First Lady's friend Anthony Cantrell entering that facility on more than one occasion."

"Rolling photos," a voice said in her ear.

"The place is called Huntington Recovery Center. It caters to wealthy and VIP clients who require extreme privacy. Earlier today I spoke with the manager who declined to comment, citing patient confidentiality. It is not clear how long the First Lady has been in residence there, nor do we know the nature of her addiction—alcoholism or something else. But we know from history that the stress of the White House has taken a toll on more than one First Lady. We should applaud Mrs. Crusoe for seeking the help that she needs, and hopefully she will be given time and space to recover privately. Ryan?"

Ryan thanked her in his best Enthusiastic tone. Did she note a touch of respect in his voice? The lights went off and Matt and Dasha exploded in applause.

"That was AMAZING!" Matt hollered.

"Goodbye, McBalls," Dasha agreed.

Grinning, Natalie looked over to see the TV lights up and down Pebble Beach switch on as camera people from rival networks raced out of the briefing room to power up their positions.

"They're all going to report our story." Matt grinned. "And they're going to attribute it to ATN. It's fucking awesome."

Soon reporters followed, racing out of the briefing room and toward their live locations. As they rushed by, one reporter after another waved at Natalie, yelling "great story" or giving her a big thumbs-up. Matt was right. This was awesome.

The ATN booth in the basement of the White House press briefing room was so cramped it could barely fit Natalie and her oversized makeup bag. But miraculously she, Dasha, and Matt had all jammed inside and were now staring at seven plasma TV screens that ran up the tiny wall of the closet-sized space. Every network was live with banners that read, "ATN reports: FLOTUS in Rehab" or "FLOTUS Fights Addiction, Says ATN."

Natalie couldn't hold back a smile. *This must be what it feels like to land a triple axel.* She'd done the stunt and stuck the landing, finally.

She looked at her phone, which was blowing up with messages from friends and Washington types she'd never met, congratulating her on a huge scoop, inviting her to drinks, and—shamelessly—asking if she'd share the name and contact info for her sources. There was an email from Karima Sahadi that read Please call me as soon as you can, dear.

She probably wants to be seen having lunch with me again, Natalie thought with a smile and flagged the email to ensure she'd remember to call her later.

"How high do you think the VOP will be?" Matt asked Dasha.

"Seventy. Maybe eighty?" Dasha said with confidence.

"Interesting, I'd say a hundred at least," Matt said. "We never found out how high it can go. It's a number with no meaning." He shrugged. "Anyway, Ryan's anchoring, so his VOP can't be that good. God, we might actually beat him."

The phone in the booth rang and Matt answered it, a little too enthusiastically, with "ATN, White House!"

He covered the mouthpiece and turned to Natalie. "They need us back on air."

Natalie frowned at him but he only shrugged in reply and said, "I don't know. They said ASAP."

Back on Pebble Beach, Natalie was squinting under the lights at ATN's camera. Why wasn't anyone talking in her ear?

The show came back from commercial, the Breaking News open rolled and it cut directly to Ryan, who was wearing a Concerned Look.

"This is Ryan McGreavy at ATN. I'm here with continuing coverage on the First Lady. I'm joined now by phone with Dr. Eric Anderson, the executive director of the Huntington Recovery Center in Phoenix."

Natalie felt a pressure a building in her chest. They'd reached the executive director, the one who wouldn't take her call.

"Mr. Anderson, moments ago our own Natalie Savage broke the news that the First Lady is in residence at your center. What more can you tell us?" Ryan asked, looking Serious and Engaged.

"Thank you, Mr. McGreavy, I'm calling to set the record straight," the voice said. "Sometimes our commitment to discretion leads to misunderstandings, and I'm afraid that's what we have here."

Natalie felt the world go into slow motion.

"Sir, please tell us, what is the misunderstanding?" Ryan wore a look of Grave Concern.

"First Lady Anita Crusoe is not a patient here, and I'm sorry for the confusion."

Natalie held in a gasp as alarms started going off in her head.

"Has she ever been a patient there?" Ryan asked.

"No, I'm afraid not. She is not in residence. Not an outpatient. Never treated here."

Natalie felt a wave of nausea rise up inside her. *Keep calm*, she told herself, the voice in her head sounding like a nervous flight attendant in a smoke-filled cabin begging passengers to proceed calmly but quickly to the exit slides. But her mind was scream-ing, *Not a patient? Not ever? What about the photos of Anthony?*

"Sir, we have photographs of the First Lady's friend Anthony Cantrell visiting the center. How do you explain those?" Ryan asked.

"As I said previously, we pride ourselves on our discretion. We never reveal the identity of our patients or their visitors, so I'm afraid I can't comment on that. But in this case I can de-finitively confirm that we have no relationship with First Lady Anita Crusoe, nor have we ever."

I was wrong. I got it wrong. On the North Lawn of the White House, I got it wrong, Natalie's mind was screaming. She could feel her legs start shaking as she stared into the North Lawn camera, her face burning with shame, her lungs filled with ice.

Ryan thanked Dr. Anderson and turned to another camera.

"I'd like to bring in our Natalie Savage at the White House, who originally broke this story." She could hear Ryan saying the words but it felt like it was happening a lifetime ago, or to someone else, or in a movie. "Natalie, can you tell us, do you have any reason to doubt the word of Mr. Anderson? And if not, how did we get this so wrong?"

She felt like she was choking, like her throat was filled with sand and if she tried to speak, nothing would come out. Open-ing her mouth, Natalie was surprised to hear her own voice.

"I got this wrong because I didn't wait for a second source," she said quietly. "In the rush to be first, I made a bad call." She felt numb. "The truth is, sometimes we get some things wrong. When we're reporting about people who aren't powerful enough to get a correction, our viewers never find out."

"Wrap! Wrap!" someone was shouting in her ear.

"But in this case, I rushed to air, and we're talking about the First Lady. I take responsibility and I'm very sorry."

"Wrap! Wrap!" The shouting was louder.

"We're going to move on now," Ryan said in a hurry. The

camera cut away from Natalie, and Ryan turned to another camera in studio. "This is a reminder that all of us are only as good as our sources. What matters is that we set the record straight." Ryan smiled and added, "As my meemaw used to say—measure twice, cut once."

Ryan went to break and the lights went off. Natalie watched other reporters rush back out to their live-shot positions, no doubt racing to retract her reporting and obliterate her reputation.

Mechanically she unplugged her microphone, pulled the earpiece out of her ear.

"Fuck! Fuck! Fuck Bibb!" Matt started shouting as soon as the camera was off. "You know this was Bibb! Bibb set us up. Bibb rigged it so Ryan would win. It's all Bibb!"

"No," said Natalie, remembering again the night the intercom buzzed in her corporate apartment. How she'd said no. She shuddered. "I bet it was Hal. And anyway, it's my fault.

"Does it fucking matter? It's all of them. They all fucked us!" Matt was yelling.

Stone faced, Natalie looked from him to Dasha and then over to the line of reporters correcting her live on air.

Her phone buzzed. It was a message from Bibb that read, Meet me in my office. Now.

Natalie was too numb to react. Like a woman in a trance, she unhooked her earpiece, dropped it on the ground, and walked out the White House gates.

27

NONE DARE CALL IT REASON

Natalie was waiting in a chair outside Bibb's locked office when she was startled by the sound of angry footsteps in the hallway followed by a swish of clothing. She saw Bibb march by without saying hello and unlock her office door.

"In!" she barked.

Feeling like she was having a flashback from fourth grade, Natalie walked into Bibb's office dazed and ready to get expelled.

"I want to know just what you think that was," Bibb barked before Natalie's bottom had touched the chair. She was pacing the floor in long, abrupt strides, so angry she didn't make eye contact. "I have given you every opportunity. This company has given you the kind of airtime anyone would kill for. And this is how you repay us? By telling the world we don't correct our mistakes? We only come clean when we screw up a story about the First Lady?"

Natalie blinked at her.

At another moment, with another boss, she would have mounted a strong defense, but she knew there was no point with Bibb. Bibb was like all predators, she could scent blood in the water, and it excited her.

"So you're not angry that I got the story wrong?" Natalie asked, piecing things together. "You're just angry that I was honest on air about *how* I got it wrong? You were the one that insisted I go on air without Phoenix," Natalie said, gaining courage. "Did you have Andrea feed me the bad info?"

"What?" Bibb had stopped stalking the office and glared down at Natalie. "You're accusing me of feeding you bad information? Are you out of your mind?" She was nearly shaking with rage.

"How did you get those photos of Anthony walking into the clinic?" Natalie pressed. "Were they doctored? You let us air doctored photos just to ensure Ryan wins?"

"You have no idea what you're talking about," Bibb spat.

Looking up at the boss, with her big diamond earrings and empty sanctimony, Natalie thought Bibb seemed not so much dangerous as ridiculous. It was suddenly clear that Matt was right: Bibb's power came from intimidating her underlings. Having spoken the truth and survived, Natalie felt invigorated, emboldened. "Why wasn't Jazzmyn in this morning?" she asked, sitting forward. "You know where she was last night, right?"

"You better watch yourself, young lady," Bibb hissed.

"With the Chief," Natalie continued, ignoring Bibb's warning. "He offered her an anchor job, then took her back to his hotel. And now she's gone. What do you think happened at that hotel?"

"You mind your own business," Bibb was pointing a finger and glaring.

"I thought truth telling was my business," Natalie said, eyes locked onto Bibb, determined to shake her boss's veneer of righteousness. "I bet you also know about Hal. About the way he stalks the girls on the news desk. Harasses them." This felt good. "He's tried it with me. So did the Chief, he made a pass at me last night. Isn't it your job as management to stop that? Surely you feel some kind of responsibility as a woman in news—"

Like a coiled snake, Bibb hissed, "Don't you dare call me that. I'm not a woman. I'm a journalist."

The words hung in the air as Natalie sat frozen in surprise. Bibb's phone rang and she lunged for it.

"Yes, she's here. I'm putting you on speakerphone now." Bibb hit a button and the sound of breathing came across the phone.

"Good evening, ladies. My wife has a no-calls policy on Saturday evening. Only emergencies, so let's make this quick." It was the Chief, sounding surprisingly calm and cheerful. "So, we had quite a little mistake on air. That was an unfortunate development."

And that's an understatement.

"Chief, I'm sorry." Natalie said, knowing what she had to do: own her part of this, stay in the Chief's good graces. "I always get a second source, but under pressure to break the news first, I ignored my better judgment."

"I understand, Natalie." The Chief sounded untroubled, sympathetic. "The truth is, it was very good TV. Highly dramatic. And it showed that at ATN we are dedicated to getting it right, eventually. In fact, I've asked PR to encourage key media reporters to watch your segment at the White House, and highlight how quickly and transparently we corrected your error. I wouldn't be surprised if we get a good bit of positive press out of this, actually."

Natalie was gripped with a new anxiety. The network was encouraging coverage of her moment of ignominy?

"Now, Natalie, I know you're a competitor and you usually don't disappoint," the Chief continued. "That's why I'd like to get you back out there ASAP, to ensure you aren't tainted by your mistake today. Bibb?"

Bibb pushed her fingers to the bridge of her nose and closed her eyes. When she opened them, they were cold hard stones.

"We have a story for you about Sonia Barbaro," Bibb said through gritted teeth. "It's no secret that Barbaro is well on her way to sleeping with every actor in Hollywood. Now a source tells us that as a teenager, Sonia had a child out of wedlock, which she apparently gave up for adoption. Venezuela is a Catholic country. That she was sexually active as a teenager is going to be frowned upon. All this should shade the perception of her rape accusation."

"Great angle," the Chief said. "Sex, lies, Hollywood, international intrigue, and a secret child. It's just the kind of narrative that could extend watch time, maybe even expand the Demo."

"We'd like you to dig into Sonia's past and tell us what we need to know about her. Who is the real Sonia Barbaro?" Bibb said.

Natalie felt the blood rush to her face. *They want me to be their news beard. ATN wants to use me, a "credible" woman, to attack Sonia Barbaro. Why? Because it excites the boss? Because he thinks his excitement is transferable and it'll rate well with male viewers ages eighteen to thirty-five? Let's use smart Natalie, the stairs person, to give this celebrity sex scandal an air of respectability.*

"You want me to slut shame Sonia Barbaro," Natalie said flatly.

"I want you to report on her. It's an assignment, not a choice," Bibb spat, looking at her with what Natalie sensed was restrained fury.

Natalie understood that the Chief had the power. And she knew that he liked her moxie, the way a murderer likes a victim who fights back. So she would fight.

Natalie walked toward the phone and leaned close to it.

"Chief, I think there is a story we are missing. Instead of chasing Sonia Barbaro, what if we look at the bigger picture?"

She thought of all the money they'd spent hyping side-stories, chasing bad leads, missing news that really mattered.

"Why is the president giving sanctuary to Lystra's son? The

Venezuelans keep saying it's a distraction. What if they're right? What if this is about something else?" The Chief wasn't dumb. He had to see her point. "Sir, if there's something behind the White House's protection of Rigo Lystra and if we break that story, it'll be a major scoop. That would help the brand and the ratings, right? All I need is a little time to do some digging."

"Do you see what I'm dealing with?" Bibb said despairingly to the Chief. "I've tried to be patient but I don't think this is working."

There was a muffled sound over the phone and then a child's voice. "Daddy, you're not supposed to be on the phone!"

"Natalie, Bibb says Sonia Barbaro is the big story." The Chief sounded a little world-weary. "And Bibb is my girl. You must understand that. I need to see loyalty from you. To Bibb, to me, to ATN, and to ASI."

Stung, it occurred to Natalie that maybe there was no path out of this. If Bibb was always going to be right, that meant she, Natalie, was always going to lose.

There was rustling and then the Chief, sounding like a different person: "Honey, don't tell Mommy, okay, and I'll give you a twenty-dollar bill? I'll be down in a minute." There was more rustling and then, "Honey, I only have this fifty, so as soon as I break it… What? Okay. Yes, here it is. That's our little deal. Hurry downstairs. I'll be there soon." There was the sound of footsteps and a door closing and the Chief was back on the line. "She's only seven and already a fierce negotiator."

After a pause, the Chief continued in a cheerful tone, "Natalie, let's look at the larger picture. In the future I see you covering the big stories, with the big anchors. Maybe even anchoring on your own someday!" He sounded like a friendly dad. "We're rebranding. And the new ATN is all about attitude, outrage, and drama. I want you to be a huge part of this. I want to put you in a promo, make you a star." He paused, and his voice changed again, now almost wheedling. "But I need you to be

on the team. And that means playing nicely with Bibb and taking her assignments."

Friendly dad with a loaded shotgun next to the front door.

His words felt like a cell door slamming shut, leaving Natalie trapped and hopeless. She shuddered as the memory of his
finger tracing down her spine came back to her.

At that moment something released in Natalie.

Her qualms and confusion, her frustration at trying to win
at a game she didn't believe in, suddenly vanished. Worry and
concern gave way to clarity. It wasn't *her* they wanted, it was a
Natalie Savage blow-up doll.

Dress her up, pull the cord, check out that smile, watch her
do it again. She's the lass that won't sass. (As seen on TV.) (Soul
not included.)

She looked at Bibb and at the wall of TVs playing the five
networks on mute.

All this time she'd convinced herself that becoming a TV
personality was the ticket to doing real news. She thought if she
became the Chief's big star, she could do investigations. On-
the-ground reporting.

Rate now, report later. Candy now, protein later.

But suddenly she saw that with Bibb and the Chief in charge,
there was never going to be a chance to do that. Under the
Chief, ATN was a candy division always in need of more refined sugar and trans fats. The irony was, he'd been honest
about that from the very beginning. He'd said it plainly. She'd
just refused to hear it.

No one had lied to her. She'd lied to herself. She'd let herself
become numb, obedient, unquestioning. All things a reporter
should never be. ATN didn't want her to follow the truth wher-
ever it might lead. ATN wanted her to get the network ratings
without questioning their choices.

Suddenly the way forward became clear. She would repay
the Chief's candor with her own. "Chief, I appreciate the op-

portunities you've given me." She inhaled, already feeling more herself. "But I'm not a good fit for your rebranding. It's not me. To be honest, I don't think I belong at ATN, at least not this version of ATN."

He chortled, apparently tickled by her reply. "My girl, I understand, you're feeling gun-shy before your big breakout." He was back to friendly, coercive dad. "So go ahead and take the weekend. Let's talk Monday." The sound of footsteps came across the speaker and a woman's voice demanding, "Are you on the phone?" broke through his words.

"Ladies, sounds like it's time to go. Natalie, think it over. You'll get used to this in no time. Bibb, let's speak later."

And he was gone.

Natalie found herself staring into space doing a recap in her mind. She had said no. She'd quit…hadn't she? Was it so inconceivable a reporter would pass on the opportunity to become a TV star, that the Chief was unable to hear it?

"I'm quitting. I quit," she said to the empty air. When she turned her head, she almost jumped at the sight of Bibb's enraged face.

"You just got an opportunity any reporter would die for, and you can't even show gratitude?" Bibb replied in a Mommy's-not-coming-back-you're-stuck-with-me-now tone. "If this is some kind of negotiating strategy, if you think that just because the Chief *likes* you, that you can manipulate me and get the White House job, you've got a surprise in store." Bibb's face was a hard, mean mask. "Childish, selfish tactics like that will not work in my bureau. And threatening me with stories of Hal and the Chief won't get you anywhere. I'm in charge here. Don't even try to outsmart me because one day you're going to find us taking what you say seriously."

When Natalie had first refused the Chief's offer, it was involuntary, a survival instinct. But now, aware that no matter how much she spoke and no matter what she did she couldn't be heard, the decision settled in her. Turned to resolve. When she spoke, her voice sounded clear, steady. "Really, Bibb, you're not hearing me. I'm not suited to ATN. Not the way you guys want it run. You need someone who—"

"Not possible!" Bibb snapped, and Natalie refocused to see Bibb was speaking into her phone.

Did it ring? Had she just lost track of time?

Bibb was pacing as she barked into the mouthpiece, "Hal, you've got to be kidding. How have you not handled this? Hold on a moment." She covered the mouthpiece of the phone with her hand, looked at Natalie, and said, "Don't think this meeting is going to be forgotten. I will see you back here on Monday. From this day forward, you do as I say."

Like a defiant five-year-old, Natalie looked at Bibb and said, "I quit. I'm quitting." But before the words were out, Bibb was back on her call, pacing the room.

"I quit," Natalie repeated as she walked out of Bibb's office and down the stairs. People nodded or walked past without appearing to hear her. "I quit," she repeated as she went into the makeup room and grabbed a handful of cloths to get the thick foundation off her face. "I quit," she said to her reflection in the mirror.

"I'm so happy for you," her reflection said back.

But Natalie wasn't sure she believed it.

THE EARLYBIRD™/ SUNDAY / 8:27 A.M.
THE E-NEWSLETTER TRUSTED BY WASHINGTON'S POLITICAL ELITE

Good morning, EarlyBirders™. Here are the morning's need-to-know stories.

BAMBAM LYSTRA TO *60 MINUTES*: "THIS IS A FABRICATED ATTACK." In an interview with CBS's Norah O'Donnell, the Colombian president alleges Barbaro's rape accusation was "manufactured by the Venezuelan government." Lystra: "THIS IS AN ATTACK ON THE COLOMBIAN PEOPLE. WE ARE ALL RIGO." Watch 7 p.m. EST, @CBS.

We wouldn't mind being Rigo Lystra for a day! Word is he's hosting the cast of The Bachelorette *at the embassy tonight. Fun, fun, fun.*

EarlyPoll™: America Loves the First Lady, Less

FLOTUS's absence is taking a toll. Her approval falling twelve points in a week, POTUS's falling with her. Another week of this and she could be underwater.

Viewer Alert: *ATN's Ryan McGreavy to guest host* The View *(in a shirt). Go Ryan!*

28

THIS CLOWN

Natalie was lying on the couch at the UnComfort Inn, blinking at the TV. Ryan was live from the White House, astride ATN's North Lawn live-shot position in his best Conquering Hero pose, chest puffed out, head up high. For what seemed like the five hundredth time, he'd just been introduced as "ATN's new White House correspondent."

"How does it feel, Ryan?" Heath asked from his state-of-the-art hologram set, a "replica" of Rigo Lystra's living space inside the Colombian embassy complete with pool table and a magisterial portrait of BamBam.

"It feels great, man," Ryan said, eyes glinting in the sun, his voice in the deep octave of a Newly Minted White House Reporter. "I worked really hard for this."

Natalie was too numb to yell, scream, or throw objects at the TV. In the six hours since she'd left Bibb's office, she'd gone through the five of the stages of I Cant Believe This Is Happening—fury, loud groaning, slightly manic laughter, depression, and eating three large bags of drugstore popcorn.

She'd been online enough of the night to know that her debacle was the talk of the media world. ATN's PR shop had issued a statement saying, "What matters is that we get it right, eventually." On TVBuzzster, speculation swirled that Natalie had been fired. Matt had gone radio silent. Dasha had emailed offering to help her "handle things," which inspired a quick fantasy involving Bibb's hunting spear and Ryan's midsection. And Jazzmyn had disappeared.

Natalie had sent her an email asking if everything was okay, but it'd bounced back from ATN's server with the message jazzmyn.maine@atn.com is not a working email.

As it had been doing all night, her mind flashed to the bottle of Xanax in her toiletries case. She resisted the urge to grab it. She thought of the look in Sarah's eyes at her mom's wedding and the disaster on the White House North Lawn. Taking those pills hadn't exactly worked out well.

To distract herself, she started scrolling through the pictures that her sister had posted on Facebook and stopped on an image of Lulu and Sarah spinning together on the dance floor. They looked really happy. Natalie felt her eyes start to water. Why couldn't she have stayed at the wedding? Stayed and been a good daughter and none of this would have happened. The First Lady. Her credibility. Her career. Her family.

There was nothing she could do about ATN, but at least she could fix things with Sarah.

She dialed her sister, half expecting her to send it to voice mail.

"Nice of you to check in." At least she'd answered.

"I'm sorry. I'm really sorry," Natalie said, quietly. "I've been a total jerk. I know it and I'm sorry."

There was silence followed by an exhale. "I think it's Mom you should be apologizing to."

"I will," Natalie said and added, "You know she wants to kill Cronkite? She said she's going to have him put to sleep."

"Oh please, even Mom wouldn't do that."

"Her guru wants her to have more flexibility to spend time with Gerald."

There was a pause. "Jesus. I can actually hear her saying that."

"I had to get out of there to save Cronkite."

"Who are you kidding? You left because you wanted to leave." She said nothing. It was true.

"Well, I'm glad you rescued Cronkite from Mom's murderous clutches."

Natalie laughed. Thank god she hadn't lost Sarah. "I'll call Mom and work it out. I promise. I'll make it up to her."

"To be honest you're lucky you left when you did," Sarah said. "Their first dance was to humpback whale music. Gerald read a poem dedicated to Mom's precious pink petal." There was a pause. "So what's going on? You don't sound like yourself."

"I don't?" Natalie dodged. Sarah knew all the sacrifices she'd made to get here, everything she'd given up, everyone she'd let down along the way—her father, herself—to land a chance at the White House. How could she explain that she'd blown it all up? By being sloppy.

"I quit my job," Natalie said finally.

"Are you kid—?" Sarah started and then stopped herself. "You're not kidding. I'm not shocked. I know you want to be at the White House, but not this way."

"What does that mean?" Natalie asked, unable to hide her surprise.

"You always said you wanted to get to the White House to do real journalism. Help speak up for people who couldn't speak for themselves. Dad did it with the law, and you were going to do it as a reporter, you know? I don't mean this as criticism, but I haven't seen you do a whole lot of that..." Sarah let her voice trail off.

It stung, but Sarah was right.

"Be noisy," Natalie said, remembering the words their dad used to say. "I guess I thought that if I was quiet now, I could speak up later when I get some power at the network. But I don't think it works that way."

"Can I say something and promise you won't get mad?" Sarah asked.

"Sure," Natalie said warily.

"Mom's the one who used to say that. Be noisy. When we were little, that was her line."

Natalie blinked. "No, Dad always used to say—"

"He was quoting Mom. Think about it. That's Mom's whole thing. I know she is a total pain in the ass," Sarah continued. "But she also doesn't take any bullshit. For her, saying what is true and right—or at least what she thinks is right—is more important than conforming and being well liked." She laughed. "Her attitude gave me the courage to come out of the closet and raise a kid on my own, even though everyone else thinks it's insane. And it should give you the courage to do what's true for you. Forget about ATN. You were never going to win playing by rules you don't believe in."

She wanted to hug her sister. "Sarah, you're such a good person."

"You're going to be great."

As soon as they got off the phone, Natalie dialed her Mom, determined to keep her promise to Sarah. She left an apology on Noreen's voice mail and stayed on the line for a moment before adding, "I love you."

She hung up and felt overcome with exhaustion. *It's late*, she told herself. *You should try to get some sleep.*

Resisting the urge to find a Xanax, she lay back, closed her eyes, and let her mind float. She replayed the events of the last two weeks. McChesty. That crazy decoy yacht. And Karima— her mysterious whispered tips. As she drifted into the memory of Karima's smile and the scent of custom perfume, she felt a sting of shame.

The woman had tried to feed her a story and she'd failed to follow up. Failed to make sense of those tips.

Sallee LLC. What was its meaning? What had she missed? Why was Karima so solicitous?

Natalie's eyes snapped open. *Who are you kidding?* No way she was going to be able to sleep.

Sitting up on the plaid sofa, she reached for her laptop and Googled who is Karima Sahadi. The site announced twenty-three million search results. There were spreads about the Sahadis' houses in St. Barts, Oman, Tahiti, Colorado, Palm Beach, the Hamptons, and Sardinia. Interviews about her art collection. Stories about her legendary parties. There were pictures of Karima looking thin and radiant with every living president and recently deceased dictator on the planet.

Glancing at the clock—just after midnight—Natalie made eye contact with the sad cowboy.

You lost. You quit. Stop torturing yourself, the cowboy seemed to say.

"I want to know what I missed," she replied out loud, pulling her laptop onto the couch. *And I'd rather read about Karima's life than spend the night thinking about mine*, she thought.

Flipping into research mode, she started reading. The first dozen articles identified Karima as the wife of Ambassador Raheem Sahadi. But one piece, a seven-year-old *New York Times Magazine* profile, described her as a member of the Mifsud family. *The Mifsud family? That's new information.* A quick Google search confirmed that the Mifsuds owned controlling shares in GlobalCom, a massive multinational corporation.

"I definitely missed that," Natalie murmured.

Toggling to her email, Natalie pulled up all the EarlyBirds from the last two weeks and double-checked. *Yep.* GlobalCom had sponsored the newsletter every day. No wonder Karima was their favorite boldface name. There were GlobalCom spots endorsing the oil summit and peace in the Middle East. Also ads for the Union of Latin American Nations and an airline with a flight to Caracas. *A Middle Eastern oil corporation is boasting about investments in Venezuela. Am I crazy or is Karima trying to send a message?*

It was a small thing, maybe just a coincidence. But it seemed like an awful lot of these threads led to South America.

You're a stairs person, Natalie thought. *You can figure this out*.

Natalie assumed that with Karima in the mix, this had to be about oil. With a little digging, she hit on a trove of articles that breathlessly described a "massive new oil field" geologists discovered in northern Colombia. According to the articles, that Magdalena oil field was worth hundreds of billions of dollars to Colombia. Colombia wanted to use something called the Trans-Caribbean Pipeline to move all that oil to the sea for export. But Venezuela controlled the pipeline and insisted on using it for natural gas.

A cold awareness shimmered through Natalie's body. Venezuela's resistance was costing Colombia billions of dollars.

Is that the real reason Lystra and Venezuela are feuding? If so, why is the US inserting itself in this fight?

She checked the clock: 2 a.m. It was too early to make calls and too late to admit defeat. She considered the information she'd just learned. It was at least possible that the White House was taking sides in a regional power struggle that would upend the international oil market and destabilize the western hemisphere. She had to know why.

But it was also possible she was spinning into a conspiracy-theory black hole. A few more hours of this and she'd probably start finding connections between her sad cowboy and Sonia Barbaro's Venezuelan hairstylist.

She felt eyes on her and reluctantly looked over at the cowboy. "I know," she said to his challenging gaze. "I can't find a White House connection, and I don't work at ATN, so it doesn't matter anyway," she murmured and lay back on the couch imagin-

ing how she could break this story—without a job—when she
passed out, laptop open on her chest.

The sound of a ringing phone jolted her awake. Bleary-eyed,
she reached for her cell and, squinting against the morning sun,
checked the caller ID. James.

"Oh god," she moaned out loud.

She'd forgotten about James.

Remembering that he still had Cronkite, she briefly wondered if maybe she should just convince James to keep her dog.
They'd be so happy together.

"Hi there, sorry I haven't been in touch," she answered,
launching right in. "It's been kind of a crazy twenty-four hours."

"I can imagine. I saw the reports," he said.

Great. She cringed. "I appreciate you keeping Cronkite overnight. When should I come get him?"

"I was thinking maybe we could all go for a walk. You, me,
Colin Powell, Cronkite. Have you been on the Washington
Mall since you've been here? It's very relaxing."

She blanched. She had to admit that she really liked him, but
since she was moving back to New York, there was no point in
getting attached.

"That's such a great offer but I'm afraid I'm not in any shape
to leave the apartment," she said, glancing down at the orange
flannel PJs she was still wearing.

"How about dinner?" James asked. "I bet you could use some
friendly company. Tonight's family night at the Hardings'. My
folks are coming over. Bet you haven't eaten a good meal all
day."

"Oh, James, I don't know—"

She was interrupted by an aggressive buzzing.

"Maybe we…" She trailed off, distracted as the buzzing continued.

"Why don't you think it over?" James said.

The buzz was coming from the wall and she remembered when she'd heard that sound before. Last week, the intercom. Was it possible that, after tanking her career, Hal thought he could worm his way into her place?

Indignant, she promised James she'd get back to him as soon as possible and marched to the intercom.

"Please go away," she barked into the receiver.

"Well, someone's been busy at charm school. C'mon, let me up."

It was Matt, not Hal.

"I don't want to see you," she said, meaning it.

"I know who set us up," Matt singsonged over the line. "It's not who you think."

Natalie considered this. She had no time for Matt and his sanctimonious *I told you so*'s. Publicly, she'd taken full responsibility for the mistake, but privately, they both knew that he'd pushed her to go live with one source. On the other hand, he had information she wanted. Relenting, she hit the buzzer.

"Jesus, this place is terrible," he said as he sauntered in, his eyes darting from the breakfast bar to the sad cowboy as he sucked on the remains of a venti Starbucks something-or-other.

She studied her ex-producer with cold eyes. "Spare me your gloating. What do you know?"

"I'm not here to gloat." He gestured to a chair opposite the couch. "You mind?" he asked and dropped into it without waiting for a reply. Leaning forward, he rested his chin on one hand and looked over at Natalie with sad puppy eyes.

"This isn't easy for me."

"You have my sympathy," she said, glaring at him impatiently.

"Can't you be nice? I'm here to apologize!" He sat back and looked at the wall. "I shouldn't have pushed you to go on air," he said as if he was reciting something he had rehearsed more than once. "I feel bad. You were right. I was wrong. I'm sorry."

Natalie stared at him.

"I'm, um, not close to many people, and it sucks that I screwed over someone I care about." He inhaled, as if gathering the courage to say something else, then turned to look her in the eye. "Honestly, Natalie, I'd hate to lose your friendship."

Friendship. He considered her a friend? She appraised him. He was making eye contact and indicating remorse. Apparently Matt had a conscience. Who would have guessed?

"And if that's not enough," he added, "Dasha's so angry that she's threatening to put polonium in my coffee if I don't find you and fix this. I'm pretty sure she's kidding around but I don't want to risk it."

Natalie had to hold back a laugh. "Dasha doesn't really joke," she said finally.

"Yes, so you see that I'm appealing to you as a humanitarian." He seemed to relax. "I should have come sooner," he continued. "But the whole thing threw me. And I wanted to figure out who was behind it. It wasn't Bibb. I was wrong about that, too."

Natalie pursed her lips, not surprised. "It was Hal and Bibb together, right?"

He shook his head. "Nope. Andrea. Well, she carried it out anyway."

Natalie couldn't make sense of what he said. "What do you mean it was Andrea?"

"Her dad died and the Chief told her that he'd give her a few days off for the funeral, but she had to pass you the tip first."

"The Chief?" She felt ice fill her veins. "Why would the Chief do this?"

Matt, who had been scanning the papers on the table, now gave Natalie his undivided attention. "Because he wanted Ryan to win."

"That doesn't make sense. Why wouldn't he just give him the job?" Natalie was confounded. "He's the boss. He's literally the Chief."

"Hello? Because he created that idiotic competition, and you were way better than he expected." Matt was speaking in the tone of a wise older sibling. "Then you actually started winning. There's no way he could take the job from the more competent female and give it to the hot dumb white dude."

Natalie turned over Matt's bombshell information in her head. All this time she'd thought Hal had been sabotaging her because she'd rejected him. But the truth was so much worse.

The whole thing had been rigged? She'd never had a shot? It'd been a setup all along.

"I can't believe Andrea did this," she said, dumbfounded. "I can't believe she didn't care about putting bad reporting on air."

"Andrea didn't know the story was BS. She thought she was hooking you up with a big story and she seems to feel awful," Matt said. "Not that it helps to hear that."

Actually it did. It wasn't Andrea's fault. It was the system they worked in. Pitting people against each other. Making it seem normal to betray a colleague or traffic in unconfirmed information in order to please the boss.

Which reminded her.

"Hey, what do you know about Jazzmyn?" Natalie asked anxiously. "I tried to reach her, but the email bounced back."

"Gone," Matt said and made a loud noise slurping from his almost empty Starbucks. "Like packed up and outta the bureau."

"Oh god," Natalie whispered, hit by a wave of guilt. "Do you think they paid her to go away?"

"I hope it was a lot." Matt nodded vigorously. "For sure they made her sign an NDA."

Natalie felt the weight of Jazzmyn's fate in her chest.

Matt surveyed the coffee table in front of Natalie's couch, littered with notes she'd taken during her reporting frenzy the night before, and held up a paper covered in especially erratic handwriting. "What's doing with the paper chase?"

"I couldn't sleep." She looked at the papers and shrugged. "I went full conspiracy theory, trying to figure out what I missed."

"And?"

She explained about the pipeline and the oil field. How there was real money at stake and the US was taking sides for no discernable reason. "It could explain what's really behind the tensions between Venezuela and the Lystras. Though I'm still trying to figure out why the White House is lining up with the Colombians," she said finally. "We need Venezuela for oil. Why alienate them?"

"Interesting," Matt said. "Too bad you don't have a place to report all this."

"Thanks for the reminder," she said.

He reached another one of the papers on the coffee table. Natalie had written *Karima* across the top. "And what's this?"

"I got a few tips from Karima I was trying to piece together."

"What, like never eat your calories when you can drink them?"

"No," Natalie laughed and recited from memory all Karima's tips. "For one thing, she said women help women. Hah. Also she told me to look into a company called Sallee LLC. And third, she said it's never too late to be wise." Natalie sighed. "That last thing I figured out. According to Wikiquote, 'it's never too late to be wise' is a quote from *Robinson Crusoe*, the book. I don't know what it's supposed to mean."

Matt scoffed. "I had a section on that book in tenth grade. Actually…" he took out his iPhone and started typing "…did you say that company was called Sallee, spelled S–A–L–L–E–E?" Matt asked, now all business.

He held up the screen to show Natalie. It was a plot summary for *Robinson Crusoe*.

"In the book, Robinson Crusoe gets taken as a slave to a place called Sallee. Same spelling." Matt held up a finger, "And you know who escapes with him? A boy named Xury!" Matt looked at her in triumph while Natalie searched her mind for the connection.

"Don't you remember the *Xury*? That's the name of the yacht we chased in St. Tropez!" Matt said excitedly. "Or Miami, whatever."

"All Karima's tips lead back to *Robinson Crusoe*?" Natalie asked, befuddled. Then, realization dawning, added, "Isn't the book about an adventurer who goes to a foreign land to make money? Then he loses his way. Wait, so Robinson Crusoe—"

"Is President Patrick Crusoe," finished Matt.

"I would never have figured that out."

"I know," Matt said smugly. "Clearly Karima thinks you're way more literate than you are."

Her heart rate ticking up, Natalie said, "So what's her point? Is she saying the president got caught up in chasing money?"

"Maybe. Oil money? Something to do with his work in Latin America?"

"I'm not sure I trust Karima's version of things," she said. "And how does this connect to the First Lady? Why did she leave the White House?"

Without asking her permission, Matt reached for Natalie's laptop and hit a few keys. "Let's see what's going on with that pipeline."

Matt was quiet as he typed. Looking over his shoulder, Natalie saw an image on the screen that was blue on one side and brown on the other, with lots of little dots on it.

"That's a satellite image of the Venezuelan coast," Matt declared proudly.

"You know how to read satellite images?" Natalie didn't even try to hide that she was impressed. "What are we looking at?"

"I know how to *find* satellite images. I didn't say I know how to read them."

"Well, how is that helpful?"

Natalie's phone on the coffee table started buzzing. They both watched the screen fill with a message.

JAMES: Cronkite and Colin Powell formally invite you to join us for dinner. Say yes.

"I'm not sure." Matt smiled. "But you know a well-connected cartographer who can answer that question."

29

PATRICK'S REPUBLIC

"I can read the images, but I can't tell you that much," James said as he studied his computer monitor, which was larger than any TV Natalie had seen in a hotel room the last six months. "It's not like the movies where you can turn the satellite ninety degrees from your home computer and read some guy's lips. It's a fixed transponder and all I can see in that location is what looks like a construction site."

Sitting opposite his deck, Natalie watched James appreciatively. He'd been so happy when she'd said yes to dinner, and so enthusiastic when she'd asked if he wouldn't mind using his cartography skills to help her read a satellite image. "Sounds like a blast," he'd responded without a hint of irony.

Of course he was being modest. Already James had made a big discovery. He'd identified the name of a company, LXX, emblazoned across the roof of a construction shed at the Magdalena oil field. Heart pounding, Natalie had texted Matt, asking if he'd try to find out who owned LXX.

As she was waiting for more morsels of information, James looked up and met her gaze with such warmth she had to look away to avoid blushing. She could have sworn that Colin Powell and Cronkite, lying next to each other on the bed, sighed in agreement. Catching her eye, Cronkite let out a quiet yap, and Natalie remembered the day her father had brought him home after a trip to the hardware store.

"A rescue. He looked so needy," her dad had said defensively.

The dog had been flea-bitten and a little wild-eyed, and her mother had agreed to let him stay on temporarily and only after he'd been bathed.

Standing outside, soaping him in the driveway with the garden hose, Natalie's father had started calling him Cronkite. Natalie said she didn't think Walter Cronkite would approve but her father had disagreed.

"My dear, Cronkite was dogged in his pursuit of a story. He never backed down and he was willing to go sniffing in places that were dark and forgotten in order to drag the truth to light. He understood that a real democracy needs people unafraid to face up to power."

Looking at Cronkite now, Natalie felt her chest go tight with sadness. At the memory, and at her consciousness of how far she'd strayed from her dad's ideal. She had been nothing like dogged in pursuit of the truth, nothing like stalwart in the face of tyranny. Everything she'd learned tonight—about the Colombians and the pipeline—had been right in front of her all along. But she'd been so caught up competing, chasing scandal to advance her career that it had stopped her from chasing down the story that mattered.

Well, that was going to change.

Natalie looked back at James and flashed to an image of him shirtless, then chastised herself to focus on the business at hand.

"Hey, can I ask you a question?" she asked. "Does everyone in DC know that Karima is from the GlobalCom family? Why doesn't anyone talk about it?"

James shrugged. "I suppose because it's understood. And no

one wants to do anything that would risk losing GlobalCom's ad dollars." He looked up and grinned at her. "Or the party invites."

"I only went to her party to develop sources," she said defensively.

"Okay." He laughed, then looked back at the computer. "I'm going to try a couple other options, see if we can get another angle," James said. "Want to come see this?"

She felt a flush of warmth as she moved to stand beside him. After a moment, they were looking at crisp clean images of what appeared to be a body of water.

"I'm not sure how much this will tell us, but this is a fleet of private satellites," he said, pointing at the images. "You can't move them, they operate in always-on mode. Still, we can get a time-lapse picture of what's been happening the last few days in the ocean."

There was more tapping and James whistled. "Whoa. That's crazy." He pointed to a bunch of dots in the ocean. "You see these formations?"

Natalie nodded yes.

"So odd," James repeated, almost to himself. He started typing, and over the satellite image, he pulled up a document. The title read, "US Naval Forces Southern Command, Fourth Fleet." He started scrolling through documents. Finally he stopped on one.

"SouthCom announced a MAGTAF last week," James said steadily, as if this meant something to her. "They've got ships from the Fourth Fleet moving to SouthCom's area of operations to conduct regional security training." He gave her a puzzled look. "Strange, right?"

She raised her eyebrows in surrender. "I have no idea what you just said."

"Oh sorry. Military speak. Basically it means we're doing a naval training exercise in the Caribbean Sea. They're moving some big ships there." Now he toggled back to the satellite image. "You see the dots? They're US ships. Surface ships. All stationed off the coast of Venezuela," James said.

"Okay," Natalie replied, wondering at the implications.

He hit a few keys and looked at the dots from a different angle.

"I spent my childhood looking at maps of naval formations. I can tell you about amphibious assault ships, cruisers, destroyers. I grew up around this. And this here is a big deck amphibious assault ship. No way that's there for a training exercise."

She looked back at the image. The dots were located just north of Maraicabo, the port city of Venezuela. "That seems unusual?" she asked.

"Yeah," he said emphatically.

"Like it's a little threatening?"

"More than a little."

They were interrupted by the sound of the doorbell followed by keys in the lock and two sets of feet walking upstairs.

"I've never even heard of cashew crema, what on earth is that?" Natalie heard General Harding's voice as he climbed the stairs.

"It's sauce made out of cashews instead of cheese," Anne Harding replied.

The couple emerged in James's living room, carrying bags of takeout and dressed looking ready for dinner at the country club: crisp khakis, pressed golf shirts, blue for him, purple for her.

"James, your mother is making us eat vegan," General Harding declared, wearing the stern look of a grandfather who'd let you sneak ice cream when your parents went out.

"It's much better for your cholesterol," Anne said, one hand holding her tote, the other on her hip.

"VIMOM," the general replied and headed for the kitchen.

"What does that mean?" his wife called after him.

"Vomiting in my own mouth. It's what the kids say at my office." The general gave Natalie and James a mischievous smile as he passed.

Ignoring her husband, Anne walked to Natalie and leaned in to give her a light hug. She was elegant with high cheekbones, hair swept up in a tight bun and only small laugh lines to show for her sixty-plus years. "Lovely to meet you, dear. I've heard so much about you." She smiled in a way that put Natalie at ease. "And I'm sorry about your terrible mix-up on television. Don't worry, reporters get it wrong all the time."

The blood rushed to Natalie's cheeks. For some reason it hadn't occurred to her that James's parents would be aware of her screwup. Now she was sure the Hardings must see her like something that had escaped from a petri dish. *Behold the accursed woman who was transformed from rising cable star into cautionary tale in less than two weeks! Shame all that great hair is going to waste.*

"You know, you weren't entirely wrong," Anne continued. "Anita does have a drinking problem. Karima hosts her all over the world and any time Anita stays, she has to have the house cleared of everything. No liquor on the premises, not even wine!" She winked.

Why did I leave the apartment? Natalie, wishing she could vaporize, shot James a look that said SOS.

"Mom, let's pick a new topic," James suggested mercifully. He looked from his mom to Natalie and back before calling out, "Hey, Dad, would you check this out?"

As Mrs. Harding moved to the kitchen, General Harding reemerged with a scotch in hand and offered Natalie a friendly handshake which she accepted, trying to mask her mortification. He moved to stand beside James and together they studied the image on the big monitor.

"Well, look what you've found," General Harding said finally.

"Why do we have two littoral combat ships and an amphibious assault warship off the coast of Venezuela?" James asked his dad. "It looks like we're preparing for an attack."

"Indeed," his dad said, taking a swig of his scotch. "After the

Rigo Lystra blowup last week, I thought we might be kinetic already, but reason has won out. So far."

Natalie blinked at the general, expecting him to take that back. Or call it a joke. Or declare it off the record.

"Is this about the pipeline?" Natalie asked, alarms going off in her head. "The president wants the Venezuelans to hand over control to Colombia."

"And the Venezuelans are resisting, so we're sending ships to make sure it happens," James concluded.

"Occam's razor, my friends," James's dad said. "The most obvious explanation is usually the right one. Follow the money."

Natalie considered the half-a-trillion-dollar oil field. *It's hard to imagine a president going to war for oil, again. And in this hemisphere,* she told herself.

"But the US will get oil no matter who controls that pipeline," James said. "Why are we siding with Colombia?"

Natalie added, "And there's no reporting about this anywhere."

The general took a sip of his scotch and smiled at Natalie. "I'm sure your friends in the press will take an interest just as soon as the Tomahawks start flying." He let his voice trail off.

Tomahawk missiles. How did I miss this story? Natalie thought.

"Enough work," Anne Harding called out. "Let's eat dinner!"

For the family of a former deputy secretary of defense, the Hardings were surprisingly easy to be around. As they passed her vegan curry and asked about her mother's wedding, Natalie smiled and nodded in all the right places, but her mind raced with everything she'd learned over the last few hours. She wanted to understand the timing and how the oil field related to Karima's tips about the president. She needed some quiet to piece it all together.

They were nearing dessert when Natalie's phone rang. She

let it go to voice mail. But the ringing started again and on the
third round, she couldn't take it anymore.

"I'm so sorry," she said apologetically. "I just want to check
that. Could be my mom."

Walking into the next room, she raced to her phone.

"You're not going to believe this." It was Matt, skipping the
hello. "LXX is the Lystras."

"What?"

"Twelve years ago the Lystras bought the president's company,
Sallee LLC. They hold it through LXX. I guess you could say
they bought the president. And apparently own that oil field."

"Holy shit."

"With this info we can get you your job back," Matt said.

"What? No. I don't think so," she said reflexively. "I mean,
the Chief won't let us report something that happened last week,
let alone twelve years ago. There's no NOWness."

"Good point. Meet me at your place. We need to figure this
out," he said, hanging up.

Whenever a big story started coming together, Natalie found
that if she let instinct lead her, she could almost intuit where
she'd find the next puzzle piece. She began pacing James's living room. Was it possible the president had been bought and
paid for? That he was threatening war in the region as a make-
good to an old investor?

Thinking about the Lystras, the oil, the president, and Karima's
tip about Sallee LLC, Natalie flashed back to her lunch with Karima
at the Bombay Club. *What did she want me to know?*

The thought was a taunt, shaming her for her current predicament. There had to be another piece of information, something obvious. The challenge grew in her head and turned until
she saw it again from another perspective. And the awareness
burst on her like a compression grenade blowing the door off
her prison.

The words Anne Harding had used earlier came back to her. She'd said that whenever Karima had hosted the First Lady, she had to get rid of all the liquor. *Everything, even the wine.*

Now Natalie remembered. At the Bombay Club, Karima had said the exact same thing when the delivery man had called. *No deliveries, not even wine. I thought we explained.* At the time Natalie had assumed Karima was emptying her house of liquor to entertain Muslim guests. But now she understood. Karima wasn't hosting visitors from the Middle East. She was hosting a guest from the White House.

Heart thudding, she reached for her cell phone and punched in Karima's number.

"Hi, Karima, it's Natalie Savage," she said as soon as voice mail picked up. "I'd like to talk to you about your houseguest. The sober one, staying at the Colorado house? Please call me back."

Electrified, she hung up. This time, she knew she was right. She had the story.

"All good?"

Natalie nearly jumped out of her skin. She hadn't seen James come in.

"Everything okay with your mom?" He flashed her that dimpled smile. "Or you just trying to sit out the tempeh spread?"

Oh god, she thought with a sinking feeling. It was happening all over again. Either she could stay for dinner and for the night, triggering the endless dance of subtle dissatisfaction that would end in three to six weeks with him saying he didn't think she was available for a relationship, and her saying no it was just her job. Or her desperation to get a job.

Or she could end it now. Like a mature, considerate adult.

"It was Matt on the phone," she said feeling guilty. "He has a lead."

"Cool, come tell us about it."

"I can't," she said, almost a whisper. "I have to go."

JESSICA YELLIN

"No, you don't. You can relax and finish dinner," he said warmly.

She imagined how James would soon remember her. *Selfish woman, used me for my satellite reading skills and my parent's bad takeout.*

"James, let's not do this," she said. "I'm probably done here. I'll be gone from DC in a few days."

He was quiet for a moment. "Well. I've become kind of attached to your dog. I wouldn't mind having a long-distance relationship with Cronkite."

Natalie laughed. "I wish the timing was different."

"You can make it different," he said sincerely. "You don't have to go."

As they looked at one another, she remembered kissing him and felt a rush of doubt. Maybe she was making a mistake. Maybe she should stay.

"God, I know that look." James laughed ruefully. "It's how my dad looked when he explained why he couldn't make my middle school soccer finals. Okay, I get it. You gotta go."

The words stung. He wasn't going to fight for her.

"I'd better take Cronkite with me," she said, feeling her throat tighten. "I'll have my sister, Sarah, come pick him up from my place."

He stood aside as she went into the next room, made her apologies to James's parents, and rounded up Cronkite. When she returned, James was waiting by the door.

She approached him, and standing close, he tipped her chin up. "It's been nice getting to know you, Natalie Savage," he told her, his thumb resting on her bottom lip. His eyes held hers for one perfect moment. Then he released her and said, "You'll get your story, don't worry. I just hope you get the happy ending, too. You're worth it."

She was shaking when she led Cronkite down the stairs.

30

ON LIES, SECRETS, AND BREAKING THE SILENCE

Anita Crusoe was standing in front of the big picture window, on the phone, looking at the landscape without seeing it. Part of her had been expecting this call. Some part of her knew it had only been a matter of time.

"Yes, I'm sure, Karima. Send her," Anita said. "I'm ready."

When she hung up, she found Anthony standing in the doorway, and she answered the question that was written on his face. "One of the reporters figured it out. The pipeline, Colorado." She let out a small laugh. "It's the girl who said I was in rehab. Patrick's games backfired."

"And what does Karima think you should do?" Anthony asked.

"Oh you know Karima," Anita said, making a sweeping gesture to indicate the Sahadis' largesse. "She has homes in Gstaad, Tahiti, Oman, Costa Rica. She offered them all."

"I'll pack."

She could tell he meant it, but it was silly and she laughed at the thought. "Really, should we go to Oman? And stay indoors for years so no one finds us?" She sucked in her breath and let out a slow exhale. "No, we're not hiding. I told Karima to send the reporter here. I'm giving her an interview."

"Anita, you don't have to do that," Anthony said, his voice full of worry. "It's not necessary."

"Yes. I want it out in the open," she said. "I want to speak. It's time."

THE EARLYBIRD™/ MONDAY / 5:49 A.M.
THE E-NEWSLETTER TRUSTED BY WASHINGTON'S POLITICAL ELITE

Good morning, EarlyBirders™. Here are the morning's need-to-know stories.

EMPTY PROVOCATION*: That's what Venezuela's President Gomez calls the Lystra family accusations. "BamBam Lystra is using the scandal involving his son's brutality to divert from the real issues."*

NEUTRAL: That's the White House posture, per **Adam Majors:** "This is a matter for Colombia and Venezuela to resolve. We won't interfere in the business of sovereign states."

NO FLOTUS: *Twelve days, three false reports, and still no word from the First Lady. Why? Why the silence? Your guess is as good as ours!*

HAIRY SITUATION: Ultra-hot VIP stylist **Osman Badem** has settled a case with explosive allegations of pay discrimination and harassment. Three former employees say they'll use the alleged six figure payout to open a rival salon, opposite the White House.

31

THE ART OF THE SCORE

Natalie, Matt, and Dasha were alone inside the formal living room of Karima's Colorado estate. Natalie thought it looked like a cross between a Swiss day spa and a carpet store. The floors were covered in overlapping Persian rugs while the rest of the place was a sea of off-white—bone-white furniture, cream ceilings, snow-white upholstery—which gave Natalie the anxious feeling she might accidentally open an artery and start bleeding over everything.

At the moment she was perched at the edge of an overstuffed white chair, spitting on her hand and using the moisture to flatten out flyaways that were sticking up on the top of her head.

"Flyaways are the surest way to ruin a good shot on TV," she could hear Bibb say.

Stop acting like a hostage, Bibb isn't here to torture you, she told herself.

But she'll be watching, her self replied. *No harm in looking good.*

Karima had called the night before to offer Natalie the interview. When Natalie had accepted it, she told Matt they would do it online. "We can livestream it on Twitter, Instagram, and Facebook, and there's nothing Bibb can do to stop us."

And yet, for the last fourteen hours Natalie had been panicked that Bibb would somehow intuit the plan and ruin it. All night, during the four-hour flight here, and the two hour drive up the mountain, Natalie had imagined arriving at the house only to find Ryan, fresh off the elevator and ready to get started.

So far, no sign of McChesty.

"Higher!" Dasha commanded. She was setting the shot for the interview and adjusted a key light right into Natalie's eyes. "Sit up! She is much taller than you." Natalie straightened to do as Dasha ordered.

"And stop playing with your hair," Matt said. "You look great. You're going to be great. Don't be nervous."

Watching them, Natalie held back a smile. Both of them had called in sick to be here, risking Bibb's ire. They'd scored the camera gear from Andrea. "She said it's the least she can do to make up for the rehab debacle," Matt had explained, then added, "And this interview will piss off Bibb, so for her, it's a twofer."

As Dasha tweaked the light, Natalie's mind jumped ahead to her plan for the interview and to any holes. She knew that whatever had prompted FLOTUS to leave the White House related to the pipeline and the ships in Venezuela and had nothing to do with the mystery man in the video. Which meant that everything ATN had reported about the affair had been wrong.

Natalie's thoughts were interrupted by the sound of Matt's ringing phone.

"Go for Matt," he barked into the speakerphone.

"Okay, all parties are primed and ready." It was Andrea. Natalie could hear the sounds of the ATN newsroom behind her. "I tipped off the AP and they're about to move three alerts. They know FLOTUS is coming out of hiding, giving an interview, and it'll be streamed on Facebook, Instagram, and Twitter. I also tipped CNN that Natalie Savage has the big exclusive, and they'll carry it live. Once it's on CNN, everyone'll grab it."

"Good plan." Dasha nodded. "Everyone copy CNN."

Beeping noises started blaring over the speaker of Matt's iPhone. It was the sound of the Associated Press moving an urgent story, chiming on newsroom computers all around Andrea. "Here we go," Andrea said as the beeps turned into a chorus and then became a roar of alarms, layered with people shouting.

Natalie imagined the scene: producers running toward TVs or printers or each other's desks, yelling, "FLOTUS interview!" People picking up phones and screaming into them for no reason at all.

"Jesus, it looks like a preschool recess in here. Either that or a prison break." Andrea whistled over the line. "Does that make me a guard? Or an inmate?" There was a pause and then Andrea whispered, "Oh boy, here she comes. Stay quiet, guys."

Natalie knew the next voice would be Bibb's. "MSNBC is reporting that the *New York Times* says that a reporter got an interview with FLOTUS. Someone tells me CNN has the livestream. We need that NOW!"

There was silence and Natalie wondered if the call had dropped. But then she heard the sound of CNN's breaking news music and Wolf Blitzer saying in his trademark placid way, "Stand by for a livestream of the First Lady of the United States, who is about to emerge from roughly two weeks of seclusion. She will be doing her first interview with Washington reporter Natalie Savage, most recently of ATN."

"Nice!" Matt pumped his fist in the air.

Over the phone there was more silence, and Natalie imagined heads turning, wide-eyed, to measure Bibb's reaction. She envisioned Bibb looking calm, suppressing any regret, rage, or remorse she might feel. That would be 80 percent Botox, Natalie estimated, and 20 percent calculation. She'd spent enough time with the woman to know that at this very moment Bibb's mind was doing the math at super speed, testing all the angles. If there was a way she could benefit from this, a way to bring the kill home, take the credit—

"Wolf needs to check his facts. Natalie is with ATN," Natalie heard Bibb declare, to her utter surprise. "Call CNN and let them know to credit ATN for this interview. This is part of our new digital-first strategy. I am so proud of my girl for landing this scoop." Then with a yell that could clear a jungle, Bibb ordered, "Get ready to get that interview on air NOW!"

"Guys, I better hop off the line," Andrea whispered into the phone. "Good luck." And she hung up.

The phone went dead. Natalie looked from Dasha to Matt, feeling elation mingled with anticipation. There was no going back now. Matt dug into his pocket and pulled out a little blue pill. "For the nerves?"

Natalie considered it and then noted how calm her mind felt. It was so different from the jumpy uncertainty she'd felt that first day at the White House briefing room, and every day on the FLOTUS story. She thought about all that energy she'd wasted wondering what would rate with the Demo, how she'd compare to Ryan, what about her hair, her cleavage, her style Bibb and the Chief would deem lacking.

"I don't need it," she said, shaking her head no. "I think I'm good. I—"

She stopped midsentence because a blond woman dressed in a black suit with an earpiece strode into the room and stood by the doorway like a sentry. *Secret Service.* Behind the woman came two more agents.

A flash of electric delight rocketed through Natalie as she stood, swallowing hard and straightened out her skirt and blouse. On instinct she glanced back to check that the camera was ready, and found Dasha two feet behind her already rolling tape. Knowing Dasha had her back, Natalie turned with confidence to find herself face-to-face with First Lady Anita Crusoe. The

woman was striking. At least five foot ten in heels, she had flawless olive skin set against a yellow blouse, with perfect posture
and soft, almost sad, eyes.

Next to her was a handsome man with salt-and-pepper hair
she recognized instantly. Anthony Cantrell.

He's here?

Suddenly everything seemed off center as Natalie felt a sharp
sting of doubt. *The First Lady didn't leave because of the pipeline?
My god. It was just an affair after all.*

Sitting opposite Anita Crusoe and Anthony Cantrell, Natalie
had no typed-out questions and no need to check her plan with
anyone. She knew the material. She was ready to go.

"Thank you for sitting down with me, Mrs. Crusoe," Natalie said.

"Thank you, Natalie," the First Lady replied in a controlled
voice without a hint of an accent. "There have been so many
rumors and false reports, I wanted to correct the record."

"Let's start with the man by your side, Mrs. Crusoe, Anthony
Cantrell. There has been a great deal of speculation about your
relationship. Are you lovers?"

A flash of irritation crossed the First Lady's face, but it dis-
solved quickly. "No. I have never betrayed my husband. This is
Anthony. He is my sober companion," the First Lady said, indicating Anthony.

Not a sex scandal, Natalie thought, feeling a new swell of anticipation.

FLOTUS continued, glancing at the man beside her. "I have
been sober for most of my adult life, but as a younger woman I
had a drinking problem. At times it's still a struggle. So that part
of your story was right, Natalie. I am a recovering alcoholic."

Natalie winced. She was struck by how awkward it felt to sit
opposite the person she'd been covering as a "character" in a

TV narrative. How strange that she, Natalie, had been one of this woman's tormenters.

"The pressures of the White House have recently begun to take their toll, and Anthony is helping me through." The First Lady turned and smiled at Anthony. "He is a steady presence in my life and a consummate mental health professional. He keeps me on the path when I need him. I'm deeply grateful to him."

Anthony nodded and said, "It is important that everyone suffering addiction understands it's okay to ask for help. I'm here to be that support for Anita. We all need support in our lives."

That explained all the photographs of Anthony with heiresses and wealthy wives—they'd paid him to be their sober companion. Natalie felt relieved that, on this, she'd been right not to make assumptions. Now they could get to the real story.

"Why did you leave the White House, Mrs. Crusoe? Why are you here?"

"When my husband betrayed me, I had to leave." She spoke with a hint of defiance in her voice.

"Respectfully, is the president is having an affair?"

"No, I don't believe he is," Anita Crusoe said, which was the answer Natalie had expected. "There are other forms of betrayal. Some more difficult to get over than sexual infidelity."

Natalie dropped her hand behind her back and did a circling motion with her index finger, indicating to Dasha she should push to crop Anthony out of the shot. Viewers would now see only Natalie and FLOTUS one-on-one.

"You said another form of betrayal," Natalie said. "You mean asking someone to betray their people? Asking you to betray your country?"

"Smart girl. Yes." A sad smile played at the corners of the First Lady's eyes. "Most of your colleagues seem to think the regional troubles are about a boy hiding out in the embassy." She shook her head. "But no. This is about economic interests. Money."

"Oil," Natalie said.

"Yes, oil. After years of violence and chaos, my country is finally beginning to sprout the green shoots of democracy. Members of my family lost their lives fighting for this democracy. My husband knows this and he claims to stand for democratic values. Yet he is prepared to destroy all that now. I can't abide it."

Natalie gestured to Matt, who handed her a photograph of one of the satellite images. She handed the photo to the First Lady. "Mrs. Crusoe, you'll see in this image US warships assembled off the coast of Venezuela. A former Pentagon official confirms to me that the US is prepared for an assault on Venezuela. The goal—to seize Venezuela's oil pipeline and hand control to the Colombians."

She paused to let the First Lady react to the bombshell, but Mrs. Crusoe remained still, almost frozen, staring down at the photos.

"Mrs. Crusoe, attacking Venezuela will destabilize the international oil market, give the Lystra family a stranglehold over the US and Latin America, and destroy the young democracy in Venezuela," Natalie continued. "Tell us, why is your husband starting this war?"

"You know my husband is a very rich man." A flash of anger crossed the First Lady's face. "My husband got rich on minerals and oil in Latin America. The Colombians were invested in these companies."

"You mean the Lystras. He owes them?"

"He doesn't just owe them. He is *owned* by them," the First Lady replied, leaning forward. Now the words came from her in a rush. "The Colombians are the source of my husband's wealth. Years ago his mines failed. His oil exploration wasn't such a success. But the Colombians kept investing. When his businesses were deeply in debt, the Lystras took them off his hands at very high valuations. No questions asked."

"Your husband owned a company called Sallee LLC. He sold it to the Lystras—"

"For almost a billion dollars," the First Lady interrupted. "He's told the American people that he earned his money honestly. Then he refused to release his taxes, and the people accepted it."

"He used Lystra money to self-fund his campaigns. First for governor, now president," Natalie offered. "In a way, the Lystras bought him the Oval Office."

"Yes." The First Lady leaned back, eyes glistening. "And now they are calling it in."

For a moment Natalie thought of Ryan live, in front of the Colombian embassy obsessing over the rape charges and Rigo's hideout upstairs—while the real story was taking place downstairs in the embassy's official offices. Developing plans to invade a neighbor. As payback to the president's debt-holder.

"The rape charge, with Rigo, was that meant as a distraction, to keep the press from covering the campaign against Venezuela?" Natalie pressed.

"Perhaps, in part. It was also my husband's way of vilifying Venezuela. How could he get the Americans to support another war for oil?" The First Lady let a sad smile play on her lips. "Imagine using a sex scandal as the match to light the conflict. It almost worked, didn't it?"

"What was your part in this meant to be?"

"My husband is not a popular man. I would have been pressed into service, to help build the case against Venezuela. Call Sonia Barbaro a liar, accuse the government of an historic provocation that threatens stability in the region."

"You felt pressured to use your position to endorse a war against your country. So you left."

"So I left."

"And the leaks," Natalie said. "Who do you think is leaking all this information about you? The video of you with Anthony and the stories about you in the Caribbean?"

"I assume my husband's team put out that doctored photograph of me with BamBam. Or maybe the Colombians did. I imagine they leaked the video of Anthony with me at the estate. They could access security video." She sighed, "And that story about me in rehab? I'm sure my husband's team suspected you were on the trail. It was just a matter of time until you connected the dots. They wanted to discredit you first."

Embarrassed, Natalie said nothing.

"But the story about the yacht in St. Tropez, that was me, and it was a mistake." The First Lady looked down at her hands. "I was feeling hunted. You had video of me, here at the house—"

"You leaked that story about the yacht?" Natalie asked, disbelieving.

The First Lady gestured to the room and her voice took on a higher pitch. "I came here for privacy, and it was as though the whole world was closing in on us. I just wanted everyone to look away."

Natalie tried to remember how that story had leaked.

"I had someone go to a coffee shop and talk too loudly on the phone," the First Lady answered before she could ask the question. "And you all went scurrying. I didn't believe it would be so easy. But a man was shot and I deeply regret it. I'd like that cameraman to know, I'm very sorry."

Natalie shook her head. There was a piece of the First Lady's story that didn't add up. "Mrs. Crusoe, why wait to reveal all this? Why not shout this from the rooftops? There's a paper trail. A history of payments. Reports of the oil field and the pipeline. There are interests in the US who would want to stop this, to say nothing of the Persian Gulf." She paused, "Respectfully, what's taken you so long?"

The First Lady looked at Anthony and reached for his hand. "Because this is a personal story, too."

Natalie glanced back at Dasha who, she could tell, was already zooming out to bring Anthony back into the shot.

"There are parts of my past about which I am not proud. If

I had spoken out, the White House would have exposed my family and I was hoping to avoid that."

"This isn't necessary, Anita," Anthony said. "You don't need to do this."

"I do," she said. Pulling her hand back, she straightened up and looked at Natalie. "They will tell you this story to discredit me. So I will tell you first.

"When I was young in Venezuela, I had a sister named Eva." Her voice dropped when she said the name. "When we were growing up, my mother was an opposition leader, and my father was a judge who dared to stand for the rule of law. The Chavez government sentenced them both to fifteen years for political incitement. When they went to prison, my sister was nineteen. I was twenty-three." The First Lady paused, seemingly lost in a memory.

"We were old enough to take care of ourselves, but still young. The conditions in prison, the stories that reached us—they were awful. We worried that we would learn our parents had died in prison from mysterious causes."

She gathered her calm before continuing.

"The head of the police force knew us. He'd visit. He'd say it was for our protection." There was a deep inhale. "He liked Eva better. He'd come at night, stay too long, get drunk. Then one night I came home to find them on the floor of the living room. He was forcing her, using her like an animal. It was disgusting. It was—" Her voice broke. "He bragged about it to his friends. We wanted to go to the police, but he was police! We didn't know what to do."

Now she leaned toward Natalie as if begging for her absolution. "You have to understand I was afraid. He was powerful. If we took it to higher authorities, surely our parents would be killed. I thought that speaking out was wrong. It wouldn't make the rape go away, but it could cost us our family."

She turned and looked out the windows, tears wet on her face.

Part of Natalie wanted to stop the interview, let the First Lady have some relief. She glanced at Matt, who was making a "go on" gesture with his hands.

Right.

She wasn't here to be a friend. She was here to get the truth.

"What happened?" Natalie asked quietly.

"A deal was cut. Eva's silence for our parents' freedom. They were released weeks later."

"And your parents were fine?"

"We stayed quiet. My father passed away seven years ago. My mother is in a home with dementia. None of us has spoken of this."

"What about your sister? I've never read about her. Where is Eva?"

The First Lady cleared her throat. "Eva killed herself a year after my parent's release. I found her hanging in the bathroom."

Now Natalie felt like a voyeur.

"It wasn't the assault that killed her," Anita Crusoe continued quietly. "It was the silence. I took away her voice. I wouldn't let her speak."

"How is it that we've never heard this story before?" Natalie asked, softly.

The First Lady sat up straight and wiped away the wetness under her eyes. "Patrick buried it well, didn't he? Wouldn't do for the future First Lady to have such a sordid past. Rape. Prison. Suicide. Addiction." She exhaled. "I loved my husband. I did. But I've made endless compromises for him. We've hidden so many things. I buried my family. Renounced my history, made myself over in an image of what he wanted me to be. Of what he believes the American people want me to be."

"What will you do now?" Natalie asked.

"My marriage is over. I'm done with politics. I need to go back to what I'm good at, where I can really help people. Maybe I'll return to my career. I was an engineer when I came to the

US. I had a scholarship. Believe it or not, I was a good at the work I was doing."

The First Lady sighed and Natalie knew she had to wrap up the interview. Bring it around to current events. "Do you believe Sonia Barbaro's story? That Rigo Lystra raped her?"

"I don't know the truth. I only know we can't silence people, not any longer. The way you all have condemned Sonia Barbaro, judged me—it's wrong. Have you noticed how Western culture still celebrates silent women? The quiet matriarch, the supporting actresses of steely resolve who keep persevering and putting up with it?

"We've all been too compliant. Me. Eva. Sonia. Playing along doesn't change anything. That's why I'm giving you this interview. Our silences were never going to protect us. It's time to speak."

Natalie felt a sudden jolt, thinking of her mother's line. "Be noisy," she said.

"That's right. Smart girl. We need to be noisy."

32

THE MYTH OF POWER

As Dasha drove them down the winding mountain road back toward the airport, it was quiet in the car, Natalie stared out at the trees dotting the mountain, in shock from the weight of everything they'd just heard.

After the interview the First Lady had thanked them and quickly vanished. As Dasha began packing up, Natalie had checked her phone and found it melting down with emails, texts and notifications. There were urgent messages from presidents of rival networks, talk show bookers, and thousands of DMs from viewers who'd just watched the interview live on social media.

"Look, we don't need ATN to have an audience," she said, thrusting the phone in Matt's face.

Without asking he'd taken the phone from her hands and powered it off. "I'm putting you on a media blackout."

Now, in the car, she turned the phone back on. It began filling with messages. The first, from her mother.

MOM: Hi, dear. I'm at Wailee Resort and we watched your interview on the computer outside the group touch room.

MOM: Honey, you did a great job with the First Lady. That poor woman.

Natalie smiled.

NATALIE: Hi, Mom. I'm so sorry about the wedding.

MOM: You know I wasn't going to kill Cronkite. Guru Steve says a dog is a great way to meet a man. You wouldn't have taken him if I hadn't forced it. Cronkite is a man magnet.

MOM: Are you going to do more interviews like that?

MOM: You could interview Oprah. People really like Oprah.

Natalie couldn't hold back her laugh.

NATALIE: Okay, Mom, thanks for the tip. Love you.

Matt's phone rang and Natalie looked up in time to see him check the caller ID. "Shit," he said and answered. "Matt Walsh."

There was silence followed by, "Any point in pleading my case?" then more silence until he said, "I see. Sorry to hear that. Yes? Got it."

He hung up and turned to Natalie, "I just lost my job."

Natalie blinked, horrified. "Who was that?" She hoped he was joking.

"Bibb," he said. "She said I should have made sure they got the exclusive on your FLOTUS interview, and she's right." He stared out the window for a minute before laughing. "Anyway, I'm fired, but you are expected back in the office tomorrow." He turned to face Natalie. "The Chief probably wants to give you a promotion."

She felt awful. She'd been so consumed with her own issues she hadn't considered how this might impact Matt and Dasha. "What are you going to do?" she asked him.

He gave her a sly look. "Actually I have an offer from a station in Iowa. They want to put me on camera."

Natalie looked at him, jaw nearly on the floor. "You can't be serious. Why the hell would you want to go on camera when you've seen everything I just went through?"

"Because I'm not a woman," he said, as in *duh*. "I don't have to deal with any of that shit. No one's going to ride my ass about my hair or try to trip me up because I'm a younger version of themselves. Actually, dudes like to promote younger versions of themselves." He considered this. "Interesting. That's true. Anyway, gotta leave this town to get some work-life balance, right? I have friends in Iowa. Laura's family still likes me."

"Laura?"

"The ex-wife," Dasha said with a sly glance in the rearview mirror.

"How about you, Dasha?" Matt asked, poking the camerawoman in the arm and changing the subject. "Want to come with me to Iowa, cover the presidential? Get away from Handsy Hal?"

"No, I stay," Dasha said, looking at Natalie in the rearview mirror, her eyes glittering fiercely. "Bibb and I have conversation. She wants I should work with Greasy. I say, okay, I make deal. I work with Greasy. You pay me double. Report to Bibb, no Hal. Is good. I stay and cash check. Fuck Hal."

Natalie reached forward to give Dasha a squeeze on the shoulder.

Matt looked at Natalie. "You don't have to go back to Bibb, you know. You could go to any network now. Hell, you could get an anchor job. Write your own ticket. You want to do a morning show? It's all wide open for you."

Natalie wasn't listening. She was reading the messages from viewers on Instagram. "Can you explain how the president got that money from the Lystras?" "Do we still take oil from Venezuela?" "Is it legal for the president to invade Venezuela?" "Are we going to war?"

"Look at this," Natalie said, mostly to herself.

"Yeah, I can't explain why they're all idiots," Matt said, eyeing the messages on her screen.

"They're not idiots. They don't spend all day researching this stuff like we do," Natalie said excitedly. "They just want to understand."

Natalie smiled shyly. "What if I just reported here?" She held up the phone.

"Seriously, Natalie? You're going to make bank on TV and be a star. No way you give that up to vlog on Instagram from your apartment. You're just overtired."

She considered what he said. It's true, she was tired. And it did sound crazy. "But if I just reported directly to real people, they wouldn't care about my hair. No gatekeepers."

Matt shook his head and laughed ruefully. "Let's talk about this once you get some sleep."

After that, they were quiet and Natalie looked at the endless stretch of thawing mountains glittering in the afternoon sun. It was a strange, fierce, beautiful landscape.

It wasn't the North Lawn, but she was starting to think she could uncover more about the country from outside the White House gates than within.

Matt looked up from something he was typing on his iPhone. "Hang on a sec. How can you be so confident you'll get an audience. Do you have something else, like another story to break?" He squinted at Natalie. "Are you sitting on a lead on something else?"

"Maybe, maybe not." She shrugged with a knowing smile.

"Tell me. What's it about?" he demanded. "Karima? POTUS? Oil? Bieber?"

"You know what they say in Reportuguese." Natalie grinned at him mischievously. "Stay tuned."

33

THAT HAPPENED

"Cronkite! Colin Powell!" James's voice was firm and commanding. The dogs had just raced past them and were careening toward a family on the other side of the Washington Monument. At the sound of his voice, they slowed to a trot instantly.

Natalie laughed. "That was impressive."

"It's all about making clear what you want," James said.

Natalie was pretty sure they were talking about more than the dogs.

She felt herself blush and, looking up at him, couldn't remember the last time she felt this at peace.

She'd even left her phone at home to ensure she'd give James her uninterrupted attention. Since she'd landed back in DC, she'd again been inundated with requests to speak to the reporter who'd broken Lystragate.

Honestly couldn't they come up with anything more creative? Natalie had wondered. She thought of the email from Bibb and the voice mail from the Chief, full of praise and pretend camaraderie. As if she'd ever consider going back. Suddenly the arbiters of advancement had determined that she was a brilliant young reporter who needed a big TV job, stat! She knew that, like everything in the news cycle, this glow of triumph would pass. It was all a shimmering illusion.

She glanced over at James in his worn jeans and navy T-shirt. James wasn't an illusion. He was real and present and seriously hot.

You can make this work.

Feeling a little flush, she pulled her hair up into a ponytail.

"You gonna let it go natural, now that you're not on TV?"

Puzzled, she saw that James was eyeing her ponytail.

"My hair?" she asked. "It doesn't work that way. All that formaldehyde is still in there." She shook her ponytail to make the point. "Takes time for it to wash out."

"Really, how long?" he asked with more than benign interest.

She shrugged, playing coy. "Maybe six months."

"Nah." He gave her a teasing glance. "There must be ways to get the real Natalie back faster."

"Well, there are some things that can be done," she said playfully. "Swimming in chlorine."

"We need to get you in a bathing suit?" he asked. "Noted."

She fluttered her eyelashes at him. "Or the ocean."

"Beach getaway, also doable." He gave her a lopsided grin and tilted his head. "What else?"

Feeling her heartbeat quicken, she forced herself to breathe. "If I take lots and lots of showers, that'll help it along,"

He moved directly in front of her and took a wide stance, bringing his chest closer to hers. "So you're saying you need to go on a beach vacation. Spend lots of time in the ocean and the shower. And then I'll get the real Natalie." He was beaming at her. "Is that right?"

"I guess that's right," she whispered.

He bent over and kissed her softly on the lips.

She rose onto her tippy toes, and when he kissed her again, it wasn't nearly as gentle. She leaned into him and felt his warmth and his strength. Crushed up against his chest, she forgot about the phone calls, her interview, her previous day, weeks, everything.

Then she was hit by a sudden worry. "Wait," she blurted. "I want to make sure you know something." She pulled back and looked him in the eyes. "I'm not done. I mean, I'm going to keep reporting."

"Well, yeah," he laughed. "That's what makes you amazing. Be noisy." Then he gave her a conspiratorial look and whispered, "But I've got a secret for you, Savage."

"What's that?"

"It's okay for you to be happy, too."

As he leaned down to kiss her, she couldn't hold back the smile that spread all over her body.

THE EARLYBIRD™/ WEDNESDAY / 5:43 A.M.
SPECIAL CRUSOE CRISIS EXTRA
THE E-NEWSLETTER TRUSTED BY WASHINGTON'S POLITICAL ELITE

Good morning, EarlyBirders™. During the ongoing crisis in the White House, EarlyBird™ is expanding our one-minute-read to bring you more EarlyNews™ on these extraordinary events.

SENATE JUDICIARY HEARINGS, DAY 1: Three weeks after filing for divorce, First Lady Anita Crusoe will testify to the Senate Judiciary Committee about the president's involvement with the Lystra family.

EarlyPoll™: America Loves the First Lady, Again

With skyrocketing popularity, FLOTUS has the American people on her side. POTUS's slumping approval rivals Nixon's pre-resignation numbers.

Savage Bombshell: In her latest *Instagram* bombshell, reporter Natalie Savage details the transactions that brought Lystra family money into Patrick Crusoe's campaign coffers. It's the fourth part in her series on political corruption and foreign interference that's already prompted Senate action. The majority leader tells EarlyBird™ he plans quick passage of the Tax Transparency Act, legislation that will require candidates to release their taxes so that "Crusoe level corruption can never happen again."

*Spotted: At **Karima Sahadi**'s soiree last night in honor of Natalie Savage's new digital media company power couples **Natalie Savage** and **James Harding**; **General Fred Harding** and his wife, socialite **Anne**; newly minted Iowa reporter **Matt Walsh**, in town for a state visit, with his ex-wife **Laura** "in tow (reunited and it feels so good?)"; ATN's **Dasha Karimov**, whose new contract with ATN is said to be the most lucrative for a cameraperson in recent history.*

Breaking Media News: American Services Industries CEO is out with a $50 million pay package. ATN Chief Reginald Bounds has the inside track on the parent company's CEO suite. Under Bounds, ATN has seen its profits surge 10 percent. With Bounds moving up, smart money is on DC Bureau Chief Bibb Connaught to get the top ATN job with either Deputy Bureau Chief Hal Thomas or Assignment Planner Andrea Jackson expected to run the DC bureau. *Check back for ongoing EarlyUpdates.*

Welcome to Washington: Lysa McGrew, new morning anchor for ATN. She's replacing **Jazzmyn Maine** who tells EarlyBird™ she's changed careers and is heading to law school where she plans to pursue employment law.

★ ★ ★ ★ ★